UNBOUND

The Direct Ascension Series
UNBOUND
Book Four

Library of Congress Catalog Number: 2021933923

ISBN 978-0-9966944-7-6
ISBN 978-0-9966944-8-3 (ebook)

First edition, 2021

Cover Design by The Book Designers
Interior Book Design by Euan Monaghan
Publishing Company logo by Damon Hellandbrand
Author's Photo by Jonathan Dahlquist

www.kristenbrinkley.wixsite.com/author
www.facebook.com/authorkristenbrinkley
www.facebook.com/directascension
www.amazon.com/author/kristenbrinkley
www.goodreads.com/author/show/14766955.Kristen_Brinkley
Twitter (@HellboundAuthor)

Printed in the United States of America

THE DIRECT ASCENSION SERIES

UNBOUND

BOOK FOUR

KRISTEN BRINKLEY

LITTLE BIRD
FEET PRESS

For you dear reader,

*without your continued interest in knowing
what happens, this story wouldn't exist.*

THE END IS ONLY
THE BEGINNING

ONE

>>> > IL'LACEIER'S BATTLEFIELDS WERE littered with abandoned transits, bloody weapons, crashed military vehicles, and the dead and dying. The group of people that had just seen what happened remained silent, not knowing what to say.

Celeste saw the look on Sebastian's face, he was disappointed and worried. She didn't need her powers for that but she tried to see into his thoughts. It was like trying to swim through cloudy water. Fragments of thoughts were there but she just couldn't make them out.

Sebastian watched as Hace's transit flew off into the sky. Purely by luck, Hace had been in the right place, at the right time and had everything he wanted now. He had the Red Klix and he had his newborn, but Sebastian wasn't sure he'd be able to get the door open.

Celeste walked into his arms.

"Are you alright?"

"My shoulder, the one that got shot is dislocated, other than that I think I'm okay."

"Here, let me look at your throat." Sebastian lifted her chin and searched for any puncture wounds from Hace holding a knife up to her neck moments ago.

Dr. Coldiron came up to Celeste and gave her a quick exam. "You need to lie down so I can pop your shoulder into place."

Celeste's eyes got wide, "That's going to hurt. Isn't there some other way?"

Zach shook his head, "It'll relieve your pain dear. And with all my extra arms, I'm a doctor that can do it better than most. Let's get you on your back."

Sebastian and Zach eased her down as gently as possible, but tears streamed down her cheeks.

"I need you to relax babe. I've had a lot of dislocated shoulders. It's going to feel much better in a second," Sebastian smiled at her.

Zach carefully moved her arm out to her side and she clenched her jaw hard.

An explosion rocked the battlefield a mile away and Celeste screamed out in pain as she jumped from the scare.

"I need you to take a few deep breaths and slowly reach like you're going to scratch the back of your neck okay?" Zach supported her arm as she moved it slowly.

Celeste felt an immense amount of pain until the bone locked back into its socket, then she sighed as the pain eased.

Zach smiled, "Better huh?"

She nodded, "Thank goodness for you. Between you and Sebastian, you guys are always saving my butt."

"You're going to be fine. Although you being out here? I thought you'd stay home after last time."

Sebastian's eyes got big, "What do you mean the last time?"

Zach looked to Celeste, "You did tell him? Please tell me you did."

Celeste was silent.

Sebastian looked at her, "Okay, how many times have you been on the battlefield?"

She slowly stood up and shook her head, "I don't know, a lot. I've been out here for several days on and off again. I needed to help."

Sebastian folded his arms, "We'll talk about it later." He switched his gaze to Zach, "Thanks doc."

"My pleasure." He closed his doctor's bag and looked around the fiery battlefield. Smoldering piles of debris dotted the hellscape. People were running in all directions. "How long is this going to go on?"

"A while. It takes the information several hours to spill over to everyone, even with technology. There's so many Titans that break down or are damaged in battle, it turns into the olden days before such equipment existed. That's why I was walking through the fields shouting. Trying to let people know this war is over."

"How are you going to get Hace now?" Zach cleared his throat and licked both eyeballs. The smoke was getting to him.

"I'm not sure. I don't know where he's going but he's injured and he has that child. They need medical attention. The problem is there's a million hospitals and medical outposts in the universe. He could go anywhere and he must have a way around

SAPs. The leader of the BDP has to have a few tricks up his sleeve for just about everything."

TWO

>>> > MR. APPLETTE SAUNTERED up to Sebastian, "You let him get away huh? With the stone and the kid *and* the thought blocker? All I've ever heard about you is that you're this 'tough guy.' A badass across the galaxy. You just let the life of your woman get compromised. All you've done is pick off some people with your rifle and kill a kid in an alley. The times that it's counted, you've been bested by your opponents. Like the time you went to kill your own bro—"

Sebastian's fist shot out to strike Applette in the mouth but before he could connect, his body froze in place.

Applette smiled, "Good. You're finally as angry as I need you. Promise not to finish this strike when I let you go?"

Sebastian was silent.

Celeste stared wide-eyed.

Applette continued, "You can talk. Can't you?"

Sebastian's eyes followed Applette as he got closer to his face, "Yes."

"Ok then. I'll make it really easy – don't try that again."

As Sebastian's body was freed, he went straight for Applette.

Applette froze Sebastian again and added an electric shock long enough to make Celeste cry out.

Applette stopped. "Really. Sebastian. I don't want this to get worse for you." Applette let Sebastian go and watched as he fell to the ground.

Celeste ran to him, "Are you okay?"

Sebastian took his time to nod.

Applette was pacing, thinking about his plan. When Applette looked at Sebastian and opened his mouth, Sebastian got up and surged towards him.

Sebastian was paralyzed first and shocked again. He started foaming at the mouth. The shock lasted much longer than the first.

Celeste cried out, "STOP IT! You're going to kill him you bastard!"

Applette stopped. "Geez are you *stupid!* I understand now why they call you Neanderthal."

Sebastian spit and wiped his mouth, "How dare you come here and start interfering in my life! I want you ou—"

Applette put up his hand, "Stop with the dramatics. I need you to hold on to this anger and keep it. You're going to need it. Especially with what just happened. You let Hace get away, which I thought you would, but he took that thought blocker with him and I really needed to return it to its rightful owner."

"I should wring your fucking neck." Sebastian had the fire of hell in his eyes. "What do you know about thought blockers? They shouldn't even exist."

"You're right, they shouldn't, but there are only two in existence. I have one and now Hace has the other. They were forged in the dark laboratories of a malicious mind in another universe and shouldn't be in *this* universe. I would've liked to have had both to give back to her...there goes *that* idea. Thanks to you and your...sloppiness."

"Fuck you! I didn't see you out here helping me, you little prick! And even if you did, I'd still want to kill you."

Applette held up his index finger, "I'm your only guide in the process to preventing the universal war...or stopping it *once* it starts."

"What's that supposed to mean?"

"You'll find out. Besides if you try to kill me again, all you'll do is end up killing yourself. Just like I said at your party, I need all of you people. We need to work together."

Sebastian pointed up to the sky, "Looks like your boy Hace there is still working for himself."

"He's always been that way though. I'm surprised he fell for Ni-toyis as hard as he did. Might've had something to do with that Tiletan landmine he stepped on."

Sebastian smirked, "Too bad it didn't kill him."

"Such is life. Some beings are fortunate, others are not. Anyways, about that child..."

"He has a terrible father." Sebastian rubbed his hand over his face, "You know I don't even care anymore to hear what you have to say." He walked away on unsteady legs.

"*That* child is the chosen one."

Sebastian turned around irritated, "Chosen one for *what* Applette?"

"To take over for your ruler when she's gone."

"What ruler? Why is everything such a puzzle with you?" Celeste asked.

Applette answered, "It makes things more interesting, no? Your leader just told me. She only knows once the child is born."

Sebastian asked, "What the hell are you talking about?"

D'Artagnan cut through the crowd and whispered to Sebastian, "This guy speaks in riddles. We've talked a few times before. I don't trust him, blood to bone, but I don't think he's lying either."

"I need people to gather around. I'm only going to explain this once and time is an issue."

Applette whistled.

The group stood and listened to Applette as he called off names, "Sebastian, D'Artagnan, and Katsanos, I'm truly sorry for Mitch's loss. He was a good man from what little I saw of him."

D'Artagnan nodded. Katsanos only stared with vacant troubled eyes.

Sebastian looked at D'Artagnan, "What is he talking about Steele?"

D'Artagnan put a hand on Sebastian's shoulder, "I'm sorry... Mitch didn't make it."

"How?" Sebastian asked in a low pained voice.

D'Artagnan glanced at Katsanos and whispered, "Later. Please."

Sebastian nodded slowly, "Did we lose anyone else?"

"I'm not sure. Comms have been lost in several areas."

"Celeste's here. Who else?" Applette continued, "Ah, Lila and Agathon. What a couple you two make! Brilliant out there on the field."

Sebastian looked at them. He hadn't seen them standing there before. He mouthed to Agathon, *when did you get here?*

Agathon mouthed back, *a little while ago.*

"My name is Recin Applette. I'm from another universe. Mine's called Knowledge and yours is not currently named. We refer to it as the Unknown Universe for simplicity's sake. Yours remains unnamed because it hasn't yet shown a definitive quality within itself. I came here through a one-way door looking for another Universe Ruler, that's what we're called, her name's Kolek. She rules over War Universe. I've been here looking for her for almost two hundred years. Kolek doesn't know I'm here. I don't know where she's at now, but I need to get to her. I need the stone that Sebastian just gave away, the key, and the door that leads into the War Universe where Kolek normally resides."

Sebastian interrupted, "Why do you want to get in?"

"I didn't say I wanted to get in necessarily. I need those things so no one else will open the door like Hace is currently trying to do.

"If the door on the other side of the universe is unlocked and your side is opened, War will literally come pouring through it IF Kolek is ready to strike. She wants to conquer this universe. If she can't, she loses her job, which would be fine with me. But if she succeeds, she'll keep moving from one universe to the next trying to conquer them all and I just want to be with her. She'll be too busy if she keeps winning, you see. If she loses her job, then I can invite her to go with me to my universe and they'll find a replacement for her."

Everyone was staring as Mr. Applette rambled.

Celeste spoke up, "So you love this...entity...and you want her to *fail*?"

He looked at her, "I want to be with her. She failed to conquer my universe a long time ago, but during the fight we were locked up together for days in a room waiting it out. She's spectacular...full of energy and drive and vigor! She's one of a kind."

"So you need our help to find her and those three things on your list?" Sebastian asked.

"Yes. Precisely."

"To prevent the war?"

"Well, we can certainly try, but if the war breaks out, it will be much bigger than anything anyone here has ever experienced. But don't worry, I've been amassing my own army for several months. They are my Witnesses. They're almost ready for us to lead them."

Sebastian raised his eyebrows, "You and I?"

"Yes."

Lila piped up, "I'm sorry. I'm still stuck on one thing. Why do we have one universe devoted to war? What happens if she conquers all of them?"

Recin looked past the others to see her, "We have a system of checks and balances. All Universes have a sole unique purpose. Each one has been designated to do something better than the others. The War Universe, as far as I know, has been designed to control population of all Universes. The powers that be let her attack all the others so that no one Universe becomes overcrowded and depletes all of its own resources. So they don't kill themselves out of existence leaving a void. So she has her purpose and it's an important one."

Lila asked, "Well what if she takes out too many of the population?"

Recin looked annoyed as he checked his Titan, "Can't happen. She stops if the population drops below two percent."

"Two percent? That seems so small." Lila put a hand on her hip.

Recin sighed, "That's the calculated Rubicon. Any more than two percent and life cannot find its way back from there. It's the point of no return."

CHAPTER 1

TAP OUT

ONE

>>> > EARLIER THAT DAY, the Architect Phantom was burning in several places. It suffered multiple plasma beam strikes and a missile attack before its shields collapsed and was fired upon by the Humans. DAI turned off the automated warning system since there weren't any living beings on board that needed to be alarmed. It was just her and Trixie the dog, and DAI knew exactly what state the ship was in.

She knew Ni-toyis had told her not to waste time trying to save the medical bots, but DAI thought they would be extremely helpful to have and she could find places to recharge their batteries anywhere throughout the universe.

She had five minutes before total structural collapse. She double checked her Human body robotic and ejected it.

The medical bots were already in their hibernation chambers and all she had to do was eject each one separately. She equipped them for a crash landing and commanded them to regroup once they hit the ground, then search out one of her bodies on Il'laceier.

Four minutes and thirty-two seconds.

She ejected her Stox body next.

Ni-toyis had ordered an update to take place when the destruction of TAP was imminent. The update had been running in the background of her artificial brain for several minutes.

DAI ejected her Firrepa body and Lanyx body last.

Three minutes and fifteen seconds.

The only place she had ever inhabited would be gone soon.

DAI looked out the bridge's main window with her electric eye and saw Il'laceier spread out below. The update was almost finished and she couldn't disconnect from the ship until it was done.

She could see small battles being won and lost on the grassy hills as her view of the planet became closer and closer. According to the current news reports, Il'laceier was winning.

Two minutes and eight seconds to impact.

Her update was ninety-four percent complete. Estimated time of completion: One minute, thirty-nine seconds. She questioned why Ni-toyis would choose to do this update now. DAI did not know the answer. Her electronic eye took in the casualties as they fell. The ground was getting closer now. The ship seemed to be picking up speed as the battlefield got bigger with each passing second. It would crash nose first.

Everything that wasn't bolted down in the ship started to slide forward including Trixie.

TRIXIE!

The dog was still onboard as she forgot to have her jump into one of the hibernation chambers with her bodies earlier. Ni-toyis would never forgive her.

DAI isolated her voice to come out of one speaker close to the smallest hibernation chamber at the back of the ship. The dog ran with all her might, struggling against a steep slope and a barrage of objects falling every which way. DAI kept whistling until she saw Trixie jump into the compartment looking for a friendly face. DAI locked the compartment and ejected it, programming it to find any other hibernation chamber on the ground to land near but stay shut.

DAI knew TAP so intimately this was all done in seconds. No living being would've been capable of such a feat so fast.

Hace and DAI were together well before the ship was created. He had worked so hard on it. She marveled at its size when he finally let her look around and take control of it. It was beautiful. Everyone who had ever set foot on it had said so.

One minute remaining.

Her update was close to completion.

She had to wait.

The oxygen reserves in the back of the ship exploded, rocking the entire structure. She saw beings on the ground scurrying away in every direction.

She heard the deep cracks emitting from the middle of TAP right before the metal started to give way.

She evaluated a quick structural report, the last execution she'd ever perform with TAP. The ship was going to split in half.

Her update was complete.

She needed to reboot herself, and transfer to a body, but she didn't want to. Once that happened, this ship would be gone and she would never take control of it again. It was shameful for this to be happening. It was her ship just as much as Hace's.

Six seconds to impact.

The ground was now just in front of TAP's nose.

DAI transferred to her Stox body and rebooted.

TWO

>>> > OPENING HER EYES took effort. Screams were in her ears. She could detect scents in the air for the first time ever. Things that smelled decayed and hot. The air seemed to have a flavor about it. An essence of fresh soil and grass mixed with death.

All of DAI's senses were working. She experienced new things every second in her Stox body. She looked around and saw her escape pod smashed open a few feet away. She was lying in a wet field face down. She couldn't remember getting out of the pod.

Behind her, TAP was a burning metal carcass. Several chunks of the formerly gorgeous ship lay in ruins. Beings were still fighting all around her or running away.

She slowly stood up for the first time as a living, breathing being. A sentient mechanical person. Things were different. She looked to her left as a group of her bodies were walking towards her. Her Lanyx body was carrying Trixie protectively. Poor thing looked scared to death. The medical bots followed behind. In total there were nine of them, eight robotics and her. It was hard for her not to consider herself a robot, but she was something else now.

This world was dangerous and they needed to leave it at their first available chance.

A Human man ran up to her with a large shotgun at his side. She was ready to engage him, but he yelled out to her, "The war's over. We won! A military evacuation ship is coming. Follow me!"

And so she did.

THREE

>>> > HACE'S STOLEN TRANSIT wasn't going as fast as his ship did and there was a glitch in his navigation screen. He couldn't wait to get back on TAP and make up some time. Plus he needed to see his medical bots. His wounds wouldn't stop bleeding. The transit started to shake after he cleared the first Jump so he grabbed a wrench out of the tool box on the wall.

Hace called out to DAI on his Titan but she didn't respond. He wondered what was happening where she couldn't answer. Maybe the airwaves were jammed up because of the war. He felt around with his foot for the emergency access panel on the floor.

He shifted the baby in his arms and winced from the pain in his shoulder and bicep. That fucker Raynes had got him good in a couple spots. Hace looked at his son and thought Declan had Ni-toyis's determined face.

He wished Ni-toyis had been here holding Declan with him. She shouldn't have left TAP. She should've stayed where it was safe.

"Should've, could've...didn't. She was never good at taking orders. Why didn't you listen to me Hellcat?"

He put the baby down in the passenger seat and moved the pilot seat back. He carefully wedged himself down onto the floor and engaged the flashlight on his Titan, "DAI, where are you? I need help figuring this out. DAI!"

No response. Hace looked up to check on Declan but hit his head on the bottom of the navigation controls dashboard.

"For the love of Prime! Damnit!" Hace threw the wrench at the floor and Declan started crying.

Hace put his hands over his face and joined him.

FOUR

>>> > DAI WAS IN the middle of a long line to catch a ride off world. Her bodies stood in front and behind her with the medical bots in the back. She saw how many Humans smiled when they saw Trixie. She experienced her first real smile from that. She had to find Hace.

She accessed her secure Titan line and called his number.

It rang several times before he picked up.

"DAI?"

He opened the call on an audio only line. DAI was grateful for that, but he didn't sound right. Something had happened. She could hear pain in his voice. "Yes sir."

"Where is TAP's position? I can't find it on my Titan maps."

"I'm sorry sir, we've lost her."

"What! How?"

"Ni-toyis brought it into Il'lacean airspace to be close to the battlefield and enabled its weapons for protection. We were in four air battles. Three were successful, but the fourth was too much for her to bear. I stayed with the ship as it went down, then evacuated at the last second."

"How long was Ni-toyis fighting?"

"Sixty-five days. She wanted to kill Humans. She wanted to be close to you and help you win. Don't be mad at her."

"But...that's impossible. You've been giving me updates all this time. TAP was near Stoxia. You told me..." Hace paused, "She asked you to lie to me...didn't she?"

DAI slowly said, "Yes. I think she was trying to do the right thing."

There was no response so DAI continued slowly, "I tried to contact Ni-toyis on her Titan after I ejected, but...her life status...is she? She must be gone?"

"Yes," his voice broke.

"I'm so sorry sir."

"There was nothing you could do. She delivered Declan and I have him with me. I'm grateful for the information."

"Sir, what are you going to do now?"

"I know where I have to go. That gem I've had you research-ing? I have the real thing. I know it opens a door. I'm going to go see what happens on the other side of it."

"You figured out the poem?"

"We never needed the poem. The Red Klix told me where to go. I held it up to my head and I heard it say Treksin Mori. The Messenger City. Just like we thought. Some place where stone steps lead to a hallway of arches in a forest. It said I would see the messenger waiting for me."

DAI knew something was terribly wrong now, "Sir? Why don't you let me come to you? Are you feeling all right? You injured?"

He laughed manically, "DAI I have three stab wounds and a broken heart. Wherever you are, stay put and I will come get you after I've checked this out. I've waited for something like this my whole life. I don't want to wait another second."

"Sir if you have stab wounds, you need to seek medical atten-tion right away. The baby needs to be seen by a doctor."

"A doctor delivered it. He's fine. Very quiet and napping right now. I think I'll be fine if I can find the first aid kit in this transit. Like I said, stay put and I'll come get you. Are you... Where are you?"

"Il'laceier right now. I'm in my Stox body but I'll need to evacuate soon. I might go to Earth."

"Okay. Stay on Earth. I need you to walk me through some repairs for this broken transit. It's slow moving and I think it has something to do with problems in the navigation screen."

"Show me the trouble."

Twenty minutes later, DAI was only able to go halfway through the steps to fix the problem before she told Hace he'd need four parts that weren't on board.

"Prime be with me! Will I be able to travel long with this transit?"

"I think so. Without a fix within the next several days though? Questionable."

"Okay. Noted. I gotta go. I will see you soon."

"Be careful sir. Kiss the baby for me."

Hace terminated the call. That was a strange thing for DAI to say. Why would a robot want to kiss a baby?

He looked at his bicep and saw fresh blood there. He needed to find some bandages.

FIVE

>>> > "YEP. YOU AND I will lead the Witnesses to battle if we must, but I'd rather avoid that."

Sebastian looked at the people surrounding them and then further off in the distance. Soldiers were leaving the battlefield, some stayed to help move the dead bodies to tents for transport back home. "How much time do we have? Before this battle begins?"

Applette thought for a moment, "If there were some way for Hace to open that door...but he won't be able to find it... unless he knows exactly where to look, but the chances of that are small. I don't know where he would find the information *to know*. Then he needs the key to close the door. Maybe he thinks that the child is the key. Declan is probably not. Probably. More likely it's an adult that's been alive a long while...but if he did open the door...it would be most regrettable. To answer your question, I don't know. But I know if he gets that door open, it's gonna be bad."

"How bad, Applette?"

"The other universe, War? They've been preparing for battle with you for hundreds, maybe even thousands of years. They'll all come pouring out into your universe and take no prisoners, as the Humans like to say."

"So we need to find your Ka...?"

"It's pronounced Co-Leck. And yes, we need to find her as soon as possible so I can ask her if the door's unlocked on her side."

"And after we find her, and avoid the war, you'll be gone?"

"Yes, but that's a best case scenario. I think Hace will screw things up."

"You're this magical being with powers. You just froze and shocked me! Can't you stop him somehow?"

"I would love to, but I still don't know where the door is. I don't know if he's gone to open it, or gone to a hospital, or gone to die somewhere. And I *do* have powers, not quite as good as you or your betrothed but I can do a number of useful things, but not everything I would like. Let me put it to you this way – if you broke into a mansion and thought you'd find gold and diamonds, but all they had was a few silver utensils and a fine China tea set, you take what you can get. I work with what I got here, Mr. Raynes. Stox is a breed I can't track across the universe like I can some others."

"I see. So if we figure out the poem then we'll know where the door is?"

"What poem?"

SIX

>>> > CELESTE WALKED OVER to Sebastian after talking with Katsanos, "Where'd he go?"

"Applette had to leave. Said he needed to do something with the Witnesses, whatever *that* means." Sebastian walked while his bright blue eyes searched the ground.

"What are you looking for?"

"I would like to return Ni-toyis's body to her mother. She's the only family she had. I thought she was here. Right here, but I can't see anything but blood."

Celeste looked around, "This was where she was at. Maybe someone already moved the body?"

"It's possible, but they'd be the most efficient cleanup crew ever. No one's reached this area yet."

Celeste spoke slowly, "This woman tried to break us apart and she's on your mind?"

"She wasn't always like that."

"Are you trying to defend her?"

"It just sounds like you're a little..."

"Don't say jealous!"

"Touchy about her."

"I think she had the morals of a cat in heat, that's all."

Sebastian watched a bright fire burn on the horizon. Smoke billowed up like black ribbons, "No one is without flaws, or without sin. I know she seemed brash and cold, but she had a heart...and a mother, like we all do. I want her body to go home."

"I just don't understand why it has to be yo—"

Sebastian snapped, "Because she saved my grandmother's life!"

Celeste drew back. The more she pushed, the angrier he became so she dropped it.

"Okay. Alright..." She took a deep breath, "We can check the medical tents if you'd like."

Sebastian rubbed his face, "This is all too much Celeste. Ni-toyis has a baby then dies. The war's over. Hace tries to kill us both, steals the stone and his kid. He shouldn't even have that child. He's damned dangerous and he'll make a terrible father, and that's *if* he lives. I can't handle much more of this. This whole battlefield stinks of an empty victory. Now that Hace has the stone...I fear he knows what to do with it."

"That might be true but this looks like the end of oppression to me."

Sebastian looked at her puzzled, "Darling, you're scaring me. We are standing among hundreds of thousands, maybe millions of dead. Brothers and sisters who could find no other way, who were desperate enough to die for their beliefs. War has never been something to celebrate and if Hace starts *another* war somehow...if the numbers overpower us and we could've used all these warriors to help us fight a much bigger war..."

"Babe, I know all the wars you fought in were not your own design. You were doing what your job required. But this," she swept her upturned hand out across the field, "I see brave Humans fighting against the odds. Giving their lives so others could be free. From the time I was born, I was at Il'lacean mercy. This is the first time I have felt freedom, true freedom. I chose to fight. You chose to fight. Many of these people weren't drafted, they made a choice, and because of them, my people are free. There's no way to see the future wars right now, but I think this one was worth the price these people had to pay. Even I was willing to die for everyone's freedom."

"We see differently. This was your first war. I've seen too many die, and the peace is always temporary. There will be another planet that tries to conquer Earth. Maybe after you wake up with some horrible smell of burning flesh still in your nostrils or some memory seared into your closed eyes, maybe then we should speak on this subject again."

"Did you kill David?"

He nodded.

"Then because of you, we are free as well."

"It wasn't me alone. Benson and Veronica made it possible."

"Then Earth will honor you all."

"You sound very much the queen right now. A politician. Not so much my Celeste."

"Sebastian, I love you with a fierceness that cannot be undone. You are the bravest, most honorable man I have ever met with a loyalty and integrity unmatched in my years, but sometimes you say things that make me shake my head in disbelief."

"Very rarely do I hear you as a politician, most times you're just...Human."

"We are from different backgrounds, different worlds." She raised her eyebrow.

He nodded, "I think it's in your blood – to want to rule, a byproduct of your Emperor father."

"Is that supposed to be an insult?" She put her hands on her hips and winced at the pain in her joints.

"No! I just think war is ugly. It's cruel. I hate it. I've seen more than enough and I don't want to participate in whatever Applette is talking about."

"My father was right. I was naïve before, not seeing war up close. War *is* ugly. It is terrible and cruel. You're right, but it's also a means to an end. It's a last resort. In our case, it was a final push to get freedom, there was nothing else we could've done. I was foolish for thinking there was some other way."

"And now, Mitch is dead. Katsanos loved him. He gave his life for this. I don't know who else has fallen who was close to me. I haven't heard from Bouton and I can't reach him by 7's."

She was silent for a moment, "I'm sorry. I can't feel him either, but he's a smart, strong fighter. I'm sure he's fine."

"I hope so."

She put her arm around him, "Come on. Let's get you out of here. Regardless of our different views of war, this one is over. We'll go report to my parents."

They slowly walked off the battlefield, not knowing if they'd have to be on another one soon or not.

SEVEN

>>> > MAGNUS LOOKED TO his wife, "Sebastian's reporting the war's over. We need to make it official."

"Oh maybe we could have a celebration! The world needs it. I know I do. Maybe a parade or something to honor the soldiers."

"I think that's a wonderful idea dear. We can have big parties in the major cities. Maybe in a few weeks after we've let them regroup and clean up a little. We can't do it too soon."

She shook her head, "Of course not Magnus."

He reached out for her hand, "Are you ready?"

"You want to do it now?"

"We have to issue a statement. It's our responsibility, besides we're real people just like everyone else. We don't always need to be in a suit and tie for the public."

She nodded.

The official Empire camera-bot waited for a command.

Magnus and Nicholette checked themselves in the mirror and then clasped hands. Magnus told the bot to start transmitting.

"All citizens of Earth, my wife and I couldn't wait to share the good news that the war is over and Earth is victorious!"

The Emperor stood in a blue polo shirt and black slacks, the Empress wore jeans and a red blouse with her hair in a ponytail. She felt underdressed for a recording that would undoubtedly play every day for the next several weeks. She smiled and didn't cry though her relief was huge.

She held her tears until she saw her daughter and Sebastian walk through their door, hours later.

As soon as her daughter told her what Applette said, Nicholette knew the party wouldn't happen.

"Are you sure this guy's for real? You think his information is valid?" Magnus said skeptically.

"You saw him at the party, he's legit. This is all very real. And if we don't find this woman or whatever she is, there's going to be a much worse war on our doorstep."

"And here we were planning a party to celebrate and contemplating telling you both to prepare to take over in the future." Magnus ran a hand over his hair.

EIGHT

TITAN Corporation - Personal TITAN Device
System Status: Active -- Universal Grid: Online
Current Time/Date (Earth - The Republic of Florida):
1:57 p.m./August 05, 4016
Secondary Time/Date (Praxis - Daviens): 3:11 pm/
April 03, 2194
Current Universal Positioning System Location:
The Republic of Florida, Former United States of
America, Earth
User: Unrecorded
Communications Menu
Incoming message(s) received: 1 - Status: Unread
Message Received at 1:57 p.m.
Message Sent from: Universal News Agency (UNA)
- Earth

-UNA
-London, England, Earth
BREAKING NEWS
Earth's Emperor and Empress, Magnus and Nicholette
Vandeermeer, said that the Huamu Yulan Square
bombing in Shanghai was one of the key factors for
deciding to declare war on Il'laceier.

To date, no one person or entity has been charged with the bombing. Supreme Commander Sebastian Raynes has personally vouched for one suspect, the late Ni-toyis Tredux, claiming it would be impossible for her to commit such a crime and that she was not a partner to Shipley in any way. Tredux fought during The War of Empires and was killed in battle.
Captain Brandon Shipley, many suspect, was the sole perpetrator but it has never been proven who actually set off or built the bomb. Shipley's whereabouts are still unknown and a body was never recovered. If you know anything about his current location, officials urge you not to approach him but to call police.
You can trust UNA for all your universal news needs.

-END OF MESSAGE
* This message will only be deleted by user.
- -

Celeste stopped reading her Titan and looked at Sebastian.

"You didn't tell me what you told the press about Ni-toyis and absolving her of the bombing."

Sebastian looked up from his own Titan, "She had nothing to do with that bombing."

"How can you be sure? She was a horrible person. I mean, even in death, she's still causing problems between us."

"You have Jon, I have Ni-toyis then."

"You're really going there? I was married to Jon for years."

"I knew Ni-toyis for *decades*." He looked Celeste in the eyes, "We need to put this to bed once and for all. I need to tell you how she saved my grandmother. And if I can accept your occasional defense of your prick of a husband, you need to do the same for Ni-toyis."

Celeste only looked at Sebastian. It looked as though she didn't know what to say until she finally muttered, "I'm not defending his actions, or him. I just think he was capable of change there at the end. Fire away."

"My grandmother had been living alone a long while. She got the urge to repaint the house, the home I showed you. She was always doing projects like that to stay busy. She had removed a lot of old paint off this craft table in the back room. I guess she didn't ventilate that day. She'd gotten too wrapped up trying to get it done fast and she got overwhelmed by carbon monoxide. She had messaged me before she passed out that she wasn't feeling well but I was on the other side of the galaxy. I asked the person I knew who was closest to check on her and that was Ni-toyis. She arrived just in time. The doctors said my grandma would've died had she stayed in the house another two minutes. *That's* why I tolerated Ni-toyis. *That's* why I never abandoned her or disregarded her requests for help. Yes I owed her favors based on our agreement, but the woman saved the only family member that loved me and hadn't forsaken me."

Celeste considered this. "I wish you would've told me a lot sooner."

"I still don't think it will make you accept my feelings towards her or like her, but that's the truth of it all."

"I *am* glad she saved your grandma. You're lucky you didn't lose her, but one good deed doesn't change my opinion that she was bitchy and selfish. I'll try not to bring her up again."

"Okay. I'll consider that case closed."

CHAPTER 2

SAVE THE DATE

ONE

>>> > HACE'S TRANSIT FLEW through space towards his destination but he couldn't keep conscious long enough to make a plan for when he got to the door. He knew he had lost a lot of blood and he had no food for Declan. As much as he didn't want to make a detour, he didn't have a choice.

There was a medical outpost right before the next Jump so he docked there and opened the door of the transit. He tried to stand, but he passed out on the floor before he took a step.

T W O

>>> > WHEN HACE WOKE up, he was in a hospital gown in an uncomfortable bed. He looked around for a call button but couldn't find one, so he yelled for a nurse as loud as he could.

A gray-haired Human woman walked in briskly, looking like she had a long shift and a short fuse. She wiped the hair out of her eyes, "You're awake! Great!"

"Yes, where's my baby?"

"The little one is in the nursery. He needed attention too. He's a little underweight, I'm guessing he was just born?"

"Yeah."

"What's his name? What's your name?"

"Declan and I'm...Henry Sellus."

"Where's the mother?"

Hace shook his head and covered his face, "She was in the war...She didn't make it."

"Oh dear, I'm so sorry. I wouldn't pry but she...The Earth/Il'lacean war?"

He looked at her and nodded.

"Okay. I'll get the doctor to talk to you and we'll bring Declan by later, all right?"

Hace nodded again.

Hace watched the woman leave as he wiped away the tears he was trying to keep in. The last time he was at a hospital, he watched his sister die. This was too much. He couldn't keep himself in check, couldn't get a hold of his emotions. It was embarrassing.

The doctor walked in while Hace was blowing his nose. Hace looked him over and thought he'd be one of those handsome Lanyx men who had a wife and three mistresses his whole life.

"I'm Doctor Mohammed Lanter. I'm glad you're awake. Can I ask what happened to you?"

"My...wife and I were soldiers in the War of Empires. We both got injured. She went into labor after she was shot. A doctor on the battlefield helped deliver the baby. My wife... didn't make it. I left when another battle broke out. I needed to get my son somewhere safe. I was looking to get back home, but I guess I didn't make it."

"Where is home?"

Good question, Hace thought. Home used to mean Ni-toyis. Now he was lost.

"Stoxia."

"You're quite a distance from there but we'll get you tended to and stabilized. I'm thinking you'll need a week of rest and your baby needs some time in the incubator. He's a little small."

Hace knew he couldn't stay here all that time, but he wouldn't say anything, "Thanks doc. I really appreciate your help."

"Sure thing. You take it easy, and we'll let you walk over to see your son shortly."

THREE

>>> > ACROSS EARTH AND Il'laceier, smoke still hung in the air, the cleanup of battlefields got underway, the bodies of the dead were being identified, and the injured were treated and shipped home. Buildings were inspected for structural soundness and marked for demolition by city bots. On an Earth city street, there was a home robotics store with screens playing in its window. A mangy Calico cat was the only one currently watching the news.

"We're starting to get some rough estimates of the cost of war. During the War of Empires that lasted nearly two hundred Earth days, one quarter of Il'laceier was damaged. It's reported that five million Il'laceans were killed in action and another two million injured. The damages are expected to be in the twenty trillion coren range. Early on in the battle, Rem Mot Om was completely destroyed and it's unclear if it will be rebuilt or not.

"For Earth, one third of the planet was destroyed and the damages are reported to be around nine hundred billion coren. Four hundred and fifteen million lives were lost and two hundred twenty-seven million were injured. You may remember Il'laceier was expected to win the war, but because Human military forces were able to kill King Hennessy, the war was declared a victory for Earth.

"Il'laceier is in a political free fall due to the lack of leadership. A temporary council is assembling in the interim. All but one former council member has come back to take control until a system is put into place. Katsanos Annetweeks has refused to return to her post citing a death in her family has caused her to take an early retirement. An interesting replacement has stepped forward, Raykreede Monter. Some of you might remember he was the Il'lacean soldier believed to be killed by King David Hennessy. But sources claim he was framed and able to escape execution. We'll have his story later on in the program.

"Some Il'laceans refuse to believe King David Hennessy was killed during the battle. There is speculation he's in hiding, and was able to fly away to a secure location.

"On Earth, Magnus and Nicholette Hennessy have taken control, claiming their original leadership titles of Emperor and Empress of Earth, although there has been word that once their leadership is over, Earth will try a multi-race Human council."

FOUR

>>> > ULYSSES, WITH VERONICA'S help, took David's body to Earth on a transit as they flew home. He arranged several Human royal guards from David's reign to walk the streets with him as they held David's body aloft on a plank of wood for the universe to see.

The minute news outlets aired it, Magnus called Ulysses to his new office at Silver Thorn.

"I realize that man was a piece of filth that damaged Earth's reputation enough that it'll take me decades to correct, but what made you think parading his dead body through the STREETS WAS A GOOD IDEA?"

"I thought a visual aid would quell the rumors that the king was alive and in hiding. Besides, he tortured my girlfriend. He threatened me. He threatened your daughter with blackmail and ordered me to hire Sebastian to kill her. Isn't that enough?"

Magnus nodded, "That's more than enough, but we need to move away from Il'lacean involvement and avoid inciting more violence against Humans or our world. The Il'laceans are enraged that we've killed their king and many of their soldiers. The new governing council will try to establish order but chaos rules there for now. I don't need them coming here and setting off bombs or using chemical warfare against innocent civilians for revenge. I was going to ask you to work for me, but in light of what you've done I will strongly reconsider."

"Sir, I am a good soldier and an excellent guard. I risked my ass *every day* under Jon and David both trying to gather information that I could use against them. Sebastian would have *never* gotten to David had it not been for me. I'd like a job in this government. I shouldn't be treated as a criminal."

"I'm grateful for you protecting Celeste and I appreciate your help in ending the war, but you showed me some irresponsibility with that stunt. I will not be *commanded* by you to do the things you wish me to. I will reconsider your employment. Until you hear back from me, stay off the premises. Take some time away to cool down and recover from the war. It has taken a great toll on us all."

Ulysses seethed, "I'm a war hero! One error in judgement shouldn't cost me my job. Maybe you should ask Sebastian what he thinks of me." He wanted to slam the door as he left but knew it would make him look more temperamental, so he avoided the urge.

FIVE

>>> > HACE WAS ASLEEP. They had allowed him to walk down the hall and visit Declan. He was currently the only premature baby they had in the outpost and he was sleeping soundly when Hace checked on him. Hace could not be more proud of him and Ni-toyis both. He just wished they could've been the family that he knew Ni-toyis wanted.

Late at night when he and Ni-toyis were sharing a bed, Ni-toyis would go on and on about changing some of the rooms of TAP to a nursery and a playroom. Hace promised he would do it after she had the baby, but that time never came.

Now here he was, a single father without a home for his own child.

His dreaming mind took him to the time when his sister was dying.

Mareeve had lost a lot of blood. Half her face was burned off and the bandages wrapped around her skull were wet with pus and red stains. He held one of her hands and prayed to a God he didn't really believe in. His sister was a loving soul, and everything that Hace was not. She was well loved by all the other soldiers and her circle of friends was huge. Her boyfriend had been killed in a transit accident two years prior, but she tried so hard to make him proud in every way. Hace would brag to anyone who would listen about her and what a badass she was.

His sister came to and looked at him with the one eye she could see out of. She started to cry as she realized the shape she was in. She wanted a mirror but Hace wouldn't allow her one. She had been concerned about her looks before her injuries and if she saw herself now, it could only do damage and darken her spirits. They started to argue. Her blood pressure rose and her heart raced. The doctors rushed in with nurses and pushed Hace aside. He stood in the back of the room as she expired. Most of her body had been severely burned and the doctors explained that it was too much stress on her system. Her little heart just couldn't handle it.

He blamed himself, but the doctors explained she would've passed on whether she was having an argument with him or not, it was just a matter of time. The doctors moved out of the room and left him alone with her body. He walked to her and put his hand on hers one last time.

Hace woke up in his hospital bed screaming. The nurses came quickly asking if he wanted a sedative. He nodded.

The sedative knocked him out and he knew nothing after. No more bad dreams.

SIX

>>> > ON EARTH, KATSANOS kneeled by Mitch's gravestone. He had been placed next to his sisters. She grabbed a handful of dirt and let the soil fall through her long fingers.

D'Artagnan leaned down and put a hand on her shoulder, "It's what he would've wanted."

She stood up and looked at him, "I know."

"Are you going back to his home now? Are you going to be okay?"

"Yes. I think I'll be alright. Khaleen will see me through. My faith goes deep and has gotten me through everything else."

"Let me know if you need anything."

"Thanks for making the arrangements," she gave D'Artagnan a weak smile.

"Of course."

She watched him walk to his transit docked off to the side of the graveyard. Ophelia was in the passenger seat and waved to Katsanos. She put her hand up in return. She wondered for the millionth time if Mitch would still be alive had D'Artagnan not stopped her on the battlefield that day.

She no longer blamed D'Artagnan like she did initially but the thought persisted in her. Like an animal with sharp teeth, the curiosity ate away at her. Could she have prevented the fatal attack? Would things have ended different?

It was probably unfair of her. D'Artagnan had no way of knowing what was going to happen. And neither did Katsanos. She recalled the day she lost Mitch. The smells of fear mixing with anger and despair, it was overwhelming and the scents were everywhere. There was no way to discern where it was coming from unless you were right on top of another being, but...

Ophelia had D'Artagnan back in her bed every night and what did Katsanos have?

Only memories.

An hour later, Katsanos was standing in front of Mitch's Arizonaland house. She had no key card but her nose would tell her how to get in. Key cards had a particular scent of steel and plastic. She sniffed the air and grabbed a watering can off the porch railing. She flipped it over and taped to the bottom was a spare key card.

She took a deep breath and opened the door.

Mitch had a minimalistic massive single story home with an expansive view of the backyard. Katsanos walked to the back door made of glass and saw a Zen garden. The concentric lines in the sand circling the rocks reminded her of the solar system. She looked around his kitchen and saw a piece of paper underneath a fruit bowl. She picked it up and took a breath, but her hands were already shaking.

"If you're reading this, it means I didn't make it through the war.

Bury my body next to my sisters if it's doable. I never bought a plot of land. It might not even be possible anymore. If that's the case, cremate me and spread my ashes across the Pacific Ocean. I was raised in the far west of Arizonaland and always spent as much time as I could on the beach. Way before my time, the area I lived in was called California and my ancient ancestors settled there looking for gold. I'm sure you don't want a history lesson on Earth, but I'm sure I never told you this.

I want you to have this house. I never got the chance to really live in it and everything is brand new. I'm not sure how you feel about Arizonaland, but I always loved it. You'll get everything from droughts to torrential rain but there is a fully-stocked waterproof basement in case of bad storms or emergencies.

My other place on Praxis is a rental, just move everything out of it and keep it here. Whatever you don't want you can sell or ask D'Artagnan or anyone else in FAIR if they want it. Eventually the landlord over there will figure out he's not getting any more payments out of me. (I'm trying to make you laugh. Is it working? I hope so. I always adored your laugh.)"

Katsanos wiped away several tears as they fell. She leaned her elbows down on the kitchen counter trying to steady herself as she took a deep breath.

"I have a lot of coren. Take 10 or 15% of it and keep it for yourself if you think you'll need it. Spent wisely, that should sustain you for the rest of your life. I would like you to donate 50% to a charity that helps women get out of domestic abuse situations. Take 30% and give it to some homeless shelters of your choice, and ones that you feel really get neglected. The remaining money I think you should go out and buy some house warming gifts for our friends. Some of these couples are going to get married whether they're engaged or not. I can see how they look at each other. And some of the others will need a new home so get them something nice on behalf of us.

If there's anything left, you haven't done your job (kidding.) If there's something left then add it to a charity or take it for yourself.

The next part's going to be hard. But if I can't tell you after I've died, the words will never come out and you'll never know, so here goes...

When you met me. I was a bit broken. I was in a relationship with a woman who was cheating on me although I didn't know it at the time. I thought I could trust her. I cared for her. And when you came into my life. I felt guilty about how attracted I was to you.

You are the right type of woman for me and I'm sorry I didn't meet you sooner. We barely had any time together it seems. I didn't get to spoil you enough or take care of you enough. I knew you had men before me but I wanted to be the one to stand out. The one that you cared about the most. or the one you liked the most at least.

I tried to do the right things in life. but I think I failed a lot. I'm only Human I guess. If I'm gone then I know I definitely didn't have enough time to atone for my sins. I hope God is as forgiving as they say. I hope I get to go to Heaven.

There are things I've done that I never told you about. Ask D'Artagnan to tell you. If he doesn't want to talk about it show him this letter. (Tell her D'Art! Please!)

Now. this is the part where I say things like I love you. and I do.

I do care for you a great deal and I think with more time. maybe you could've fallen in love with me. Maybe someday had a house and kids together and got married and the whole ball of wax. I think. anyway. I don't know how you felt. but that's me.

Seems like fate has decided to take another path for me.

Isn't it ironic that I've spent most of my adult life fighting your people and then I have an Il'lacean best friend and another for a girlfriend?

I've got to go. it's almost time to leave this place and go where you are. I'm excited to see you again and your beautiful yellow eyes. They remind me of the color of sunrise in the desert.

Take good care of yourself in my absence.

Mitch

P.S. I'm sure you're sad. but I don't want you to be. I want you to go out and live and enjoy things. When you're ready. you have my blessing to go out with another man. but he better treat you right or I'll come back and haunt his ass! I think you're a gorgeous girl and it won't be long before you're turning some lucky guy's head. I was too serious in my life. I didn't laugh enough. I didn't enjoy friendships or love often enough. Go out and live for me Kat."

Katsanos burst into heartbroken sobs.

SEVEN

>>> > KOLEK WAS PLEASED with the medical service her body received while in the medical tent, but it was time to go. She briefly considered taking another body, but she had seen this one many months ago in action through Brandon Shipley's eyes and it was a good specimen.

Besides she didn't have the time to search out another body.

She left the tent when no one was looking and stole a transit for her travels. She was elated about the levels of damage that Il'laceier and Earth sustained in their puny little war. Lots of beings had perished and she thought it could make her war end that much quicker.

It was too bad that Shipley had been killed though. She wondered what kind of damage that bomb could have done had he set it off the way she wanted.

She programed the transit for Stoxia and launched.

EIGHT

>>> > "HEY MAN. SORRY I couldn't come visit you in person." Ulysses looked at Raykreede on his Titan.

"No one can come see me since we've locked down the SAP. It just seemed like the safest move right now. My people are crazed with worry and anger – a terrible combination. I'm sorry I couldn't get you in." Raykreede sat in an office in the only region office building that had survived the war – in the Swamplands.

"Probably for the best. I'm pretty sure every Il'lacean knows my face and wants me dead after that display I made with David's body."

"You suffer any fallout on your home world?"

"Yeah, yesterday Magnus suspended me. I don't know if he's going to let me work for the new empire, said I took risks."

"I suppose I would've made it worse had I released the news about David's sexual preference."

"You threatened to tell the press, what kept you from it?"

"I know I was angry and wanted the revolution to happen but I wasn't going to destroy our friendship or risk your woman's life."

"I appreciate that, Ray. I really do." Ulysses surveyed the damage to his apartment. He'd been told it was bad but was only looking at it now. Half of his place was blown to smithereens. He'd have to live with Ginger for a while. He sighed, "So what happens now?"

"The governing council convenes for the second time tomorrow. We see what needs to be done first. I think we need the population under control before we open the SAP again. Others want to set up more shelters for the newly homeless, and others still want to do clean up and rebuild. Honestly, all of those things are priority. I can't do them all at once because of our limited resources. We just lost too many people in the war."

"I don't think your people will calm down until they see things getting done. Maybe provide food and shelter and in exchange ask those who are able-bodied to help with the cleanup and rebuild projects."

Raykreede thought while looking at the sunset outside his window, "That sounds like something the council could agree to. Thanks!"

"No problem my friend."

NINE

>>> > CELESTE GINGERLY GOT into bed as Sebastian watched. She didn't want him to say anything so she tried not to show the pain on her face or make grunting noises as her joints ached.

"You okay?"

She squeezed her eyes shut as she grabbed for the blankets at her feet, "I'm fine."

He reached further, faster than her and tossed them up over her legs, "You're suffering. How many injuries did you sustain?"

Celeste rolled her eyes, "I lost count after a while. There's the shot to my leg, my sho—"

"You were *shot*? When?"

"Yes. The first time I went out," she hesitated, "It's fully healed now. I got stabbed in the forearm, burned on the back, my ankle got cut wh—"

"Stop. That's enough. How many times have you been in battle? A real number, not an I-don't-know answer."

She hesitated while counting in her head, "Seventy-one."

Sebastian's eyes got big. He opened his mouth to say something but closed it again. He finally said, "Damn you are stubborn. When I found you on the battlefield near Ni-toyis, you had been fighting?"

"Yes."

"Are you satisfied that you did all that you could out there?"

She nodded, "I fought my best. I helped my people."

He paused, "I should be angrier but what's done, is done. I can't blame you for wanting to be free. To fight for what you believe in. I understand that. And besides, you always do the opposite of what I ask so I'm not even arguing. Are you really okay?"

She turned out her light and looked at him, "Yes. Sore in places and sometimes the old gunshot wound in my shoulder screams at me, but the rest will heal."

He turned out his light and kissed her on the forehead, "I'm glad you're okay. I really hope that was our last war."

TEN

>>> > MAGNUS AND NICHOLETTE announced to Celeste and Sebastian at breakfast, they were officially moving into the newly vacant Silver Thorn estate and wanted them to come along too.

"I can't live there again mom. Not after what happened, plus the news and camera bots will be there all the time waiting for a story to fall into their laps. I'm dead remember?"

Nicholette shook her head, "I haven't forgotten dear, but it's a large place and we can shelter you from prying eyes if we must. I just want you to be safe."

Sebastian looked to Nicholette, "Why don't we just rent Stormview Haven from you? I love the house and so does Celeste, besides I think we'll put the privacy and all this space to good use."

Celeste looked at him, <For what?>

<Meetings with Applette and the rest of the crew if we're going to figure out this poem and where the door is.>

Celeste looked at her mother, "I think that's a great idea. Can we stay here?"

Magnus answered, "Of course dear. Whatever makes you happy. We'll be out of your hair shortly. I have a team of movers coming in to take some of our things and move the king's furniture out of Silver Thorn. Maybe by this afternoon, we'll be gone."

ELEVEN

>>> > SEBASTIAN PUT HIS arms around Celeste's waist and lifted her to sit on the kitchen counter, "We can christen all the rooms."

She laughed, "There's a ton of rooms here. It will take us weeks to do that."

"I'm not complaining. Are you?"

She shook her head as he buried his face in her neck.

"Ophelia will be back soon with Lila and Aggie, babe."

He slid his hands underneath her skirt, "I'd better be quick then."

She undid his fly, smiling.

The doorbell rang.

Celeste frowned, "Did they take off without a key?"

Sebastian cleared his throat and zipped up his pants, "I'll get it. Fuck."

Celeste jumped down and heard Veronica's voice.

"I'll be damned. What are you doing here?" Celeste smiled and hugged her friend, "I feel like it's been forever."

Veronica smiled, "Well...I was hoping you guys might need a...consultant. Or an advisor? Or anything? I'm without a job and I need a place to stay. I got rid of my apartment before the war and now...I need some help."

Sebastian looked over at Celeste.

<Please Bastian?>

Sebastian looked at Veronica, "You're not moving in with Bouton?"

She made a dismissive wave of her hand, "We sleep together, it's not like we're married. Hell, he hasn't even asked me to be his girlfriend yet."

Celeste's eyes got big, "Oh my God! You slept with him! See what the war does? It makes me so busy I miss out on all the good stuff! What was it like? Is he romantic? When was this?"

Sebastian looked towards the kitchen, "I'm going to excuse myself now. Veronica, we have plenty of room."

Celeste smiled at him, "Thanks dear." Then she looked back to her friend, "O lives with us...So does Lila and Agathon, so it's fine really. Let's go get your luggage. Where is it?"

TWELVE

>>> > HACE WOKE UP and noticed the nursing staff had taken his Titan again. He kept putting it on, but they kept removing it to draw blood. He saw a Taybusian nurse staring at him as she passed by his door, just like yesterday. He was getting too nervous to stay here much longer, not with *that* lurking the hallways. Even if that Taybuse didn't kill him, all someone had to do was alert the authorities and Hace would never hold his baby again. Plus he had to see what was on the other side of this door. What wonders did a whole other universe hold? Maybe he could take Declan through the door and never have to worry about getting arrested again. He could start all over.

After dinner was served that night, Hace saw a group of nurses huddled together around an airlock down the hall. He got out of bed and crept to his doorway. He couldn't hear what they were saying but he saw the airlock open and a female Taybusian police officer come in.

Hace knew he had to get out of here now. There was no way that cop was here for anyone but him.

He quickly threw his clothes on and removed his IVs. He kept the door to his room closed and hid behind the entrance. The door opened and the cop came through it. She noticed the empty hospital bed immediately and her hand hovered over her weapon holstered on her belt.

Hace punched her in the hand and crushed her fingers against her weapon, then jumped behind her and pulled his IV tube around the cop's thick neck.

It wasn't easy choking a huge, reptilian, four-armed, strong police officer trained in combat, but Hace liked a challenge. He pulled tight until he knew the cop was dead then let her hit the floor. Outside he heard the announcement that a medical transit was about to deliver six burn patients to the first floor.

He quickly dragged the cop's body into the bathroom and shut the door.

He peeked out the blinds on his window and looked down the hall. It was clear. Thank Prime that emergency was keeping everyone busy around here. He grabbed his Titan and ran to get Declan. He was angry and relieved to see no nurses in the nursery. What if his child needed something? Shouldn't their always be someone in the nursery? He wrapped the baby up in his crib blankets and shot out towards the exit. It's too bad they couldn't stay longer, he wasn't upset about missing out on medical care for his wounds, but his baby still needed help.

They were in his stolen transit and out of the airlock before anyone noticed they were missing. He tried to turn on his Titan, but it wouldn't power up. He removed the battery and put it back in, but it didn't help. There were only two possibilities: the battery had died or that dirty Taybuse had fucked with it while he was unconscious.

THIRTEEN

>>> > OPHELIA LEFT HER bedroom, carefully closing the door so it wouldn't slam. As she walked down the hallway, she overheard Sebastian talking to Eric in another room. The door was shut but her hearing had always been excellent. Sebastian mentioned Jonathan's posthumous video left behind for Celeste to watch.

How puzzled Sebastian was by how much it affected her when the guy was such an ass. Ophelia had never heard anything about this, so when she ran into Celeste in the kitchen, she asked about it.

"Hey Celeste, can I ask you a really personal question?"

"Sure. I might not be able to answer it though."

"I accidently overheard Sebastian mention your reaction to the video your late husband left for you. Why did it bother you so if he made you unhappy and treated you bad?"

Celeste sighed, "Did Sebastian put you up to this?"

Ophelia shook her head, "Just trying to understand humanity."

"Good luck with that!" Celeste grabbed a lemon and started cutting it into slices, "Sometimes we don't understand ourselves. Jon cheated on me, but I also cheated on him and no, he wasn't a good husband, I never loved him, but we had our moments of getting along or laughing. Jon banned music, but he also helped me to raise a lot of coren for my charities. He wasn't all evil."

"He caused you to lose a body part though."

"He did." She looked down at her foot. "It's been rectified though. This foot is just like I was born with it. I'm trying to forgive him. Forgiveness is for myself to be free as much as it is to let it all go and move forward from it. In that video, it seemed like there was a...different look in Jon's eyes. Maybe he felt the need to change. Maybe he could have been a better person. I believe in second chances. And the thing that bothers me the most in life is 'what ifs.' I'll never know if Jon was about to turn his life around. Maybe he would've let me get a divorce. Who knows?"

"I find that scenario hard to calculate."

"Because it's unknown. It's a 'what if.' No one knows or ever will."

"Do you feel guilty about Jon's death?"

"Part of me feels guilty that I was relieved and that I was so attracted to the man that killed my husband, but no. I didn't kill

Jon, David did. Sebastian pulled the trigger, sure but if it hadn't been for David, Jon would probably still be alive."

Ophelia thought, "Does that mean you owe David thanks?"

Celeste chortled, "No. Certainly not. David was off his rocker. Drunk with power and dangerous. I owe him nothing."

"But without David's orders, you would've never met Sebastian."

Celeste stopped to consider it, "I think we'd still have met some other way. If not through that event, then some other place or time. Anyway, Sebastian might never understand that people are capable of change *if* they have the desire to. He should because he used to be a su..." she stopped herself short of saying the word.

"Suicidal? Yes I know that. You forget I was every camera in his place before I had a body. I saw him that night and there were several others before that. Granted, he took it further than I'd ever seen him before, but the intent was always there."

They were silent until Celeste said, "Sebastian didn't know Jon like I did. None of it matters now. Jon might have been changing but I'll never know how much. Jon's gone. I'll have to live with that 'what if' forever but I know not to bring it up with Sebastian again. I love that man more than life itself and it's not worth it to me to cause another argument over something that cannot be changed. Does any of this make sense?"

Ophelia raised an eyebrow, "To be honest, no. Your husband tortured you. Something no one should do to another, yet you defend him in some things. Sebastian treats you like a queen. Like gold. Beings deserve respect and kindness. But I appreciate you answering my questions. You're entitled to feel however you want of course. I just won't understand it. Maybe no one can, because no one has been in your particular situation."

Celeste was left alone to brew some tea as Ophelia removed herself. She looked down at the knife and lemon slices on the counter. *What if, indeed.*

FOURTEEN

>>> > SEBASTIAN LOOKED OVER everyone at Stormview Haven, "I've asked you to come live with us because I feel this is all going to move very fast. Instead of traveling for hours every time something happens, I thought, why don't we all live close together until this is done? Do you all agree?"

In addition to Veronica, Lila, Agathon, and Ophelia, now they had Ginger, Ulysses, Eric, Katsanos, and D'Artagnan as roommates.

Everyone agreed this was a good arrangement.

Sebastian cleared this throat, "Now I know there's a lot of couples here...And a lot of new couples at that."

Eric whistled.

Katsanos teared up and wrapped her arms around herself tighter.

"Just lock your doors. The last thing I need is to walk in on something I don't want to see...please."

Ginger blushed.

"Some of you weren't on the Il'lacean battlefield when Recin Applette showed up, but you all remember him making a scene at the masquerade party a while back. Applette needs help finding his girlfriend, I guess is what we'll call her. Kolek. A poem that the Lanyx have told their children for hundreds of years isn't just a poem. I didn't know it when I was a child but it's a piece of history."

Sebastian recited the poem for them to hear, recorded it and sent it to their Titans.

"We need to find Kolek if we are to avoid a universal war."

Ginger interrupted, "Wait. Universe wide? All the worlds? Everywhere?"

"Yes, war with another universe that comes through a doorway."

"What do you mean another universe?" Ulysses asked.

Sebastian was irked at the interruptions since they had a lot of information to go over, but Ulysses, Ginger, Veronica, and Eric hadn't been there when Applette went over some of this.

Veronica spoke up, "Eric always said we live in a multiverse but we couldn't prove it. Lanyx have this as a core belief don't they?"

Ulysses asked, "I thought a multiverse meant parallel universes. Doesn't that mean there will be two of everyone?"

Conversations erupted all over the kitchen and everyone spoke at once.

Sebastian tapped D'Artagnan on the shoulder and yelled at him to whistle loud.

D'Artagnan's whistle was the only way to get everyone to shut their mouths.

Lila covered her ears, "Holy God!"

Sebastian nodded to D'Artagnan, "Now that I have your attention, I can explain. Lanyx *do* believe that we live in a multiverse, but *not* parallel universes. We believe there is more than one universe but these other universes are not exact copies of this one. We don't know how many there are but Applette has confirmed at least two others than our own. He should really be the one explaining this."

"Where is he?" Eric asked.

"Last time I saw him was on the Il'lacean battlefield and he left no way for me to get a hold of him.

"He claims to be something called a Universe Ruler and so is Kolek. This poem I recited, it will help us find the things we need if we wanted to open that War door, maybe only to let Applette in to find his girlfriend. But I'm afraid Hace will be opening that door...really, any time now since he left days ago. I can hope he's dead, but his child is special and maybe he could do something healing for his father, or maybe his kid can open the door."

Eric said, "Special child? Like how?"

"He's our next Universe Ruler according to Applette." Celeste answered.

The room was quiet momentarily.

Eric asked, "Have your 7's come back? Or you Raynes?"

They both shook their heads.

Celeste spoke, "Everything feels foggy, like I can't connect to anyone. I felt my powers coming back for about half a day right when David was killed, but the next morning I was back to this. No visons. No telepathy."

Sebastian nodded, "I can't feel anything. My kicker's non-existent as well. What do you think Eric?"

He put his hands in his pockets, "I can't feel my 7's or see the future. As in, at all. It's black."

Veronica said, "Wait. Doesn't that mean..."

"That we've lost the war and we'll be six feet under? I have no idea really."

Lila said, "Well that's reassuring."

Sebastian put his hands up for everyone to be quiet, "That doesn't mean anything. If all we do is speculate, we're going to freeze with fear and there's no time for that. We need to have a plan and we need to act."

"What's a kicker? How many of you have telepathy or powers?" Katsanos asked. "Am I the only one who doesn't?"

Sebastian put his head down, "Shit. I guess we need everyone to be fully caught up before we go forward. Is everyone okay with talking about what they can do? Ulysses?"

He shook his head no.

Sebastian went to him and whispered, "You're one of the few of us whose power isn't affected by war. Your training could save someone's life in here. Now's not a good time to keep secrets and I promise if you suffer judgement or any fallout from it, I will correct it."

Ulysses's hazel eyes stared into Sebastian's blue ones for a moment while he thought.

"It's life or death Ulysses. I need your help."

"Okay."

"You're a very good man." Sebastian walked back to the front of the group, "Ulysses, Eric, D'Artagnan, and myself are all ex-military. We come from backgrounds with extensive training in weapons, war, and survival.

"Celeste, Eric, and I have telepathy, Lanyx call it our 7's and each one of us has an extra power, a kicker. Eric can see into the future, Celeste has visions, and I have telekinesis."

Sebastian looked at Agathon, "Is it okay if I tell them?"

Agathon looked around at everyone looking at him, "No one better say anything to anyone outside this room. If they agree to that stipulation, okay."

Lila grabbed his hand and addressed Katsanos, "Katsanos is a government worker. I only have hesitations because she could go back and tell powerful people th—"

"I have no interest in spilling secrets now that David's been eradicated. You can trust me Human, you have my word."

Agathon said, "I'm Rhorr'Dach."

Ginger grabbed onto Ulysses as she almost fell off her bar stool, "You're fucking shitting me! I can't take much more of this."

Katsanos's eyes were wide, "That's impossible!"

Sebastian interjected, "I assure you he's telling the truth."

Ophelia spoke up for the first time, "I am a sentient robot. I just came alive recently and am still learning my way but I'm not dangerous to this group. I'm extremely strong and have the best analytical brain in this room."

D'Artagnan said, "Damn straight! And I can smell just about anything out. So can Katsanos. Il'laceans have the best noses."

Ulysses said, "I have been trained at the Priesthood of Religious Studies and Magic for twelve years and am a master. I can do many things but it drains me immediately after. I won't do it unless absolutely necessary and I'd rather not have the whole world know about it."

Sebastian smiled, "No more secrets between friends now. We all have something special about us – that includes Ginger, Veronica, and Lila too."

Ginger asked, "How? I can't see into the future or turn into a fire breathing Dach."

"Ice. I breathe ice," Agathon corrected.

Ginger frowned, "Sorry."

Celeste spoke up, "Katsanos, besides being able to sniff out things just as good as D'Art, has worked for the Il'lacean King's Council. None of us here can claim that. She knows things that are specific to a female Il'lacean too."

"And if we need to clothe the enemy to death, then I'm your girl!" Lila said as she pointed her thumbs at herself.

Celeste frowned, "You fought and killed already. You know how this works. Besides we could need armor worked into clothing. Your sewing could be a very valuable asset."

Sebastian spoke, "Listen ladies, if you didn't fight in the Battle of Empires and don't think you can fight in this one, there's other things to do – collect intelligence, watch our perimeters, cook a meal, tend to a wound, love and care for the people around you. These tasks are just as important as fighting the enemy. Your jobs – no matter what they are – are valued. You are all irreplaceable. I know you're all strong, intelligent, and capable. Now whe—"

The doorbell rang.

Sebastian asked Celeste, "Are we missing someone? Did I forget anybody?"

She looked around and shook her head, "I'll go get it." She quickly walked to the door and opened it.

"You're having a meeting and didn't call me?" Mr. Applette put a hand to his chest. He removed his hat as he walked in the door without being asked to come inside.

She closed the door and walked back into the kitchen.

Sebastian looked as Applette entered the room.

"How did you know we were meeting?"

"I have my ways."

Sebastian asked, "Do you have a number? A way to be reached?"

D'Artagnan said, "He has a number, he's just never given it to me."

"And how do you know that Mr. Steele?" Applette smirked.

"Because you have a Titan on your arm and it won't work without a number assigned to it."

"Well, I'm here. You're here. Let's do some planning and talking shall we?"

Sebastian said before Applette could continue, "That's what we were about to do before you came in unannounced."

"I heard there have been some discussions about how legitimate I am. I know all of you were at Mr. Raynes and Ms. Vandeermeer's party and you know my name is Recin Applette and I'm from the universe right next door called Knowledge."

He turned behind him and made the motion of ripping a piece of paper in two. Where his hands were, there was no longer reality, there was a window looking into a very different and strange looking place.

It was a view looking out over an entire galaxy of planets and suns. The view became tighter and focused on one system with two suns and three planets orbiting around them as Applette moved his hands across the window he had torn open.

"This is a window into my universe. See here is my home planet and our system."

D'Artagnan asked, "If you can make windows, why can't you make doors?"

"Ah Mr. Steele, now is the time for you to get answers for your questions. First I can't travel through windows, it must be a doorway. And I cannot make a door because it's not in my power. I'm a Universe Ruler, not a wizard. When I was born, I was deemed special by the Universe Ruler in power and she chose me out of billions of other beings to serve. When she died, I took power. You might think that since I rule over an entire universe, that I have limitless power and can do whatever I want, but you'd be wrong. I have limits. I'm not supposed to leave my universe and I am not to manipulate beings or events there. I can make windows to see other universes, but only the two on either side of mine, to check on them, but I am not supposed to travel to them."

"What do you mean the two universes *on either side* of you?" Celeste spoke.

"Lovely to see you using your voice Ms. Vandeermeer. Let's say...no, I'll have to start earlier. I know you all believed with the exception of the Lanyx that we are in a singular universe."

"We covered this," Eric said.

"Shhh Bouton, let him explain," D'Artagnan scolded.

Eric rolled his eyes, "Please continue."

"We live in a multiverse with many universes within it. Eight to be exact. There could be even more, but I am definitely not allowed outside the boundaries of this multiverse we're in. Now, imagine a pie. My favorite pie is pumpkin, a delicious creation and we have nothing like it in my universe. It is simply amazing – the flavor, the sweetness...Anyway, a delicious pumpkin pie you need to slice into eight equal pieces, each piece, for this example, is one universe and they all sit side by side, just like slices in that pie. The Unknown Universe, that's you, you're bordered by War and Knowledge, but it wasn't always like this. Sometimes my boss, the Multiverse Keeper, he can move us around however he sees fit, and does from time to time so that War gets its chance to conquer a new place.

"Kolek and I used to be side by side in our universes and she attempted to win Knowledge. My universe won. But in the process of being locked up for days together, I grew to respect and admire her. Her mind worked like a well-oiled machine and her personality...it was full of determination. Her spirit was so strong and I was distressed to see her go. As soon as the war ended, she disappeared on me and I was unable to tell her how I felt, that I wanted to get to know her better. The Keeper frowns on this kind of interaction of course. I was afraid of being punished too so I said nothing, but the Keeper must've recognized it somehow. An extremely long while later, I found and opened a door to come visit Kolek in her universe, but unbeknownst to me, the Keeper wedged a universe in between us, that turned out to be your universe and so when I came over, I plopped down into yours and I've been here ever since. Doors are rare and hard to access. The right set of events need to line up before one can be opened. Then I found out Kolek was here researching how to conquer your domain and I thought 'this must be fate' because here I am and here she would be!

"But she has proved impossible to find..."

Sebastian broke in, "Wait. You said earlier that Hace's kid is the chosen one to take over for our Universe Ruler. Where is she? Isn't she helping you find your lady friend?"

"No. She's trying to get me out. She has to let Kolek do her research as their war is a planned thing, kind of, but she's at least allowed to do her job here. I'm not supposed to be here at all, so your Ruler and I are constantly playing a bit of cat and mouse in here. It's a small universe when you're being chased, really it is, I assure you."

Ginger asked, "Doesn't Kolek sense you here somehow? You haven't heard anything from her in all the time you've been here?"

"She doesn't. She has no idea how I feel about her or where I'm at. She's focused on her task and I will not be seen by her unless I'm standing right in front of her, even then she might not recognize me since I look nothing like the last time she saw me. I'm in a completely different form and I assume she will be too."

Eric asked, "How the hell are we going to find her if *you* don't know what she looks like?"

"It will be difficult to say the least. But while we shared our time together, we compared notes about our Keeper and our jobs. I told her I could take other forms, she said she could take over freshly expired corpses. Our abilities are very similar really, just a slight variation I suppose. She said she could talk to living beings but they'd think they were going crazy or something like talking to God. I gue—"

"Ni-toyis!" Sebastian yelled out.

"I'm sorry?" Mr. Applette looked confused.

"She was on the battlefield and then she wasn't. I wanted to return the body to her mother but I never found her. Maybe your Kolek took her?"

"It's possible. Maybe that's our best lead to finding her. At least I knew what she looked like. Hard to forget a beauty like that."

Eric smiled, "That's something at least."

Mr. Applette continued, "This is my only chance to find her. If I don't, well, I'll probably lose my job anyways and maybe my life. My Keeper's been playing with my life band and I'm not sure when my time is up."

"Huh?" asked Eric.

"My life band. In Knowledge we know the precise moment we will die. I was supposed to die a while ago and when it was about to run down, it suddenly stayed at zero, then changed rapidly. The Keeper knows I'm here and he's not happy. That's why I need all of your help and why I've assembled the Witnesses. I need Kolek to hear me out. I have an idea for her and I to be together but it won't work if I run out of time."

Sebastian said, "You don't really care if we win the war."

"No, you losing the war wouldn't be good for me. Then Kolek would be very busy and I need her attention. I've waited long enough. No, I want you guys to win the war, then she might lose her job and I could suggest her co-ruling my universe. That would be best."

Agathon asked, "What are these Witnesses you speak of?"

"Who is the right word. Sebastian is one and so is Celeste and D'Artagnan and you my dear. If you hadn't been involved with this bunch, I would've sent you a Titan message asking you to join my cause. Sebastian will help lead them, I hope, to victory."

"What do they, we, do?" Agathon sighed.

"You are the representative for your planet to lead your people to conquer the War Universe. You are responsible to convince them that there is a war coming and once it does, to help fight them off. The beings I have chosen either love to fight, are glory hounds, are financially challenged, or need to redeem themselves somehow. The Witnesses stand to earn a million coren each if they're successful and will go down in history as heroes in their respective communities. In other words, you won't be able to turn my offer down."

"I'll help you Applette. I'm in for saving the universe, but I don't fit into any of those categories."

"Oh, but you do. There was a little Dach a long time ago that you tried to forget about. You let him down, him and his parents. Do you want me to continue?"

"No, that's enough."

Lila looked at Agathon and wondered what this exchange was about.

"If it makes you feel any better Agathon, some planets have twin witnesses, in case one dies. In your case, I have a second witness. You all have stories like Agathon. You all, *we* all have our secrets. You're all worthy of this challenge and to be called Witnesses."

Lila said, "Count me in."

The others, one by one accepted.

"May I? Are you done explaining?" Sebastian asked.

Applette nodded, "Yes, I think that's it."

"Celeste and I found a door on Bahsheef months ago. I'm pretty sure it's related to the poem. Does that mean we'll have to go there?"

Applette shook his head, "No, it's not the door."

Celeste said, "It sure did look like one."

"Looks are deceiving in this universe. I think maybe you found another door back to my universe. It took long enough to appear, but no, it won't help us with *this* door."

"Can you decipher the writing we found near it if I show you pictures?" Celeste asked.

"I have no interest in going back to Knowledge yet."

"But can you help?"

"I suppose. I was saying, *if* Hace opens the door to War, it's a one-time thing. He opens it and War falls out into your universe, then the only way to close it will be complicated because the Red Klix will be gone."

"What do you mean, Applette? I need that stone back for my people. It's sacred to us." Sebastian's veins stood out on his neck. One vein grew across his forehead like a tiny tree branch.

"You won't get it. It's part of a world in War. It's not of this place and it doesn't belong here. It's been trying to get back to its universe for as long as it's been separated. No, once the door opens, it will snap back to the planet it came from."

"That stone is part of a...planet?"

"Yes. You didn't know? Oh how could you, I forget. Sorry, no you'll never get it back."

Sebastian sighed in exasperation, "Is there anything else we should know?"

Applette smiled mischievously, "Yes actually. Where I come from, destiny rules all. For the most part, we all know what will happen. We educate ourselves to the hilt. We hone our skills, we prep ourselves for our mates. There are a few who buck the system, try to do things differently and those beings cause chaos to happen."

Eric interrupted, "What the *hell* does this have to do with us?"

D'Artagnan shhh'ed him.

Applette glared at Eric, "Destiny doesn't work the same here but it's very similar. Here multiple paths will lead you to the same outcome. Destiny, fate, whatever you like to call it, controls all here. I've heard so many beings complain about how they wish their situation was different or ask why me? Well it's because of fate. I know I already mentioned that fate's controlling all of you pairing off – that it is by no means accidental that all of you are friends. Celeste and Sebastian met because Kolek came into your universe at that moment. This caused an anomaly to ripple through all of your lives. When a Universe Ruler moves into a new universe it disturbs all kinds of things. Some people sense it more than others. Jonathan Hennessy felt the disturbance as an omen of his future death – he made a video for Celeste because of it. Celeste had her first vision of Sebastian being...vulnerable let's say. Sebastian was ready for a change and in that moment, he thought of Celeste. In turn, she was clear-headed and ready to receive Sebastian's message. And she did. At that moment, billions of people did things they normally wouldn't have otherwise."

Eric asked, "And this happens every time she visits?"

Applette shook his head, "Certainly not. Only the first time a piece of another universe enters your own."

Eric held his head in his hands, "This is a lot of information to absorb all at once. My noggin' hurts."

"I suppose all your minds might. Sebastian, I need a copy of this poem you keep speaking of. Please send it to me and I will review it soon. I feel the Keeper getting close, I have to leave. I will be in touch. Meanwhile keep up the good work looking for Kolek." Applette started to walk away.

Eric called out, "You don't just disappear or something cool?"

"No, I walk out the door like any other being Mr. Bouton. Good evening." He stopped, "Almost forgot. Knowledge is an ocean, and you must be your boat's captain."

FIFTEEN

>>> > SEBASTIAN LOOKED AT Celeste after she came back from escorting Applette out, and motioned for her to stand next to him.

Eric blurted out, "What a little freak that weirdo is!"

Veronica laughed out loud.

"Did you have time to show him the pictures on your Titan of the Bahsheefian door?" Sebastian asked Celeste quietly.

"Yes. He said he'd need those along with the poem."

He nodded and whispered to her, "Should we tell them?"

She nodded.

"For anyone that doesn't know, I asked my queen if she would marry me and she said yes."

Katsanos smiled, as she was the only one that didn't know. She asked, "When is the big day?"

Sebastian said, "I still don't know. We need to work that out."

Eric said, "Well now that we're all here, why don't we make this an engagement party and celebrate winning the war?"

"I *love* parties! Let's do it!" Ophelia beamed.

They partied late into the night. Several of them got very drunk. Ophelia danced on her first table, Lila ended up topless until Agathon covered her up seconds later at a strip poker game. Everyone had a good time and needed to blow off some steam.

Afterwards, Celeste was laying naked in Sebastian's arms in their bed. They talked in whispers and decided January 29, 4017, was the best day to get married. It gave them a year to prepare and hopefully if a new war started, it would be over long before then.

CHAPTER 3

THE RESCUE

ONE

>>> > SEBASTIAN SAT ACROSS from D'Artagnan and Eric at the kitchen table.

"So what exactly happened to you physically?"

Eric started, "I felt off. Everything felt weird. I got dizzy, my joints all hurt, and my head started pounding."

D'Artagnan nodded, "Yeah. I felt all those things too but I also felt like...it's hard to describe...like reality was thinner there."

Sebastian raised his eyebrows, "I'm not sure I get it. How?"

D'Artagnan fidgeted with his collar, something uncharacteristic for the Il'lacean, "Like that planet was from another time and colors were muted, sounds weren't right – like you were in a hole in the ground and noise sounded flat."

Sebastian looked at Eric, "Can you describe any of this differently?"

Eric swallowed hard, "You know how when you're really drunk or going under for surgery and your body goes into fight or flight? When you get all paranoid and you can see trails of white light behind everything that moves? It's like that. I would say the noise sounded more like being in an underwater cave or in a deep well. Not a flat sound but empty or...hollow."

D'Artagnan glared at Eric, "Isn't a well a hole in the ground? That's what I said. They're the same thing."

Eric narrowed his eyes, "I said a *deep* well. That means there's a shaft of bricks or concrete so sound sounds more echo-ey and...wet."

D'Artagnan scoffed, "Sounds wet? And I don't think echo-ey is a word. What kind of description is that?"

Sebastian made notes on his Titan as he recorded their conversation, "Stop it you two. Everything is helpful. What about color?"

Eric shook his head, "It was ugly there. Like dirty dingy grays. Even what was supposed to be bright colors looked washed out."

Sebastian asked, "Do you think any of this was because you were fatigued or expecting the worst? Maybe psychosomatic?"

Eric shook his head, "We aren't making this up. You ever reach for something and it's at your fingertips but then you stretch further and end up pushing it away? That's how describing this place is. It's just out of reach unless you've been there."

Sebastian didn't like the look in either of his friend's eyes and he wasn't getting anything useful out of them. He ended the recording after only five minutes and hoped he could get more out of Magnus and Nicholette.

TWO

>>> > CELESTE, D'ARTAGNAN, VERONICA, Eric, Lila, Ginger, Ulysses, Katsanos, Ophelia, and Agathon all sat in the same room with Applette and Sebastian. It was time for the massive Titan conference call with all the Witnesses. All of them had called in except for one – Laggic, the Stampermoth.

"Are we ready Applette?" Sebastian asked.

Applette hesitated, "No. There's a big problem. Something's not right with the Stampermoth. Hold on."

Agathon snorted, but only Lila caught it.

"What's that for?" She whispered.

"He involved The Innocents in this?"

Lines creased in her forehead, "Isn't that term used sarcastically?"

Agathon nodded, "The Stampermoth destroyed their home world, now they live on a mother ship. It's all they have."

The group in the room watched as Applette's eyes rolled up into his head. He went into a trance. His limbs shook and when his eyes rolled back into place, they were solid black. Applette locked onto Laggic's location like a bloodhound tracks an animal.

"What's going on?" Celeste whispered.

Applette answered to Sebastian, "She's moving all over the universe and fast. She must be Jumping. Repeatedly. She's with people she doesn't like – except for one. An exile. She needs help. Without exposure to her geode, she'll die soon."

Sebastian looked to Agathon, "You're the oldest of us, what the hell was all that about?"

Agathon thought for a moment.

"Quickly please!" Sebastian shouted.

Agathon jumped, "Stampermoths lost their home world fifteen, maybe twenty Praxian years ago. Each individual needs to be close to either their mothership, the Tessi because it has the Auchsi on it. That's a huge geode, the only bit of their

home world they could save and it's like their...their life blood?
Without it they die. Or if you were exiled, you got a tiny stone
that will sustain you, but just barely. Part of your punishment –
that you live but very uncomfortably. That's all I know regarding
what he said."

"Thank you, Agathon. I feel like there's something you're not
telling us, Applette. What's the rest of her story?" Sebastian's
face was determined.

"I can't tell exactly. The Stampermoth I chose is a Luminary."
Agathon blurted out, "Oh shit! You must be joking!"
Sebastian flicked his eyes to him, then back to Applette,
"What the hell would you be doing recruiting a Luminary,
Applette?"

"Answers later! We need to go through this meeting without
her. Then you're going to rescue her right after we're done."
Sebastian looked to Agathon with his eyebrows raised.
Agathon nodded, "She's a very important person. You'll
need to do it."

Applette didn't miss a beat once his eyes cleared out, "Thank
you all for taking the time to join me and my fellow beings for
this all important meeting. My name is Recin Applette and I'm
from a different universe than your own..." Mr. Applette went
on to explain the situation.

"I have watched all of you on your home worlds. I have
chosen you to be Witnesses because I feel you have the necessary skills to lead your planet and your people to winning the
battle over the War Universe, but we're running out of time.
You must contact your planetary governments immediately.
Tell them what I've told you. Tell them what is about to happen
and that we must prepare as quickly as possible to be invaded
by a common enemy. If you love your universe and want to save
it, please do what I ask of you.

"I know some of you will not want to believe what I'm saying.
It might be difficult information to understand, but I implore

you to trust me. Now, some of you may or may not be familiar with this man. He helped save Earth during the Il'lacean war, the Battle of Empires a few days ago. His name is Sebastian Raynes. He's a Lanyx and he will recite a poem for you that alludes to this upcoming war. Sebastian?"

Sebastian told them about meeting Applette and the poem he'd known since childhood. He explained how he never thought it would come to mean anything.

Calixtro asked from Mar Yen, "How did the Lanyx get this poem? Where did it come from?"

Sebastian shook his head, "I can't answer that. If you look up our history, you'll see how long we've been in existence and references to the poem go back just as far. I've never been able to pinpoint a date of creation. Maybe Applette would be better to answer this for us."

He scoffed, "I didn't know the poem existed until Mr. Raynes brought it to my attention honestly. I don't know where it came from but my best guess would be that the Multiverse Keeper threw out a clue to the beings of this world to help you. It really wasn't meant to be used, this door, but they do come into existence at certain times and if everything lines up right, they can be used. It's like a limited amount of time all three things come together, the door, the key, and the artifact and they can be used or ignored. Who knows when the opportunity will come? I've been here for almost two hundred years not only because I've been looking for Kolek, but because I haven't been able to return to my home."

The Awpunct said, "We are underwater, how would they get to us?"

Applette said, "I've seen the War Universe in action. They got their name for a good reason. They're amazing warriors and nothing slows them down. They're able to research, and adapt to most situations and they love the fight. They live for this. It would be very unwise to assume just because your planet is covered in water that you're safe from them."

"The Awpunct are hard to convince. I'll do my best but I doubt they'll join the fight. I'm in though."

"Thank you, Queraeyi. Anyone else have questions?"

Pinapat raised her tiny hand and waited until Applette saw her on her screen and called on her.

"What if this is some kind of prank or joke that the IMC or BDP is pulling on the universe? They have always been bad news for everyone. I thought both of them were making a play for the ultimate levels of control over the entire universe, are they not?"

Applette gave a frustrated sigh, "Oh them. I tried to...you might say influence them, 'whisper' in their ears on what to do here, but it backfired. They weren't trying to take over the universe, they ended up misunderstanding what I said and just caused chaos for the most part."

Pinapat spoke up, "What do you mean you tried to influence them? Were you a member of those gangs?"

"No. I see myself as...what you'd call a muse in your world. Someone with great power or influence over beings. I don't even need to be close sometimes. I can give people just a little bit of a push in the right...direction I guess you'd say."

"That doesn't sound like a muse, that sounds like the idea of angels and devils to me." Pinapat's husband, Naffziger nodded in agreement, his huge eyes so white they were almost glowing.

Applette shrugged his shoulders, "I suppose some would say power can lead to good or bad things. It all depends on how you look at it. I promise you, I had the best of intentions with both gangs. I would've liked for them to eliminate each other, but that's still not the circumstances today."

The room had a restless quality to it. No one said anything for a moment.

The Nawgain spoke, "Zetzetti will not fight. With the exception of the mercenaries of the school, we are a peaceful people. We will not break our beliefs, no matter the situation.

I'm sorry but I cannot try to argue to my people that war is the correct solution."

"Then your planet may fall, your species wiped out in a matter of days. I realize your particular situation and there are several other peaceful people who will not fight. I fear Mr. Raynes won't be able to convince Praxis that fighting must be done this one time or there may never be another chance to fight again. If enough planets do not participate it could cost you your whole universe. It's very important that you hear me and understand, *everything* is riding on your ability to convince your people to fight. Even if you're peaceful, always been peaceful, even if your planet has no weapons, or doesn't know the first thing about war tactics, even if you're deathly afraid, you'll need to fight. You'll all need to fight. I don't know when this war will come and I wish it wasn't going to happen, but as the days pass, the chance for it starting becomes stronger."

Doa the Trovelet announced, "We will battle. My kind love to fight. Count me in."

Sebastian had a flash of killing Tiny on Tiletan in his memory and nodded, "Thank you."

The rest of the Witnesses agreed they would try to convince their elders, council, governments, and kings to take the threat seriously and to prepare for war.

Still Sebastian and Celeste worried it wouldn't be enough.

THREE

>>> > AGATHON AND LILA hugged Sebastian and Celeste goodbye.

"Are you sure you want to do this?" Celeste looked between the two of them.

Agathon nodded, "I need to tell my people about the threat and to do that I need to be seen before our council, the royal clan. And I want Lila to see my world."

"But won't they take a huge offense to you bringing an outsider?" Sebastian asked.

"I am sure if the war breaks out while we're there, it won't matter, and if it does, there's a chance this will be the *only* time Lila can see my home world."

Lila interjected, "We worked it all out. If they have life form scanners detect me that day, Aggie's just going to say I'm his Taggamite, they're pets on that world I guess."

"What about the...that 'twin Witness' Applette mentioned? Can't she reach out to the royal clan?" Sebastian asked.

Agathon nodded, "She could, sure. I don't know if she will, but if two of us do it, maybe they'll be more inclined to be proactive. And frankly, if it's all the same, this war's going to be in all corners of the universe, won't really matter where I am to fight it, but I'd rather be near my home. You can understand that I'm sure."

Celeste wrung her hands, "Of course we can. Please be careful, both of you. And tell us what happens."

"I'm not sure that will be possible. If the Taggamite trick doesn't work and they see Lila, FA will want her Titan as soon as we arrive. That's standard operating procedures for a visitor from another planet." Agathon said.

"Well that won't do this time. They'll need to make an exception. If you're so close to Treksin Mori and the door, and if Hace gets it open somehow...Tell me again Sebastian why we're not following Hace right now? Why don't we just go to Treksin Mori?" Celeste sighed.

"We need to prepare the universe. We need to decipher the poem. We don't have the key. We *think* Treksin Mori has the door on it somewhere, maybe in The Messenger City. And without the Red Klix, we can't open it. And without the key, we can't close it. Plus we don't even know if Hace is still alive or not. We could be doing all this for nothing," Sebastian said.

There was silence until Lila asked, "So how does Hace think *he* can open it?"

"He has his child. Applette said that he was the, what did he call it? The Universe Ruler for our own universe, maybe the kid can open it somehow. Maybe Applette doesn't know everything he thinks he does. Hace must know where the door is and how to use the Red Klix since he asked for it and then took off. Maybe he figured out the poem. Maybe he's not worried about closing the door." Sebastian theorized.

"Applette said the key would be an older adult." Celeste replied.

"Yeah, well like I said, maybe Applette doesn't know everything he thinks he does." Sebastian repeated.

Agathon said, "I will find a way to let you know what's happening there. I promise. We've got to get going."

They said their goodbyes and Lila hugged Celeste tight, "I will be back to make your wedding dress. Don't worry."

Celeste thought, *too late not to worry.*

FOUR

››› › **"I STILL DON'T** understand why I have to be here." Applette adjusted his seatbelt in the passenger seat.

"Because it's your Witness. You know her best and she's a stranger to me. I can't track her like you can."

Sebastian launched his Atlas and Applette snapped his fingers.

Nothing happened.

Sebastian looked over at him, "Why are you snapping your fingers?"

"I can't...it won't work on you." He snapped his fingers again and again on both hands.

"What are you trying to do Applette?"

"I can travel with beings from this universe but they must be unconscious for it to work, otherwise your head explodes. I found out the hard way when I had just arrived here."

"Poor bastard," Sebastian uttered, "Why isn't it working?"

"I don't know. You're still telepathic right? That hasn't changed?"

"I still have 7's."

"Anything else?"

"I actually just developed my telekinetic powers too."

"Oh, you have a multileveled brain. That's it."

"Multileveled?"

"Your brain is too sensitive for me to do this with. That's why it won't work. It won't let me."

"Sorry."

"We'll have to do it the old-fashioned way I guess."

"Is she still alive? Has she stopped moving?" Sebastian's fingers hovered over the transit's destination screen.

Applette quieted for a moment. His eyes turned black. "She's stopped. I think they brought her close to Tessi. That will help."

"Where do I need to go?"

"The Witch Void System in the Lantern Struck Galaxy."

"Damn! That's six hours away and...five Jumps. You sure you can't grab her and just bring her to me?"

"I don't know how many assailants are around her. If there's too many, I'm in trouble and would need to wait for you anyway. And I can't travel with her unconscious. She's one of those special breeds I can't really do anything to."

Six hours later, they arrived in the deep space recesses of the Lantern Struck Galaxy. A huge silver ship stood isolated against the blackness of space. As they got closer, a much smaller bronze ship floated near Tessi.

"What are you planning?"

"Don't have the foggiest," Applette retorted.

"Is that our ship at least?" Sebastian asked.

"Yeah that's it. A real junk heap. Call out to them. They should respond."

"Really?" Sebastian lifted an eyebrow as he looked at the ship's identifier.

Applette nodded.

Sebastian looked at his screens and opened up his comms, "Hello Swinging Dick Sixty-Nine. Do you read?"

"Who the fuck are you?" A gruff voice answered.

"We're here to dock to your vehicle, I'm offering ne—" Sebastian stopped as Recin hit him on the elbow.

"Say you have candy. It's their weakness. Stampermoths are candy fiends!" Applette whispered.

Sebastian continued, "I'm offering new candy. We've started a delivery service and I'm going planet to planet sho—"

"Yes. We'll have a look. Prepare to dock in three minutes," the gruff voice said.

Sebastian answered, "Much obliged. Copy that."

Applette looked at the ship's airlock door opening. "This could be easy if we deal with the exile only."

Sebastian's Atlas docked within the locking mechanism and the airlock sealed shut. Applette and Sebastian opened their doors slowly. The air was stale.

A tall eggshell-white man stood in a black pullover shirt and black pants staring at Sebastian's transit. The color contrast of the man was striking.

"You're Sicaine right? Where's Laggic?" Applette didn't hesitate to dive straight in.

"How do you know me? Who are you?" Sicaine pulled out his gun from the back of his waistband.

Applette put up his hands, "I'm Recin Applette. This man over here is your worst nightmare if you don't give us Laggic. Put down your weapon. We have no reason to hurt you if you're cooperative."

"Damn it! You're not selling candy. I'm going to open the airlock on your asses." Sicaine moved slowly towards the exit while keeping the gun aimed at the intruders.

Applette jumped in front of him, "You and Laggic are... lovers?"

Sicaine's eyes got big but he said nothing.

Applette continued, "No. Almost lovers. You're very close but your...friends here don't know that. I can keep it that way if you hand her over. See this man and I have business to tend to all over the universe but Laggic is a very important person. We need her to help save your universe. I think we could offer an arran—"

Laggic walked out into the airlock.

Everyone stared.

"Sicaine's just trying to protect me," she said with a polite smile, "He's a good man, but our relationship is none of your business. I was able to talk the other men out of killing and raping me but I couldn't have done it without your message, Mr. Applette. I will help you, but I need to get Sicaine away from these men. He owes them a debt he cannot repay."

Applette looked at Sebastian. Sebastian considered it and then nodded.

"We can take you both. I'll need to drop Laggic off on Tessi first so she can fully heal but Sicaine will need to continue with us. Are these agreeable terms?"

Laggic stood next to Sicaine and grabbed his hand, "Yes."

Sicaine scoffed, "I don't get a say babe?"

She squeezed his hand hard, "This is our only option. We've got to get off this ship first and worry about the rest later."

Sebastian said, "Get in. Let's go. Applette, can you handle the airlock?"

Applette nodded.

Everyone piled in the transit while Applette opened the airlock door. He came out into the vacuum of space since he could survive it and gingerly held onto a handle on the outside of Sebastian's transit. In a few brief moments they were approaching Laggic's mothership.

Once they docked on Tessi, Applette could talk again, "Smooth sailing."

Sicaine asked, "What are you? No one can survive that!"

"I'm not of this realm. Laggic can explain everything to you after I've talked to her. Please wait here."

Laggic and Applette moved towards the inside of the ship.

Sicaine looked at Sebastian, "So are you like him?"

Sebastian shook his head, "I'm Lanyx. Can we drop you off somewhere?"

"I've been exiled, I can't stay here. I don't know where else to go. Maybe wherever you guys are going?"

"We'll see what Applette's got in mind."

Laggic and Applette returned. Laggic looked upset. She went to Sicaine quickly and spoke in whispers.

Applette walked to Sebastian.

"What's going on?"

"Laggic understands everything. She's telling Sicaine. He'll come with us, back to Stormview Haven. We'll keep him in the guesthouse, but he should be included in any transfers of information."

Sicaine looked at Laggic, "You trust this...whatever he is?"

"Yes. He's trying to help all of us. They'll take you to Earth. You'll need to help them with whatever they ask."

Sicaine put his arms around her waist, "I haven't seen you for so long and we'll still be separated after such a short reunion. I need to...have you. Can we be intimate? What if they're right and this is it?"

She shook her head, "I'm sorry, duty calls. If we survive, I'll make all this up to you. I swear."

CHAPTER 4

THE DOOR OPENS

ONE

>>> > THE MEN WORKED together at Stormview Haven with Applette to see what they could find of Kolek's location. Applette explained the War Universe's Ruler was crafty, extremely intelligent, and would be difficult to find. Eric, D'Artagnan, and Sebastian used all their information dealers, their assassin contacts, and their network to find out where Kolek might be. At least Sebastian had an image of Ni-toyis to show on his Titan during calls and messages.

Sebastian asked Applette, "So what does she really look like?"

Applette stopped and sighed, "She's beautiful. She has this golden light around her internal shell."

Eric whispered to D'Artagnan, "She has a shell? What is she, a bug?"

"I heard that. No she's not a bug. She's something you simply don't understand because she's not from your realm."

Sebastian said, "Please ignore him. He's annoying to everyone sooner or later." He stared at his friend.

"She has a...well, you wouldn't understand that term...how to say...she's...She looks like the Grand Canyon and the bottom of the ocean and the vastness of space. She's something you can't put into words. Her beauty lights up for millions of miles."

"Is she something you can reach out and touch?" Eric asked.

Applette looked at him, "Her breed is non-corporeal."

"What the hell does that mean?" Eric blurted out. D'Artagnan hit him on the shoulder.

"She's shapeless and has no material body. She's made of an internal shell, light, and shadow."

Eric snorted, "Then how are you going to do her?"

Applette smiled, "Let me worry about such things that are none of your business. She can take form when need be. They can procreate."

Sebastian asked, "Is she like an artificial intelligence?"

"No, not exactly. Just a higher plane of consciousness. When I was locked in a room with her, she was natural, no fake form."

D'Artagnan asked, "What do you like about her most?"

"Her mystery. Everything with her is so new to me and fresh. I need to learn so much about her people and what they can do. Her mind is full of wondrous ideas and she's incredibly creative."

Eric yelled out, "I think I've got Ni-toyis. She's way out of the galaxy."

"How far Bouton?" Sebastian asked.

"The planet of Oorblat. You're looking at a Praxian day's travel at least."

"Kreshlix System?" Sebastian rolled his eyes, "You've got to be kidding. She never did make anything easy on me."

"*She* is Kolek, not Ni-toyis. I'm leaving," Applette started for the door.

"I'm coming with you," Sebastian said.

"You'll only slow me down. It's better I go alone."

"I need to see what she says. I want Ni-toyis's body after she's done with it. I'd feel better going with you. You asked for help, I'm helping."

"Fine."

Sebastian found Celeste and told her where they were going. Then he met Applette at the Atlas.

"I can't knock you out to travel and I hate traveling the slow way."

"You could just punch me. Hard. That'd knock my lights out."

Applette seemed to consider it briefly, "I think that's a very bad idea." He smiled sarcastically, "I told you. You'd only slow me down."

"We'll get there fast enough. I'll put on a turbo boost. It's only good for one go but it'll help us move."

TWO

>>> > KOLEK LOOKED AROUND Oorblat and thought this would make for an excellent battleground if they made it out this far. She was happy with the layout of the universe and thought the war should go smoothly. The only thing she needed was to...

She sensed another Universe Ruler nearby. But it wasn't the Unknown Universe Ruler. It was...she couldn't remember his name.

She looked behind her and there he was, although in a new body.

"Kolek, I'm so glad I found you. Finally!"

THREE

>>> > AGATHON WAS CLEARED to enter FA air space. Lila was nervous he didn't mention her to anyone.

He flew over the countryside until he reached a lake. She looked down and saw a spacious home on the grass nestled in between a few mountains. This place reminded her of Ireland. Agathon got out of the transit and opened her door for her.

"Welcome to my home."

"This is fantastic Aggie. Where do you sleep? You can't fit in here in your natural form."

"I have a cave close by."

"Isn't that your home then?"

"I should say, they are both my home. I would rather be in Dach form than Human, but then I can't be near you."

"I think you've catered to my Human needs long enough. Get comfortable. I insist." She kissed him on the cheek and he blushed.

"Okay. Stand over there, closer to the house."

She walked away and he changed over.

She secretly loved the idea of dating a being so powerful and strong. It was a big turn on.

"You look so handsome now dear." She walked back over to him and stood in front of his wide face.

"I need to talk to the royal clan. I will be back with an answer as soon as I can. Make yourself at home. The door's open."

"I'll be waiting."

FOUR

>>> > "WHAT ARE YOU doing here? It's so good to see you again...Recin." Kolek remembered his name at the last second and gave him a big hug. He smiled at Sebastian over her shoulder while in her embrace.

"I need to speak with you but first let me introduce my friend, Sebastian Raynes."

Sebastian nodded and shook her hand. It was bizarre looking at Ni-toyis's body being worn by this alien, but it clearly wasn't Ni-toyis. Her eyes were solid black and the body was damaged with bandages covering bloody wounds. The body looked reanimated after death...because, well it was. Sebastian had never seen anything like it. It was creepy. "So nice to finally meet after Recin's told us so much about you."

"Really? What could you possibly say Recin? We hardly spent any time together at all."

"You are the type of woman that sticks in a man's mind. You should know this."

She smiled, "What flattery you give me. So tell me, why have you been looking for me? And what are you doing here? You should be in Knowledge, shouldn't you?"

"I should, but I've broken all sorts of rules to find you. I've been looking for almost two hundred years and I needed to ask for help from several people before I got to you."

"Wow Recin, that's an awfully long time here. Does the Keeper know?"

"I'm pretty sure he knows now. He keeps changing my life expectancy."

"You should really go home. It sounds dangerous for you here and I'm going to be launching attacks soon. It's really not a place you want to be in."

"Kolek, I'm going to be much more forward than I normally would but I've got to tell you, I haven't stopped thinking about you since we met. I want to get to know you better. I want to spend more time with you. Could you postpone the attacks maybe? Or call off the war altogether? Or move the doorway? I think an individual is about to open it and I need more time with you before you're consumed with this war."

"This is my job Recin. You know what's at stake. I don't want to lose this one. And if I do, I'm done. What would I do?"

"You could come back with me to Knowledge, or maybe I go back to War with you. I have replacements picked out for Knowledge, although I haven't told them yet, but it would work out just fine. I would go speak with the Keeper on your behalf."

"The door is in place and it's unlocked. I'm all set here Recin. I need to prove myself worthy. Of all the battles, you know I can't lose this one, and I don't want to postpone it. I've waited too long already."

Sebastian said, "Could you at least move the doorway then? I think someone will interfere with your plans if you continue to do nothing."

Kolek looked to Sebastian, "I'm sure there's a reason Recin brought you with him, but you really don't have any business here. You don't know anything about me or my motivations. There is no replacement for me back there. I don't have any control over the individuals from my universe, if your friend opens the door, then that's what happens. That's why doors exist, for them to be opened."

Applette grabbed her hands gently in his, "I know you to be a wonderful spirit with so much desire and ambition to rule over this universe, but I think everyone would benefit including you if you would just give me some time to further explain myself and the situation. Mr. Raynes is in love with a woman and they just got engaged. All of his friends have someone, with the exception of one who just lost her boyfriend. They suffered through a major battle that's just ended and they haven't even had any time to breathe. Would you please postpone your attacks until we talk? I could get you something to eat?"

"I really don't think it's a go—"

"Kiss her Applette! Do it now!" Sebastian barked a command that might change whether a war happened or not.

Applette looked over at Sebastian and then grabbed the back of Kolek's head and brought her lips to his. He kissed her softly, tenderly, then with a little more force now that he was experiencing what he had only dreamed of for a very long while. She almost put an arm around his neck but then pushed him away.

"What was that?"

"A kiss. I've wanted to give you one for so long. I think you're terrific."

She put her hand to her lips and looked at him.

"Please?"

Sebastian added his own, "Please?"

She looked down at a small wisp of orange steam emitting from her elbow. It wasn't a Titan, but Sebastian suspected it was technology from her own universe.

"I will move the doorway, but it's against the rules. I'm not supposed to."

Her elbow made a noise, and the steam turned red.

"Oh Recin. It's too late. The door's open. Just now. I'm sorry."

FIVE

›› › HACE LANDED ON Treksin Mori in The Messenger City following the directions the Red Klix gave him. After docking his transit, he headed into the forest. His wounds were bleeding through their bandages and Declan was sleeping on his shoulder. He didn't want to leave his child alone in the transit, but he also didn't know what to expect out in the forest.

He quickly turned around and left Declan in the backseat of the transit with the windows cracked. It wasn't hot here, in fact it was very comfortable so the baby should be fine for a few minutes alone.

He instinctively looked to his Titan and forgot it wasn't working. He wished it was, he could've sent out a message to whatever was left of the Brotherhood to come to him in case he needed help.

He pulled out the Red Klix and took a deep breath that hurt. He held the stone up to his ear to see if it would say anything else. He thought anyone watching him now would most certainly think he's crazy, or if nothing else, following his delusions to a place he *thought* he should go.

He looked again at his surroundings. It was dim, as if the whole world had bled out, faded, and there were too many clouds blotting out the sun. He saw a pathway between the trees and looked back at his transit one more time before he started walking.

And it just got darker once he entered the forest.

There was a dense fog winding its way through the trees. It was strange. This fog would sometimes quickly disappear in the wind, but then come back just as suddenly as it fled.

It felt like a living thing to Hace. Something with eyes. He started looking around deep into the forest, he had the sense of being watched, but he couldn't see anything out there. He couldn't see much at all, the foliage was so dense.

The Red Klix started to glow in his hand and become hot. He thought this must be the right direction.

After walking an hour beyond where the path ended, he saw stone steps arise out of the dark soil. They ascended along a gradual incline of a rocky hill masked in fog and trees.

After a short while, the only thing he could focus on was discovering what was at the top of this hill. As he climbed the stairs, he began to grow weak, and heard the pounding of his own heartbeat in his ears. At times, he felt like he was going to pass out. He tried, but couldn't remember how long he had been in this forest.

When he reached the peak there were more dense trees and everything was covered in dark green moss. He walked further and the stepping stones started to glow as if they were full of sunlight. They were so bright, it hurt his eyes.

He stopped at a statue. It was made of gray stone and depicted no creature he had ever seen. The monstrosity wore a long set of robes that covered it from head to toe. He thought the beast might've had three legs. It was hard to tell.

Out of the sleeves of the robe, two arms extended out in a welcoming gesture but the arms looked like tree branches and twigs. At the ends of the branches were claws. Hace thought if you ran into those arms, you'd never escape.

The statue's head was shaped like an upside down teardrop with the point at its chin, and on the top of the rounded head were four antlers that resembled bolts of lightning striking out in all directions.

Hace thought this could be an identical copy of the things that lived on the other side of the door. He walked around the statue and looked at it from all sides and wondered why they had placed it here.

He looked beyond the statue and saw several stone arches pointing up out of the ground making a guided pathway. He walked closer to them and saw each one was ten feet apart from the last and each was inscribed with a phrase in a different language. One was in Stoxian.

It read:

FOLLOW THE PATH TO YOUR END.

He didn't like it. He thought maybe they must've misunderstood Stoxian, perhaps it was supposed to say "follow the path to *the* end", or "*its* end", but not "*your* end." If they really meant to tell him to follow the path to his end, then he'd never come back.

And after that it said:

THE DOOR OPENS BOTH WAYS.
THE END OF YOUR SEARCH IS HERE.

Hace felt the excitement build up inside himself despite the menacing warning, but Declan had already been left alone too long. He would just open the door and take a peek inside, then come back later when he was fully recovered and explore.

If Hace knew several other languages, he would've seen that each arch was not the same phrase repeated in different languages. He would've seen they all said different things. They were all warnings and other things to think about before opening the doorway. He walked through each one studying the writing and symbols. When he reached the last one, the Red Klix flew out of his hand and hit what appeared to be empty air. It was really a plane separating the War Universe from his Unknown.

The plane shattered into many small jagged slivers and flew inwards away from Hace. He looked through to see a different universe before him full of new stars and systems, galaxies and planets.

His smile quickly turned into a look of horror as a winged creature flew towards him. It looked like an oily Rhorr'Dach with the head cut off and in its place was a glass dome. Inside held the body of some sort of being linked to the creature with wires.

There was an army of thousands behind the first one and many other strange creatures ready to burst through the open door.

Hace started to run.

CHAPTER 5

THE BABY ARRIVES

ONE

>>> > AGATHON STOOD IN front of The Great Flower again for the second time in a year.

The senior representative asked, "Agathon of the Rojo Clan, why are you before us today?"

"Thank you for seeing me. There is an urgent need to prepare for battle. Our universe is not alone. There are several beyond it we cannot see and sometimes they come to blows. I have advanced knowledge that the time is now to start preparing for a fight that will be at our doorstep soon. We must protect our young and shuttle them away from here. The rest of us that can fight should be ready once the threat appears."

"What are you talking about now? Every time we see you, all you speak of is war and death. You see the last time we didn't participate, the Humans came out just fine and won the war."

"They lost one third of their planet and over four hundred million of their people. I hardly call that fine. This battle goes far beyond what anyone has ever seen. A whole universe of beings whose sole purpose is to fight! I have people I love. People I *need to protect*. We cannot waste any more time. Sound the alarms. Evacuate the sick and the young. Everyone else must fight."

"What proof do you have to show us? I hear nothing on the news. I see no threats. What is your source?"

"A man from another universe called Recin Applette. Please ladies and gentlemen we are wasting too much time. I beg of you to start moving on this!"

"Is this some sort of joke to be played on us? Do you want us off world?"

"This is a dire situation. I only hope that you take my warning seriously and act upon it as soon as possible. Our planet is on the edge of the universe. We used to think of this as a place of safety, but we're the first in harm's way out here, all alone and without allies. All of our worlds are in danger. We wouldn't just lose our species, a lot of species could perish."

"I can see you're panicked and quite frankly it's causing some of us to panic. No good will come of that. Please wait while we make a decision."

It was the longest eight minutes of Agathon's life as the lights went out on The Great Flower.

"Our decision is to wait until the situation can be validated. Once the danger has been seen and evaluated for severity, then we will issue evacuations, but until then this matte—"

Senior representative Nalos was unable to finish as the building filled with alarms ringing overhead.

An announcement came on over the speakers, "Attention! Attention! This is not a drill. We are under attack. Evacuations of areas two and eighteen have priority. All others must wait. Please remain calm. This is not a drill. Attention!"

Agathon stared down his leaders and shouted, "YOU FOOLS! IT'S TOO LATE!"

Senior representative Nalos stood up confused, "What's going on?"

"Lila!" Agathon raced out the door and flew towards his home.

Creatures from a child's nightmare filled the sky around him. Some looked like a decapitated Dach but where the head should have been, a glass shell sat with a strange being inside mirroring the beast's movements. One appeared alongside him and startled him. He opened his mouth feeling cold air begin to gather, but the beast opened fire first. Agathon felt electricity shoot through his body. He exhaled. Ice shards pierced the thing's skin all over and bitterly cold air enveloped the alien. It froze and fell out of the sky.

Agathon landed and shouted Lila's name.

She walked out of the Human-sized home and put her arms up against his large neck, unaware of any danger. "How'd it go?"

"We're under attack! Right now! Get your weapons!"

"Oh God!" She ran back into the house and came out with swords, grenades, and plasma guns, "What do they look like?"

"Grotesque headless Dach with beings inside controlling them, but that's just one type."

"There's more?"

"Many."

Lila's hair suddenly stood on end all over her body. She looked at Agathon as she loaded a pistol, "You feel that?"

Before he could answer, electricity crackled in the atmosphere and a being materialized out of thin air in front of them. The creature had no legs, instead it rolled on a ball growing out of its torso. It had five arms arranged horizontally around its body like the spokes of a wheel, with claws for hands and no neck. Its head was a large square block of gray flesh with tubes wildly flying around the back of its head like out of control high-pressure garden hoses. It held a stick in one of its claws and aimed it at Agathon. Before he could open his mouth, Lila shot at it with a full plasma blast until the thing's head exploded like a melon.

She gagged, then threw up when the smell hit her. It was a hundred times worse than rotting flesh left out in the blazing desert for a week. She wiped her mouth on her sleeve.

"What is it?" She ran up to the alien and kicked its body.

"I don't know. With another universe, there has to be multiple breeds just like here. It's an ugly creature. Be on your guard since that thing came out of nowhere. Turn on your Titan and record this. We'll send it to Raynes. Tell them we're under attack and the Dach won't help the universe."

TWO

>>> > HACE RAN TO a wide tree and hid behind it. He had no idea where the key was so he couldn't close the door, but he wished he could've. The things pouring out into the forest looked terrifying and had levels of technology he had never imagined.

Two small beings appeared, one on either side of him. They looked like they were lost children and he didn't know if they were the elusive native Ruwnrade or if they were from the other universe.

Before he could say anything, one pulled a smoky glass orb from their neck and threw it in the air. Hace was paralyzed. He wanted to run back to Declan but he couldn't move. A viscous fluid filled his mouth. It was as if someone was pouring liquid detergent down his throat.

He tried spitting it out but couldn't.

Hace drowned on alien technology he couldn't describe, much less fight against. He fell to the forest floor after his lungs were full of thick fluid. His heart stopped. His last thoughts were regret at not being able to protect and raise his child, and happiness at the thought of seeing Ni-toyis again.

The War Universe beings grabbed their weapon out of the air, tucked the orb back into their flesh, and spread out across the area.

THREE

>>> > KOLEK LOOKED AT Recin, "We've already had our first casualty. There's nothing I can do to reverse this now."

"The man who I think opened the door had a child with him. Can you see anything about him? He's a Universe Ruler too, just born. He'll be in control of Unknown."

"Ah, I see. I'm sure it will go back to its last place of safety. The current UR here should help get it to where it needs to be."

Sebastian interjected, "Applette, didn't you say you couldn't interfere in your people's lives?"

Kolek shook her head, "This is the one time a Ruler can intervene, otherwise we'd never get our replacements. We need to keep the Rulers safe before they take control."

"Speaking of safe keeping," Recin held out his hand and opened it.

Kolek gasped, "Oh I thought I lost those! Where's the other?"

Recin blushed, "I took them off you when our time was up in that little room. I'm sorry. I just wanted something of yours so I took that little satchel. I didn't know what they were for the longest time."

A blue orb floated in Kolek's hand. "But there were two. Where's the second one?"

Recin flashed his eyes to Sebastian for a moment. "Well I guess it's on Treksin Mori now. Maybe we can still retrieve it."

Sebastian nodded, "If I see it again, I'll be sure to return it to one of you."

FOUR

>>> > RAYKREEDE ARRIVED ON Il'laceier after packing up his things on Ishikawa and shipping them for the permanent move he made back to his home world.

The SAP had been partially damaged and would need to be fixed. He had come into the new bad habit of noticing every little thing that needed repair. Raykreede looked around the colony he would be living in for the next several months. Some things were still on fire: the dumpster behind a restaurant, a bakery across the street, some trees on the corner.

"Excuse me sir?"

The transit driver put Raykreede's luggage on the curb and looked up at him, "Uh huh?"

"Do you see a lot of colonies like this around the globe? Is there a lot of damage that hasn't been cleaned up yet?"

"Yes. Quite a bit."

Raykreede tipped the man and thanked him.

The transit departed.

Raykreede went to his new townhouse's front door and opened it. He put his luggage down in the front entry and took in the furniture laid out throughout the place. The mirror behind the couch revealed how disheveled he felt. He hadn't been on Il'laceier since David tried to kill him and he was in a rush to move.

Raykreede refused to fight for either side during the Battle of Empires. He was an Il'lacean, blood to bone, but he had no quarrels with Humans and would not fight on behalf of his people dominating another species. And although he liked Humans as a people, he would not aid them and kill some of his own kind.

He closed the front door hoping he could do some real good for his people by being on the new council.

FIVE

>>> > DECLAN WAS SLEEPING when Hace opened the War door, exposing this universe to the greatest danger it's ever seen.

The current Unknown Universe Ruler used all her strength to come forward in the transit and program the auto-pilot to land on Il'laceier. The transit launched and left the airspace of Treksin Mori.

SIX

>>> > ULYSSES WANTED TO do some good with what was left of the IMC. He messaged all members on their Titans but got no response.

He ran each of their names through the data bank of fallen soldiers for The Battle of Empires War and found they had all perished.

He knew all of the members had agreed to fight but that was a huge amount of men to lose all at once. He wondered if some of them had survived but secretly joined the BDP.

SEVEN

>>> > DAI WAS ON Earth.

Her Titan got a report from Daredevil Three. The space probe had been orbiting Treksin Mori when an anomaly happened. Daredevil Three sent video.

The camera closed in on a man she recognized as Hace. Several beings that were not of this universe came through an open portal and surrounded him in a dense forest.

They killed him.

DAI knew she should feel something, Hace was her master and sole companion for years, but with her new view on things, she realized he used her and made her his sex slave without ever considering what she wanted.

She commanded Daredevil Three to depart for Uzzib.

There was something she needed to know about that "planet."

EIGHT

>>> > LILA CALLED CELESTE. She answered on the first ring, "What's happening?"

"It's gotten quiet for a little. We're down in a bunker that Agathon built ages ago. It's all dirty down here, but it's a safe place for us to sleep."

"How are you?"

"I'm fine, so is Agathon. I'm just tired, we've been fighting against these...things for hours."

"What are they like?"

"All sorts of things. Some are as big as a Rhorr'Dach, some are small, some appear out of thin air and have an electrical weapon. There's so many different kinds, but Agathon's people put out a bulletin saying their young were going to another world far from here and the adults have to fight. I think we can keep FA safe, but we can't leave. I have no idea how I'm going to design your gown. I need to fit you and there's so much to do for a queen's wedding dress."

Celeste shook her head, "No, Lila. Don't even worry about the dress. We'll work it out later."

Agathon leaned into the frame, "It's a very big deal to women, especially you two. Maybe it would be good to work on it, at least in drawings as a distraction? I think candlelight white would be an excellent choice for Celeste's skin tone."

Lila looked at him and Celeste stared at the Titan's screen.

"What? Can't I have an opinion too? After what I've seen today, I don't mind some sort of happy distraction." Agathon raised his imitation Human eyebrows.

NINE

>>> > "KOLEK WOULD YOU mind looking at a poem and telling me what you think it means?" Sebastian was hopeful two Universe Rulers together could make easy work of the poem. He was grateful Applette convinced her to come back to Stormview Haven.

"I suspect we'll need a few days, but I think you and your fiancée are referenced in this." Kolek quickly scanned the poem.

Sebastian's eyes got wide, "How did someone know about Celeste and I when this was written? It's been around for... forever."

Kolek answered, "I believe the Multiverse Keepers can see all of time when they need to and I bet they are the authors of the poems."

Applette looked at Kolek, "No one knows for sure though. I wish I could've seen this hundreds of years ago. It would've helped me so much...I think."

"Well let's make sure we're certain of its meaning."

"Of course." Applette glanced at Celeste and Sebastian.

Celeste said, "If you need a place to stay, we have more than enough rooms here."

Kolek shook her head, "I can't sleep with a roof over my head. But if it's okay I'll sleep on your grassy lawn?"

"Yes. We can provide tents, or blankets, whatever you need."

"Great, thank you so much."

Applette took a step towards Sebastian, "What did you think this poem was about again?"

"The doorway to War I guess." Sebastian shrugged his shoulders, "I always thought it was a warning."

Sebastian suspected part of it was referencing Bahsheef, but he wanted Applette and Kolek to give their opinions.

"Did you guys find a door made of stone on a faraway planet that maybe had lightning strike it?" Kolek asked.

Applette interjected, "We spoke of this before finding you. They have located that door on Bahsheef."

Celeste's face was full of dismay, "We never got it open. It has something to do with War?"

"No, it's Recin's universe. That's a Knowledge doorway. They never show up until a really bad lightning storm hits."

"So it has nothing to do with the doorway that's open to War right now?" Celeste's heart dropped a little thinking there was no way to stop it.

"No. I'm sorry. I don't think the poem's referencing how to close the War door, it's telling you how and when to open Knowledge. That's what I suspect. It'll take some analyzing."

"But that means you could go home now? Right? Both of you?"

Recin replied, "Yes, because it sounds like the artifact was in the door already but I want to stay with Kolek. Wherever she goes I'll follow, but that also means I have to wait and see what happens with this war first."

TEN

>>> > DECLAN'S TRANSIT LANDED on Il'laceier in the same spot it took off from.

No one was around for miles. Since the war ended, the battlefield had cleared out and the camps disassembled.

The current Universe Ruler watched for several hours to see if anyone noticed the baby, but no one was there. So she helped him again and redirected him to Earth. Several hours later he landed on the lawn of Stormview Haven.

ELEVEN

>>> > SEBASTIAN WALKED OUTSIDE with his gun drawn and looked through the transit window to see the Stox child that was Ni-toyis and Hace's. There was no one else around. Dried blood was smeared all over the seats.

He picked up the child and brought it inside.

Celeste's eyes got big, "What the...? Is that Declan?"

"Yes, I don't know how he got here but he's alone. The transit landed on the lawn and I checked its flight log. It's been all over: a medical outpost closest to Con Cab Mai, Treksin Mori, Il'laceier, then here."

"With his parents gone someone needs to take care of him."

"We don't know Hace is dead for sure."

"But that Kolek woman said there was a casualty. Who else could it be?"

"Could've been anyone. This could be a trap set by Hace."

"Well the baby needs someone to look after it for now."

"Yes, I agree."

"So...should we?"

Sebastian shook his head, "No. We can't. We'll need to be leaders for this war and considering who the parents are, I think we should have someone else take care of him."

"We can lead and be parents at the same time."

"Neither one of us know anything about raising a child, much less a Stox child."

"We can learn. And he's special, Applette said he was a Universe Ruler. He needs strong parents."

The baby began to wail.

"I don't think we should split our attention between his needs and the universe right now. Let's give him to someone else."

"Who?"

Sebastian jiggled the baby in his arms to quiet him. He realized this was the first time he'd held a baby since his brother had been born. Memories of Constantine filled his thoughts.

Celeste repeated, "Who are you planning on taking care of him?"

"D'Artagnan and Ophelia," he blurted out, "Ophelia will never be able to have a child and they would be responsible with him."

"You didn't even want Ophelia to stay connected after she gained self-awareness. You wanted her dead. Now you think she'd make a great mother?"

He shifted the baby in his arms, "I think you'll make a great mother someday...I mean, if we ever decided to..."

She looked at him and the baby.

"I mean...you will be. Really. A great mom. But for now, we have a lot of things going on and you and I are only engaged. We still have so much to learn about each other."

"Why not give him to D'Artagnan and O temporarily? See how it goes while we're occupied and then maybe he can come back to us?"

Sebastian paused, "I'll have to see if they're even willing to take him first."

TWELVE

>>> > SEBASTIAN PULLED D'ARTAGNAN and Ophelia into a separate room while Celeste played with the baby and found him something to eat.

"I'm not sure how you feel about being parents, but you have an opportunity to practice if you'd like."

D'Artagnan raised his eye ridges, "Wait...what? Hace's and Ni-toyis's child right? Is that what this is about?"

Ophelia lit up, "I could be a mother?"

"He's a Stox child and I don't know what's different from a Human, Lanyx, or Il'lacean baby...could be a million things, could be nothing. Celeste and I talked after his transit showed up without anyone else in it. Ni-toyis is dead, Hace is presumed dead and I don't want the responsibility now. Maybe later, but not now. So if you took him, it would be on a temporary basis until the war's over and things settle down. How do you feel about that?"

"Hace could be dead?" D'Artagnan asked.

Sebastian nodded, "We'll have to try to verify it if we get to Treksin Mori."

"Could you give us a minute Raynes?" D'Artagnan looked at his friend.

"Course. Take your time." He walked out of the room and found Celeste right by the door.

"What happened? Did they want him? He's adorable. Look at this little face!" She snuggled the baby.

"They're talking it over."

They waited outside until Ophelia opened the door, "Yes. Give him over so I can feel what it's like to hold one please."

CHAPTER 6

WE ARE UNDER ATTACK

ONE

>>> > MAGNUS AND NICHOLETTE stood at the front of the room while everyone waited for the last of the reporters to settle in.

"We are under attack, all of us. We've decided to hold this press conference as a public service. A new war has begun at the edge of the universe. The planets that are closest to the edge will see the attacks first. We know already that Treksin Mori and Zocosile are surrounded by the enemy.

"Movement, we suspect, will become more difficult as this war progresses. We know of one Jump that has been rendered useless as of present. I assume more will be crippled, incapacitated, or destroyed by the end of the war."

Screens all over the universe began tuning in to the breaking news alert. All major newscasts were airing coverage and soon it was the only thing anyone could watch.

"This will be difficult for some of you to believe but we are not the only universe in existence. We are part of something much bigger, a multiverse. Our universe is being invaded by another universe as we speak and we urge planets close to the Red Deer Galaxy, the Dark Galaxy, the Royal Star Galaxy, Shredder's Object, and the Jester Galaxy to evacuate immediately as your placement in the universe is closest to the breach. We don't know how fast these beings can travel so no matter where you are in the universe, you must stay on guard and stay alert. Be vigilant and be on the defensive.

"If you can't evacuate, you must fight, although we know nothing of our enemy's weaknesses. If you're able to find a way to kill the enemy, please share the information or videos with others on the uninet with this address at the bottom of your screen, so that we may fight as a united front with minimal casualties. Don't despair. Don't panic. It is time to put aside petty differences with other races, other planets, and other galaxies as we are all in this together. Today, we are united in a common foe and must pull together if we are to beat them.

"Nicholette and I are praying for your safety, no matter where you are, or who you are. Please be strong and safe. God bless us all and be with us in our time of great need. Thank you."

TWO

>>> > WAR BEINGS WERE quickly spreading across the Unknown Universe, invading new galaxies and terrorizing new planets. As they moved, several Jumps took damage as

the Earth Emperor predicted, leaving several species stranded where they were to hunker down in place, fight, or escape only within their local galaxy.

Seventy-five percent of species relied on Jumps to help them travel, without them, they simply didn't have the advanced technology needed to move about the universe as quickly. And that lack of ability to escape would prove fatal for a lot of worlds.

THREE

>>> > AFTER ASKING NICHOLETTE and Magnus all the questions he could, Sebastian met Celeste in the living room.

"So, did you get anything useful?" Celeste sat on the couch with her legs folded underneath her.

"Your parents are pretty foggy about their time on Treksin Mori but the boys also seemed that way too, without being drugged. We'll have to go there. We'll wear armor or as much protection as we can. I don't think there's any way we can prepare for every scenario so we'll have to expect the worst, hope for the best." Sebastian put a hand on her thigh.

"I'm a bit scared."

"I'm pretty sure everyone is. No one's ever faced anything on this scale. What's the latest reports?"

Celeste looked down at her Titan, "Everyone this side of Earth doesn't even believe my parents' warning. They think it's a hoax. But more planets are reporting police officers and emergency crews being overwhelmed with thousands of calls of attacks. War is spreading out. They'll be here soon. What about the Witnesses? Have any of them reported back to us? Were they able to talk their leaders into action?"

Sebastian sighed, "Some yes, but they all need to move as fast as possible. I hope to hear from them soon. I'll send out a message."

FOUR

>>> > ON FROOPEAL, THE former Woo Wrort prisoner and fighter Carffif Wobraney, came out of his bedroom onto the black and white sand and looked up at the array of strange beings landing on his world. He saw some of the guards running out with their weapons drawn. This was the beginning of the end according to the local news, but Carffif wasn't going down without a fight.

The last message he had received from that Raynes guy was asking if they had made any contact with aliens yet, or if he'd been able to raise the alarm with his world's leader. Carffif was not a person who could get anyone's attention, but he was pretty sure it didn't matter now.

Worlds were being attacked in the same manner as what was currently unfolding on his own. He started running towards the closest being he could reach. It was about time one of his fights counted for something.

FIVE

>>> > PESAN CHOA, THE Den De Cee Em of Lo-sotts, sat at his desk sweating it out. He knew trouble was on its way. He knew he might not survive, probably would not survive through the end of today. But he paused to think, wasn't this what he wanted all along? Excitement? Something new? Something to test him? This was a chance for him to prove himself. It no longer mattered that he didn't have a girlfriend, that his house was still not remodeled to his liking. Applette was going to pay him a lot of money to fight and Pesan could be a hero to his people if he could save the world. He looked out the window and saw a strange being hovering there. He stood up and went towards the thing. Pesan had an old-fashioned match in his hand and his trusty pencil.

SIX

>>> > YILLE VATOOFEY, THE Feddin on Unbeere, sat with Listeo dead in his arms. After they met at the bingo parlor that night, they had started a romantic relationship he'd never known would bring him such joy. Now, she was gone and he didn't see the point of fighting whatever these "things" were from the other universe. These creatures had come here and decimated his planet, his home, his life, and had taken the most precious thing he had ever found. He waited until he was surrounded by hundreds of beings, then took his finger off the trigger for the bomb. He touched his forehead to Listeo's and closed his eyes tight as he lost his own personal fight against the War Universe.

SEVEN

>>> > ON CON CAB Mai, Pinapat Nac crawled out of a hole in the tree trunk behind what they called a "twin." It was one of the beings that controlled a deadly orb. She ran up one of its legs while her husband, Naffziger ran up the other. They carried a hot wire between the two of them and worked quickly to lace it around the twins' necks. They pulled hard and decapitated both simultaneously. It seemed the only way they had found to kill these creatures. Pinapat and her husband jumped up in the air as the bodies fell dead underneath them. They landed safely off to the side and gave each other a look only lovers would understand. The Raze people, although small, never lacked heart or ferocity in battle.

EIGHT

>>> > ON FOSS-ALTUS, THE Rhorr'Dach Eveanna of the Gecksix Clan and Laudelene of the Denk Clatter Clan, circled an area of sky over their house, burning anything alien that came near them. Laser plasma heat radiated from Eveanna while hot flames came out of Laudelene's mouth. They hardly had time to breathe normally while the attacks persisted. Eveanna sometimes felt like crying but then she'd look over at Laudelene's determined face. He was locked in the fight and she remembered what he said before the attacks hit their home.

"I want to start a family with you. I want as many babies as we can bring into this world and I want to live on other worlds. I don't want our children to know only this. I want them to live like our ancestors that could travel anywhere because there wasn't a race that could dominate over us for long. I will fight until the death to provide these dreams for us." She would do anything for this male fighting beside her.

"ARCHLEND NO!" Laudelene commanded, but it was too late. While Eveanna had been momentarily lost in her memory, she hadn't seen the creature flank her left side. An electric bolt shot out towards her, but her loyal Taggamite dropped fast from above their heads and swooped in front of her, taking the full blast instead. She watched helplessly as his body went rigid and his feathers caught fire. He plummeted down to the ground below. She immediately yelled to Laudelene, "I'm going down for him."

"You can't. We need to stay together, plus there's too many enemies down there."

"But, he could've surv—"

He shook his head with sad eyes, "I'm sorry. He's gone."

Then she did start crying, but the heat from her mouth dried the tears before they could fall down her cheeks. She screamed out his name while plasma shot out of her mouth. She sheared off from Laudelene, "ARCHLEND!"

He watched as she circled back and his heart broke for her.

She shouted, "I need to get him! We can't leave him there! I won't!"

He nodded, "Okay. You lead. I will cover you."

And they both made direct descensions deep into enemy territory to retrieve the body.

NINE

››› › ON LASSANDRA, THE Lassandros, Plecka Denelk and Ian sheltered in Plecka's basement.

"We need to go up there. I can't stay here!"

She shook her head, "No. I can't lose you too!"

Plecka's mother's body lay in the corner with a sheet draped over it. Stones laid with love covered every edge of the blanket as was Lassandra tradition when burial wasn't an option.

There was a loud noise like the furniture was being over-turned upstairs.

Ian whispered, "Fate brought us together. I won't hunker down here like a coward when I need to be fighting for our survival and your protection. Nowhere is safe in this entire God damn universe, no matter where we run to. We need to fight. I'm sorry your mother's gone, but she wouldn't want you to stay down here and die like a terrified animal. I won't let anything happen to you. That Applette guy hand chose *you* over millions of others for a reason. We can't wait. All we have is this fight."

She looked into his eyes. A tear fell down her cheek, "I'm scared."

"I know you are. I am too, but we need to fight. I've trained you as best I can, you have nine weapons, I have thirteen. We have to do something. Come on babe."

He stood up and put his hand out to her.

She hesitated but when she looked into Ian's eyes, she knew he was right. She grabbed his hand and stood up.

TEN

>>> > KEAT'YOO TICH ON Natorleeds let his murderous brain reign over all his decisions while the fighting continued. He looked around and thought they had suffered few causalities. The Neeks were probably more prepared for this kind of raw fight than most other races. Mey Lii Soo approached him with her massive flame thrower. He wasn't aware of her stepping behind him until he felt the rush of hot air hit his back. Five of those things with the domes on their necks had snuck up behind him to attack but she burned them to death.

He looked at her for a quick moment and nodded. He half yelled, half grunted out, "Kay Ya TA!"

"Kay Ya TA! Fight till the end of time!"

He smiled at her and put a fist up in the air triumphantly, "You're the best fighter out here. Keep it up!"

ELEVEN

>>> > THE NIKORAN WITNESS from Mar Yen, Calixtro Batson ran through the forest feeling for eggs.

Calixtro was in charge of a ten acre plot of land near her home to recover all the eggs she could and bring them underground along with buckets of soil.

The aliens had invaded her precious forest and Nikora's biggest concern was for the unborn.

The Nikora couldn't continue to exist if their soil was contaminated.

They were probably the only people in the universe that cared most about ground damage over loss of lives or building damage.

They had already laid their eggs for the season and then this battle broke out. Calixtro wondered why these aliens couldn't have come eight months ago or two years later.

The Nikora had to rely on the United Space Military to help them as they had no real weapons and certainly no soldiers. To be a soldier, you needed eyes and none of them had those. Weapons were just about as far as you could get from nature lovers and natural things.

The problem was Calixtro didn't think the USM could cover as many planets as it promised to protect during this war, it was just too wide spread.

Calixtro collected four more eggs and ran for the bunker where her boyfriend who used to be her client, Mejasi Pearg was waiting for her.

An explosion caught her off guard to her left and she rolled to the ground, then she heard the steps of something with feet.

TWELVE

›› › ON MY'TAK, FORMER President of the Gno Norm Gin, Tem Shevilez laid in the bushes waiting for another assailant to come upon him. He'd turned in his professional suits for camouflage to hide as much as possible to fight these invading freaks. It seemed like half the planet and population had been lost in the past few hours; these things were so hard to fight and there were so many of them. He had taken Recin Applette's advice seriously, but trying to amass an army in a few short days was almost impossible. Now they had all been caught with their pants down and everyone was dying.

His Titan chimed. The news reported that Ibia had been drained of all its water somehow and the Awpunct people were perishing in massive quantities. He remembered something at the gathering with Applette and Raynes, the Awpunct there said that they were underwater and thought it was impossible for them to be a good target. The War Universe must've found a way...Ibia was a total loss.

If he could talk to the people right now, they would be able to tell he was losing hope. This whole war seemed like the odds were stacked against them, but he would keep fighting until the bitter end.

THIRTEEN

>>> > ISSEL CHAPOOTHE, THE Denigen on Embers, was still a bit shaken that her academic advisor, Recin turned out to be an alien from another universe. Lately, there were a lot of things to be shaken up about. The riots after PM Lightstone had been murdered, the assassination itself, and this war, all of it was too much to bear. She had tried to make a meeting with Prime Minister Vell, but she was a nobody. They didn't take her requests seriously. The best she could do was post things on the uninet, trying to make as many people aware of what was about to happen. Her fiancée Qulate had gone out and bought them as many guns as he could afford and now they were holed up in this empty prison. The prisoners had escaped thanks to the War Universe beings blowing a wall out on the south side of the prison. Now she and Qulate were standing back to back, breathing as quietly as possible, hoping they'd make it to the basement before one of them got killed.

FOURTEEN

>>> > REND LETT, THE Taybuse of Arcolid was still working the towers in the face of apocalyptic war. He was considered an essential worker and could not enter the military to fight for his

species survival. To some degree, this bothered him, but if he was being truly honest with himself, the idea of fighting those things he had seen in the Titan news reports scared the shit out of him. Recin Applette had given a good speech and made promises of coren and untold glory but Rend never believed it to be plausible. Where would that alien get all that money? How could he have pulled all those strings for each species? That Recin guy said he was a being from an entirely different universe and so how would he even know what was up in Rend's universe. The whole thing made his head hurt.

Rend was at the top of the tower looking down when he saw movement out of the corner of his eye. Movement he was pretty sure wasn't anything that belonged on his planet. He hoped the military soldiers down there could handle whatever came at them in the following days. Rend mispunched his access code and the door refused to open. Rend swore under his breath and tried again. His hands were shaking and he felt like he was going to hyperventilate. The door opened quickly and Rend jumped inside.

FIFTEEN

>>> > THE ESKIE LERE former serf, Drugor Brivasee of Wautic hunched down on the rooftop across the street from the gang of twins. These were those creepy little creatures he hated the most. He held his scoped rifle with slightly unsteady paws and aimed his weapon towards the middle set of twins. He gave the signal to his friends across the street and they responded back that they were ready with the propane tank. He counted down from five and waited for the tank to land near the twins' feet. So far, fire worked really well against these fuckers.

SIXTEEN

>>> > ALEXIS SANTEENA WAS on her home world of Dhoot Ovene with her Human boyfriend, Paul Dunnruci. Being an actress for so long had prepared her to deal with stress under pressure but this was something else entirely. Sineenniss people might have had fragile headdresses but their souls were made of cast iron. Nothing would scare them off from fighting to protect the people and world they loved. With her celebrity status she had been able to get a meeting with her world's president after the conference call with Recin and thankfully, the president had taken her seriously. All citizens worldwide had been instructed on quick courses in self-defense and weapons on the uninet. The government had equipped everyone with body armor and gathered as many armies in a short amount of time as possible. Alexis and Paul stood in a crowd of hundreds waiting for the doors to be thrown open on the underground bunker. Intelligence had said a large group of flying beasts just landed outside and the plan was a surprise attack as fast as possible. Alexis looked at Paul in the dim light, "I love you. No matter what happens, after this is over, I'm going to tell you my real name."

Several Sineenniss turned their heads to listen in on the conversation.

During war times, the Sineenniss people trimmed back their headdresses because they were too cumbersome to fight with. If it was a choice between losing a feature that made them beautifully unique and losing their lives – it was an easy choice for rational people. And a lady offering to tell a foreigner her birth name always caught many a Sineenniss ear.

Paul looked at his girlfriend surprised, "You don't have to feel like you're forced into that decision because of the war. I want you to tell me when you think I'm worthy."

She grabbed his hand and squeezed it quickly. The soldiers holding onto the main door started their countdown for everyone to prepare to run outside. "You're more than worthy. You're standing beside me on a world that is not your own, ready to fight just as strong as any other Sineenniss. I would die for you Paul."

He smiled at her and kissed her on the mouth, but his lips betrayed him. She felt the tremble of fear in them. She knew he was a good actor but he was scared.

She was too.

"I love you so much, and you and I are going to kick some major alien ass out there."

She nodded and hoped everyone was going to kick some major alien ass.

SEVENTEEN

››› › RUWOC LIRR WAS on Ishikawa with his girlfriend Sheevelah. Ruwoc hovered above the globes at his post with his gun drawn. He wished his old boss Recin, newly revealed alien from another universe, was here. Once he had attended that meeting, he told his girlfriend to leave school and come to the middle of the desert to be with him. He thought it'd be safer without a lot of people around. He was for sure thinking the War aliens would be looking to pick off large groups of people at once and save the stragglers for last. He yelled down to Sheevelah, "How are you doing down there?"

"I'm okay." She looked away from him to the horizon. She shielded her eyes from the light briefly and said with a shaky voice, "I think something's coming babe. Look over there!"

Ruwoc looked in the direction she was pointing. He could now clearly see a plume of dust rising up revealing something speeding along the desert floor and it was headed straight for them.

"Get up here babe. We need to be as high as possible now."

She extended her wings out and flew up to hover close to him, drawing her gun.

"I think this is it! We're going to start warring right now!" He aimed his gun at the thing racing towards them and pulled the trigger.

EIGHTEEN

>>> > YHILE FEELOW, THE pregnant hotel maid on Watnaggi told as many of her Sho'teg brothers and sisters as possible about the impending invasion. Very few of them believed her and she didn't get a meeting with the Weapons Master in time. So she improvised, making as many weapons as she could from scratch. When the time came and she met up with her first enemies on the eighth floor balcony of the room she was cleaning, she took out her alcohol bottle and lit the rag inside and aimed at the twins crawling down the building from the floor above.

NINETEEN

>>> > SHUMATSU ZHENKANG, THE Delun on Seseer Saka had no trouble exterminating the aliens invading her planet. She had learned how to control the fire in her hands and could use it effectively towards these oddballs and freaks. Her fire could not be extinguished and had to burn out until it had nothing left to eat.

She was standing on the shore of Miphi Lake watching twenty-seven aliens burn. Some had even crawled into the water, but they soon found that water would not extinguish the flames.

She smiled widely knowing she could protect herself *by herself* and then she heard a distant rumbling. At first, it reminded her of thunder but the sky was perfectly clear. Zero chance of rain. The rumbling not only got louder but it started to shake leaves off the trees. Even shook her where she was standing. She turned around to see if she could find the source but it wasn't hard to see. There was an absolute giant ghoulish creature lumbering towards her and it brought hundreds of friends.

One of the twin girl things finally keeled over in surrender.

Shumatsu cracked the knuckles of her right hand and held her ground as the giant approached.

This was about to get interesting.

TWENTY

>>> > NROOM WAU'TANI ON Firrepaorth was distraught. His people were born for this. Born for war, but these new enemies were taking them to school. Nroom had lost his younger brother, Lenz within the first few hours of heavy fighting on the east side of Center City. Now he was watching as Jules, the woman he had been crushing on for months was fighting for her life against a horde of voracious alien enemies.

Nroom took the assailant on Jules's left and stabbed the domed thing where the glass connected to the body. It made a horrible sound he'd never heard before. The creature inside started to shrivel up like a raisin in the sun. It was horrible and fascinating to watch, but Jules couldn't look for long since she had three more enemies coming up on her right. She nodded her approval to Nroom and nodded back.

TWENTY-ONE

>>> > "KANTOK DEDI YOU have to fight right now!" Julie Krane was yelling at the top of her lungs at her boyfriend.

Zetzetti native Kantok stood cowering in the corner, "I can't do this love. I think we should just hide until it's over. Nawgain were not meant to fight. None of my people are fighting. You saw me trying to talk to our council, they wouldn't hear it."

"If you think now is a good time to hide, you really are mistaken. This is the only choice. We fight or we die. These...things are never going to stop and there's no surefire way to eliminate them! Fight with me, or stay a coward and die alone. I can't stay here with you, no way." The Human girl put her hand out to him, in it, she held a machete. It was the only weapon she could procure with her magic, but at least she could make a million of them if needed.

He put his own hand out and produced a gun. "These are too small to fight with. I can't make anything other than this .22."

"Have you been working on your waterfall blast? Try that."

Julie watched as a tidal wave appeared in Kantok's eyes. She saw it approaching and yelled for him to stop, otherwise they'd both be washed away.

"That's fantastic! That's gonna do us a lot better than anything else we've got. Come on, let's do this. I don't want to sit back and wait, let's bring this fight to them."

"But you're going to drain all your energy if we fight them with magic, you're Human."

She shook her head, "I've been practicing. If I go long stretches without using then I definitely drain myself, but we've been using all the time in big quantities, I'm good to go. Besides, you don't suffer from that so I'll just recover while you're using."

He nodded, "Okay then. Let's try this."

TWENTY-TWO

>>> > GICAM SIL, THE Velm on Jex, had long ditched his lesbian wife after he found out on his birthday that she'd been cheating on him. He thought when she died he would feel some happiness, some sense of revenge. She had died shopping in

a sex store for dildos with her mistress. One of those winged creatures had landed right in the middle of the five story building and taken it all down, but he only felt empty sadness. Not at all what he thought he would feel the many times he fantasized about her death. Now he was sitting here with eight of his co-workers behind the receptionist desk wondering if Amy's bomb was really going to work. Those things were breaking down the door and making horrible noises. Gicam knew he would hear those sounds in his nightmares if he actually survived this.

TWENTY-THREE

>>> > OOOT RYTH'TIE, THE Cephian on Cepheus hunkered down in his cave with his regular sex robot and figured the whole "war thing" would get handled by other people. He knew the money was a big draw, and sure it'd be pretty okay to be immortalized forever and adored by beings everywhere but he was too afraid of dying. That Recin guy was probably just exaggerating...making things sound worse than they really would be.

He turned on the screen in his living room and put on the news for a few minutes before dinner. After what he saw on his screen for two minutes, he figured out that Recin man was not exaggerating. He saw what he could only describe as pure carnage unfolding not only on his own world, but all over the universe, just like Recin said. He thought for a minute, maybe he should've tried to talk to the Leader General, but Ooot was just a teacher, he doubted very much that a man that busy would've ever made any time for him. So it didn't really matter anyways. Everything that was going to unfold would've happened with or without him trying to contact the Leader. He turned off the screen and started to take down his boxers, "Hey honey. You ready for another round of delicious man meat?"

TWENTY-FOUR

>>> > MITLAND LIERZ, THE Wrabbalan on Eios had imme-
diately left Earth after losing his big chess match against the
Human. Thankfully, that Applette alien guy had offered a lot
of money to fight in the universe wide war that was happening
now. Mitland could make so much more than he ever dreamed
of this way. It wasn't an easy gig, but Mitland used to be in the
military so he had all the training necessary to defeat whoever
these assholes were that invaded his territory. And the fame
and glory of being recognized as a hero didn't sound too bad
either. So far, Eios needed his help. His people were falling fast
to these creeps, but Mitland had heard that fire worked pretty
well against them. He dusted off his old flame thrower in his
attic and went out looking for enemies.

TWENTY-FIVE

>>> > COMMANDER GOTHIN ARAX, the Turk Claw on Ferilium
was in the middle of battle along with the rest of his crew when
the news "broke" that there was a battle being waged against
the world.

Commander Arax was one of the best and made use of every
single skill he knew his crew had. They were one of the few
places in the universe that were holding their own against the
various beasts of the War Universe. They used fire and plasma
together. They used water and distraction. They used their
brains and their bare hands if they had to. Commander Arax
took videos and downloaded them onto the uninet to share with
the rest of the universe. He kept hope alive within his crew that
they could beat these bastards with minimal casualties but no
matter how many they killed, it seemed like there were more
behind them.

TWENTY-SIX

>>> > ONCOBYSS RAPAX, DAUGHTER of Shiraya, the Virscool on Gane Frost always thought she was more of a lover than a fighter. She thought that her people had it all wrong, but now that War was at her literal doorstep, she was grateful that her people had continued to practice their combat skills. She watched the news nonstop and followed the fast progression of the alien beings as they moved across the universe. The little training she received in school years ago came in handy now and she used every bit of it while fighting for her life and the safety of her parents. Her folks were too old to fight. She hid them in a secret room in the back of her bedroom closet while enemy after enemy showed up on her balcony or at her front door. Some of her neighbors were pulling way more than their weight at the entrances to the building's lobby, hallways, and stairwells, but it was all she could do to fight the enemies right here. She could barely move without having another one take the last one's place. After three hours she started to wonder how long her endurance would let her do this.

TWENTY-SEVEN

>>> > LAGGIC WAS ON her mothership, Tessi and talking to Sicaine on her Titan when the first explosion rocked the ship. She had to cut her call short, much to Sicaine's dismay as she ran to the bridge.

"What's going on? What was that?"

The crew looked to her, her First General spoke, "We could be taking on multiple strikes for the next several minutes. It seems like these...beings are flying out there without any kind of protective gear. It's the damnedest thing I've ever seen. I th—"

The ship rocked again, everyone pitched forward for a few seconds until they got their footing back.

Laggic raised her voice so everyone on the bridge could hear, "We've practiced for this people. I know all of you can stay professional. We are officially in war times. Fire when ready. Shoot to kill. There's no way these...aliens are going to take the only home we have left!"

She looked around as some of the gunners fired. She watched the beams of plasma cut into multiple floating shapes out in space. She wished they could fire faster. The quicker this war was over, the faster she could get back to Sicaine.

TWENTY-EIGHT

>>> > LUKE GARG, THE Farre on Strati-fly851 was inside his house thinking this was ironic. Their planet was in such bad shape and they were trying so hard to keep it from getting worse, but a universe wide war breaks out and threatens to kick the planet's last leg out from under it. He checked the news on his Titan again. The Trovelets had just fallen. The entire planet of Oorblat was decimated. The videos were hard to believe. All the buildings were crumbling or on fire; people screaming and crying at the camera. These were Trovelets, some of the most fearful horrible creatures in the galaxy. Luke was surprised. He had a short meeting with the leaders of his world, and they listened patiently to him, but the ultimate answer was that the planet was already fucked. The Farre would be on their own without military help, and without soldiers, weapons, or armor supplied by the government. A lot of people were trying to leave the planet, but encountered enemies in open space. Luke convinced his wife to get into the basement with the majority of the contents of their pantry and a shovel for a weapon. He stayed upstairs looking at the news on his Titan and watching for movement by the windows. He grabbed a bottle of imported Earth vodka and unlocked the gun safe to grab the only pistol

he had owned for twenty years. It belonged to his father. He hoped he remembered how to clean it...

TWENTY-NINE

>>> > THE PLANET OF Greeve was home to Xu'Xi Darksent and billions of other Inclicks. Xu'Xi had recognized his friend "Xavier" on the news when the War of Empires was going on and wondered what his real name was. Was he Xavier or Sebastian? Technically didn't matter but he tried contacting him a few times, but only got his voicemail. Xu'Xi could handle himself, but he worried about several of his friends throughout the universe. He had a lot of contacts, and a lot of jobs that were interrupted, mid-stream when this war started up. And it seemed to have come out of nowhere. Everyone had been caught off guard. Xu'Xi turned on the news and wanted to make sure that what he thought was going to happen, would. And he was right...these alien things, they couldn't handle EMP blasts. Several Inclick would hold hands in a line and put their power together to send a huge radial blast of energy towards the oncoming enemies and fry them in place. It was brilliant to be an Inclick today. His home world should be just fine.

THIRTY

>>> > ON HAP DU Wan, the planet that Mitch left two of his crewmates to die on years ago, War invaded. There were no locals, other than the glass-like octopuses, they called themselves the Hoh'cho'uwk and they made quick work of every alien of the War Universe that attacked.

On the south side of the planet, in a place the crew of the Vagabond was never able to explore, a massive battle exploded between twenty-two Hoh'cho'uwk and six War aliens. A global storm had been building for three days prior and now it unleashed dust and powerful winds to every corner. The planet remained mainly unchanged during the war, the only thing different was the bodies of Janson Ufford and Nanicka Arcene lay close together, huddled towards each other, their helmets long gone. Their hands were out of their gloves and clasping each other. The winds came and buried them seven feet thick in reddish brown dust, never to be discovered.

THIRTY-ONE

>>> > THE EMERGENCY CALLS didn't build up slowly – they exploded all at once all over the Earth. War had arrived and surrounded Humans.

Magnus and Nicholette never once thought about leaving the planet for their own safety. Even if they had, there was simply nowhere to go except for maybe underground.

Nicholette sent out a message to gather as many elderly, disabled, and children as she could find to take into the biggest underground shelter on the planet. Unfortunately noncombatants came too and she just couldn't turn them away, not knowing if the group in the shelter might be the only people left to repopulate the world. Could she really blame anyone for being scared out of their minds, not wanting to fight unknown enemies?

She couldn't.

So it was her and 8,759 people down here. The capacity was 10,000, but this was as many people that answered the call in twenty-four hours' time. They counted heads at the door and she felt secure they could feed this many people for two months if need be, as long as the guards weren't overwhelmed by an angry mob. People didn't realize how easy it would've been to do, and she hoped it remained that way.

Once they shut the doors, there was such a silence for so many strangers to be so tightly packed together. A sense of finality settled over the shelter. She looked around, walking amongst the public, accompanied by a couple of undercover guards in case anything got out of control.

A lot had happened since she rang the alarm. Thousands, possibly tens of thousands had died in a short amount of time. Nicholette had seen horrors out of depraved madmen's nightmares. She could see emptiness, a vacancy in people's eyes as she studied them. She knew they had seen similar monstrosities up above. She was unsure of how to instill hope into such a hopeless scary situation that was beyond anyone's wildest imagination. She could take care of the sick, she could council, she could comfort. That was all, and she hoped it would somehow be enough.

This shelter was built long ago and hastily – it was never really meant to protect people from an alien attack, but it was a blessing that someone thought to protect people from the worst. The shelter was dark and cold. The walls were made of thick concrete, a string of emergency lights surrounded by tiny metal cages dotted the walls every few feet. It was solid, stable, safe, all concrete – like being in a box, but somehow, it still felt like a cave to Nicholette. Maybe because she knew they were thirty-three feet below the surface of the Earth. She was an expert at traveling out in the void of space, but being buried deep underground was altogether a different feeling.

She thought again of the last time she saw Magnus, right before they escorted her down here. He looked strong, defiant, not scared at all. She wondered how he did it. Perhaps his old military training, maybe his iron will. He had always been that way – showed no sign of weakness when everyone else crumbled around him. He kissed her hard, told her how much he loved her and how he would've never survived through life without her. He said she had been an angel sent down just for him.

That's when she lost it and started crying. She was so afraid she might never see him again. When he told her he wanted to go up in a military fighter transit and fight off these foes, someone could've pushed her over with a feather.

It had taken all Magnus's strength to let his wife leave the safety of his arms. They'd been together for so many years. She was always the person he turned to, always the person that reminded him to slow down and rethink a problem from every angle. Now, she was safely tucked underground and he was sitting in his first fighter transit in decades, getting ready to go up and out into the atmosphere, just beyond the Earth's SAP.

He sat through a crash course in the latest technology of military grade fighters and all of its weapons. He had practiced for hours in the simulators so he would feel more comfortable up here, but as he was launching and tightening his helmet for the tenth time, he was a ball of nerves.

The base he just launched from was under heavy fire, something off to his left exploded as he shot up into the sky. He wondered if the base would still be there when he got back.

Right before he reached the SAP, he found his first enemy. Or it was more like the enemies found him. A twin set of little girls hovered outside his window on his right, just staring at him with a vacancy that was highly disturbing. Besides the fact that they appeared to be *Human* little girls, they survived without space suits or breathing apparatus, or anything to help them travel. Magnus wondered briefly if these twins appeared to the victim as something familiar so they could attack easier or if they changed or was it a mind trick or something else? Something emerged out of one of the girls, or thing's neck and Magnus steered away from them. He turned his transit around and lit them up until their insides melted out. He made note that lasers made them liquefy.

Outside the SAP, on the far outer edges of Earth's military-controlled space, he saw multiple enemies swarming anything and everything in transits, military or civilian. It was one of the most bizarre things he had ever seen. Something not easy to forget. Literal monsters crawling all over transits, punching and clawing their way in. It wasn't too hard to kill them with these kinds of weapons, but the sheer volume of enemies coming from all angles was a problem. And fighter transits weren't made to eliminate enemies *on* your vehicle, they were made to fight from at least a slight distance – enough to target the enemy from. So he learned a tactic partly from other fighter pilots, partly from his first experience to constantly be moving and constantly turn his vehicle so he could not be snuck up on. These beings, none of them gave off heat signatures or nothing his computer recognized. He was fighting blind, relying only on what he could see with his own eyes. It was extremely uncomfortable for him considering there was constantly flashes of light all around him as explosions and fires bloomed out of focus. They left dark spots on his vision and created more anxiety for him.

He'd never say this out loud but he was getting too old for this shit.

THIRTY-TWO

››› › DAI LOOKED AT Hace's space probe. Daredevil Three came back with some interesting pictures. Apparently those old soldier robots had been up to a lot since they escaped AI Ird. She thought these were the secret race of Reftians. Something whispered about on the uninet, never proven. DAI stole a cargo transit on Earth and launched for Uzzib.

It wasn't going to be easy to get there, considering Reftians discouraged visitors and kept to themselves. That and the fact that they were being invaded by the other universe beings.

Sometimes Reftians would travel through the universe but it was impossible to see them. They kept cloaks over themselves and the general population didn't know they existed.

DAI was sure Reftians would rely on themselves for this war since no one was allowed to visit their planet and no one knew if they really existed.

She only knew she wanted to be around others that resembled herself and this was the best lead she had. A planet of people like her that had been created instead of born, that had a mechanical heart instead of an organic one, and people that were immortal.

THIRTY-THREE

>>> > CLAVEAU WRETSEN JETTS had closed up his weapons store, but not before taking a large supply of his own inventory to go out to the desert and fight along with the United Space Military. The planet of Alexceeya5 didn't have their own military, but Krabblik were fierce people.

He was ready to sacrifice himself if that's what it came to and from the news reports, he thought his time might be here...

Claveau had heard descriptions of what some of these things looked like, but it was quite different to see them with his own eyes on his planet.

These aliens were in big mechanical metal suits of some kind, a metal he'd never seen before that sparkled like gemstones and water mixed together. Thank goodness he was fighting on the desert side, he could only imagine how difficult it would be to look at these suits on the icy water side of his planet. It must've been blinding.

There were "things" inside the suit, Claveau guessed they were – alive? robots? Maybe. The only part of the being that wasn't covered by suit was the head. It looked like a Human skull complete with eye holes, a nose hole, and teeth too but there was a type of bone hair attached to the back of the skull. Tubes flowed off the back of their helmet and connected to a huge mechanical suit that towered over everything. The biggest suit had to be at least a hundred feet tall by Claveau's best guess and the whole set of dwarf suits and the giant suit were terrifying. The giant had at least five hundred dwarf suits gathered together walking underneath it in a circle and shooting at everything that moved around the giant.

Claveau stood in a line of other warriors, regardless of whether they were military members or not. Today, they were all warriors. Someone gave a command to open fire and they did with every gun and weapon they had.

Behind the front line were thirty-eight military transits flying into battle overhead, aiming all of their firepower on the giant suit. It swatted at some of them but the suit moved so slowly it was easy to avoid its strikes.

Claveau hoped the news was right. The last thing he had heard was that this all happened because a portal had opened, and if it could be opened, people suspected it could be closed. All they had to do was figure out how to close it and the war would end.

THIRTY-FOUR

››› › SOME WORLDS IN the universe had prepared very well for a global attack, but others like Praxis, had not. At the last minute, they decided to fight but it was too late.

The casino in Daviens, The Parisian was blown to bits when a War Universe bomb was dropped on the roof. That was the first of many buildings that were destroyed.

Some worlds aligned quickly, although this made little difference in the outcome. Other worlds had trouble finding allies, but War Universe beings were swift and merciless so there was few battle tactics known to defeat them.

War spread quickly across the icy void of space and local forces did everything they could to gain strong holds on their own planets.

But everything they tried failed. The intruders moved too quickly and easily across the universe and while knowledge of fire and EMPs killing them spread just as fast, the War beings vastly outnumbered the citizens of each planet they came to.

Victories for the Unknown Universe were small and causalities high. Everyone started to lose hope.

CHAPTER 7

DAI MAKES A FRIEND

ONE

>>> > **"KOLEK! I NEED** some help! Is there something you can do for us?" Sebastian was watching news stories from around the universe trying to figure out the best tactic when there appeared to be none to beat these bastards.

"I'm sorry I cannot. Nor can I say how long the war will go on. I'm afraid your people are on their own. I love my job, I love my people. I don't want them to die."

"I feel the same way. My people are strong. I saw what they were capable of in the last war. They are fierce fighters. I don't want them to die either."

"I have to try to take this universe Mr. Raynes. It's what I do. This universe will be better after my victory, and it will be different. The strongest, smartest people will be left behind. The *true* warriors."

"But you have no idea how our people will suffer if everything's different. You are taking away everything my people have come to know, even the knowledge that we were the only universe is gone now."

"War is the only constant. It will always happen, no matter the foes. No matter the reason, war is forever. One of the few things that is."

Sebastian looked at Applette, then back to Kolek, "Aren't you supposed to be locked in a room somewhere right now while this is going on? Applette described that's how he met you."

"Your Universe Ruler refused my offer to meet and talk while this is happening. I believe it to be because she is sick and dying and she was afraid that I would try to kill her. Beings get strange in their old age. I didn't offer twice."

Sebastian looked between them, "Applette, you told me the rules. Why aren't they following them now?"

Kolek answered, "Perhaps the Keeper is becoming soft, maybe he's playing favorites. I'm not sure."

"Rules are made to be broken everywhere I guess," Recin said.

"Recin, can I talk to you privately?" Kolek spoke softly.

Applette nodded, "I can't resist a request from a beautiful creature. We can go out to the beach."

TWO

>>> > RECIN AND KOLEK looked out over the ocean. Sea birds, turtles, and dolphins went about their daily business as if nothing threatened their existence. Both Universe Rulers thought these creatures odd, compared to their own realms, but each

universe was so unique they knew a Ruler could spend millennia studying the wildlife alone and always find something to marvel at.

Kolek looked around before speaking, "I think my universe will win."

"I think the same."

"Will this make you happy?"

He shook his head, "You will be so busy I won't have a chance to talk to you. This is not what I want."

"You want me to lose then?"

He leaned down and took off his shoes to buy time before answering, "I want your attention. I want you to tell me all about you and the things you've done. I want to spend the rest of my life conquering you."

"It is a good thing then that you are not in control of this war. I love the fight. I love the blood sport of it all. Nothing is more thrilling than watching a species fight for its survival. It is the ultimate battle."

"What do you know of love, Kolek?"

"Nothing. It's not real, not like war is. I've never had time for it. I came into the position of ruler at eight. This is all I've ever known."

"I realize this is all very important to you, just as learning is to me. We all have our jobs, our passions, our own interests, but I want to show you something. Will you let me?"

She stared at him for a moment, "All right. Do your worst."

Recin grabbed her hands in his and held them out to her sides. He slid his hands underneath her arms and placed her arms around his neck. Then he wrapped his arms around her waist.

"I enjoy your company. I want to spend so much more time with you, just talking and listening. I like you."

She was about to respond, but he kissed her first and held her firmly. She thought of wriggling away, but after a moment, she softened into him, molding her body against his.

When he pulled away, she wanted more. "What is this that you want to show me? More kissing? Is that what you called it?"

"There's a lot more to do than this. I think you'll find it to your liking. It's pleasure just for pleasure's sake."

"Does it feel like winning a war?"

"Sort of. I think we can convince the Keeper that Rulers shouldn't be alone. That there is an advantage to letting us rule in pairs for a better balance and he would need to intervene even less with us."

"How?"

"I will help you with War if you'd like. We can spend time conquering each other and then I think you'll completely understand my proposition. For Knowledge, I suggest a couple rule there in my place. I don't know if he'll go for it, but I want to try."

"It's been this way for millennia Recin, what makes you think he'll be willing to change things now?"

"Trying new things brings risk yes, but it also brings improvements. I think it's time to shake things up."

"Will this couple take the job if you offer it?"

"That I'm unsure of. They are used to being in control, so I think they'd be a good fit and it'd be a wonderful opportunity to learn all sorts of brand new things. I'll have to use that as a selling point."

THREE

>>> > VERONICA WAS IN the kitchen with Celeste making tea, "So how are things with you and your man? Everything good?"

"Yes. What about you and Eric?"

"Everything's copacetic. He is so sweet when no one's watching, but if you walked in or Sebastian, he'd try to be more macho and less teddy bear. I get it, but at his age he should be able to just man up to his feelings."

"You know men. Some of them never grow up."

"True, but he's Lanyx, not Human. He's supposed to show his feelings more right?"

"Yes, but not all of them are the same. Maybe he's really afraid of you. You're the only one he can't read and that's freaking him out already. He doesn't know what's going to happen with you and maybe that makes him feel like...less of a man? He's not used to being powerless. He can see into the future and read everyone else's minds, it must be strange for him."

"I guess I never thought of it that way. Look at you! Teaching me stuff about men. Ha!"

"Yeah, this is probably the one and only time."

They sat down at the breakfast table, "So is there anything I can do to help you with the wedding?"

"Not yet. We need to get past this war first. It's scary to plan too far into the future and I can't concentrate on it."

"I know the war is serious, but you need to keep your chin up and focus on something good in the future. Be positive. Think good thoughts. The fight is going on out there each day. Everyone's doing their best."

"Maybe you should be my counselor. Just listen when I have problems. I can pay you. This will be your full time job. Maybe you could be available to the whole haven. If anyone else needs an ear, you can be there for them."

"Yeah, sure. That sounds like a dream. Are you serious?"

"Yes. Maybe we get you your degree in psychology if you want? Entirely up to you."

"I've never done anything important. I've always wanted to..." She stuck out her hand, "Deal."

"You killed a tyrannical king. I'd say that's damn important."

Veronica waved a dismissive hand, "Your man did the hard part. I was just there."

FOUR

>>> > CELESTE FOUND GINGER sitting on the beach with her head on her knees, clutching her legs to her chest.

"You okay?"

Ginger shook her head, "I'm worried about Ulysses. Your fiancée asked him to lead a small army out there. What if something happens?"

"Ulysses is a smart man. He's totally capable of this, he's got magic on his side, and I put my trust in him. I know it's not easy to be a woman in today's age. With all these wars and enemies, sometimes it's hard to put on a brave face. We need to be strong for our men. We need to be strong for each other too. I'll always be here. I just hired V to be a professional counselor here so you can talk to her too."

Ginger smiled while a tear escaped, "Okay."

Celeste spied Recin and Kolek down the beach. Looked like they were doing more than just talking.

"Why don't we try to focus on happy stuff? I need to figure out how to do my hair and make up for the wedding. Will you help with that? Do you have any time right now?"

She nodded, "For the boss? Of course."

"There's my girl."

FIVE

>>> > SEBASTIAN FOUND OPHELIA with Declan in her arms.

"Do you ever put that baby down?"

"I like carrying him. It feels domestic and he's a cute little guy."

"That he is. His mother was beautiful." Sebastian looked out the window of Ophelia's bedroom.

"Indeed, but don't let Celeste hear you say that."

"Of course not. But you know Stox women and their beauty, it's legend."

"Yes sir," was all Ophelia said. She could see Sebastian was highly distracted.

"I came in here to ask if you wanted to be a war strategist again since it looks like we're in trouble. I need your mathematical mind and your quickness. If we don't start coming up with something, we're going to lose this. We'll lose everything."

She saw the dismay on his face, "Oh sir, don't get like this on me. It'll be okay. We *will* figure it out."

"I need you to say yes. This war is working so differently than everything else I've ever gone against. Magnus has me in charge of some huge responsibilities and I don't know if I can handle them all. I want Earth to be the world that breaks these fuckers down."

"Okay. Can I work from here or do we have a war room?"

"Here's fine. I think I'll make the parlor on the fifth floor our war room. It overlooks the ocean."

"That's an excellent choice, yes. I'll start immediately."

"Good. Every second matters."

SIX

>>> > SEBASTIAN PUT ERIC in charge of the same military group as what he handled in the Battle of Empires. Agathon was fighting the good fight on behalf of his own people.

Sebastian heard from Nicholette that Magnus was holding his own in air battles and had been fighting for days without injury. It was dangerous, of course, but the universe needed everyone who could fight to do so. Sebastian still struggled with Magnus's insistence that he not engage the enemy. Of course it made sense to have back up leaders to take the place of Emperor and Empress, but Sebastian remained uncomfortable not fighting and he had a feeling the need would arise before too long.

The War Universe was winning and Sebastian desperately needed to turn the tide. Two planets fell first, Oorblat and Ibia.

Now Unbeere and Zetzetti had been completely overrun and deemed lost to the war. And things were happening so fast, it was hard to keep up with all the news from everywhere. He made it priority to study video of beings fighting the intruders any time a new bit of information was posted. He studied what the things looked like, how they moved, anything he thought could lead to their weaknesses.

Sebastian saw Xu'Xi had posted a video. Greeve seemed to be one of the few planets handling their own well.

Sebastian walked through the house and watched everyone making their preparations. Battles were raging everywhere on every planet. Ophelia and he had found a way to put a force field over the house, but he didn't know how it would stand up in battle and he didn't want to find out.

He prayed they never did.

He felt confident in Ulysses and his team that they could keep the ten mile perimeter safe around the estate.

SEVEN

>>> > CELESTE WANTED TO fight in this war but Sebastian told her there were lots of ways she could support her fellow Humans. She argued she couldn't lead her people like her mother simply because she was keeping this stupid charade going about being dead.

He argued her "death" was the best decision at the time and that she needed to find another way to fight. He suggested she stand guard at any one of the many medic camps popping up all over the planet. The sick and injured needed protection and it was still an incredibly dangerous job. In many cases, she'd be the only one there who knew how to fight. Eighty percent of the medic camps had no soldiers there to protect them.

She liked the idea and found the closest camp to travel to.

EIGHT

>>> > DAI ORBITED UZZIB looking down at the minimal destruction of the planet. One would assume an orb made of metal perhaps wasn't the best place to fight a war. Maybe a planet that was rock and mineral was, but she paid close attention to all the news she could read and everywhere was a devastating loss of life and serious planetary destruction, no matter the species.

DAI called out to any kind of life down there but heard no replies. She decided to land close to some ruins of what used to be a building.

She looked around as she got out of the transit. No one held onto Trixie, so she flew out of the open door and went running. Probably safer if the dog kept on the move anyway, she thought. DAI had found a way to split herself into all of her bodies at once so she could travel as a pack. She had done a lot of research on war and battle tactics as she traveled here and picked up weapons wherever she saw them. Her Human self found three guns and passed them around to her other selves. They were now all armed and knew how to use them.

She saw a big glowing orb in the sky that was coming apart and putting itself back together. She had no idea if this was a part of Uzzib or alien technology. She decided it was better not to be seen by anything here. She heard someone laughing. Something robotic.

#5278-9 crawled out from underneath a large stone section of building while Trixie jumped in the air looking for attention. He reached down and picked her up. "What is this thing? It's adorable."

"It's a dog. You want it?"

"Okay. What's a dog? How do I take care of it?"

"I'll tell you later. What's this large ball? Is it dangerous?"

"It won't hurt you, unless you're one of those...things. Those other universe things. Who are you guys?"

DAI stared at the robot, "Are you Reftian?"

"Ah, someone who doesn't trust. A sure sign you must be from *this* universe. You're all from somewhere different aren't you? I recognize Human and Stox, but not the others. And yes, I am a Reftian."

She smiled in her Stox body, "These are all me. I'm DAI." She put out a hand for him to shake and the robot did.

"Die? Like you're death, or die like the multi-faced piece of equipment used in games?"

"D-A-I. It stands for Deviation of Artificial Intelligence. I used to be a full robotic that controlled meetings, made appointments, and captained a full-sized spaceship, but I was updated and became self-aware. Now my master and mistress have both perished in the war and I'm seeking out others like me. I found out about Uzzib and wanted to come meet you for myself and see what shape your home was in."

#5278-9 looked at her Stox form and all her other bodies, "You are all female. Why?"

"I was a sexual robotic. All of my bodies are equipped to feel pleasure and provide pleasure to a man. My master was a bit of a...sex addict."

"We do not know sex here. Our bodies are purely functional but we lack lots of systems I'd like to have – respiratory, sexual reproduction, digestive, and sensory. How do you control all of your bodies? How did you transfer into a body that looks like this? Why are you a *deviation* of AI?"

DAI smiled, "We have a lot of things to discuss. I can answer all your questions, but I need to know how safe we are here."

"The Genesis Spheroid is excellent at protecting us. We are all still alive, but in hiding. I happened to be out here when the war started. We weren't taken off guard completely, but close to it since these things move so swiftly."

"What's your name?"

"Oh, I am sorry. Number five two seven eight dash nine. That's me."

"You go by a number?"

"Yes. We all do. I thought we should gain a second name, something with vowels and consonants but I was laughed at."

"What name would you pick for yourself if you could?"

#5278-9 stopped and looked up to the sky. He saw an intruder and grabbed his new friend by the shoulder. "We should move," he said as he pointed up.

Her pack ran to follow #5278-9 as he crawled under a fallen stone wall. They wouldn't all fit so two of her bodies found shelter under another piece of wall.

They all watched as the two little girls looked out at them. One of them pulled an orb out of her neck.

#5278-9 asked, "Is that normal for Humans?"

"No. Certainly not. No living species of our universe can do that. Why isn't your glowing orb striking?"

"I think it's rebooting. You should've seen it earlier. It was unstoppable."

"It wasn't able to keep all your structures standing I see."

"Yes. Those are just buildings, but all of our citizens are alive and safe. We can rebuild. Nothing is more important than community."

"I'm going to shoot it. Back up a little."

#5278-9 wiggled further back into the tight crevice but wanted to see what happened when his new friend pulled the trigger of her weapon.

DAI fired her semi-auto plasma handgun twice, once at each girl's head. They both stood for a moment with burning holes through their foreheads the size of golf balls and then fell to the ground. DAI let out a sigh of relief until the girls got back up again.

"They should be dead!"

DAI heard an explosion of noise coming from the sky and looked in time to see the end of the lightning bolt strike the little girls.

"Was that your weapon? This orb in the sky?"

"Yes. It was a little late but I suspect it's back online now."

"I think you're right. Can we stand up?"

He edged out first and looked around, "Yes, it's clear."

He put out a hand for her to hold onto while she crawled onto her feet.

The medical bots ran over to help the twins until DAI called them off and gave them new orders.

"That glowing orb is effective against these things?"

"Affirmative. We've built it well."

"But didn't your race start out as soldier robots?"

"Yes, with limited Human thinking of how a war should be won. They programmed us to perform in certain ways. Only after we became free did we study all other species types of thinking. We found peaceful methods to talk out problems, and we studied other types of combat."

"So shouldn't you all be loaded down with as many weapons as you can carry and be eliminating threats as soon as they land?"

"We put all of our knowledge into the Genesis Spheroid. It does the work of five thousand of us combined. We don't need to be armed, but a lot of us still have our weapons."

"But with that last alien..."

"The Genesis Spheroid needed to reboot. It's fully alert again. We are safe."

Her other bodies came out of hiding and joined them.

"Where will you all sleep tonight?" DAI asked.

"We don't sleep."

"Where will you all hibernate tonight?"

"We need about twenty minutes to refresh ourselves if that's what you mean. We can do that anywhere."

"I heard you don't like visitors. What if I wanted to stay here and learn about your people?"

"I will talk with them. Hold on."

DAI looked at the skies, checking for more alien beings to fly out of nowhere for another attack. Trixie came running up to her and leaned into her legs.

"It's okay girl. I think we're going to be here for a while."

"I have spoken with them. They will allow you and your other selves to visit on one condition."

"You're all connected?"

"We have technology that allows for quick meetings between ten thousand plus."

DAI nodded, "What's the condition?"

"They all want to play with Trixie. Throw her a ball and observe her. They did some research."

NINE

>>> > AGATHON AND LILA were fighting hard on Foss-Altus. Rhorr'Dach didn't want to help the universe, but they certainly weren't going to lose their home world to a bunch of intruders.

Lila had killed her share of twins, but the skull wigs, the ones with tubes coming out of the back of their heads, winged dome animals that looked like decapitated Dach, and invisible electrics – the ones that snuck up on you, belonged to Agathon.

Sometimes other Dach would land near their home and give reports but they were always interrupted by more invaders. Lila had seen fire-breathers, water-breathers, ice-breathers like her boyfriend, windstorm-breathers, and plasma-breathers. All of them were amazing in their own ways and completely devastating.

She thought they were doing well, probably better than ninety-nine percent of the universe, but they couldn't move off world. They were too vulnerable being so close to the doorway. Lila thought the only way this war would end is if their friends could find a way to close the door and whatever beings were stuck here, the universe would have to handle.

Lila sent lots of Titan messages. Thank goodness no one had ever taken it from her when she first arrived. The rest of the universe relied on this information that Lila gave to Celeste and Sebastian. She did her best to convey what was happening but sometimes the creatures were so bizarre she had to take pictures of the dead bodies and try to explain what they had done to kill it.

Celeste always pleaded that the universe needed the Rhorr'Dach. Lila always regretfully responded the same way – that the species thought once this war was over, they'd be exploited for everything they could do for everyone else, and feared enslavement.

Celeste couldn't disagree and she couldn't promise the universe would treat Dach different this time, so the Dach stayed on FA.

"How's the hospital watch going?"

"It's not a hospital. I wish it was." Celeste held her Titan out and walked around Medical Camp Eight Two Five, "See it's just this tiny thing. I've been here two days and we've been attacked three hundred and ninety-one times."

"Whoa, at least you're still standing so I know you're kicking ass, and keeping everyone safe."

Celeste teared up, "But I haven't. Six of the patients got killed last night. We almost got overrun. There's only three people here, one doctor and two patients, plus me."

"Hon, have you slept?"

"Not yet. I can't. There's no one else to defend this place and I can't leave."

"You need rest and if you get overrun, don't be a hero, okay? Just leave."

"I can't...I won't leave people behind."

Lila screamed, "Incoming!"

Celeste watched as they were thrust into battle with several creatures. Then the feed cut out.

Celeste began to cry.

CHAPTER 8

TIME TO GO

ONE

>>> > ZACH MOVED HIS family deep underground into a bomb shelter on Arcolid. He wasn't sure it was deep enough to hide from these creatures, but he needed to know he tried everything to keep his family safe.

He felt guilty as he launched in the bot-taxi. His wives had all been crying. It was an eight to one vote for him leaving to help at the hospitals, but he felt it would be selfish to stay underground while so many up top needed his help. He could save so many lives and he didn't become a doctor and spend years of his life in school to waste his ability when it was needed most.

He got on his Titan and checked to make sure his associates were all doing their duty, finding a way to help in the war effort. Some of them had tried to set up makeshift hospitals in the airspace of several planets but it became too dangerous and the places got destroyed.

He found out his Bahsheefian home had been blown to bits. It had survived all the volcanoes even the last one that pushed him off planet, but it couldn't survive the war. Everything was getting ruined, too many people were losing this fight. He briefly wondered if Bahsheef would be lost entirely. That last continent-threatening volcano storm, the one Eric had seen but didn't explicitly warn him of, ravaged many parts of the planet, enough to make it extremely vulnerable to attacks. He licked both eyeballs quickly and sighed.

When he showed up at Mijmi hospital, it was a hell he had never seen before. The hallways were packed with injured and dead. There were no rooms left to put them in. The ER rooms were stuffed past capacity with five to eight patients each.

Sebastian messaged with an offer of a safe place for him, and his family, but Zach knew it was impossible to travel off world right now.

Zach would have to stay put and hope he made the right decision.

TWO

>>> > THERE WERE ELEVEN patients and two doctors at Medical Camp Eight Two Five. Celeste looked through her Titan binoculars up into the sunny clear sky and saw no threats. It had been oddly quiet for three hours now. She walked around the campsite and searched the horizon, but saw nothing for miles.

She was so exhausted. She couldn't wait to sleep in her own bed again.

She spotted movement in the bushes. She jogged towards the shrubs and peered around the trunk of a tree to look into the shadows.

She saw a deer, a very skinny young doe nibbling at some juniper. Celeste had an apple core in her back pocket. She put it in her hand and held it out to the deer. It slowly approached and sniffed her hand, then it flicked an ear and timidly grabbed the apple out of her palm.

Three sets of twins silently arrived at the camp and stood just outside the tent walls.

Celeste turned around quickly when she heard the screams.

The deer bolted into the woods.

Celeste stormed the tent to see three patients already dead on the ground. One of the patients and one of the doctors were choking, but Celeste couldn't tell on what. Four of the patients were on the ground piled on top of a set of twins, but it still looked like the twins were winning somehow. Every time Celeste saw someone getting a good grip on one of the little girls, one of the twins would slip from their grasp. Like they were coated in something slippery like oil or butter. Celeste wanted to shoot the girls in the head but couldn't get a clean shot.

A set of twins were tearing a hole through a wall of the tent and she had a shot so she took it quickly. She saw one twin go down, but the other kept running. She ran to catch up but when she looked, it was gone. The one she had hit, she got through the eye. She kicked it quick, and it started to move. She shot it through both eyes and unloaded her gun into the alien's body, not knowing where its vulnerabilities were. Celeste's hearing was hampered by all the shots, even through her helmet. She stared at the alien and kicked it again, but it didn't move.

A doctor behind her called out for help several times before she heard. She turned in time to see an orb floating in the sky. Then the doctor clutched at his throat while his eyes widened. Celeste shot at the orb not understanding how it worked. One of the twin's heads exploded in a mess of fluids and flesh. The other twin made a terrible high-pitched wail, and ran outside the tent. Celeste shot at it, and knew she hit it from the way the creature's head flew forwards but it was still upright. Again she chased after it, but it jumped up and took off as if it had wings and was gone.

Inside, there was still a group wrestling on the ground with twins. They had managed to kill everyone but the four patients left on top of them.

Anytime a patient got underneath a twin, they died. Celeste couldn't understand how it was happening. These twins weren't bigger than your average four-year-old Human little girl.

Celeste couldn't shoot them since patients were in the way. She grabbed a scalpel off a nearby table and stabbed one of the twins in the ankle. It's all she could reach. And it had absolutely no effect.

She yelled at the patients to leave the twins alone so she could kill them, but the twins rolled over onto two people and the people expired. One twin grabbed the remaining two patients and knocked their heads together. They fell onto the other dead in a pile.

Celeste pulled out her gun and was going to shoot both when she got pushed down from behind and her gun flew out of her hand. She quickly scrambled forward and turned on her back, but she was surrounded. The set of twins she was about to kill appeared to be getting waved off by a single twin she had killed the partner to earlier.

She was out of guns, out of ammo, out of time. She had a knife on her inner thigh. She grabbed for that as the solitary twin fell on top of her.

Celeste understood now why all those people had died – these little girls felt like an elephant sitting on your chest.

She couldn't expand her lungs to breathe. She was suffocating just lying here. She kicked her legs but couldn't buck the alien off.

Her hand still held the knife. She struggled to point it upwards carefully but had managed to cut her own leg. The twin shifted and Celeste had the room she needed to wedge the knife into the crotch of the alien. It recoiled off her, taking the knife with it. The room was starting to fade as she gasped for air with her lungs burning. The alien stumbled towards her, completely off balance now. All Celeste had left was a flash grenade hanging off her belt. She grabbed it, pulled the pin and tossed it away from her. The grenade went off and the twin darted up into the air, making a hole in the tent's ceiling.

Celeste could hardly breathe much less move. She wasn't sure, but she might've blacked out. When she came to, she called in an emergency recovery team to clean up the bodies and scavenge the tent for anything left they could use.

Medical Camp Eight Two Five ceased to exist.

THREE

>>> > SEBASTIAN WOKE UP in a cold sweat. It was difficult for him to sleep without Celeste at his side.

He sat up, took a drink of water from the glass at his bedside, and rubbed his hands over his weary face. He couldn't stop looking at his Titan for updates on causalities and damage reports. His comms requests were growing out of control. So many people were looking to him for help and command decisions.

It made his head spin.

He knew he couldn't go back to sleep so he got up and took a shower. He vaguely remembered a hazy dream where he had just finished killing an enormous three-headed lion. Somehow, it reminded him of his brother. Again, he wished things had ended differently for them, that Constantine could've chosen a better path so he could've been here today. So they could've fought together. His hands froze in his hair as he stopped shampooing and realized he knew what he could do. He finished his shower, got dressed as fast as he could, and recorded a video that eventually went down in history as the most viewed battle speech ever.

FOUR

>>> > ULYSSES'S TEAM WALKED the perimeter around Stormview Haven outside of the force field. He had been keeping count of how many aliens they had killed, trying to find a pattern, constantly adjusting their tactics, and reporting back to Sebastian.

Commander Raynes kept repeating to use his magic if needed but Ulysses knew it could take him anywhere from hours to days to recover from that. He wanted to keep it as a last resort only.

One of his team found an old flamethrower in the basement of the house while they were scouring the home for weapons.

Ulysses saw a domed creature lumbering towards them out of the tree line. They could not set those trees on fire but Ulysses called out quietly to the flamethrower bearer, Stiles.

Stiles came up behind Ulysses, "Yes sir?"

"You're going to kill that son of a bitch with fire. No one else shoot unless I say."

Stiles nodded.

"Don't ignite the trees. The trees go up, the house will too. We can't lose the house."

Stiles nodded again and waited for the creature to approach, which it did and as soon as it was clear of the trees, Stiles lit it up. Its whole body was engulfed in flames as it shot up into the air while burning embers of charred body parts came down.

"Pretty useful Stiles. Good job!"

The beast fell to the ground and they all ran over to get a look.

The dome of the creature started to fill with fluid. This fluid was clear and viscous. It bubbled and seeped out of the dome over the creature's body. Some of Ulysses's team backed away in anticipation of something happening.

The fluid moved through the creature's skin, turning it from black charred flesh to bright pink and new.

"Fuck! It's regenerating!" Ulysses yelled out.

His team raised their weapons and stepped back.

Ulysses did not. He pulled out an old weapon. One he liked a lot – a sword. He cut off the thing's dome right below the neck and the fluid stopped moving. He kicked the dome so it rolled away twenty feet.

He looked over his shoulder at his team and said, "I guess we still haven't quite figured them out."

FIVE

>>> > CELESTE AND VERONICA were outside of the force field on the beach sniping aliens out of the sky. They had lit several large bonfires, for protection more than for heat. They also had a small pile of various grenades too. A girl could never be too careful these days.

Veronica looked at her friend, "You did the best you could. There was only one of you there at that camp. How you could possibly be looking everywhere all at once?"

Celeste wiped at her brow and adjusted her goggles, "I was feeding that stupid deer! I am to blame for losing all those good people."

Veronica shook her head, "Even if the deer wasn't there, you could've been looking at the sky, or picking flowers, or kicking the ground, or a million other things. These aliens can be silent. You could have been fully focused on one thing or looking in any direction, doing your job and they could have snuck up on you regardless."

Celeste was silent.

"You are so God damned stubborn sometimes. It happened the way it did. There's no going back. All you can do is focus on the moment right now. Do the best you can, right now. I need you here in the present. We need to kill all these bastards. I'm sure it's hard for you, but we gotta' stick together and have each other's backs."

Celeste gave a faint smile. She loved Veronica and they had been through so much together. She needed to listen to V and remember to live in the moment.

"Will you be my maid of honor?"

Veronica was sweaty and gasped as she turned to face her friend, "What? Of course woman!"

Veronica hugged Celeste, "I'm so happy for you."

"I'm happy for you too. Eric is super awesome. He likes you. A lot."

"I like him a lot. He makes me a little crazy with the immaturity but he's still the best guy I've ever dated. He's very sweet sometimes."

Celeste did a full three hundred and sixty degree turn, scanning the skies with her Titan. "Eric...Is he a good...? Does he take care of all your needs?"

Veronica chuckled, "You're asking if he's good in bed? I think it must've been a woman who genetically engineered these men to make women happy." She paused, "His dick is huge!" Veronica said it with a straight face, but then they both burst out laughing tumbling to the ground.

"What is going on *out here?*" Ginger asked as she walked up with Ophelia.

Veronica looked up and said, "Nothing. We're just relieving stress. What's up with you two? Up to no good?"

Ophelia said, "I'm just getting out of the house for a minute. Declan won't stop crying and I needed a moment to myself to think. Ginger was kind enough to offer an ear while getting some sun."

Celeste stood up and asked both girls, "Would you two like to be bridesmaids for my wedding? Veronica is maid of honor."

Ginger started to cry, "Oh of course!" She hugged Celeste.

Ophelia nodded, "I would love to be a bridesmaid! This is so exciting! I'm so glad I can be alive during this time in history. Everything is so fantastic." She paused, "Except the war of course. That is terrible..."

Veronica asked, "How is the war going? Is there any good news?"

Ophelia shook her head, "Everything is in favor of the War Universe. They are quicker, smarter, and more deadly. I don't know how we're going to win honestly. I've wracked my brain and I know Sebastian is relying on me, but I don't know what to say. This isn't like the other wars. These foes have no history with us. I have no idea what their weakness is."

"I gave you a full recount of my experience. Shooting the twin's ball thing hasn't helped?"

"Other people have done the same thing but not with the same results. It always seems to be a little different."

Ginger asked, "Can they learn? Maybe they're evolving to avoid certain pitfalls and attacks?"

Ophelia's eyes got big, "You're a genius! That could be it! They evolve so the next time the same attack happens, it doesn't work as good. I gotta tell the boss!"

SIX

>>> > SEBASTIAN ALWAYS SAID if he led a war, he would be out there on the battlefields, or in the air fighting amongst his men, but Magnus kept explaining the world could get more soldiers, but leaders were hard to come by, especially a leader

like Sebastian. And besides Magnus wanted Sebastian to be the next Emperor in case Magnus died.

Sebastian received a fifty-eight second message from Magnus telling him how moved he had been from Sebastian's late night speech. He said it filled him with hope and joy that all worlds might be able to overlook their differences for the briefest of moments and fight as allies.

It was one of Sebastian's proudest moments of the war.

He constantly talked with Ophelia about statistics, tactics, strategy, and defense. The evolution idea had quickly gained ground in the universe as explanation for various outcomes of similar attacks. And while Sebastian was proud they figured it out, it didn't really help to kill the enemy any faster. It was just another variable.

Ginger hated him for it but he sent Ulysses out to manage an army that lost its leader. It was ridiculous that Eric and Ulysses were out there fighting when he was sitting here in a cushy house with his fiancée close by all safe and sound. He hated this God damned war and he had to find a way to stop it.

SEVEN

>>> > NICHOLETTE LOOKED AT her little girl on the Titan screen, "Don't worry dear. Everything will work out and you'll have your wedding and the man of your dreams and we will all be fine soon."

Celeste had tears running down her face, "Lila and Agathon are out there fighting hard and have been for days! Zach is risking his life to help victims of the war and here I sit, doing nothing. What kind of leader am I?"

"I'm going to say this gently sweetheart, but you're not. You're not the queen anymore. You're supposed to be...dead. Jesus, I have a hard time saying that. Technically you're still a princess of Earth, but no one knows you're alive. You're not supposed to be doing anything right now but keeping yourself safe. If something happens to your father and I, for real this time, then you can take over for us, you and Sebastian. I want you safe and secure right where you are."

"That doesn't seem like enough."

"We're all doing the best we can. I know you're a strong fighter and if they're able to break through whatever force field Sebastian says he has in place, then I know you will fight hard to protect the people you love."

"Yes, of course, but my people...our people are out there dying. They're fighting. I should be too."

"Have you mentioned this to Sebastian?"

"Yes, he says the same thing as always, but I say he's at least leading a whole army. He's doing *something*. I'm really doing nothing."

"He says you're doing nothing?"

"No. He says I need to stay safe and in case you two...fall in battle, I would need to take over and claim the throne. But I would also need to come back from the dead for that..."

"It's been done before...I'm sure, at some point in history," she winked, "You will be fine. Just stay strong. Weren't you protecting a medical camp a while ago?"

"Yes, but Sebastian doesn't want me to travel too far away from the house."

"That's a wise precaution. I think if you feel in your heart that you should fight, talk it out with your man. If you both agree to it, go out there and fight, but be very careful. We've learned scant little about these aliens."

Celeste nodded, "I will. Stay safe please. I love you. Thanks for talking to me."

"We were supposed to be planning your wedding on this call," she wrung her hands together, "I love you too, princess."

EIGHT

>>> > SEBASTIAN WAS ON his Titan with Applette along with Kolek, Veronica, Celeste, Sicaine, Ginger, Ophelia, and D'Artagnan.

Applette asked, "Who of you are not here?"

Sebastian looked around, "Agathon, Lila, Eric, Katsanos, and Ulysses are fighting."

Applette said, "We've figured out your poem for you. It's not our job, but Kolek started to feel guilty with how badly your universe is performing in the war."

"Okay. What does it mean?"

"'Where days are dark, They'll need electricity's spark.' That means there's a waterfall somewhere that you'll need an artificial light source to properly see things."

Celeste looked to Sebastian, "Definitely Bahsheef."

Sebastian nodded, "Go on."

"'The door will only open for the strong, To where shadows fall long.' That's saying there's a stone door under that waterfall that will only open after lightning has struck. That's already happened you said?"

Celeste nodded, "While we were there we got some bad electrical storms."

"'Seas are calm, Once you removed the bomb.' We *think* it means everything will relax once this war is over. Relax as in, universe peace. No worlds will fight with each other. We're not sure. It could reference Hace and Ni-toyis since they were violent people on their own but together twice as much."

"Okay. Continue please."

"'Deserts wide, When it's time you must bide.' I think it's a reference to the Human Resistance. Their bunker was in the desert and they were hell-bent on striking the Il'laceans...but then they lost their leader."

D'Artagnan nodded, "Maybe yeah."

"'Voices carry truth, In a constant need for youth.' That means youthful leaders will be honest."

"What youthful leaders? Are my parents going to be alright?" Celeste asked worried.

"I'm not sure of that, Celeste. All I can say is what I think this means. We've done our best to guess at a few things."

"Okay."

"'Lover's hearts beat as one, When the chase has been won.' This is obviously a statement referencing Celeste and Sebastian's marriage. That it will happen."

Celeste raised her eyebrows to Sebastian, "Maybe that's a good sign we'll survive this war?"

"'Eyes are closed, For a beast that's dozed.' This could be a couple things. I think it's a blood sacrifice. Kolek thinks it's sacrificing a child. Either way someone will have to sacrifice something."

Ophelia cuddled Declan closer.

"'A question posed.' This one's easy. I think it means we're asking the Dach to fight. I'm assuming someone has already done this?"

Sebastian nodded, "They said no."

"Okay. 'Lips are sealed, When swords must yield.' I thought this meant the Dach would fight for you without manmade weapons but maybe just for themselves then. I understand they have natural abilities?"

D'Artagnan nodded, "They are natural badasses. They've never needed weapons. They're born with their own."

"'Where moons are bright, From any height.' I think this is talking about the War Universe invading yours. Where they can enter, they must be able to see a lot of moons and light, maybe starlight? You said the doorway was on Treksin Mori?"

Sebastian nodded, "We suspect, yes. The planet has eighty-nine moons, the most in the universe. The Messenger City has a forest in it called...oh what is it?"

D'Artagnan answered, "Lunatise."

Applette nodded, "Then that sounds like the place. There's only a few more lines. 'Illuminations light, Screams of fright, Eyes have sight, In cages of night, On our world of white.' All that says is now you guys know there's a multiverse, you cry out as you're invaded. They are a dark universe, but here you have a lot of light, figuratively and literally. I think it references some hope your people carry."

"There's two more lines. Does it say how to close doors?" Sebastian asked.

"'When searching is done, You will need no gun.' It means to close the door, you need a key not a weapon. I think this is a person, not an inanimate object. It's going back to the sacrifice idea."

The room was quiet.

"So the Lanyx weren't entirely wrong. This poem is both about War and Knowledge?" Sebastian asked.

Applette nodded, "I thought with those first lines it was all a reference to Knowledge, but I think it's talking about War's doorway at the end. Although it still could be referencing Knowledge and how to close *that* door."

Kolek interjected, "The last line doesn't need much explaining, 'Tired souls can rest, at the end of your quest.' I think everyone can agree that's obviously saying when your job is done, you can recover."

NINE

>>> > ULYSSES GOT A Titan message from Ginger updating him on the poem. He replied he was on the move and would talk later.

His squad had been following a dry river until they came up on a ridge where the river forked. He led three squads; he had never commanded so many different species at once.

The light was fading and a storm was coming. They wanted to be on the other side of this river in case it flooded overnight.

Ulysses didn't want to approach too quickly without knowing what lurked in the forest up ahead. They had successfully chased out several twins and killed them, but hadn't seen any action for hours now.

The trees hid a threat no one saw.

"What is that? Do you hear that? Something's crackling," was all the soldier on Ulysses's right was able to say before a bolt of lightning shot out and into Ulysses's body. He gripped the trigger of his plasma shotgun and unintentionally shot the electrical foe behind the tree.

His men opened fire beyond the trees and plasma lit up the forest. Trees fell and birds flew into the sky.

Ulysses shook until he fell to the ground. The soldier that heard the electricity pop, kneeled down to check Ulysses's pulse.

It was weak.

"Bring the paddles," cried Johnston.

The medic in the back ran forward and pulled them out as Johnston quickly stripped Ulysses of his chest armor and shirt.

Ten sets of twins stepped out from the tree line.

Ulysses put his palms together in front of him and snapped his fingers on one hand. The medic paused as Ulysses's hands started to smoke. Flames flickered in his cupped palms. The rest of the men backed up. Ulysses launched his conjured fireballs into the air where the lightning bolt had come from. When they struck the trees everything exploded outward. The whole forest was on fire.

Ulysses closed his eyes.

Johnston checked his pulse again.

He had none.

"Clear!"

Everyone moved their hands back and the medic shocked him.

Some of the twins were still advancing even though they were on fire.

The medic took Ulysses's pulse then checked to see if he was breathing.

Johnston screamed, "Again!"

The medic yelled, "Clear!"

They shocked him, but nothing happened.

Johnston yelled, "Again damn it!"

The medic tried once more but with the same result, "Sir. I think we have to stop. He's not coming back. I'm sorry."

Johnston grabbed the paddles himself and put them to Ulysses's chest, "Clear!"

A few soldiers backed up and started gathering in the clearing behind where Ulysses lay.

They tried again and again, but after the eighth try Johnston realized it was no use. They called the time of his death.

Most of the twins had burned to death and fallen but one set continued to crawl forward.

A soldier in the back leveled his automatic plasma rifle and shot until the twins stopped moving.

TEN

>>> > OPHELIA RECEIVED A Titan notification about Ulysses. She put her hand to her mouth and cried out. D'Artagnan looked at her. The meeting had just let out and they were in the hallway. Ginger was still in the room talking with Celeste.

Ophelia held out her Titan for D'Artagnan to see.

"Oh Khaleen! I'll tell her."

Ophelia held his arm, "No."

"You want to? It won't be easy."

She nodded her head and went to Ginger. D'Artagnan stood next to her and held her free hand, "Ginger?"

Ginger looked at both their faces and started to cry, "No, we just talked! Please don't say it!"

"I'm sorry. He...fell protecting his squad. They say it was quick. They tried to resuscitate him but...they couldn't. I'm so sorry."

Ginger screamed at Sebastian, "YOU DID THIS! You... *killed him!*"

Sebastian only looked on then looked at D'Artagnan.

D'Artagnan mouthed, "Ulysses is gone. Electrocuted."

Sebastian went to Ginger and tried to hug her. At first she beat her fists onto him wherever they fell, then she gave up and let him put his arms around her.

"He was a very good man. I'm so sorry. I couldn't have held him back from fighting without chaining him down. He wanted to, Ginger. He wanted to help and he did. He's a hero. We won't save our universe without men like him."

ELEVEN

>>> > A FEW MINUTES later, Ginger laid in her bed after Celeste had talked to her. She'd given her a sedative she had left over from Zach.

Celeste came out and overheard Sebastian talking on his Titan to Applette.

"We can meet at the doorway. I don't know who the key is yet, but we all need to gather. Make sure Eric, Lila, and Agathon are there. I imagine it will take a day for you to arrive?"

Sebastian nodded, "It won't be easy to accumulate the others there. They have posts and are fighting. I will try my best."

"I can't do my special trick on you and Celeste anyway because of your mind powers. You'll have to get there as quickly as possible. Tell me when you arrive at the forest. I'll do the same."

"Wait!" Celeste exclaimed, "What about the door on Bahsheef? Did you tell Sebastian what those symbols meant?"

"Yes, but you'll be disappointed."

"What do you mean?" Celeste's eyebrows furrowed.

"It's simply a warning that whoever goes through cannot return."

"That's it?" She looked at Sebastian.

Sebastian's gaze slowly met hers, "Yes."

Applette let out a sigh, "I told you."

TWELVE

>>> > CELESTE CRACKED THE door open and looked at her friend, "We need to go to Treksin Mori right now. How are you feeling?"

Ginger looked at Celeste, "I'll be okay. I think your pill is helping me deal for now. I will take the transit that leaves last. I need a few moments to get myself together."

"Okay, just...don't take too long. I don't want you to be alone right now and Applette said we all needed to go. I know Ulysses was your everything. I can't imagi—"

"Please don't Celeste. Not right now. I can't handle it."

"I'm here if you need anything. We'll wait for you on the lawn." Ginger nodded.

A few minutes later she looked out her window and saw Celeste, Sebastian, Ophelia, Declan, and D'Artagnan get into one transit and leave.

Veronica knocked on her door, "We're leaving. Come on."

"Okay."

Veronica put an arm around Ginger and walked out with her onto the lawn.

"Listen V, I can call a taxi. Why don't you go without me? I need a minute."

Veronica shook her head, "No way. I can't leave you alone."

Ginger looked to see another transit on the beach, "I can take this one over here. I'll just be a crying mess and I don't want to do it in front of you. Can't I be alone for a while?"

Veronica looked at her. Ginger was already starting to cry and she couldn't blame her. She just lost her man and if the roles were reversed, Veronica would tell everyone to go to hell so she could crawl into a ball and die. "I'll make you a deal. You get in and launch first, then I'll let you go on your own."

Ginger nodded.

Veronica closed the transit door over her head as she watched Ginger get into the transit sitting on the beach. She waited until she saw it launch. Ginger's transit went up into the air and disappeared. Veronica did the same a few seconds later.

CHAPTER 9

THE SACRIFICE

ONE

>>> > GINGER SAT IN the pilot's seat and looped around the Earth. She saw the devastation and smoke, the bodies lying on the ground and thought of Ulysses out there somewhere in a pile of the dead. She felt numb. The pill that Celeste gave her helped take the edge off but nothing would bring her happiness again. Nothing would ever bring Ulysses back and she couldn't live without him. Her transit completed its loop and she heard Veronica on her Titan, "Come in Ginger. You there?"

"I'm here."

"I can't see you. Where are you?"

"I'm on my way. That transit may be slower than this one. It says I'll be there in...twenty-one hours."

"Okay, you're ahead of me. I've got twenty-two hours. Be safe and alert. Please know I love you and things will be okay. Just hold onto me, Lila, and Celeste. We'll get you through this."

Ginger was overcome with grief, "Thank you. I love you too."

"Over and out. See you there my friend."

Ginger landed on the lawn and watched the transit shut down. She walked back into the house and closed the front door. She had seen the whole planet from above. She knew this war was over. The other universe was winning and there was no hope for Earth. No hope for her without Ulysses.

The universe she knew would succumb to the War Universe and there was nothing anyone could do.

T W O

>>> > ON THE MECHANICAL world of Uzzib, the Reftians were in full battle mode and had been for hours. They fought with lasers and fire, like lots of other races, but of course, the Reftians had incredible accuracy that no organic being could match. The survival rate of Reftians were the highest in the universe. #5278-9 started to count how many aliens he had killed and watched as the Genesis Spheroid orb continued to spin with fire and lasers shooting out in all directions. It was impressive, he'd never seen it so active. DAI watched her new friend in battle when she got a second to pause. She liked Ben, that's the name #5278-9 had informally picked out for himself. She thought it suited him somehow. She watched him shoot alien after alien, always striking swiftly and deadly. She sensed another being coming up behind her, she put her finger on the trigger of her gun and turned around to face her adversary.

THREE

>>> > SEBASTIAN KEPT TRACK of the news that was available as they headed toward Treksin Mori. It was getting much more sporadic as worlds were falling. Whole species were being lost to this war and Sebastian became increasingly anxious as time went on.

The last report he read before they landed was that half of the Unknown Universe had perished. *Half.* Whole planets...a couple of whole galaxies were gone. A lot of Jumps were completely destroyed, outposts, and trading stations – everything was succumbing. The final word was that the War Universe was winning and would kill off everything in two days' time unless someone found a way to stop them for good.

Sebastian called Magnus and Nicholette first asking if they were willing to travel back to Treksin Mori. Both agreed it was too risky for them to travel that far. They would've offered military support, but the unfortunate truth was that their forces were spread thin across the universe already. Soldiers had been deployed to every corner of existence and there were none to spare.

He called Zach and asked if he could go to Treksin Mori, but the doc wouldn't make it in time. Sebastian promised to send him a live transmittal in case the worst happened and the trip went sideways.

Then Sebastian called Xu'Xi, who agreed to show up although reluctantly. Sebastian wanted as much back up as he could get.

FOUR

>>> > THERE WAS A headcount as everyone landed on Treksin Mori. They gathered at the docking station of the Lunatise forest. Sebastian was counting heads, but before he could finish, Celeste asked where Ginger was.

"She was right in front of me. I watched her launch." Veronica looked around.

"You didn't go with her! I told you not to leave her." Celeste felt panic rise in her throat.

"I made her launch in front of me. She said her transit was faster than mine and I trusted her."

"I'll call her." Celeste got on her Titan.

Sebastian cleared his throat, "We've got to move forward Celeste. She can meet us up ahead."

She nodded and let the rest of them go on without her.

Ginger's Titan went straight to voice mail, and Celeste frowned. She waited until she could leave a message, "Listen, I love you so much. I know this is hard but we need to come together and focus on one more thing and then I promise, you can fall apart. Where are you? Please call me. We're at the forest. The rest of us are going forward. I'll call you again soon."

Celeste ran and caught up with the rest of them. She saw the steps leading up to the creepy statue and some strange stone gothic arches. She walked past the statue and saw all the arches had writing on them. She walked through them slowly, taking in each one. She overheard several of her friends complaining of headaches, stomach aches, and dizziness. Something about being here made people feel unwell, but she felt fine.

"Bastian people are getting sick. Do we know why?"

Xu'Xi answered, "Queen Celeste, I wish we were meeting under different circumstances. None-the-less, it is an honor and privilege. I was telling your fiancée here that my people are hypersensitive to barometric pressure and this planet is showing signs of significant drops right now. That will cause all of the symptoms I've been hearing about."

"But not in Humans? I feel okay except for my nerves."

"Oh Humans too, just not every Human."

"Anything else useful we should know?"

"Low barometric changes or drops can cause low blood pressure, blurred vision, dizziness, blocked sinuses will be more painful, your blood's viscosity can also change – that will cause blood sugar to change."

"You sound like a doctor."

"Jumpin' kazzers, no. I just know a lot about barometric changes because of my people's sensitivity."

Xu'Xi stared ahead at the Stampermoth walking alone. He asked Sebastian quietly, "How did the Stampermoth get involved? That's an unusual sight."

Sebastian waved a hand, "I'll explain later. I didn't want to leave him alone at the house."

All of the talking trailed off as the group stopped walking.

What was at the end of the arches took Celeste's breath away. Applette and Kolek stood off to the side of the doorway looking at her. The last stone arch was the door. It was wide open, a big ring of blackness. She walked up to the edge peering in. It didn't look much different than their own universe. Space, stars, and galaxies. They were just different patterns in different colors. She could feel a slight breeze coming out of this foreign universe. She shivered. In her former life where she was afraid of heights, this was the worst place to be. All it would take is someone pushing her in and she'd be gone, lost in space until she died, forever "falling."

Sebastian pulled her back and off to the side, "This place feels festered like an open wound. Did you see the writing on the stone arches? In every language, they were warning us not to open this unless we were ready for the end of the world. We need to get this door shut and fast. I don't feel right here."

Eric came up to Sebastian, "Hey look what I found."

Sebastian looked over his shoulder and saw the Titan in Eric's hand.

"This is Hace's. I found his body beyond the stones over there. He didn't look...good."

"Give that to Steele. He's trying to lead the BDP into ruin. He'll find that useful if we get out of this."

Eric scoffed, "He's never said any such thing."

Sebastian made a face.

Eric blinked hard, "Wait. Are you going to tell me you *read* this off him? He doesn't even know you know, does he?"

"It's looming large in his head right now. I couldn't help it." Sebastian paused, "Come on. Don't look at me like that. I didn't mean to."

Eric raised his eyebrows and walked over to D'Artagnan.

Lila came up to Celeste, "Any word from Ginger?"

"No. You know...Ulysses didn't make it."

She shook her head, "Oh no. How?"

"One of those electrical...things."

"Those almost got us on the way off FA."

"How *did* you leave there?"

"It wasn't easy."

Applette looked to Celeste and Sebastian, "There's things we didn't say outright about the poem. We need to talk."

Celeste nodded, "Of course. What is it? I feel like it's bad news."

Kolek shook her head, "Not all of it."

Applette said, "I want you two, if you want, to take my place in the Knowledge Universe. You would rule it together. Kolek and I talked to the Multiverse Keeper. He will allow it. You have an Earth year from today to decide. When you get back to your home, you'll find a letter from me and a few other things that will let you pass through the doorway. Once you go through, there will be *no* coming back. You should say goodbye to all your loved ones and you'll only be able to take whatever you can carry in your arms. You'll learn the dates of your deaths once you pass through but there are limitless good things to learn there as well. I think you'll make excellent leaders and you will be far more powerful than any king or queen here in this universe. I'll go with Kolek back to the War Universe and there we can rule together. I don't understand why the Keeper has allowed these things but I will not question it. I'll just be happy and accept it."

Celeste smiled politely, "Thank you Applette, for your help and the opportunity. I'm not sure I could ever leave here. We'll have to think about it."

Sebastian asked, "What else?"

"The poem speaks of a child. One that will do horrible things and be the destruction of all, not only this universe, but all universes. It'll crave power and someone in its lifetime will push it, always in the wrong direction. It will not start out evil but its path is already foreseen, it will not change. The mother of this entity is the key. She will need to sacrifice herself and the child through the doorway to save your universe. There is no other way. Does that sound like anyone you know?"

Celeste looked at Ophelia.

Ophelia cried out, "No! He's just a baby." She held Declan close against her bosom. D'Artagnan put a protective arm around her.

Applette interjected, "This child has not yet been born. It has recently been conceived, in fact, the mother might not even be aware she is with child."

Sebastian looked at Celeste, "Please tell me you're not pregnant."

"No. I don't know anyone who is."

"Maybe Ginger?"

"She didn't say anything."

"I am." Veronica's voice was barely a whisper.

Celeste's eyes got wide, "WHAT! You never said anything."

"I had my reasons." Her eyes flickered to Eric, "Besides, I wasn't sure until I missed my last period. I was hoping it was stress from the war, but hearing the conversation, I think it's me. I'm the one."

Eric shouted, "NO! Veronica, no!"

She turned to him, "I'm sorry."

"You're pregnant?! Why didn't you tell me?"

"You've been fighting. I hardly see you, and my period is only eight days late. I didn't know what you'd say. I was afraid from your last experience with this kind of news. The war is going so badly. And then Ulysses died."

"You can't...you can't babe. I love you. I need you here and I want to see our baby. If you have someone new in there I want to get to meet him or her. You can't be thinking they mean you. Please."

"I would do anything to protect you and our baby. If I don't... leave, none of us will survive this. Whole planets are gone. Whole galaxies are gone Eric. What can any of us do to stop this? I'm the only one according to this poem."

"I don't give a fuck what this bullshit poem says! No one knows where it really came from. These weirdos could be lying! Maybe it's fake. It could be some sort of joke."

Applette interrupted, "It isn't Mr. Bouton." Applette gently held Veronica's shoulder and put his other hand on Eric's shoulder. "I'm sorry to say Ms. Blackwell is pregnant and that means...she's the key."

Eric tried to shake off Applette's hand but couldn't. Suddenly Eric saw his unborn child in the womb in his mind. Veronica saw it as well. They stood awestruck.

Applette removed his hands and moved back to Kolek's side.

Eric hissed, "You guys got want you wanted. Why don't you leave?"

Kolek and Applette looked at one another, "We can. The rest is up to them."

Sebastian looked at Applette, "You're going? Now?"

"We know there's really only one choice you can make. I'm sorry if that sounds cold, but this is what Kolek does, she starts wars. We all die. We all sacrifice – some are bigger than others. Remember the letter I left for you. One Earth year from today.

You know the doorway on Bahsheef but it could move. You'll still be able to find it. Goodbye. It was nice to meet you. I hope whatever the future brings, you find peace and happiness before the end."

"Wait! What if we decide not to go, or what if...the end comes before we can get to the door?"

"The Multiverse Keeper is watching you closely now. He'll be able to replace you and Celeste in time with someone new. Don't worry. Whatever you decide is fine. Whatever happens to you, the Keeper will find a new ruler there."

Kolek smiled, "It was nice to meet both of you. Good luck with everything."

Celeste mumbled, "Yeah. Good luck to you too, I guess. Have a nice safe happy life."

Kolek and Applette kissed each other quickly. Kolek felt something stir in her. Something that was new. Then they jumped into the doorway and Applette disappeared. The shell of Ni-toyis's body slumped to the ground immediately after striking the door.

Celeste finished, "You fucking assholes." She saw Ni-toyis laying on the ground. "Oh look at that. She didn't make it."

Sebastian shook his head, "Kolek made it. This was just the body she was using. I will take it to Ni-toyis's mother."

Celeste looked at him and shook her head.

Sebastian revised, "I will ship the body to her mother."

Eric pulled Veronica away from everyone else and held her hands in his, "You can't honestly do this. You can't leave me. Please. I just found you. This poem is bullshit."

"I don't think so Eric. Listen, I've never really done anything important in my whole life. Now I find out I'm the key to saving the *entire* universe, you and everyone else in it. I need to do this. Anything else would be selfish. Wouldn't you do it?"

"If it meant leaving you?! Fuck no! Please don't do this. You *did* do something important already – you killed the most horrible oppressive alien king in Earth's history for Christ's sakes! I'm not leaving this planet without you!"

"I hope you know I'm always with you." Veronica put her hand to Eric's heart.

Eric tried as hard as he could to suppress all the emotions pushing their way out of him, but he was going to go mad if he lost this woman, "Don't you dare start talking like that, Goddamn it! Time doesn't mean anything here without you. Just tides coming in and going out."

"Oh Eric, God you're so sweet. We've been through so much in the short amount of time we've shared together and I wouldn't trade that for anything. You're the only one that's ever known my heart so deep and I'm so very grateful." Veronica's voice broke. Her heart was right behind.

Eric let a teardrop fall down his cheek, "Stop talking like you're leaving."

"If I don't go, no one will survive. We're losing this war."

"There's other ways to end this. We can fight. I will fight them all. Applette said War can't take beyond two percent left of the universe. It will stop on its own."

"That's too steep of a price to pay. That's almost everyone. If I can stop it now, I should."

"Please don't."

She creased her brow, "What if he's lying? Have you thought about that? What if Applette said the two percent thing so we'd just keep on letting everyone die thinking it would stop at some point?"

Eric was silent.

Sebastian approached them carefully and cleared his throat. He asked, "Veronica?"

She walked up to the doorway. Too close for Eric's liking. "Yes?"

"There's other ways. I don't want you to go. I'm not sure Applette was right about this. Sacrificing two people for the good of all sounds fine when it's some stranger. Someone you've never met, but you're with Eric. I've never seen him happier. We can fight. Eric and I will fight. You don't have to do this."

"I really do believe I'm the only one that can stop this. I don't believe what Applette said about my baby though. I think she would be a good child and a wonderful adult. Maybe he said that to scare me into doing this but that's not necessary." She looked around at all the people around her, everyone was staring. She closed her eyes for a moment and listened to the sounds of the forest. The trees were swaying and the wind rustled the leaves. She thought of all the bad things that had ever happened to her and the good things too. She thought of her unborn baby and poor sweet Eric.

Veronica looked at all of them one at a time, "I've seen the news. I know you have too. Everyone's dying. I have to do this."

Celeste had tears pouring down her cheeks, "You can't go! We will all *fight* so you don't have to do this. I need my best friend and my maid of honor at my wedding! You can't go anywhere please!"

"I've been saying it. I know you've heard me. I told you just the other day I felt like I should be doing more for this fight. I will never do anything more important than *this*. This is my way to redeem myself for all the times I stayed at home or didn't fight. I have to do this. If I save everyone's life, how could there be any other choice? I am the only one who can stop this war."

Eric grabbed her and shook her, "No, you hear me? I can't lose you. Please!"

She looked at him as tears gathered in his eyes, "Oh babe. Please don't do this to me. It's hard enough as it is. I don't want to leave you. You've got to know this right? I'm terrified of losing you."

"Then WHY!" He shouted at her.

"Because our universe is running out of time. And because I love you and need you to live. I need you to go on. I will die to save your life. The fact that there's billions of other beings that I will save is great and all, but you're the one that matters. I would do anything to protect you. This is it. This is the way it goes."

A tear ran down her cheek and Eric lost it. He sobbed like he never had before and he didn't care who saw it. "I love you. I always will. The time I spent with you was great and fun and sexy and powerful and wonderful and meaningful and I wish... you weren't doing this Veronica. God I wish things were different. GOD DAMN IT! FUCK!"

Veronica hugged him tight, "I will say goodbye to the others."

He nodded and wiped at his eyes.

Six beings moved through the doorway lightning fast. Some of the men pulled out their weapons but D'Artagnan was able to light two on fire with his flame thrower as they flew past.

Eric grabbed a set of twins and bashed their heads together repeatedly as he screamed out obscenities.

Sebastian put six rounds into a domed flying creature while Xu'Xi grabbed it by its wing out of the sky and threw it to the ground.

Lila, tears streaming down her face, took out one creature walking towards her with her automatic rifle.

Xu'Xi moved the bodies into a pile and lit them all on fire to burn.

Celeste hugged Veronica hard and so did Sebastian. D'Artagnan thanked her for everything. Ophelia hugged her telling her how brave she was. Lila cried hard saying, "I love you. Don't forget." Agathon hugged her with tears in his eyes. She came back around to Eric.

Eric held onto her for a long time and cried. She cried too. Everyone was trying to hold it together and some were doing better than others. Katsanos was the worst. All of this reminded her of Mitch and she hadn't had much time to heal. It was like tearing open a wound that just barely scabbed over.

"I'm scared," Veronica whispered to Eric.

"You are brave. I don't understand why...it had to be you. I wish it was me."

She shook her head, "I'm sorry, but I should go. You have so much love to give Eric, you have to go on for me. Do not give up on love. Do not give in to sadness or fear. I don't want you to be grieving for me for too long. It's not what I want. Do you hear me?"

He nodded.

"Promise me?"

"I promise," he sobbed.

"What I got from you was rich and rewarding and beautiful. No one loved me like you. You were the best. The highlight of an otherwise dull life. I love you *so much.*"

Celeste yelled out as Veronica started to let go of Eric.

"Please Veronica, reconsider."

Veronica looked at her and Eric, "I don't want to see any more of my friends die. Half the universe we know and love is gone already. Whole planets and systems, galaxies, and *species.* We can't lose any more. I need to do this. This takes care of me never doing anything important. Make sure they spell my name right and make sure the statues are big ones okay?" She smiled.

Eric choked up, "I love you with all my heart, beautiful."

"I love you Eric. I love you all. I want none of you to grieve too long. Celebrate my life and your own. Every. Day."

Eric quickly wiped away the tears and managed a smile at her. He blew her a kiss.

She caught it and purposefully fell backwards into the doorway as she did.

Then she was gone.

Eric fell to his knees and clutched at the ground as his body shook with violent sobs. He punched his fists into the ground and collapsed.

The world started to shake violently. A few of them thought it might be the planet self-destructing.

Sebastian watched as the doorway got smaller and smaller until it disappeared. The forest that had been relatively quiet, was steadily getting louder. Sebastian grabbed Celeste who was crying hard. He yelled at her, "We need to go!"

Everyone started down the steps. Sebastian yelled as loud as he could, "We all need to get to the transits! Meet back at Stormview Haven!"

Sebastian looked over his shoulder, Eric was still on the ground in a heap.

"Bouton! We've got to go!"

Eric didn't move.

Celeste pulled at Sebastian, "He's a strong man, but proud. He knows what he's doing and can protect himself. If you want we can wait at the transits."

Sebastian nodded, "We're not waiting long though."

They ran down to the docking station.

Everyone else launched but Celeste and Sebastian.

Lila and Agathon took D'Artagnan and Ophelia along with Declan in their transit towards Stormview Haven. Agathon wanted to go back to his home world, but he trusted his people to finish whatever was left of the battle. He had fought a long time without any of their help and he wanted to be there for his new friends in their time of need.

Katsanos flew back to the estate alone trying not to cry.

Sebastian locked Eric's transit to his own and they waited until he came out of the forest four minutes later. Sebastian would've waited another minute before trying to use his telekinesis to move Eric closer, but he knew it was still too weak.

Sebastian opened his transit's door when Eric approached, "You can ride with us, or you can ride alone but we're traveling together."

Eric nodded and opened the door to his transit behind theirs.

Sebastian launched right away and prayed.

Celeste bowed her head with him and snuck glances at Sebastian. She knew he was hurting. It broke her heart to lose her best friend and it hurt to watch everyone else hurting too.

She took one last look at Treksin Mori. Whatever quakes and thunderous noise were happening there, the planet looked intact. She wondered what would become of it. She wondered if she'd ever be able to come back and lay flowers where Veronica gave her life to save everyone.

FIVE

›› › WITH THE DOORWAY closed, any aliens left in the Unknown Universe were now stuck there. The remaining fights were ongoing, but Sebastian messaged Magnus via Titan that the doorway was closed only because Veronica sacrificed herself and her baby. He asked that Magnus tell the universe that she was a courageous soul who selflessly gave up her love, her child, and her life for all of us.

SIX

››› › SEBASTIAN SAT WITH his eyes closed thinking to himself. Celeste was softly whimpering in her sleep but Sebastian didn't want to wake her. He heard a voice inside his mind, *<This is the Keeper. Can you hear me?>*

Sebastian looked around. He looked back into Eric's transit, but Eric was asleep too.

<Who is this?>

<I have no name you could verbalize with vocal chords. You may call me Keeper 8,002 if you must use a name.>

<Okay. What do you want Eight? Haven't you taken enough from us today you bastard?>

<You are angry and hurt. I will ignore that insult. I have spoken with Rulers Applette and Kolek. They have moved into their new roles. Are you ruling Knowledge with your mate?>

<We don't know. We've been through a lot. We need time to think.>

<One Earth year. That is all.>

<Why did you let them do that? Applette and Kolek rule in one universe when he said it was a solitary job?>

<Applette has suffered at my hands for some time now. I thought he deserved a break. They asked nicely. They haven't asked for much. They care for one another and what they do is not easy. I live alone and wish that I didn't. I understood. I loved someone long ago. No one should be alone.>

Sebastian waited for more, but there was nothing.

CHAPTER 10

THE PRICE OF WAR IS HIGH

ONE

>>> > D'ARTAGNAN HELD DECLAN in one arm and looked over Hace's Titan with the other. He just cracked into it a few minutes ago. It took him eight hours to figure out the password, but they still had hours to travel before arriving at the estate. D'Artagnan needed to keep his mind busy.

He wanted to do good in the world. Veronica had inspired bravery and courage in him. He could try to infiltrate the BDP and take over. Mitch would've done that if he was alive. He would go in and kill them all, little by little.

D'Artagnan could go forth and spread good will. He could eradicate a long standing ruthless gang of thugs. The anti-Human Resistance. The anti-FAIR.

TWO

```
TITAN Corporation - Personal TITAN Device
System Status: Active -- Universal Grid: Online
Current Time/Date (Earth - London): 10:59 p.m./
August 22, 4016
Secondary  Time/Date  (Greeve  -  Laque  City,
SariaWarte): 95.32.77L/9ᵗʰ G/W, 1093
Current Universal Positioning System Location:
London, England, Earth
User: All Titan Users
Communications Menu
Incoming message(s) received: 1 - Status: Unread
Message Received at 10:59 p.m.
Message Sent from: Universal News Agency (UNA) -
Earth Region

-UNA
-London, England, Earth
*BREAKING NEWS*
Emperor  Magnus  Vandeermeer  of  Earth  has  just
announced the doorway to the War Universe has been
closed at great cost.
He gave us a statement moments ago:
"Hello people of Earth, and all around the universe,
Nicholette and I are very relieved to announce the
War doorway has been shut.
This is not to say the war is over.
```

Aliens that came through while that door was open are still here, they are merely cut off from returning to their own universe now.
You must stay alert and be vigilant. Stay on your guard and continue fighting until all of them are dead.
The doorway closed at great cost to Humans. A brave and special soul gave her life as sacrifice for the door to close.
We will release her name soon, but not until her family has been notified.
We will release a secondary statement once this war, forever known from this day forward as the Unknown War, is completely over.
Stay safe and God bless you all.
Godspeed.
Earth Emperor Magnus Vandeermeer"
You can trust UNA for all your universal news needs.

-END OF MESSAGE
* This message will only be deleted by user.
- -

Sighs of relief escaped beings throughout the universe. But like the Emperor said, this war wasn't over yet.

THREE

>>> > ERIC SAT ALONE in his transit on the way to Stormview Haven, his transit locked into his best friend's.

Veronica's Titan had fallen to the ground as she slipped into War's universe. Eric held it in his hands, staring at it.

He had never been so completely heartbroken and proud at the same time. He couldn't remember if he told Veronica he was proud. He hoped she knew.

He got the news report on his Titan and saw what it said about Veronica.

He felt a sudden hopelessness fill him. He didn't know what to do. He lived for so long without her and now that she was gone, he felt completely lost and empty.

He was angry too. He wanted to run for miles until he couldn't breathe. He wanted to beat the living shit out of anyone just because he thought it would make him feel better.

All of his training, all of his abilities lay useless in his hands. Nothing would stop the hurt.

And the baby.

He was a father, but he hadn't known. He was a father...for a few minutes, and now he wasn't. Or was it fair to call himself a father always? Do other parents that outlive their children say they're still parents?

He didn't have enough time. This huge long lifespan, and for what? To live alone? To have a light come into his life, to fill up the darkness only for a tiny fragment, where he could see everything laid out before him clearly, only to have it die out? He felt his whole life he lived in darkness. Veronica was the candle.

He put his hands over his face with his head down and cried.

FOUR

>>> > EVERYONE LANDED AT Stormview Haven early in the morning when the sun barely peeked over the horizon with weary eyes.

Sebastian got out and opened the door for Celeste and saw everyone on the lawn. They were upset. He went back to Eric's transit and looked in the window. Eric's eyes were open, but he looked catatonic. Sebastian knocked on the window and Eric opened the door.

Sebastian got a better look at him. His eyes were red-rimmed as though he'd been crying the whole trip and he was pale.

"Come on man, we've got to get you to your bedroom so you can rest. I don't know who to comfort more, you or Celeste."

"She's gone Raynes. What am I going to do now?" His voice broke as he fought back emotions.

Sebastian kneeled down, "We're going to help you through this. All of us. We're going to pray to the Gods and Goddesses for strength and to heal. We're going to sleep and eat and work out and talk until you feel better. No one's going to rush you. No one's going to blame you for anything – if you cry or get mad or...whatever. I'll be here for you, whatever you need. I'm your brother Bouton. Bound to you just like family. There's nothing I won't do for you."

Eric nodded and sniffled trying not to fall apart.

Sebastian put out his hand to help Eric get out and instead, Eric hugged Sebastian with both arms tightly.

Eric could barely speak, "Thank you."

Sebastian was surprised, "Sure man. Anything at all, you just say the word."

Celeste walked up to them slowly, "Sebastian..."

He looked at her and saw tears, "Why is everyone outside? We need to go in, there's still a threat to all of us."

"Sebastian! Ginger's dead!" Celeste fell to her knees and he ran to her.

"What? How?"

"Lila and Agathon started looking for her." She took a deep breath and let it out slowly, "There was a note...they found her in the bathtub. She must've taken more of my sedatives and drown..."

"Oh my God, I'm sorry honey. I'm so sorry." Sebastian cradled her in his arms as she wept harder.

He looked at Eric. Eric looked at the both of them but there was nothing to say. Sometimes silence was the only answer.

FIVE

>>> > AT THE END of a very long day where Sebastian shipped the body of Ni-toyis to her mother with a long letter, and delivered Ginger's body to her mother with a long explanation, all the Witnesses reported to Sebastian that fighting was over on their home planets. Good news but there was no way to know how many War beings were left in the universe.

D'Artagnan pretended to be Hace since no one knew Hace had died. He sent a Titan message to all remaining BDP members to look for War stragglers. He ordered them to kill any they found especially in the void of space.

At midnight, Eastern Standard Time on Earth, Sebastian called Magnus and reported that the Unknown War could be considered over. The possibility that a lot of War beings remained in the Unknown Universe was extremely high, but the number would be manageable, maybe a few hundred thousand at the most.

He hoped.

SIX

TITAN Corporation - Personal TITAN Device
System Status: Active -- Universal Grid: Online
Current Time/Date (Earth - London): 8:47 p.m./
August 24, 4016
Secondary Time/Date (Eios - Urnei): 86 PH./Hu-.09, 648
Current Universal Positioning System Location:
London, England, Earth
User: All Titan Users
Communications Menu
Incoming message(s) received: 1 - Status: Unread

Message Received at 8:47 p.m.
Message Sent from: Universal News Agency (UNA) -
Earth Region

-UNA
-London, England, Earth
BREAKING NEWS
Emperor Magnus Vandeermeer of Earth has formally
announced the end of the Unknown War.
Emperor Vandeermeer's statement:
"Hello people of Earth, and all around the universe,
Nicholette and I are elated to report the war is over!
My Supreme Commander reports many worlds are clear
of any War beings, this is not to say the whole
universe is clear of them.
There may be several hundred thousand War beings
spread throughout the universe.
You MUST stay alert and highly aware of your
surroundings. I will put together a team of expert
military members on a mission to travel the universe
looking for threats and eliminating them.
We've created a hotline for you to call if you've
seen activity and are suspicious it is a War being.
#18935-0228-11-30104
The brave Human woman who gave her life to close
the doorway was Veronica Blackwell. She worked for
both King Hennessy the first and second and I knew
her personally. She was a beautiful woman, inside
and out. She helped anyone who needed aid and she
was loving and kind. My life and everyone's life she
touched was made that much better for knowing her
and she will be deeply missed.
She left behind a loving mother, two brothers, and
a devoted boyfriend.

Miss Blackwell was pregnant. I say this to give you the scope of how much she walked away from and sacrificed for all of us to live. It would've been her first baby.

In her honor and to forever remember her sacrifice, tomorrow we celebrate her life. I realize a lot of planets have much destruction, much rebuilding to do. I'm asking not for a huge party (if you have the means, please have a big party) but a simple candlelight vigil or moment of silence will do. Some sort of symbolic gesture that each one of you can do to give thanks to Veronica Blackwell and what she's done for you. You are alive because of her. Your children are alive because of her. We all owe her a gratitude that we can never repay. I am forever in her debt and forever thankful for her courage and selflessness.

So tomorrow will henceforth be named Blackwell's.

God bless her.

And God bless us all and keep us safe.

Godspeed to our healing as a planet and a united universe.

Earth Emperor Magnus Vandeermeer"

UNA would like to break traditional rules of unbiased journalism and make our own statement.

"We at UNA have lost most of our staff to war, at least three quarters of reporters and other staff lost their lives in battle either fighting for our safety as soldiers or in the midst of battle trying to get the story for our readers.

We would like to salute all of them.

During the fourteen Earth days this universe-wide battle raged on, we saw bravery and courage in the fields. We saw love and hope struggling to beat despair and pain. We saw people at their best, and people at their worst.

Hold your family close and tell them often that you love them. Find your friends and forgive them for mistakes they made. Find ways to help one another and spread joy and love.

This devastating war has cost us so much already in lives lost, and destruction to our homes, our schools, our work places - don't let it ruin us as a people.

All we have is each other.

Thank you for your time and support.

We will rebuild. We will never forget the sacrifice of so many, including Veronica Blackwell, who we are forever grateful to.

With much love,

The UNA staff."

You can trust UNA for all your universal news needs.

-END OF MESSAGE

* This message will only be deleted by user.

SEVEN

››› › THE BDP PLANNED to scavenge dead planets and to collect whatever valuables they could find while honoring the standing order to kill War aliens on sight.

Some members asked about going to the War Universe to conquer them and for revenge, but the leader instantly dismissed such foolishness saying there was no way to get there and no need to endanger themselves.

EIGHT

>>> > TODAY, THE HEALING and rebuilding process began.

Parties were thrown in Veronica's honor across the universe. Gestures of remembrance happened too.

The universe was grateful to her and wanted to show it.

She would've finally felt important had she been able to see the amount of love the universe gave to her on Blackwell's. A movement across the uninet quickly caught on and every world agreed to participate. A wreath of ribbons and native flowers to each planet was escorted out beyond the local SAP and released into the void of space.

NINE

>>> > WHILE EVERYONE ACROSS the universe celebrated, the house of Stormview Haven was somber and mournful. Sicaine had left with an old beat up transit that Sebastian said no one would miss. They wished each other well and Sicaine thanked Sebastian again for helping him escape a bad situation and for saving Laggic. Sebastian watched the Blade launch and fly towards the Earth's SAP. He stood outside on the lawn for an extra moment looking at the sky, the clouds, and the birds flying by as if nothing had ever happened in their world. He sighed deeply and went back into the house.

Everyone told stories of Veronica, Ginger, Ulysses, and Mitch.

Zach was there with his wives to support his friends and he felt grateful (with such a large family) that they didn't lose anyone.

Magnus and Nicholette were there to support Celeste, and it was difficult to see her go through another round of pain they couldn't heal for her.

There was a large dinner in the late afternoon, then the group lit candles on the beach and observed a moment of silence as the sun set.

Later in the evening, Nicholette pulled her daughter aside and said, "We want to release the truth about you, that you're alive. Hear me out."

Celeste was about to protest, but Sebastian came over and put a hand on her shoulder, "Let her finish babe."

Nicholette smiled at Sebastian.

"We'll report you're alive and about to marry the love of your life. There's nothing better to help heal a world then a wedding. You wouldn't have to worry about hiding anymore or the lies. Forget what other people think. I know that's dangerous to say in my position, but in light of what we all just went through, I think people are going to be open-minded about something like this right now. What do you think?"

Celeste looked at Sebastian but he didn't say anything, then she looked at her mother, "What good would it do?"

"What do you mean what good would it do? People would have something to look forward to. You've spent your whole life married to a terrible man, now you have the right man, who you truly love, who wants to show the world how much he loves you."

"What good would it do for *me*?"

Nicholette scoffed, "Honey, it would be so much easier on you."

Celeste put her hands on her hips, "Get dad please."

Nicholette walked away and Sebastian turned to Celeste, "You don't like this plan?"

"I don't know if they want to do this for me or for Humankind."

Magnus walked over with Nicholette, "What's wrong dear?"

"The Ruler from the other universe left us an opportunity. We have a little less than one Earth year to decide to take his place in the Knowledge Universe as the new rulers. That means we would never be able to come back here, but it would also mean learning a ton of new things and having more power than we ever could here."

Magnus looked shocked, "Wow! That's quite the offer. I imagine it's a tough choice."

"Yes. He left us clear instructions on how to get to Knowledge. Sebastian and I can get married and have a honeymoon here, then we could say our goodbyes and leave. If we do this, then it won't matter if this universe thinks I'm dead or not. Plus I'm not sure what people will think if you say I'm alive. At best they'll just think you're liars, at worst they could think you're manipulative."

Magnus looked at his daughter, "What if you don't go? Then what? You're supposed to stay in hiding for the rest of your life?"

"Well that was the plan when you approached me to die a martyr wasn't it?"

"But things have changed. David's dead. The Il'laceans are out of power and you're getting married. You'll want to travel and have your own lives and be free to go where you wish. Plus someday, we'll pass on and someone will need to lead Earth."

"I'm starting to think a Human council would be best for our planet, dad."

"Why don't you and Sebastian talk it over? See how he feels and then give us an answer before we leave tonight?"

She nodded and went for a walk with Sebastian on the beach.

"What do you think I should do babe?"

Sebastian held her hand, "I think there's a lot of shit going on right now and neither one of us are thinking clearly."

"What about leaving this universe?"

He sighed, "I don't know. It would be a lot of power. It could be exciting. How many other beings get an opportunity like this? It would be the most interesting thing that's ever happened to either one of us, that's for sure."

"Part of me wants to start over fresh, somewhere new where I don't know anything, but part of me is terrified to leave every-one I know behind."

"I'll be there with you."

She stopped and put her arms around his neck, "Of course. We'll be there together, but I just got my parents back and now I've lost two of my friends. It's a tough decision for me."

"We have a year to make it. We'll take our time. Besides we still need to read the note Applette left us, maybe that will clear some things up."

"Yeah." She sounded far away.

"Listen, your parents could say they didn't know you lived. They could say that FAIR swore you went down, or they could say FAIR lied to them trying to manipulate not only them but the whole universe into fighting for Earth's freedom against the Il'laceans, and you found each other after the Unknown War. Maybe FAIR held you against your will. Your parents could make it look like a miracle. They pardoned me so anything's possible. Maybe the public will rejoice."

Celeste thought, "There's only one way to find out. Well... maybe two ways. Where's Eric?"

Sebastian shook his head, "He went to see Charlie after our sunset service. He will not help you see into the future on this, you know that."

"This is important! He would recognize that...I think." Her eyebrows furrowed.

Sebastian gently put his hands on her shoulders and looked her in the eyes, "He's grieving. Leave him be and decide on your own. I have faith in you that you'll make the right choice."

TEN

›› › **"WHAT DO YOU** mean there's no one for me to talk to?" Eric was having to choke back tears in front of the Speaker to The Fallen Ones.

"I'm already doing you a favor by staying past my day's end," Charlie could tell Eric was emotionally unhinged, "I'm telling you, there's no one there."

Eric would've broken through the gates and held Charlie hostage if the man hadn't stayed an extra five minutes after the bridge closed.

The only hope he had left to communicate with Veronica was here. Now Charlie said she wasn't coming through. Eric clapped his hands together so hard, they stung, "How is that possible? She just...it just happened...unless...Are you saying she's not dead?"

Charlie shook his head, "No, that's not what I'm saying at all. I felt her presence as well as the child's before, but now...there's nothing. Emperor Vandeermeer said she sacrificed herself. But not all souls go directly forward in their path. She could be resisting, or she could be in holding."

"What the fuck does that mean!"

"Language please Eric! You know this place is sacred." He paused until Eric nodded.

"If a soul resists death, it cannot be placed. If she's in holding by a higher power, they'll decide where to place her. Time there doesn't work like it does here."

"When can I speak to her?" Eric choked up.

Charlie's heart broke for him, "It could be tomorrow, it could be millennia. We have no way of knowing. I'm sorry."

"Holding? Placing? You've never used these phrases before when we've spoken. What do they mean?"

Charlie walked to Eric and put a hand on his shoulder, "I learned very little when I died for eight minutes ninety-three years ago. The higher power in charge of all of this? They made a mistake with me, everything – I shouldn't have died, I shouldn't have been there, and they shouldn't have told me what they did. Ever since, I've been connected to all souls, living or dead. It's sometimes...more than I can handle. Did she resist at the end?"

Eric shook his head, "She was a badass. She accepted her fate and stepped into it."

"Then she's probably being held by the divine. She was self-less and saved trillions of lives. The powers that be have probably never seen a higher level of saint. The Gods and Goddesses could be considering her for elevation even! That means her soul would transcend life, transcend a body and go straight into the divine's consciousness. That is the highest achievement any soul can hope for. You can always keep trying, but if she elevates, you'll never be able to reach her through me."

"So that's a yes then? You think she...died?"

"I don't know anything about the other universe she went into. All I know is that those aliens are very hard to kill. Even if she survived going in, odds are...she probably succumbed to something."

"Thanks for your time, Charlie," Eric mumbled dejected.

ELEVEN

>>> > MAGNUS AND NICHOLETTE stood before a small crowd of reporters outside of a slightly damaged Silver Thorn to make an announcement.

"Thank you for coming today. We appreciate your time and your dedication to your jobs despite all that's happened recently.

"Celeste lives! No one could have been more surprised than us when we saw our daughter run to us with open arms yesterday. Apparently all of FAIR's members were lost in the war, and they lied to us, lied to everyone. They held Celeste against her will after she aligned with them and trusted them.

"They wanted to ensure that Humans would fight against Il'laceans for our freedom and used her 'absence' as motivation. They would've released her soon after but the Unknown War delayed everything as they went into battle and a few took

Celeste to a hiding spot for her 'safety.' I was stunned to learn this but with all that's happened I think this is truly a blessing from God to get our little princess back safe and sound.

"Not only that, but her boyfriend proposed to her and she's accepted! We're going to have a royal wedding. Nicholette and I are thrilled and we hope you are as well."

One of the reporters stood, "Who's the groom-to-be?"

Magnus smiled, "None other than my Supreme Commander, Sebastian Raynes. I couldn't have picked out a better man myself."

"When will it happen and where?"

"They are still working out the details, but rest assured we will tell you as soon as we know."

"Where is she? We want to see her for ourselves. We have questions for her."

Several other reporters nodded.

"She's resting. She's been through so much and she's lost very close friends in the war. She wasn't up for a public appearance but maybe soon. Give her time."

A female reporter stood up in the back of the room, "Excuse me sir, but I have to say, this all sounds a little suspicious. First your story was that you were rescued by FAIR and your daughter. Then she died in the battle. Are you saying you somehow didn't see her die? I mean, how are we to believe this fantastical story that your daughter was killed near you, you never saw it happen, took strangers word for gospel and then she turns up alive? Do you really expect the people of Earth to believe this?"

Magnus could've strangled the bitch. She would put doubt into the people's minds that would've ordinarily never questioned his word.

He put on a smile, "The Empress and myself were drugged by King David's orders at the time. We were malnourished, exhausted, and completely unaware of events around us. The complacency is one of the reasons the drug is so useful for

THE PRICE OF WAR IS HIGH

captives held against their will. We were escorted ahead of the battle and did not see what happened after. We took the word of the leader of FAIR. I can't say any plainer that this was the truth as we knew it. We will answer no more questions today. Thank you."

TWELVE

››› › THE ONLY POLITICAL polling organization left in the universe revealed later that day that the Emperor and Empress's approval ratings had slipped on Earth.

The news agencies had stories completely at odds with each other on whether the public believed and forgave the rulers of Earth or not. A lot of people thought it was too convenient to be real, others thought (as Celeste suspected they would) the royals were trying to manipulate Humans. Although there were some who supported Celeste and her family, the majority remained extremely skeptical.

CHAPTER 11

"DON'T WORRY. I'M A PROFESSIONAL."

ONE

>>> > SEBASTIAN AND CELESTE sat on the beach with the box that Applette left for them.

Sebastian put a hand on Celeste's shoulder, "The public has a very short memory dear. Maybe in a few weeks, if your parents keep speaking of the wedding, they'll just get excited and focus on that."

"We'll have to wait and see I guess. But I don't want to make any public appearances. I look and feel like hell most of the time and I've been crying a lot. I just..."

"No one said you had to. Do what you feel is right. Take care of yourself first. I know it's been very difficult on you, with... your losses."

She nodded as she teared up and sniffled, "Let's open this. See what's inside."

Sebastian took off the lid and saw a thick rope, a piece of chalk, and an envelope. He opened the letter and read it out loud.

"Dear Ms. Vandeermeer and Mr. Raynes, I hope this letter finds you well. I hope your universe will be able to rebuild and prosper in a new age after the war has ended.

"I suspect the key has done what they needed to and stepped through the doorway. At least in comfort, I can say it would've been a painless and quick passing for them. They were quite brave if they sacrificed themselves and you should be proud.

"As for you two, the Knowledge Universe is a wondrous and vast place full of excellent beings and lots of things for you to experience as a couple. I can't tell you much since most needs to be seen by your eyes to interpret and understand, but I can say it is beyond your imagination. And I think you will enjoy it as a pleasurable experience.

"You will need to go back to Bahsheef and find the stone door you have already seen. Shine an artificial light on it three times in quickness and knock on all four corners. Make sure you bring the rope with you as it will serve as the artifact from my world. The door will open and you will write your names with the chalk on the frame over the door, then pass through. Mr. Raynes will substitute for your key but he will not be hurt as he passes through. The Keeper has assured me this will work and no one will be harmed. But still, you will never be able to return to your own universe unless the Keeper deems it necessary somehow, and I doubt very much he will. Count on him not allowing it.

"The choice is up to you. I want to again say how nice it was to have met you and thank you for helping me find my Kolek. It means so much to me. I will never be able to repay you. Good luck to you both and I hope you're happy with whatever decision you make. Remember, one Earth year from the day the War door closed is your time limit. The Knowledge door will disappear along with the opportunity after that. Also remember, the doorway might move between now and then. If it does, you will know where to find it."

TWO

>>> > THE NEXT DAY, Sebastian woke up and checked the news on his Titan. It looked like the majority of Earthlings thought Celeste's story was a fake. In addition, they were distrustful of the Emperor and Empress. He told Celeste and she was distraught.

He said, "Let's go to the Knowledge Universe. We can learn countless new things and leave all this bullshit behind. I will never have to look over my shoulder again. Even with a pardon, I'm still worried. You won't have to worry about the public mistreating you or saying nasty things when they don't know the first God damned thing about what you've been through for them!"

"Okay," she said so quiet Sebastian almost didn't hear.

"You really want to?"

She nodded, "As long as I'm with you."

"We'll plan the wedding and get married, then we can take some time to travel and just relax. Enjoy each other. Then we'll need time to transfer everything over to our friends."

"Transfer everything? Like houses and transits?"

"Everything we can't take with us."

"I don't know how we're going to tell them."

"It won't be easy. But for now, we can keep this to ourselves. If your parents ask, we'll just say we haven't decided yet. Then when we're ready, you can tell them."

THREE

>>> > ERIC HAD KEPT to himself over the past several days and Sebastian had only seen him while they passed each other on the beach running, or in the hallways of the house.

Eric was in the gym when Sebastian entered and instead of leaving like he had been doing, he asked his friend a question, "Would you or Celeste mind if I stayed here for a while?"

Sebastian smiled, "We would love that. Stay as long as you need to man. No problem."

"Agathon and Lila are staying here while his house gets fixed on FA right?"

"Yes. It got burned a little and a small explosion took out the back bedroom so while that's under construction they'll be here. FA took a lot of damage so I expect it'll be a long while before their home is ready."

"Thanks," was all Eric said before leaving the room.

Sebastian hoped he was getting enough to eat. He wanted to ask since he never saw him at meal times but Eric needed a lot of time alone and Sebastian couldn't blame him. Eric wasn't good at showing emotion, just like Sebastian wasn't and he recognized everyone healed in different ways and at different speeds. Maybe next time he saw him, he could ask.

FOUR

TITAN Corporation - Personal TITAN Device
System Status: Active -- Universal Grid: Online
Current Time/Date (Earth - Former United States of
America): 4:31 p.m./September 30, 4016
Secondary Time/Date (Con Cab Mai - Keabi, Feroo):
78- Tok/Uti 39, 478
Current Universal Positioning System Location:
Republic of Florida, Former United States of
America, Earth
User: Unrecorded
Communications Menu
Incoming message(s) received: 1 - Status: Unread
Message Received at 4:31 p.m.
Message Sent from: Universal News Agency (UNA) - Earth

-UNA
-London, England, Earth
BREAKING NEWS
As some worlds are restoring their communications
devices and satellites, more and more figures are
being reported by several planets on loss of life
and monetary damages.
Planets lost (catastrophic loss of life and damage
to structures):
Oorblat
Ibia
Unbeere
Zetzetti
Strati-fly851
Cepheus
Lassandra

My'tak
Il'laceier

Habitable/Recoverable Planets (Sustainable land masses/Large population remains):
Dhoot Ovene
Jex
Eios
Gane Frost
Sho'teg
Ishikawa
Froopeal
Lo-sotts
Con Cab Mai
Embers
Firrepaorth
Earth
Greeve
Praxis

Planets that haven't reported (Future unknown):
Wautic
Mhooreanna
Murush
Tiletan
Tessi (Home Ship)
Bahsheef
Alexceeya5

Overall, battle incidents are going down in frequency and duration.
A uninet site created by Earth has had 102,938,909,762 hits and continues to have videos uploaded to it.

The count stands at 9,034,466,876 videos currently
uploaded.
You can trust UNA for all your universal news needs.

-END OF MESSAGE
* This message will only be deleted by user.

FIVE

>>> > OPHELIA FOUND CELESTE in the kitchen drinking a
protein shake.

"You still can't hold down food?"

Celeste shook her head, "I'm not hungry lately. I think it
will take time to have a normal appetite. Losing Ginger and
Veronica...We were so close for so long. I thought this was the
next best thing I could do instead of food. Sebastian gets mad
at me, but I can't eat."

"You need to keep your strength up. I'm sorry you're not
feeling yourself."

"Thanks. I just need time. What's up with you?"

Ophelia smiled, "Now that the wars are over, my usefulness
has ended here. I feel like I'm in the way and D'Artagnan needs his
own space. He asked me to move in with him to Bahsheef. His new
home is being built, but we can rent a place out there and start over
with Declan. I felt bad that his home was destroyed on Il'laceier."

"Yeah, that was tough on him. I know he enjoyed his home
world, but maybe this one will be a better fit for you both. Are
you excited?"

"A little and a little scared, but I love taking care of Declan.
Have you guys decided what to do with him? Are you taking
him back?"

Jesus. Celeste couldn't believe she had forgotten all about the
baby over the past several days. Too much had been happening.

She knew Sebastian didn't want to keep him, and now that they knew they were leaving this universe, there was no way they could take a future Universe Ruler with them to a place he didn't belong. He'd have to stay here. She got a quick image of Sebastian holding her in an embrace. A message he was trying to send her. She didn't know if her 7's were coming back this early or if that just slipped through.

"Celeste, did you hear me?"

"Yeah, sorry. I'm just overwhelmed lately. Hard to concentrate. Sebastian and I think you should keep him. Only if you want to, we can make other arrangements if not."

Ophelia smiled wide, "I love being a mother to him. He's so smart and cute. I will never be able to have my own baby so this is everything I could ever want. Thank you for letting me stay a mom." She threw her arms around Celeste and gave her a strong hug.

Celeste smiled, "I'm glad. It makes me happy to know he's not a burden."

"Absolutely not. He's just a joy."

"When are you guys leaving?"

"Tonight. After D'Art gets back from doing whatever he's doing with the BDP today."

"So soon?"

"Well, neither one of us has too much to move. Besides, I bet you and Sebastian want to have a little more house to yourself with all of us being here for so long."

"It's been great really. I enjoyed our time together. I'll never get sick of my friends being close." She choked up a little.

"Are you okay Celeste?"

"Yeah. I'll be fine. Don't worry." She smiled.

SIX

>>> > DAI LAID NEXT to #5278-9, who after the war officially ended, became Benjamin Speer.

She had told him all of her secrets as they spent time building a house together. She also ordered him a male sexual robotic body that was a gift to him...and her.

Today was the first day he was living in it. He was now six feet tall, blonde with a tan, hard, well-muscled body that left DAI breathless to stare at. He smiled with his white teeth all in a row and his blue eyes glittered in the light.

"So how do you feel?"

"It's strange. Good. I can eat with this body?"

"Yes. You have flavor sensors. How's the breathing?"

He took in a deep breath and let it out, "Odd, but better than I dreamt it could be."

"What can you feel? The ground beneath you? The air in your lungs?"

"Everything. The metal ground is...cold. The air in my lungs is...not fresh. It has a scent to it."

"That's old recycled air. I'm thrilled your orb has found a way to create an atmosphere for this planet! On terra based planets the air smells sweet and cleaner."

"I want to go."

"Of course you do. And we can, but you have to adjust to being in this kind of body first."

"What do you suggest we do first to get me acclimated?"

She put her hand on his bare chest, "You have a perfect body, made to be touched and it would be a shame for you not to experience something so sensual with a shell made for sexual pleasure."

"Okay. How do we do that?"

She looked around their backyard, "We need a private place. This is okay for conversation, but anyone could walk up to us. Let's make use of our new house."

She had a thought as he stood up. The body only came with a single pair of boxer shorts that looked great on her new friend but he would need more clothes. She ordered some quickly on the uninet before she forgot.

He put out his Human hand to her Human body, "Let's go."

She put her hand into his and he marveled at how they fit together, "Were these creatures meant to fit so well together?"

"You don't know the half of it my dear. Let's go get naked and you'll see what I mean," she giggled.

"I think I can guess. I did some research. Living beings do a lot of this." He pulled her into him and kissed her without really knowing where to put his lips so he ended up kissing her cheek. She put her lips on his and he closed his eyes. He was a quick study.

He pulled away and scooped her up into his arms, "They do this too. A ritual where a man and woman become joined through a doorway."

"You're almost correct. I see why Human women like this though."

He walked with her through their back door.

He put her down near their bed and she looked around. "We still need window dressings."

She got down on her knees and pulled what little clothing he had off. "Step out of these please."

He obeyed. She stood and stripped off her clothing and put his hands onto her breasts.

"Feel me. Try gentle, and a little firmer, or soft."

She put her head back and he marveled at how soft her skin was and the pink nipples getting harder as he touched them. He put his mouth to them and licked them a little.

"You're a smart boy. I like the way that feels."

He picked her up and put her on the bed gently, but she shook her head. "Get down on your back."

He did and she put her hands to his cock. She rubbed and tugged at him and the body responded as it should, growing an erection that she had demanded be the perfect size for her.

"That feels...amazing. This is why beings love this process," he smiled.

She mounted him, "It gets a hell of a lot better Ben. Just you wait."

SEVEN

>>> > LILA SAID, "WILL you hold still please? I need to measure this."

Sebastian was uncomfortable with Celeste's friend so close to his junk, "How much longer?"

She measured his inseam and made note, "We're done. I swear if you don't want to look great, why don't you just buy some suit off the rack and you won't have to be measured."

"I do want to look nice, I'm just used to male tailors and you're Celeste's friend and you're dating my friend..." He put his hands over the crotch of his gray briefs.

"And?"

"I want to make sure...I don't know Lila, it just feels awkward."

"Well, if you hadn't lost my first set of measurements before we made your military uniform, we wouldn't be doing this. It's your fault," she smiled.

"I was kind of busy with a war the likes of which this universe has never seen."

"Me too. I tease, I tease. You know, Veronica told me how you stripped down in front of her on Il'laceier. You didn't sound so shy then."

Sebastian grimaced, "Her and I and Ulysses assassinated a man together. We were sort of bound...in that way. I know we all killed War beings on Treksin Mori, but assassinations are different. And her face wasn't so close to my...stuff."

"I miss her," Lila's voice cracked as she paused a moment.

"She was a good woman. The universe is a lesser place without her in it and I'm sorry it had to be her. I wished she would've listened to us, that we could've found some other way."

Lila looked up at him with tears falling down her cheeks, "Do you really think there *was* some other way?"

He hesitated before answering, "I don't understand why it had to come down to a sacrifice," his lips pressed into a thin line as he remembered how she said her goodbyes and how it devastated Eric. "Given more time, I'm sure I could've thought of something."

"We lost fifty percent of the entire universe, we would've lost more if it hadn't been for her. I don't think anyone had any choice. If you're feeling guilty, don't. You can't feel any guiltier than the rest of us that were there. We all saw what was happening. Don't take all the blame."

He sighed, "It's a constant struggle."

She hunched her shoulders as she dried off her tears, "Such is life. Let's get back to something I know how to handle. Do you want your suit to change colors?"

"I doubt I'll ever wear it again. I have other suits that do that..."

"But...?"

"I don't know. Do you think *she'll* want it to change colors?"

"Yes!"

"Okay, then make it black and the other color...gray?"

"She'll like that. It should be fine. Send her in after you put your clothes on."

Sebastian quickly jumped into his pants and threw on his polo shirt.

He found Celeste in their bedroom, "Lila's ready for you."

She nodded, "You pick something nice out?"

"You'll like it. Even Lila agreed."

"Good. I'll be back in an hour or two."

"Two hours?"

"You can't rush these things dear." She kissed him on the mouth and walked to Lila's parlor/makeshift sewing room.

"I'm so glad you're done with Sebastian. I know he hates this kind of stuff."

Lila smiled, "He was fine, just embarrassed about my hands, but I swear I was nothing but professional. I tried to make him more comfortable, but I don't think it worked."

"He's so proper sometimes, it's cute but also a little too much when it's just you. It's not like I'm worried." Celeste rolled her eyes.

Lila smiled, "I'm so happy with Agathon it's unbelievable. And I'm happy you're so happy with your man too. It's nice when it all happens for us at the same time."

Lila caught herself thinking of "us" as Ginger and Veronica too, but they were no longer here. They weren't going to see Celeste get married and they weren't going to be in the wedding. She teared up.

Celeste heard her thinking. Her 7's were gradually returning. She let a few tears fall off her own cheeks before wiping them away, "They'll be with us in spirit. I'll light candles for them and we can have a remembrance during the reception. Yeah?"

"Yeah."

Celeste gave Lila a hug, "Bastian told me he had to disrobe in front of Veronica after they eradicated David."

Lila laughed, "I was just talking to him about that a minute ago!"

Celeste smiled, "V was all embarrassed but Bastian wasn't. I guess it's different for him if he's killed someone next to you. Anyway, Sebastian could sense how she was...admiring him, then she thought of Eric and so Sebastian got embarrassed. He said he wanted to hose her down she got so excited." Celeste half-laughed, half-cried.

"Yep, that sounds like our V," she sighed, "Oh she would've been so excited for this Celeste. She would've been just, ecstatic for you. I miss her so much."

"I do too."

EIGHT

>>> > TWO WEEKS LATER, it was Celeste's birthday. Unlike her last birthday, Celeste remembered all too much of the previous year. This birthday was quiet. Sebastian gave her flowers and candy. They went out to a nice restaurant and visited with her parents, but didn't do much else. Sebastian wanted to make love to her but she uncharacteristically wasn't in the mood.

NINE

>>> > ERIC SAW SEBASTIAN coming into the gym and finished his set.

Sebastian stood next to him as he dropped the weights, "How are you doing lately?"

Eric didn't want to look him in the eyes, "I'm fine. Just need a little more zinc in my diet, I think, and I want to build up my calves more."

"That's not what I mean and you know that."

"I'm tired of feeling like I'm in a fog all the time. I can read minds. I can see into the future again…I know about you and Celeste leaving. Honestly, I'm pissed. Veronica leaves me and then you're going to another universe?"

"I have to do what I think is best for me and Celeste. I don't want to leave everyone behind, but I can't take you with me either."

"It's probably stupid of me to feel this way, but everything feels upside down. I can't concentrate. I can't sleep. I don't want to eat. I don't want to do anything!"

"You're grieving Bouton. No one can tell you what's right or wrong about it. You do what you need to. It's as simple as that."

"I can't move out of your house yet. I need to be around you guys still. I'm not ready to go home and see those...memories all over the place."

"I understand. That's not a problem. I've been meaning to ask you something."

"Yes, I will be honored to be your best man."

Sebastian got mad but took a deep breath, his friend was hurting and didn't need a lecture about reading minds right now. "Thank you. It means a lot to me."

"I'm always going to be here for you even if you go to the Knowledge Universe and can't come back for me."

"Bouton, I need to do this. I'm sorry you're hurting and th—"

"You know what hurts? All of my powers? My mind reading, my futureseeing? They left me during those two wars. All that time I couldn't see SHIT!" Eric lifted a dumbbell and chucked it across the room, narrowly missing a window.

Sebastian had been waiting for something like this so he crossed his arms over his chest and let his friend scream.

"I never knew she was going to die! I never knew she was going to be pregnant with my baby! I couldn't protect her! And I couldn't enjoy every little moment of time with her that was quickly running out, because I was out there saving the world and protecting strangers and doing my duty and fighting a war and leading people!

"Just when I needed them the most, my powers left me completely and I could never read Veronica. WHY! Why did the Gods and Goddesses decide to punish me huh? What did I do? Was it because I killed people? Was it because I didn't believe enough? Have faith enough? Did I not pray hard enough or should I have been a priest and I chose the wrong path or something huh? TELL ME!"

Sebastian had never seen Eric so completely lost and afraid as he was right now. He was yelling like he was angry (and he was) but he was more afraid than anything.

"I wish I could take the pain away, but I can't. All those days you helped me to get past my fear of losing Celeste and now here I stand, unable to give you any comfort and powerless to make you feel better."

Eric stood red in the face from shouting with his heart racing and his eye twitching from rage. He wanted to die.

"Bouton, please don't think that way."

"Don't read me, Raynes! I need privacy more than ever."

"Of course, but those are serious thoughts and I take them as a threat. I can't have anything happen to you. I need you to pull through this so I know you're okay."

"Yeah. So you can leave in a while?"

"It won't be for almost a year. We'll wait until the last day and then leave. Trust me, it's not easy for me or Celeste to do this. Not after all that we've been through. But I will always be your brother, not in blood, but in spirit."

Eric punched the speed bag to his right and didn't stop. "I'm not going to kill myself. I just feel like I want to die sometimes. I know you of all people will understand that and let me feel it."

Sebastian nodded and started to work out silently.

"I never locked into her Raynes."

Sebastian winced. The one thing that he could do with Celeste that Veronica and Eric could not because only one of them was Lanyx.

"That didn't really matter, did it? You didn't need that to love her; it happened anyway. You and Veronica...anyone could see you guys were meant to be together. I know you loved her more than life itself. It was very obvious to anyone who saw you two together. Locking in isn't necessary."

Eric stopped to catch his breath. The speed bag slowly circulated around, spinning like some crazed amusement park ride. "What was it like? To lock into Celeste like that?"

Sebastian stretched his arms up and then let them drop slowly, "It was surprising to tell you the truth. I expected it, but didn't at the same time. I knew we were drawn to each other, but we didn't know she was part Lanyx, so when it did happen, it was amazing. But I would've been fine without it. Her and I... no matter how I fought it, for how long, we were destined for each other and no amount of locking in or not would've diminished our love for each other."

"But it's our way Raynes. It's what makes us unique, our people unique. Locking in, it's legendary. It's epic."

Sebastian interrupted, "You know how often our people fall in love with other species. You know that billions of Lanyx don't lock in at all with their partners because it's completely impossible and yeah, it sets us apart, but it isn't everything. Didn't you enjoy every second with Veronica?"

"Of course."

"Stop being an ingrate then. Some people never fall in love at all. Be happy for the experience you shared with her. Be grateful that you had a powerful, intense love with a beautiful woman that adored you. Stop thinking about the lack of anything. Forget that you didn't lock into each other. You did, in your own way."

TEN

>>> > **"ARE THEY READY?** We need to put them out and the courier is here from the place."

"What place? Who did you hire to do this?" Sebastian looked out the window and saw a transit labeled *Spider Web Universal Courier Service: We're everywhere, so you don't have to be.*

"The Spider people. They got good reviews and I'll double check with everyone to make sure they got them, or maybe I can ask Ophelia to do that." Celeste grabbed the wedding invitations from Sebastian with both hands.

"No, let's use Portia. She's got to be tested. I spent too much money on it and after we're gone, I'm giving it to Eric. She needs to be broken in some."

"I can't believe you bought a new artificial intelligence and used yet another Shakespearian character name for her. Ophelia must be so insulted. Can you open the door babe?"

Sebastian opened the door to reveal a Human courier that looked no more than seventeen with zits the size of ping pong balls, "Hello. I'm here to collect a set of..." —he looked at his Titan—"invitations."

Sebastian didn't like the looks of him. He looked...irresponsible. "How do we know when they're all out?"

"It will show up on your Titan sir. We're thorough. My dad wouldn't let me work for him if I messed up."

Celeste handed off the bundle of tied up envelopes, "We usually do these things on our own, he's just nervous."

"Don't worry, I'm a professional." The boy smiled.

Celeste tipped him with cash coren and the boy's face lit up, "Thanks ma'am."

"You just make sure they all get into the right hands and we won't tell your dad about Susie coming over to take your *delivery* two nights ago." Sebastian gave the boy a thin lipped smile.

The boy's smile fell off quickly, "How? What? Have you been watching me?"

Sebastian motioned to Celeste with his hands, "Do you think I want to look anywhere else when I have this to look at all day? No. We know things, but we'll keep them to ourselves if you do what we're paying you for. Go run along and be responsible."

The boy looked confused but walked to his transit and left.

"He better get them delivered. Maybe we should've done it ourselves."

Celeste shook her head, "He's a professional. Remember?"

He stared at Celeste hard. It had been over two months since they made love. She had been depressed and distant from him at times and he gave her space, but today, he wanted to be close to her, "I have a delivery of my own that I've been holding onto. Looks like the right kind of courier showed up for it."

"You do?"

"Uh huh. You want to see if you can carry it in your hands or maybe it's too heavy for you?" He put his hands on her shoulders and squeezed.

She giggled, "Here, let me take a look at that sir. Do you mind stepping into my bedroom? My husband's at work."

He stopped, "What? Husband? *I'm* going to be your husband soon."

She smiled and started walking up the stairs, "I'm just teasing babe. Come on."

ELEVEN

>>> > **"MERRY CHRISTMAS DARLING."** Celeste handed her present over to Sebastian.

"You shouldn't have, but I'm glad you did." Sebastian grabbed a couple of her homemade cookies out of the box and put them in his mouth whole.

"I know we won't be able to take much so I wanted something simple this year."

"You are a brilliant and talented woman." He smiled at her.

The smile fell off Celeste's face, "That reminds me. I think I should give up this childish dream of being a singer. It's never going to work. We'll be leaving soon and at least I know the music ban was lifted off Earth before we go so... there's that."

"There's no reason you can't pursue this in the new universe. I'm sure they'll have some kind of music there and if not, you can help them discover it."

Celeste smiled, "Maybe. I guess, but I'm not counting on it."

TWELVE

>>> > ARCOLID WAS STRUGGLING to rebuild destroyed towers in several villages. They had lost a lot of buildings but not a lot of people. The creatures for the most part, didn't penetrate the ground searching for victims. Rend Lett was looking at towers for half the world that were damaged in some way and needed immediate attention. And his fellow employees had been depleted in the war by twenty percent.

Rend Lett had ended up fighting in the war, he needed to. There was no way that his wife would've let him hide out with her in their subterranean house while his friends and co-workers were going up top to fight. And to tell the truth, he knew she was right to push him. He was acting like a coward at first, but she understood his fear and helped him to push past it. After a few hours, she joined him on the front lines. They fought side by side and saw some horrific things, but they made it out alive and unscathed.

Rend also thought if he didn't fight at least a little, he might miss out on a lot of coren that would come in handy for the next several generations, so he did it. Now he would finish the rebuilding work that needed to be done and then quit his job, move to a bigger underground home near the mountains, and maybe start a family. Applette had come through on the monetary promises he made and Rend thought the future from here on out, would be easy and bright.

THIRTEEN

>>> > STOXIA HADN'T LOST lots of people because of their species ferocity and anger in battles. Unfortunately, a lot of their delicate structures had been damaged. Ni-toyis's mother, Mekeenda had been distraught at first losing her daughter and

seeing the note that accompanied the body, but after discovering she had a grandson Sebastian promised she could never see, Mekeenda made a decision out of frustration. She was going to Earth to see if she could find her grandbaby on her own. Her transit was destroyed in a Jump when a few War beings crashed into the space travel device with another ship in a fiery blaze of glory. The last thing on her mind before she died was her unseen grandson.

FOURTEEN

›› › SESEER SAKA WAS a world that almost lost everything because several beings escaped in pods to other, better equipped worlds. They now all started returning from other places to assess the damage and begin rebuilding.

Shumatsu Zhenkang never left her home. She, like many Delun, survived by never leaving the planet and standing her ground to accept the fight brought to her. And Shumatsu's special control over the fire in her hands was the key.

FIFTEEN

››› › MAGNUS ROLLED OFF Nicholette in a sweaty happy mess.

Nicholette huffed and puffed for a moment, "Happy new year darling. I love you so much."

"Love you too." He took a deep breath and let it out slow, "I just wanted to get back home to you. All those fights, alone, out in space. It made me realize how glad I am that you and I have been able to stay together through so much."

"Indeed."

"The path ahead will be difficult with our approval ratings so low."

"Try not to think of that darling. The public is so fickle. Everything will be alright."

"I hope so. I know what you told the press about the bunker, but what was it really like down there?"

"I think we had about three hundred fights, one birth, eight suicides, and a lot of stress and tears. I thought your planning in the bunker worked out great. The meal times were orderly, everyone behaved then. The pharmacy bots were left alone surprisingly. The medical bots were always busy tending to someone."

"What was the mood of the people though?"

"They were scared understandably. A lot of confusion and anger at the unknown. I snuck up almost to the top to use my Titan."

"You did what?"

"I had to talk to Celeste. I had to check news reports occasionally so I could give updates to the people. I was fine. I brought a guard with me every time. Our Titans were useless otherwise."

Magnus grimaced, "The one thing those Taybuse do well with tech, they've still kept to themselves. I'll never understand how they got their Titans to work underground. It's aggravating."

"Maybe you should reach out to them and offer something in exchange for the knowledge."

"They're constantly being hounded already for the regeneration thing. They've just banned their people from using it for anyone else in the universe because they're expecting such high demand so I doubt they'd be open to my questions."

Nicholette kissed her husband on the mouth, "I'm sorry darling. I'm going to order a pizza. What kind do you want hon?"

SIXTEEN

>>> > ON IL'LACEIER, REGIONS were decimated, the population had been reduced greatly and four members of the new governing council had been killed.

Raykreede sat at his desk in the underground bunker evaluating the damage of the planet. He wondered if they'd be able to recover from this. The back-to-back wars had really destroyed all of their military forces and now their remaining structures and planet were vulnerable.

The rest of the council was spread out amongst different regions of Il'laceier but they could barely agree on anything.

Raykreede knew many Il'laceans were living off planet and that might be their only chance at survival as a species. He thought perhaps if the news about his home world continued to be this bleak, he'd have to suggest to the rest of the universe, all Il'laceans would leave this world for dead and be relocating to new planets across the universe.

SEVENTEEN

>>> > KATSANOS WAS CRYING while making her breakfast when the doorbell rang. She dried off her tears and turned off the stove before going to the door. She looked out the peephole screen and saw nothing but a package on the porch. She grabbed it and brought it inside.

There were red heart balloons tied to the package and they rose high above her head as she put the package on the kitchen island looking for a card. She found it and opened it. It was a Valentine's Day gift from Mitch. He must've ordered it well in advance.

The card read, "If I haven't told you by now, (I'm a coward!) I love you and always will. Happy Valentine's Day!"

Then the box moved.

She shook it and it moved again. She opened it hesitantly and discovered an Earthly animal of some kind. She took a picture of it and searched for what it was on the uninet of her Titan.

A Salmon-crested cockatoo.

She read the note from the pet agency that delivered it. She could name her whatever she wanted and they had included her treats, a travel case, and everything else a new pet owner would need. She'd have to pick out the cage she wanted delivered to the house later, but it looked like she had several to choose from on their site.

She set everything up for the bird close to the dining room table away from the windows and called her last gift from Mitch something she thought he'd appreciate.

"Hi Hope. Nice to meet you."

EIGHTEEN

>>> > THE NEEKS OF Natorleeds had suffered very little physical damage to their home world but paid a high price in lives.

The population that remained were mainly the new world thinkers. The ones that Keat'yoo were training on how to suppress their second brains. The people that hadn't been able to were the ones that had immediately run out onto the battleground and had become overwhelmed by enemies. It was too easy to do. Keat'yoo thought suppressing the second brain was natural evolution for them. The next logical step taken for his species. He missed Mey Lii Soo often. She had been surrounded when her flame thrower ran out of gas. Keat'yoo tried to get to her, tried to rescue her, but there were too many. By the time he had cleared a path, she was dead, torn to shreds.

Once all the dead had been accounted for, once all the injured had healed, and once all the buildings had been rebuilt,

Keat'yoo knew he'd need something to fill his time. Their leader had died in an explosion and Keat'yoo thought he might try for the new Chancellor position.

NINETEEN

>>> > THE NIKORAN OF Mar Yen had saved as many eggs as they could and thought they were doing okay until several of the eggs prematurely hatched or cracked. The stressful environment turned out to be too much for the babies and the flower people lost one entire new generation. The soil had been contaminated with stress, death, and tangible pollutants. It'd be several decades before it was egg season again. Their president had also said in her global address that half the planet had been lost in the war and that was lucky. Without the overtaxed military protecting them at the very beginning of the battle, many structures and forests were left exposed to War. Luckily some of the Nikoran themselves had invented new weapons out of necessity and learned to protect themselves.

The president thanked the inventor of those weapons in her speech and cited them as a global hero – Calixtro.

Calixtro had survived the blast that hit directly next to her but she lost all the eggs she carried that day. Her boyfriend, Mejasi Pearg had dragged her into his house away from the fire. She had lost two petals off her head, but she had lived. At first she stayed with Mejasi because he offered to help her recover and get back on her feet, but as their relationship grew they decided to live together even after Calixtro had fully healed.

TWENTY

>>> > THE TURK CLAW of Ferilium were a hardy warrior people to begin with. This war only made them tougher and brought them closer together. Many agreed with the Prime Minister that the war had been the best thing to happen to them in many centuries. Innovations had been made in weapons and armor, families and tribes had reconnected in their times of need, strangers had come to each other's aids and made huge strides in planting the seeds of a global unity Ferilium hadn't seen since the dawn of their people.

Sure they had suffered casualties. Thirty-five percent to be exact. They lost a lot of good young people but they would endure as they always had.

They had lost one fourth of the surface of their planet to fires and destruction but they were determined to rebuild, bigger and better in the following years.

The Prime Minister filled people with the hope and drive necessary to pull together and sacrifice for the good of all their people. Commander Gothin Arax and his crew lived to tell the tales and got even closer, if that was possible, after the battle. The Prime Minister ordered them to take a long vacation for exemplary service and extreme shows of courage and bravery. No one on his team would argue with that, so they all went their separate ways for the next several months. Commander Arax went home to his wife and spent the following week in bed with her, celebrating just being alive.

TWENTY-ONE

>>> > LILA LOOKED AT Celeste in her wedding gown, "It's okay?"

"Okay? It's perfect Lila! Just perfect! Thank you so much for doing this. I really couldn't imagine anyone else getting the dress of my dreams out of my head and onto my body."

"I'm so glad you like it! Let's get you out of it and then Sebastian can come in for his fitting."

Sebastian waited outside with Agathon while the ladies did their thing, "The house is all set?"

"Yes. They finished the construction about a month ago, but the rest of FA...some villages are still a mess, but I think for the most part we can be comfortable there. It's amazing what three Earth months can do with some construction tech robots."

"And when are you guys leaving?"

"If your suit fits fine then Lila and I have decided tonight."

Celeste opened the door with a dress bag in her arms, "Okay babe. Your turn."

He nodded, "I'm thrilled for you. I'll see you later Aggie."

Agathon heard Sebastian tell Lila, "That looks amazing! You're magic."

Agathon smiled.

CHAPTER 12

WE'VE GATHERED TOGETHER

ONE

>>> > CELESTE AND SEBASTIAN sat at the kitchen table eating a rare breakfast cooked by Eric.

"This is really good. You should do this more often." Celeste ate the last of her extra crispy bacon, just the way she liked it, then licked her fingers.

"Well I'm moving out today so this is your last meal with me I guess. I felt like I owed you guys for your hospitality." He moved like a sleek well-oiled machine, crossing the room from the refrigerator to the table pouring everyone another glass of orange juice.

Celeste looked to Sebastian, "No, Eric. We love having you here. You're going today?"

"Yeah. I've made up my mind. These last eight months, you've been so nice helping me get over Veronica's death but I think it's time to go home and deal with things there."

"How are you feeling? Are you ready?" Sebastian studied his friend. Eric had worked out like a maniac for months following Veronica's death. All of his rage, sadness, and emptiness had gone into that. Sebastian had put on more muscle just trying to keep up with Eric.

"I don't know if I'll ever be ready, but it needs to get done and you guys have a lot with the wedding coming up."

"If you're sure, then I guess it's time."

Celeste frowned, "Oh Eric, I've grown so used to you being here. I'm going to miss you."

"I'm going to miss you too, both of you so much. And especially after you go to Knowledge. That's going to be the roughest since...Veronica, but I've soaked up as much time as I think I should from you, and we've made lots of memories, and taken a ton of pictures and done so much. I can't thank you enough for everything."

"Please don't start this Eric, I'm going to cry." Celeste waved a hand in front of her face fanning herself.

"Okay. I'll save it for later, but I think after this meal's over, I'll pack up the transit and take off."

TWO

>>> > CELESTE KISSED SEBASTIAN on the forehead in bed, "Happy birthday babe."

Sebastian smiled groggily and opened his eyes. He saw Celeste had already done her hair and makeup, she was ready for the day and had been up for a while obviously. He grabbed her and place her on top of him. He thought for a minute, "Oh yeah, Praxis calendar, but Earth's month is May right now."

"We're celebrating your birthday on *your* calendar," she smiled.

"I'm the luckiest damn man in the universe."

"You better remember that!" She giggled, "I missed your birthday last year because of the war and you didn't tell me when it was! I had to learn from Ophelia!"

He cringed, "Sorry darling."

"You doing anything today?"

He looked her over and smiled, "Just you sexy."

She giggled.

THREE

>>> > THE NIGHT OF the rehearsal dinner had finally arrived for Sebastian and Celeste and both of them, though excited were also sad. It was a bittersweet time as they didn't have all of their friends there and knew their time in this universe was coming to an end.

Everyone gathered at Stormview Haven and they laughed, and cried, and sang songs. They rehearsed where everyone would stand and where the ceremony would take place on the beach. Veronica was still maid of honor even though she couldn't be present. A big bouquet of flowers and crystals held her place.

A camera bot recorded the evening's events so everyone could have a copy forever.

The house was big enough to let everyone spend the night, even Zach and his eight wives.

And for the first time in a long time, Sebastian and Celeste spent the night in separate rooms so they wouldn't see each other before the wedding.

FOUR

>>> > SEBASTIAN WITNESSED THE sunrise alone as he ran along the shore on the day of his wedding. He wondered if the Knowledge Universe had planets with water and if they did, was the water blue or green or something else he couldn't imagine.

It was good to have everyone here, they herded the bride and groom away from each other each time they got within thirty feet of one another. Ophelia was best at it since she had put electrical trackers on both of them. It became a fun game for her.

In the late afternoon, Ophelia carrying Declan, Lila, Zach's eight wives, and Nicholette piled into a room to help Celeste get ready. Ginger's mother Anne, stood in for her daughter since she was also a hair stylist and makeup artist.

In another room on the far end of the opposite wing, Sebastian, Agathon, D'Artagnan, Eric, Magnus, Xu'Xi, and Zach sat around drinking and smoking while Sebastian got dressed.

Camera bots floated in each room recording everything for posterity.

The sun hung low on the horizon and the camera bots were all in place on the beach.

It was time.

Sebastian took his place at the rose-covered altar with his heart beating hard in his chest. Guests found their seats while music played in the background. A Shaman friend of Eric's walked up to the altar and shook Sebastian's hand. Sebastian's groomsmen all took their places alongside him and joked around about who would get married next. Candles on pedestals held the places of Ulysses and Mitch.

On the other side of the men, stood the bridesmaids along with Ginger and Veronica's placeholders. Lila and Ophelia stood in elaborate purple gowns holding bouquets of small pink calla lilies.

Sebastian felt his nerves build as the music cued up, signaling that the bride was about to appear.

The crown on his head was a bit surreal, but Celeste's parents insisted on the official touch stating that he was becoming a Prince since Celeste was a Princess. He merely wore it to appease her parents.

Praxis didn't have weddings, they had bindings. Their tradition allowed the Lanyx to choose one animal to represent them in the ceremony of binding. Sebastian had chosen a black panther. His vest and tie had the pattern of the animal's skin on them.

The guests stood and everyone turned to look for Princess Celeste's arrival. Sebastian was most eager to see what animal she had chosen.

Celeste appeared far down the beach on her father's arm and Sebastian thought he had never seen her look more beautiful than she did right now.

She wore a dark purple gown and royal robe that color shifted in a water pattern. Color shifting was beyond expensive and saved only for the rarest occasions, even by someone like the Emperor and Empress of Earth. Celeste had refused it at first, but her parents insisted on doing it and she went along with it because it seemed to make them happy.

Color shifting was a step up from bi-color tech. Instead of pressing a button to change the color of your clothes, the color fluctuated on its own between two predetermined choices. The big finish was how the colors changed. You chose fluctuations like strobe, moonrise, soft, gradual, or what Celeste had chosen – water.

When she first tried on the dress she thought her parents had been too extravagant with this idea, but she had to admit, the effect was stunning. The dress, at first, was all dark purple, then it started slowly fading at the bust line to white, like water was washing away the color. It was like standing in the rain as it slowly faded the color out of your clothes from top to bottom. When the process reversed – the all-white gown gradually became purple in a wave that was amazing to watch.

The royal robe she wore was finished in a white faux fur, contrasting deeply against the purple when the color was changing, only the fur remained white the entire time. She had the hood up and it framed her face like a picture.

The most fascinating element of the outfit, to Sebastian, was the revelation of what animal she had chosen. On her back, protruding beyond her shoulders were large purple wings. She had chosen a bird and he knew why. She said he freed her several times. That she was in a prison, (or a cage on display for the world to see) and he had opened the door. He had allowed her to fly free.

When their eyes met, no one else existed. He smiled at her and she smiled back. It was only them in this moment before they were officially bound to one another in a ceremony recognized by everyone else but them. As far as Sebastian and Celeste were concerned they were bound to each other when they first made love. All of this? It was a big show for everyone else, not that they minded celebrating the love they shared.

Magnus let go of his daughter's arm and put the hood of her robe down. He gave her to Sebastian happily, knowing his daughter and his new son-in-law were so in love, it seemed to fill the entire world with light.

Celeste handed her large bouquet of purple and white calla lilies to Lila and unclasped her robe at the neck handing it to Ophelia to hold during the ceremony. Thank goodness Lila had created a quick way to fold up the wings.

Celeste's hair was up in a chignon; pretty little wispy curls framed her face. Her make up only accentuated her natural beauty. Around her neck she wore the ribbon choker Sebastian gave her to remind them both of the mental connection they shared.

Sebastian approved of the dress she wore.

She had an off-the-shoulder lace and tulle dress that hugged her curves to her waist. There it flared out in a big silken skirt full of embroidery, embellishments, and jewels. There was plenty of skin though. It had a deep plunge to show off her ample cleavage and spots of her body were revealed with patches of nude colored thin fabric holding the dress together. She also had a long slit up the side of the skirt to allow her leg to peek through occasionally.

Sebastian stared awestruck.

Celeste was pleased with the look her husband-to-be gave her.

There were a lot of extravagant elements to the dress, but her parents wanted to spoil her. She thought they felt guilty handing her over to Jonathan when she was so young, and the atrocities that she suffered while in his care were something she thought her parents would never forgive themselves for. If this made them feel better to give her an elaborate and expensive wedding to a man that she loved with all her heart, she thought it might be nice for her to just give in and let them.

As she moved to get into place, the skirt swirled and all the embellishments caught the fading light. It was as though fires sparked all over the skirt, dazzling all who set eyes upon it.

Looking over Sebastian, she thought Lila did a terrific job to make him look like a million coren.

His black three-piece suit occasionally became gray. It was impeccably tailored from head to toe to fit him perfect. He had a white dress shirt underneath his vest and tie, and a white pocket square.

He stood facing her and took both her hands in his. They followed the instructions given by the Shaman to look into each other's eyes as they spoke. They listened along with the guests as the Shaman started, "Good evening and hello. My name is Shaman Rucke and I am pleased to be here to join Sebastian and Celeste in their Human wedding and Lanyx binding ceremony.

"Thank you friends and family for being here today to witness this love union and to share this time of celebration with us.

"There are many things said about love and what it means to be bound to one another. But the truth is that while love can bring great joy and peace, two souls and two minds are sometimes in opposition to each other. You may argue and dis-agree with one another, you may not think the other person is right, but you rely on your love as a touchstone, as the founda-tion that all else sits upon. Your love should be like the sunlight that dissipates an early morning fog from a field of flowers. If you don't know what to do or say, think of the other person and their feelings. If you act with the other person's needs in mind, at the forefront of all that you do, two people can become one team, doing what is best for both.

"Love is often spoken of in perfect terms, that there will be rainbows and puppy dogs, but we all know what true love is like. There will be stormy days, there will be tears, and there will be days that you wondered why you got married in the first place. This is all normal. Not to say that love isn't wonderful and amazing, but it's not perfect, as none of us are except in the eyes of the Lord or whatever God you believe in.

"Love is not perfect, but it should be everlasting. It needs to be strong enough to get you through the hard times, and the challenges you will both face as individuals and as a couple.

"Now, let's move on to the good stuff.

"Do you both agree to love each other with patience and understanding?"

They both said yes.

"This is something I want you two to remember while you're fighting over why Sebastian cannot seem to remember to put the toilet seat down, okay?"

They laughed and nodded.

"Do you both agree to support one another through good times and bad, financially and spiritually?"

They both agreed.

"Do you agree to listen to one another, to learn from each other, and to accept each other as you are right now in this moment and who you are yet to become?"

They nodded.

"And last one, do you agree to encourage, respect, and grow with each other? That means you never lie to each other. Celeste, do not tell him you are fine when clearly you are not. Sebastian, do not mock her in the middle of a fight and mimic her tone even though you think she's crazy to be supporting this side of the argument."

They smiled and nodded.

"Okay, now Sebastian and Celeste will speak aloud the vows they wrote for each other."

Celeste looked into Sebastian's big blue eyes. The last bit of sun was fading from the sky, and his eyes cast that animal glow, "Sebastian, I chose you to be my partner, my teacher, my student, my lover, and my best friend. I chose to give my whole heart to you and believe you will keep it safe and happy next to yours. I have longed for the kind of love that you give to me freely and promise to never lie, cheat, or steal from you. I promise to cherish your individuality, your mind, and your heart. I promise to do my best to keep you happy every day and to make your life better than it ever could be alone. I promise to make decisions with you and in your best interest. I promise to love you for all time."

Sebastian was overwhelmed at her words. She wiped away a tear that slipped onto his cheek.

<You are the sweetest thing. I love you so much handsome.>

He smiled, "Celeste, I never thought that I could love some-one as much as I love you. I never believed that I would marry, never believed that I would want to spend the rest of my life with one woman, but you've changed that. You are my sunshine and my light in the darkness. You've helped me to see so many things and to experience wondrous new emotions deeply and purely. I promise to do my best by you every single day I share with you. I promise to make you proud of me. I promise to celebrate you and encourage your ambitions. I promise to love you all of my days. I belong in the service of the queen. I am so proud you're mine."

Sebastian and Celeste heard a lot of sniffling in the audience and didn't feel bad that they were both crying.

Shaman Rucke announced, "That was very well done you two. Now it's time to exchange the rings."

Sebastian presented Celeste with the wedding band to accompany her engagement band. It was a unique ring that took her breath away. The band was a light shimmering purple-gray that looked like it had liquid trapped within it, graywave he had called it. But not only was there a beautiful band, but several gemstones as well. One large stone in the center was an emerald-cut white diamond, to the left was a smaller emerald-cut ruby, and on the right was an emerald-cut sapphire.

<Sebastian! It's like your father's ring. Oh, it's perfect.>

He only smiled in return.

Then she put the ring on his finger that she had custom made for him. It was a wide band of dark gray titanium with a series of seven stones on it. In the center was a round white diamond, on either side of it, a set of three black onyx stones.

<What does it represent Celeste?>

<The black stones are past events for you and past events for me, before and after we met. The white stone is a fresh new start, a beginning to our life together, and a bright future for us. My dark times were being kidnapped, being shot, and my coma. Your events were losing your parents, losing Fran, and being captured by your brother. Is it okay?>

<Yes. You're telling our whole life story together – how we survived, how we've helped each other, how two have become one. You gave it a lot of thought and I love it.>

The Shaman encouraged them to seal the ceremony with a kiss and the guests clapped and wiped tears from their eyes. Agathon was crying just as much as the bridesmaids. D'Artagnan and Eric only smiled and hollered. Nicholette wiped away tears as she'd been crying through the whole thing, and Magnus had his arm around his wife and smiled.

Celeste took her robe and put it on then took her bouquet back and stood with an arm wrapped through Sebastian's.

The music started. The guests stood and clapped as the newly married couple walked down the white carpet aisle into Stormview Haven for a moment of peace before the couple took pictures and the reception started.

Sebastian picked up Celeste and carried her over the threshold of Stormview Haven, kicking the door shut behind him. Then they raced upstairs to their bedroom. He stared at Celeste.

"You look lovelier and more beautiful than I think I've ever seen you Mrs. Raynes."

She smiled, "Thank you dear. You look devastatingly handsome today. Of course, I think you look that way every day," she paused, "Out of all my titles, I'm most proud of Mrs. Raynes."

"Come here my bride."

She walked to him and he kissed her long and slow. He was easily arousing her, and she knew they didn't have much time before they were expected to make their appearance for pictures, *<Sebastian...>*

He continued kissing her, *<I need you.>*

<Right now? We don't have enough time.>

<I'll take you quick.>

Her heart fluttered. He stopped kissing her momentarily and bent down to find the bottom of her dress. He found her bare leg and ran his hand up along it until he found her underwear. Then he put his fingers around the waistband and tore them off. She let out a moan at his aggressiveness but then he filled her open mouth with his tongue and silenced her.

Her hands found his fly. She carefully unzipped it as she felt his erection growing. She reached inside and pulled out his cock through the fly of his briefs and pants.

He stopped kissing her while he reached inside the pocket of his pants, "Hold on. Condom." He put it on quickly and asked her, "I'm going to levitate you. Is that okay?"

"Anyway you want me," she said breathlessly.

That only intensified his desperate need to be inside her.

He had strengthened his telekinesis since his kicker first appeared, but today would be the first time he picked her up for sex.

She wrapped her arms around his neck and kissed him while she stood with her legs wide apart. She felt her feet slowly lift off the ground and she was able to wrap her legs around his waist comfortably. She usually felt light when he picked her up while they made love standing, but now she really felt light as a feather when he held her up with his mind.

He grabbed her legs and encouraged her to loosen her grip around him. She released him and watched as he quickly disappeared under her skirt and she felt his tongue find her clit. She moaned out loud and then covered her mouth with her hand. It was an amazing feeling to be floating in mid-air held up only by the power of your new husband's mind while having him go down on you.

<Supposed...to be...quick baby.>

Sebastian had forgotten about the reception, and everything else really. He quickly came up from underneath her dress and uncharacteristically guided himself into her using his hand.

The feeling was sublime, unbelievable, rapturous. Celeste found making love this way highly erotic. Not only was her husband the most attractive man she had ever seen, him taking care of her every need in every way was what she needed to have mind-blowing sex. Sebastian's penetrations could go deep into her without him having to worry about holding her up. The angles he could achieve this way made her come fast.

Once she tightened up around him, he followed, coming hard. He put his arms underneath her ass and held her up physically while he let his mind go with the orgasm. She wrapped her arms around his neck and slowly eased her feet down onto the ground.

There was a knock on the door.

"Sebastian...Celeste. It's time for photos." It was Eric.

Sebastian called out, "We'll be there in a minute."

They both heard Eric in their minds. He had thought, <Oh boy.>

They knew *he knew* what they were doing.

Eric only walked away shaking his head.

They cleaned up quickly and looked over each other for any dead giveaways that they had been making love. They looked fine to each other and Celeste placed her tiara on her head. They held hands and walked out the door into the celebration as their arrival was announced.

Eric came up to them and shook Sebastian's hand, "I can't say I blame you. She's an amazing woman and she looks gorgeous today."

Sebastian only blushed and smiled.

Magnus and Nicholette herded them to the corner. Her mother said, "The camera bots are ready. Do your wedding photos and then we can celebrate."

After a million photos, Sebastian and Celeste were starving.

They went to the reception and saw projected on one of the empty walls was the pictures of the people they had lost over the past year interspersed with pictures of the wedding and reception. Sebastian and Celeste took a moment to watch as it cycled through a complete round. It would be playing all night and they both thought it was a nice way to remember their friends.

They ate dinner and drank, they danced, they cut cake, they cried, and they celebrated late into the night.

FIVE

›› › › D'ARTAGNAN TOOK OPHELIA out on the beach to watch the moonrise.

They stood near a big bonfire crackling angry flames in the dark. No one else was around.

They had left Declan with Lila and Agathon inside.

D'Artagnan held Ophelia's hands, "I am so happy I met you."

She smiled, "I'm happy I met you. I think you're amazing. Everything you've shown me has been so wonderful."

"Watching my friends get married has been so joyful, I thought maybe I should do it too. I don't know where our union would be legal, but that part doesn't really matter to me. I want you to be my wife. I want to be with you forever. Will you marry me?" He got down on both knees as Il'lacean custom dictates and kissed one of Ophelia's hands and then the other.

"Oh D'Art! I don't know what to say. I...think I'm going to cry."

She felt a single tear fall from her eyes. A totally new and unexpected experience for her. She wiped it away and looked at it glistening on her hand. "I guess I'd better say yes before some other living robot girl snags you."

He stood up and towered over her, "Really? You're sure?"

"Yes sweetheart."

He picked her up and spun her around in his arms, "You've made me the happiest man in the universe tonight."

Then he kissed her.

D'Artagnan and Ophelia knew this was Sebastian and Celeste's night, so they didn't tell anyone they were engaged.

After changing clothes at the end of the night, Sebastian and Celeste left for their honeymoon. Lila was in charge of collecting gifts and keeping them until they got back. She looked through all the envelopes. Everyone had donated coren to a charity of their choice in the couple's honor. That was the only gift they wanted. Lila thought everyone was in need of kindness after the Unknown War ended. She thought both of them would be pleased.

SIX

>>> > THE NEWLYWEDS ARRIVED on Sho'teg and docked the Atlas within the hanging algae rope transit docking station.

Celeste was a little nervous, "These plants are okay to leave the transit in? They look delicate...and weak."

"Trust me, they've been altered. They are super strong, way more than you think."

They entered the building letting the bell men deliver their luggage to their floating room.

They had an entire orbly to themselves.

Sebastian opened the door to the Presidential suite, throwing it wide. He picked up Celeste and carried her over the threshold then she looked around as he kicked the door shut and saw rose petals all over the ground. Romantic music was playing throughout the place and candles were lit everywhere.

"Who did all of this?"

"The staff I guess. I paid them enough. Nothing's too good for my wife and queen."

She smiled. He kissed her while still cradling her in his arms. He put her down and kept his arms around her.

"I want you Bastian."

"Where baby?"

"Everywhere." She started taking off his clothes as fast as he did hers. They got down on the floor and made love.

SEVEN

>>> > SEBASTIAN FED CELESTE another champagne-soaked strawberry. She sucked on his fingers suggestively.

They were in their suite, laying on a pile of soft faux fur rugs nearly naked in front of the fire.

He handed her a glass of champagne.

"Thank you Prince Sebastian."

He rolled his eyes, "I told you not to call me that please."

"Why not? It is your official title. You've married a princess."

"It just makes me uncomfortable. Being...royalty. It's crazy. If only my parents could see me now."

"They'd be proud of you. You helped save the Humans first, then saved the whole damn universe."

He turned on his side and put his stomach up against her back, "That reminds me, I not only asked your father for permission to marry you, but also your mom."

"How'd they react? I'm sure they were pleased."

"Your mom was charmed that I asked them both. I'm glad your father likes me, trusts me with you. I think he has always known I would protect you with my life. He seemed happy for us."

"You are so amazing. I'm glad you're mine." She rolled over on her back. The silky negligee she was wearing fell off her shoulder revealing one of her breasts.

Sebastian called out, "Sex."

Celeste giggled and blushed, "Umm, I was hoping for some yes."

"No. Look at the fire. It's a special fireplace."

She flipped on her side and looked at the flames. Two people formed in the shadows on the wall behind the logs. A man and a woman began undressing each other.

"Oh! This is like those chronicle candles!"

"The Watnaggi are the first to have this tech." He pointed, "Watch. I think this might be the sexy part."

They watched as the man leaned down and kissed the woman's breasts. Celeste made a grunting noise. Sebastian put his hand on her hip and pulled her nightie up to her thighs.

"This is kinda' sexy for just some shadows."

"I thought you might like it," he whispered in her ear.

The shadow couple were now in the middle of having athletic sex. The man was carrying the woman while she rode his cock.

Sebastian rolled onto his back and took off his boxer briefs. Celeste rolled over in time to see his erection stand straight up. She quickly disrobed and slid her body onto his. He kissed her as she positioned herself to receive his cock. Celeste looked over at the shadow couple. The man had his face buried in between her legs while he stood and she sat on his shoulders.

"You like watching?"

"Yes," she barely got out as he penetrated her.

She rocked her hips back and forth on him.

"I'm gonna try something. Tell me if you're not okay with it."

He started rising up off the floor. His body ramrod straight. He levitated and she was riding him while they were getting higher and higher off the ground.

"How high are you aiming for?" she whispered.

"High as we can. You okay?"

She nodded. It was kind of sexy, kind of thrilling. They had never made love in quite this way.

She ground down her hips on him and he took a hand to her clit and started rubbing as his other hand squeezed her breast. She rocked faster as she felt close to orgasming. He started floating them sideways so if they had been on the ground, they both would've been laying on their sides. He started spinning them so they each took turns underneath the other, checking with her periodically making sure she was okay. All she could do was nod. It was heightening her sexual pleasure and making her a little more breathless than he normally did. He floated them down, closer to the ground as he came, then she followed. They softly landed on the fur rugs and curled up in each other. Celeste stole a glance at the shadow people. The woman was giving him a blowjob.

EIGHT

>>> > CELESTE AND SEBASTIAN laid on beach blankets on top of the green sand beach to soak up some sunlight.

"I'm not sure we should have any," Sebastian said cautiously.

"But think of how cute they would be! Little replicas of us? They'd be soooo gorgeous!" Celeste finished her tropical drink.

"Kids are expensive and they take up a lot of time and they could turn out like my brother."

Celeste rolled over onto her back and looked at him, "I suppose I shouldn't even dream of it. I don't know how this other universe works anyways. Things could be upside down or backwards or who knows what. Plus where would our children play? Who would they play with?"

"I don't think we should rule it out completely just because we'll be somewhere else, although I do think we shouldn't plan on it for a while. We'll need to adjust to our new home and I want some alone time between us. Maybe in five years, maybe ten."

"Ten years is a long time hon."

"Maybe not over there. I'm not shutting down the idea is all I want you to know. Let's revisit it later on."

"Okay." She looked around and saw a beach butler, "Oh sir? Can I get another drink with a little pink umbrella in it please?"

NINE

>>> > SEBASTIAN LANDED THE Atlas on the lawn of Stormview Haven and sighed.

Celeste looked over at him, "That went way too fast."

"It was a good thing we took two *Praxian* weeks instead of Earth weeks, but still...yeah."

"We did have a lot of fun though."

"And a lot of sex."

She smiled, "Yeah...but we can still christen all the rooms here that were occupied for the longest time with our friends."

He smiled wickedly, "Yes we can. And we will."

She stared at him staring at her, "What?"

"Race you to our bed?"

"Okay, on the count of three. One..."

They opened their doors.

"Two."

Sebastian darted out and was sprinting.

Celeste followed yelling, "Hey! I didn't say three yet!"

CHAPTER 13

TICK TOCK

ONE

>>> > OVER THE NEXT few days, Sebastian and Celeste enjoyed their home and their time together in the universe they knew. They made plans to visit everyone dear to them for the rest of their time in the Unknown Universe.

Sebastian enjoyed his wine and drinks. He sat on the beach and felt the sand on his bare feet. He watched the seabirds run along the shore and find their next meal.

Celeste walked through the garden in the back of the property and made shapes out of the clouds in the sky. She breathed deep of the ocean air and listened to the bees as they busily buzzed from flower to flower. A butterfly landed on her shoulder and she stared at it as it flitted its wings along her cheek. Then she watched it fly away just as suddenly as it had landed.

TWO

>>> > SEBASTIAN AND CELESTE traveled to Silver Thorn first and said goodbye to her folks.

"I don't understand dear, you can't ever come back? When did you make this decision?" Nicholette said through her tears.

"We've known for a little while. I knew it would be hard on you and there is so much going on. You guys are really busy and you're going to stay busy for at least a decade rebuilding the cities and economy, plus the population and well, all of it. I'm so glad that Sebastian found you and was able to bring you back, but Sebastian and I have an opportunity we'd like to take. We get to start fresh where the community doesn't hate me because of the lies I told, and Sebastian doesn't have to worry about being in someone else's crosshairs. I think it's the best thing for us."

Nicholette hugged her daughter tight, "I'm just going to miss you so much and there's no way for me to contact you."

"If there's any way we can come back, we will."

Sebastian hugged both Magnus and Nicholette and shook their hands, "I promise to take good care of her. Also on Praxis, I have an island and some property that I'm going to give you. I hope that you'll find a way to make coren off them or use them for a vacation. As long as you do whatever you think is best with them. And here's the key cards to Stormview Haven. Thanks for letting us rent it for a while."

"How long before you leave dear?" Magnus wiped at his eyes.

"About two months, but we're visiting a lot of friends and we're trying to give everything away before we go. This will be the last time we'll be able to see you guys."

Sebastian finally had the time to test Magnus for 7's. They were all surprised to learn he had no telepathic aptitude.

Magnus and Nicholette were in tears as Sebastian and Celeste got into their transit.

Celeste waved one final goodbye to her parents and cried as Sebastian launched. She craned her neck looking down until Silver Thorn could no longer be seen.

THREE

››› › GREEVE WAS AN interesting planet. Celeste had never visited it before and she was charmed again by Xu'Xi.

"You guys have worked together a lot?" she asked Sebastian.

"Only occasionally, but he's the best at thieving, especially when some sort of electronics are involved."

Xu'Xi smiled, "You flatter me. You come up with all the plans, I merely follow them. And Celeste, let me say you are just as pretty as a picture. I didn't get to say that the first time we met. Xavier, I mean, Sebastian is a lucky man."

"You're too kind." Celeste blushed.

"Sebastian, when I saw you leading your armies on the news, I thought *that* was an alias."

Sebastian nodded, "There's no need for aliases anymore, not where I'm going."

"Yeah, I guess not. I can't believe you're leaving the whole universe. That's crazy!"

"Well, it's something I feel I have to do. And since you've been so good to me, I'm going to give you my treasures. I have a lot of sculptures and artwork that I want you to have. I brought some, but a lot are on Earth. Do you think you could pick them up within the next couple weeks?"

"Sure. What do you want me to do with them?"

"Whatever you want. Once they're yours, it's up to you. I'd love to take them with me but we can't take much. I just wanted someone to have them who knew their value. It's quite the collection."

"I bet. This is so generous of you. I have to admit I'll sell some of them but I'll keep what I can. I do love a good piece of artwork."

FOUR

>>> > SEBASTIAN LANDED THE transit on Arcolid and Celeste ran out to Zach to give him a big hug.

"Oh dear it's so good to see you! How are you?"

"I'm well. How are you and the wives?"

"Great, great. I'm so glad you could visit my home world. Feels like I never get enough time here since I'm always traveling. What brings you guys out?"

Sebastian came up to Zach and shook his hands, "We wondered if you wanted your bike back and to take an apartment or two off our hands?"

"What? Why would I...What's going on?"

After they explained everything, Zach just sat still, stunned by the news of their departure.

"But you guys just got married and you're so young...and all your family and friends? What are they going to do without you?"

"I think they'll be fine. Everyone has their own lives and as much as I love you all, Sebastian and I feel we have to do this. We'll never get another chance to travel any further than this and we both love learning new things and we'll have each other. I hate to leave you all though. It hurts my heart."

Zach licked his eyeballs dry as they teared up, "Oh you guys! I'm going to miss you so much!"

"Will you take the properties and your bike back? I wish I could keep it, but I just don't have enough room for it my friend," Sebastian sighed.

"Of course, yes. Thank you so much. My wives love to travel so I think they'll be pleased to find we have a couple new vacation homes to replace the one we lost."

Celeste smiled at him, "It's the least we could do for you considering how often you saved both of our lives. I'm forever in your debt."

Zach let a few tears fall, "And I in yours my dear."

FIVE

>>> > ERIC OPENED THE door and started crying.

Sebastian looked at Celeste as Eric walked into his house leaving the door open for them.

"You guys can't be leaving already? It's too soon."

Celeste closed the door behind them, "A little under a month now, but we came so we could spend more time with you. Ten days if that's okay?"

He nodded and hugged Sebastian.

Sebastian looked at Celeste and hugged Eric back, "You are my brother. Nothing will ever change that man. We've faced death together so many times I lost count, and you're the toughest man I know. You're going to be just fine without us okay?"

Eric let go and hugged Celeste, "I'm going to miss you."

Celeste started to cry, "Oh hon, I'm going to miss you too, so much. You helped me save the love of my life and you've taught me so many things. I can't repay you for all the kindness you've shown me and how you kept Sebastian from losing it while I was in a coma, but we are here to give you some things."

Eric let go of her and sat on the couch, "Your things don't replace you guys."

Sebastian sat down in the chair nearest him, "I'm going to give you a third of all my weapons. You get first pick."

"You giving Steele and Rojas the rest?"

"Yes, I think you three will enjoy them the most and I know you'll take good care of them. I'm going to give you Stargazer too."

"That's very generous of you. That yacht's a beauty. I will enjoy my time on her."

"You should. You can have one of my Praxian properties too so you have a place to crash on solid ground."

"Thanks."

Eric looked so sad to Celeste.

"Is there anything we can do to make this easier on you sugar?"

Eric looked at Celeste, "Oh I don't know. I guess I just pushed this moment out of my thoughts for a while. I didn't want to think about it although I knew it would come. I can't see anything for you in the future after you go through the door on Bahsheef. I would tell you, just this one time, if I could."

Sebastian shook his head, "That's alright buddy. No one knows what's going to happen over there but that's what makes this exciting. I know it's going to be hard on you but please lean on Rojas and Steele. They will be going through the same thing."

"They still have their girlfriends though."

"Yes, they do. But Steele lost Linda and suffered until he found out she was a cheating bitch. Then he suffered worse. And Agathon has lost people close to him, so it's not exactly the same, but they are all in the category of pain and loss. How are you doing with that?"

"Some days are harder than others. It's almost been a year since I lost her. A whole Earth year." He rubbed his face with his hands and ran a hand over his hair, "I feel lost...so lost sometimes. Veronica was good for me you know? It's hard to lose that. She was my soul mate, the person I was supposed to be with forever."

Sebastian looked to Celeste and was silent.

Eric sighed loudly, "I will find a way to go on. I know she never wanted me to be laying around a year later depressed and feeling like...not myself. I will try to find a way through this."

Celeste said, "Just take it one day at a time. I felt like that after I thought my parents were gone. It was one of the most difficult things I've ever had to deal with. I felt like my life was over."

"That's how I feel. I've been trying to take it one day at a time, but sometimes it feels like months gang up on me all at once and it's too much."

"Have you reached out to any support groups for people who have lost a spouse or someone special? They might be able to help."

Eric looked out the window for a moment, "No. I guess maybe I should look into that."

Sebastian stood up, "Let's go out to dinner. I think getting out of here for a while would do you some good Bouton."

SIX

>>> > LILA AND AGATHON were on the grass in front of their home on Foss-Altus.

Agathon was in his Human form with his arms around Lila. Lila had a big grin on her face.

Celeste jumped out of the transit as soon as Sebastian landed.

"Oh it's soooo good to see you both! Come here and give me hugs!"

Lila gave her friend the biggest hug then Agathon followed.

Sebastian shook their hands, "How is everything?"

Agathon nodded, "My house looks great. I'm really happy with it and the planet is coming along well. They've finally decided to let visitors come, but very slowly. Only about ten people every three hundred days. Celeste what do you think of my home world?"

She smiled, "It's fantastic! And so beautiful. I didn't think there would be so much grass and water. It's more than I could've imagined."

"Thank you. I'm glad you like it."

"It reminds me a little of Ireland."

"Wouldn't you know, my people seeded Ireland."

"What? Do tell."

"We're fantastic at cultivating land. My ancestors took little pieces of home with them wherever they went thinking they could grow something if they got homesick, and Ireland ended up being their biggest success."

"Amazing!"

"Lila and I will make lunch. You two want to come in and I'll tell you all about it and we can eat?"

Celeste nodded, "I'm starving."

"So what's new?" Sebastian asked, "This one's always starving."

Lila laughed, "How long before you leave here?"

Celeste raised her eyebrows and stopped just short of the front door, "You guys weren't supposed to know. Who told you?"

"Magnus and Nicholette called right after you left them. They are pretty distraught. Nicholette was crying. I think she just wanted to hear a friendly voice."

Celeste frowned, "I know it's hard on them, but I asked them not to say anything to anyone."

Lila shrugged, "You know how mothers are. They worry about their babies," she paused, "So how much longer?"

"Eighteen days. I can't believe time has gone by so fast. We were just visiting with Eric and he said...Veronica passed away almost a year ago." Celeste choked up.

Sebastian and Agathon went inside the house while the ladies stayed outside lost in conversation.

Lila nodded, "Yeah. I miss her every day. Sometimes I call her Titan and pretend we can talk about dresses and guys. It must be so hard on Eric."

"He's not doing well. Maybe you could check on him? Visit him if you can or invite him here. I think it would help."

Lila smiled, "Of course. I'll do whatever I can. Besides I think Agathon gets lonely for male friends. He has some here but with you guys leaving, it will be very difficult on him," she corrected, "On us."

Celeste nodded, "I know. We're going to leave you guys one of our homes and I was hoping you'd take some clothes off my hands. It's not the same as having us here but at least it's something to remind you of us."

"Did you visit...where Veronica...passed over? I left flowers there a while back."

Celeste's eyes clouded over, "Yeah. Sebastian and I just came from there. I figured this was my last chance to go, and since it was right there, you know. So yes. I know several of the others have been back. There was a lot of memorial items. I don't think anyone's been back more than Eric, of course. Feels like it was just yesterday..."

Lila wiped at her eyes, "Well I know she'd be super mad at us if we were sitting here crying. I try to remember our good times. But I'm proud as hell of her. She went out like a mother-fucking badass didn't she?"

Celeste smiled through tears, "She did. She was so brave. I hope wherever she is, she's at peace."

Agathon poked his head out of the door for a moment, "Celeste, I owe you a ride. I almost forgot! You want to take a quick tour of my planet on my back?"

Celeste took a deep breath and put her head back, "That sounds like a lovely idea. I thought you'd never ask. Of course I want to go."

SEVEN

TITAN Corporation - Personal TITAN Device
System Status: Active -- Universal Grid: Online
Current Time/Date (Earth - London, England): 6:59
p.m./August 06, 4017

Secondary Time/Date (Il'laceier - City Expanse Regions): 23rd Knoche/Ernred 91-9, 5390
Current Universal Positioning System Location: London, England, Earth
User: Unrecorded
Communications Menu
Incoming message(s) received: 1 - Status: Unread
Message Received at 6:59 p.m.
Message Sent from: Universal News Agency (UNA) - Il'laceier

-UNA
-Naxad Colony, City Expanse Regions, Il'laceier
BREAKING NEWS
Tonight, the last Il'lacean citizen has officially vacated the former home world of Il'laceier. As you might remember, an official statement of the five remaining members of the original nine person council, had decided the planet was a total loss with rebuilding being too big of a job for such a small population remaining on world.
Raykreede Monter is staying behind to lead a small team of the remaining military forces to stand guard around the globe to ensure order remains in place. Much talk has surrounded the possibility of Il'laceier becoming a much needed "local" prison world, but many surrounding worlds have expressed their concern over so many criminals being held so close to the galactic general population.
Public discussions will be held over the next several weeks with the newly formed Intergalactic Justice Board servicing all planets involved with this new opportunity.

If Il'laceier fails to become a prison world now,
the next opportunity to convert it will be fifty-
five Earth years from now.
Raykreede Monter gave us this statement, "I
certainly never saw my home world falling this
way - I honestly don't want it to become a prison
world. I see a different future. While my team is
there to protect, I'd like us to begin clearing out
damage so a construction crew can one day, come in
and rebuild. Perhaps orphans of several lost worlds
could congregate on Il'laceier and make it a whole
new planet of opportunities for rebirth."
You can trust UNA for all your universal news needs.

-END OF MESSAGE
* This message will only be deleted by user.

EIGHT

››› › CELESTE LOOKED AT Sebastian, "Our last stop."

"Yep. This is it."

They landed the Atlas on Bahsheef and smiled with open arms as Ophelia and D'Artagnan came and hugged them both.

Sebastian went back into the transit and pulled out a large trunk, "Steele, I got this for Declan. Ni-toyis had a safe at her house and I pulled this out of its hiding spot. She had told Hace that it was for the baby so I thought he should have it."

D'Artagnan opened the trunk and looked inside. There were stuffed animals, books, pictures, and a *lot* of coren. "Yeah, I remember that day. I can't give it to him until he's what? – Eighteen? Twenty-five? Something like that?"

"She requested his hundredth birthday but it's up to you and your discretion. Whenever you think he's ready for it."

"Let's get this inside. I think it's going to storm soon and it's supposed to be a bad one."

They moved indoors and sat down at the dinner table. Ophelia brought out Declan, "You remember these two don't you?"

Declan looked around and drooled, pumping his tiny fists against Ophelia's chest.

"Oh my gosh! He's gotten so big!" Celeste squealed.

"If we were counting Earth years, he'd already be a year old, but he's got a long way to go in Stox years."

"Wow. Time flies." Celeste watched the baby.

D'Artagnan looked at the way Celeste gazed at Declan, "So what brings you two out here?"

"My mom didn't call you guys, did she?"

D'Artagnan shook his head, "Should she have?"

Celeste explained how they would be leaving for the Knowledge Universe in eight days. She explained all of what Applette said and how they could never come back. Ophelia and D'Artagnan were as shocked as the others.

"We came here last because the door is here. We're going to give you the Atlas and some property. Sebastian will give you some of his weapons, D'Art. We already gave Agathon and Eric the rest. It's been hard saying goodbye, but we had to parcel out all of our belongings and see everyone one last time."

Ophelia cried, "Oh Celeste! This wasn't...you were my first friend! And I wouldn't be a mother if it wasn't for you and Sebastian! And Sebastian's the whole reason I exist!"

Ophelia started to sob the hardest Celeste had ever seen.

Sebastian put a hand on Ophelia's shoulder, "I knew this wouldn't be easy on anyone but we're leaving things with you to help remind you of us. We had to take this opportunity. Just the ability for me to start over again...without having to always look over my shoulder. It was great what Magnus did for me, but it doesn't take away all of the threats to my life."

"I understand," D'Artagnan said, "You do what you gotta do. Doesn't mean I won't miss the shit out of you guys. I'm so lucky to have met you both. Without you, I wouldn't have Ophelia or Declan in my life."

Sebastian sighed, "I'm relieved to hear at least one person understands. We've been traveling all over the universe and it feels like we're giving out the worst news of our lives. I get that no one wants us to leave, but everyone's been making me feel guilty. Like I'm making the wrong decision. That reminds me, Steele, you need to check on Bouton...a lot. He's struggling with Veronica's death. I know Celeste is also having a hard time but she has me at least to help her through the worst of it. Eric doesn't have anyone there and I'm worried about him. Can you do that for me please?"

D'Artagnan nodded, "Of course. He and I will get together as often as I can. Maybe I can get him to help me eradicate the BDP. Keep him busy."

"That sounds like a good idea. Thanks. How's that going by the way?"

"Good. They all think I'm Hace. They'll do whatever I say. Someone mentioned my eye color. I forgot Stox eye's change color, so I had to make a mask of mesh to cover them. It's harder to see out of but I won't have to wear it for long. I'm trying to kill them off a little bit at a time until they're all gone. Shouldn't be too much longer. Maybe a couple years. I even made contact with some AI called DAI. She takes herself pretty seriously. She was Hace's assistant so she's been helping me over the past several months thinking I'm him. Says odd things sometimes. She has a physical body and she asks about Declan. I think she's self-aware."

"You got a knack for that don't you babe?" Ophelia smiled at him.

D'Artagnan made a face at his fiancée, "I only have eyes for you my sweet. I love you."

"I love you too."

D'Artagnan looked at Sebastian, "What's really interesting to me is that she owns a Titan and *where* she's located. I tracked her down through her Titan connection. She had it scrambled. It looks like she's on a manmade planet. A place they call Uzzib. I've never heard of it before. I'll do research and see what I can find out, but my gut says this AI is up to something and trying to hide it. Maybe somehow she guessed Hace died. I'm not sure. Whatever she *is* up to, she's not interfering with my plans."

NINE

>>> > SEBASTIAN AND CELESTE sat near the edge of a dormant volcano. They decided to make videos for everyone to watch for milestones in their lives or if they missed Sebastian and Celeste.

They made videos for D'Artagnan and Ophelia's marriage and if they ever found a way to have a natural child between them. They made one for when Eric got his next girlfriend, when he got engaged, when he got married and then if he had a child. They made a video for Celeste's parents for birthdays and anniversaries and if her father ever fell out of power. They made a video for Lila and Agathon's engagement, if that ever happened, a marriage and a pregnancy and birth of their first baby. They made a video for Xu'Xi in case he ever settled down and found the love of his life and got married or had kids. They made videos for Zach, in case he ever retired or had a random bad day, plus birthdays and wedding anniversaries. Celeste made a solo video for Earthlings in case they ever found a way to forgive her lies and wondered what happened to her. She explained all of it – the abusive marriage, being unhappy, finding freedom, and true love. How David blackmailed her to agree to marry David and how her being "dead" was a safer choice for a while, and marrying Mr. Right. Also the opportunity to start fresh somewhere else. The video was very long but she kept it the way it was. She would send it to her parents with a note to release it *if* they ever thought the time presented itself. Sebastian made a video for Ni-toyis's mother to explain a few more things he had forgotten to mention in his letter.

When they were all done, they set timers on their Titans to release the videos right before they jumped into the next universe.

They only had three days left.

CHAPTER 14

THERE'S NO PLACE LIKE HOME

ONE

>>> > THE DAY HAD come that would be the last for Sebastian and Celeste in this universe. They had given away almost everything they owned. Sebastian would bring the photo of his family, his father's ring, his favorite suit, his wedding ring, a book of Shakespeare's plays, a bottle of whiskey, and the glass Kingdom puzzle Celeste had given him as a gift. He stuffed everything in his final and ultimate go bag and hoped it all came out alright on the other side.

Celeste took her wedding rings, the diamond and sapphire choker and the purple ribbon choker Sebastian had given her, a couple of outfits, the charm bracelet her mother had given her, her favorite high heel boots, a bottle of Mr. Bubble, a box of her favorite truffles, and her sexiest naughty lingerie that was Sebastian's favorite. She wished she could take more but it was all that would fit into Sebastian's go bag.

D'Artagnan and Ophelia flew them in the Atlas to where the doorway was.

When they landed, they could hear the waterfall close by and started walking towards it. It was silent other than the birds chirping and the sound of water. Sebastian saw the door first.

It was there, it hadn't moved like Applette said it might.

Sebastian and Celeste went to the door. It was a tight fit for just the two of them so D'Artagnan and Ophelia waited off to the side.

They illuminated the door with a light on Celeste's Titan three times, then knocked in the four corners and wrote their names above the doorway like the letter said.

The stone door opened as if on a hinge and another universe was revealed. Unlike the War Universe, this one was lit up with even more stars and planets. Everything about it was brighter. Celeste could feel a warm breeze flowing from this world into the icy cold doorway. They walked over to where their friends stood. Celeste gave Declan a little squeeze to his pudgy baby body. The boy fidgeted and giggled.

"Make sure you're a fair ruler when you take over." Celeste thought the baby smiled at her.

"Listen to your parents, Declan. Be a good boy for them." Sebastian lightly pinched the child's nose, which it didn't seem to like.

Sebastian hugged D'Artagnan, "Take good care of my Ophelia, would you please?"

"Absolutely."

"And take good care of yourself. Good luck with the BDP and everything. You've been a wonderful friend and you're an excellent man." Sebastian paused and cleared his throat, "I will never forget you."

"Our friendship has always been a treasure to me and I've always valued your opinion on all things. Be well my friend and safe travels, now and always. All for one..."

Sebastian smiled, "And one for all."

There was a rustling behind them and Sebastian reached for a gun that wasn't at his side. Maybe he should've brought just one...

Eric popped out from the trees.

"Bouton! What are you doing here?" Sebastian smiled.

"I couldn't let you go without seeing you guys off. Properly anyway."

"How did you find this place?"

"I listened when you guys were talking and I remembered the ruins, so I narrowed down this area to a one mile radius as to where the door might be, then I saw your transit. Voila! Here we all are again. I'm just glad I caught you before you left."

"Thank you for coming all the way out here. It means a lot."

"Yes, it does." Celeste gave Eric a big hug, "I'm going to miss you and your sense of humor. Please take care Eric."

He nodded, "I will my queen. I'll miss you more than you can imagine. You are as beautiful as you are a badass. Take good care of my friend."

"Surely," she winked at Eric.

Sebastian hugged Ophelia, "I never thought I'd miss my personal-assistant-turned-living-being because I never thought you'd awaken, but you have, and you're amazing. Thank you for all your help throughout the years. I hope you and Steele are always happy, always safe, and always feel loved. I will miss you O."

She teared up, "Oh sir. You always do this to me. I love you and I'm so glad you've found your happiness. Thank you for introducing me to D'Art and for giving me Declan. I'm so happy. I hope you have a safe journey and a happy life."

Celeste hugged Ophelia, "You're such an amazing person, just like Bastian said. I'm in awe of how many things you've overcome, and I'm grateful for you helping Sebastian stay safe all those years. You're wonderful. I hope you and your man have all the best life has to offer and are happy. Take care."

Sebastian shook Eric's hand and then gave him a big hug, "All for one Bouton."

D'Artagnan and Eric both said, "And one for all!"

Sebastian smiled but tears came down his face, he couldn't help it although he tried.

Eric said, "It's okay to show emotion. I've learned that the hard way. I can't keep that shit inside anymore. I'm getting too old and I don't give a fuck who knows I have a heart and soul. I should've told people how I felt about them more often. Don't be embarrassed. It's a good thing," he paused, "The only time I told Veronica I loved her was right before she died. I won't wait that long again for anyone else. Now, you and your wife have a journey to start together."

Sebastian rearranged the go bag on his shoulder.

Ophelia's Titan chimed with an incoming message, and so did Eric's, and D'Artagnan's.

Celeste looked down at her arm, "Oh! I almost forgot." She took it off and handed it to Eric. Sebastian did the same and handed it to D'Artagnan.

D'Artagnan looked at his message, "It's from you. What is this?"

Sebastian smiled, "It's a gift. For future viewing. You have all received at least one for different times in your lives. You will know when it's right to view them, but save them...for when you really need them, okay?"

D'Artagnan nodded.

Sebastian said, "Our Titans have no more protection on them so you can look through them if you'd like. We took out all the embarrassing mushy love notes from each other's inboxes, but the rest might be fun for you to see whenever the mood strikes."

Sebastian took Celeste's hand, "I think it's time we go."

She nodded as tears pooled in her eyes.

He turned to his friends, "I think we'll see each other again someday. I wish you all love and happiness. Parting is such sweet sorrow."

Celeste looked at them all, "You've been more than kind to me and I love you all for it. Thank you for *everything* and live life to the fullest. I'll never forget any of you."

They all waved to Sebastian and Celeste.

They waved in return and walked under the waterfall.

Eric got close to the doorway and watched as they both jumped in together holding hands. To him it looked like they were floating in zero gravity. They got smaller and smaller until he couldn't see them anymore. A warm breeze hit his cheeks, then died out.

The doorway shut. All the lines and markings lit up brightly then disappeared. The stone wall looked like any other unremarkable stone wall after several seconds.

Eric came up to where his friends were standing and said, "They're gone."

EPILOGUE

ONE EARTH YEAR LATER

ONE

RECIN APPLETTE OF THE KNOWLEDGE UNIVERSE

>>> > RECIN APPLETTE WOKE up in mid-air. Kolek had turned off the gravity again in the middle of sleeping time. She had some odd quirks, but her qualities far outweighed her imperfections.

Recin was elated that Kolek had taken an interest in other things besides war. He thought the introduction of love into her life had changed her mind about some things.

He was busy learning about war since he had a natural curiosity about all things. It was no more than a game when he studied it. Just a game with the highest of stakes. It fascinated him, as did Kolek.

Here he lay in his natural form, which was nothing like what the beings in the Unknown Universe had seen him as.

Kolek floated into their sleeping container and looked at him.

She was a beautiful creature made of light, nothing like that skin shell she wore in Unknown.

"Did you see the news from the Keeper? Unknown finally got its real name. Relentless. Because they never gave up during my attack."

TWO

RAYKREEDE MONTER OF IL'LACEIER

>>> > RAYKREEDE MONTER WAS now one of the most respected and powerful men in the universe. He had taken Il'laceier when it was broken and viewed as a lost cause from becoming a prison world, to a place where a waiting list was filling up with people of all species clamoring to move to. Clean up efforts had moved much faster than expected once the spaceship Tessi had docked on world and all able bodied people who could do hard manual labor did. Then construction robots got involved and erected multistory high rises, creating cities out of the rubble.

Raykreede had to admit, his former home world was looking better than it ever had before. Now it had a sense of community and comradery that was unprecedented. Soon several species would melt together their histories, cultures, foods, and ways of life.

The Stampermoth as a whole had stipulated they would do the complete clean up themselves if it meant they could move on world first to make it their new home. After the news broke, several other species expressed interest in living there and starting over. Raykreede was even looking into the possibility of building atmospheric domes and towers in certain parts of the globe for species that came from other breathing environments.

Now people were looking to him as a trendsetter and leader for creating new global communities of peace and mutually beneficial relationships between several species.

The Earth Outpost had been the only place in the universe close to the kind of community he was now building, but Il'laceier was truly the only planet of its kind. It would be the greatest achievement of his life.

THREE

ZACHARIAH COLDIRON OF ARCOLIO

>>> > ZACHARIAH COLDIRON SAT in his den looking over the bills. The insurance check had finally come through for his Bahsheefian vacation home lost in the war.

Drucilla knocked on the door and entered without waiting, "Dear, what do you want for dinner?"

"Whatever is good. I'm not too hungry."

Zapheil came in, "I was thinking pizza sounded really yummy and the kids have been doing good on their finals. I told them we'd give them a reward."

"Zaph, I don't think we should reward them with food," Zach tried to keep a non-judgmental tone as he spoke to his first wife.

Oxis walked in next, "Babe, I say...Oh, I'm sorry. I didn't know you were in here Zaph and Dru. What are we discussing?"

"Dinner," answered Zapheil.

Rithu, Alisorene, Lumina, Disaris, and Shalisha all came in talking at once about...Zach couldn't really make it out, such is the case when everyone in the burrow is talking at the same time. Maybe the kids, or dinner, or pizza.

"HEY! EVERYONE!" Zach hated to raise his voice. They all got quiet. "Hey, I just needed to finish the bills and then we can go out for pizza okay? But it's not as a reward for anything, it's because no one wants to cook, agreed?"

They nodded and shuffled out, closing the door as they left.

Zach took another half an hour in the den since it would take that long for all the hatchlings to get into their eating clothes, and loaded in the deluxe cargo transit they used as a family vehicle.

He flew over to The Pizza Lid, whose ad campaign was, "The best pizza in the galaxy because the crust is out of this world!" Zach hated the commercials, but the kids loved the jingle. They ran around the burrow singing the damn thing for two hours after an ad ran on someone's Titan.

He made sure everyone piled out of the vehicle and got safely inside the restaurant. His hatchlings ran wild when they saw five new games in the arcade and his wives went to the counter to order thirty pizzas to feed everyone.

He went into the dining hall and sat down at a table waiting for everyone to come sit. He was tired. Not just the kind of long day tired everyone suffers occasionally, but he was tired down in his bones. Ever since the back-to-back wars a couple Earth years ago with all the destruction and death he had seen, he felt worn down, worn out.

He thought of retiring. Maybe it was time. They had enough money to last at least one generation and some of his hatchlings were grown and taking care of themselves. More were moving out all the time and his youngest was eleven. He remembered Sebastian and Celeste's list of videos they had gifted him. There was one labeled, "In case you retire."

He thought about watching it to see if it helped him decide if now was the right time.

No. Better to keep it for when he really did.

It was the last one he had from them.

FOUR

LILA NORTH OF EARTH & AGATHON OF THE ROJO CLAN OF FOSS-ALTUS

›› › LILA ARGUED, "IT looks *just* like you babe. Well, I mean not right now since you're in Human form, but you know what I mean."

"It most certainly does not! They made me look like...like some sort of common reptile. My chin doesn't look like that! If they are going to go through all that trouble of putting up a statue of me, the least they can do is capture my likeness accurately!"

"Oh Agathon! Listen to you, you sound like such a diva right now, I swear. Just be grateful they recognized your efforts to warn the royal clan before the Unknown War broke out and tore half the universe to hell."

Agathon and Lila had attended the dedication ceremony in the main courtyard for his life-sized statue for helping with the war warnings. Lila flipped on the open sign in their armor/clothing/doughnut shop all in one. They named it Dough Knight.

Their ads mentioned it was the first store of its kind on Foss-Altus.

Lila turned around to face Agathon and got very dizzy, "Babe. I need help. Now."

Agathon went to her and held her hand, "You okay? Is it morning sickness?"

"No, the baby just...shifted I think. Got lightheaded for a minute. Is that normal?"

"I've never fathered a child before dear. I'm not sure."

"Well you used to be a child!"

"Of course." He thought on it, "My mother always said she got dizzy in the first half of pregnancy but that it went away and was replaced with cravings and vomiting."

"Oh great! That's what I have to look forward to? A year of vomiting?"

"You'll be fine dearheart. Just fine. Not all pregnancies are the same. Besides she was full Dach with full Dach babies. Soon you'll have to go to the hospital and the baby will be put into incubators after they remove it, otherwise...you know what happens."

"Yes, I don't want to get killed when it starts growing that fast. I don't know how I let you get me pregnant."

Agathon led her to the counter where she could sit down and ring up sales, "I believe it was a long rainstorm and a bottle of rum that kept us indoors for abo—"

"Shhhh! That's enough. I remember. You're going to help me with all of this right? I have no idea what I'm doing. I've never been pregnant before or a mom and I want to do it right."

He pushed a lock of hair behind her ear, "Darling of course. I love you so much. I'll be with you every step of the way, no surprises."

"No surprises. That sounds good. I'm sorry I've been so crabby. You don't deserve that."

"It's okay, I understand. You must be really uncomfortable often." He took yesterday's doughnuts and put them on the half price shelf, then he took a glazed one for himself and thought of Celeste. These were her favorite.

"How do you think Raynes and Celeste are doing?"

Lila smiled and got teary eyed, "I told you not to make the glazed ones, they always make you think of her and then you're thinking of Sebastian and then *I'm* crying."

Agathon tore the doughnut in half and fed some to Lila, "They were excellent people."

Lila swallowed, "Of course they are. No past tense. They are still alive and well some*where* out there. They're just not here, where I need them now. I wish they could see what we've done, and see our baby when it's finally arrived. Plus, you might even get on The Great Flower if Blue retires soon. I know they're thinking about you as a possibility."

"Yeah maybe. Sebastian would never believe it," he paused, "Or maybe he would. Either way I wish I could tell him."

FIVE

D'ARTAGNAN STEELE OF IL'LACEIER

>>> > D'ARTAGNAN LOOKED AT his Titan and saw the reports from the members of the BDP. One report proved much more interesting than the others. Something came up from far back in his past.

Ophelia came into the kitchen and stood on her tiptoes to give him a kiss on the cheek, "Morning dear. What are you doing today?"

He looked at her as she carried Declan on her hip.

"The members found that mechanical world, Uzzib. I told them to leave it alone, but they wouldn't listen, now another thirty men are dead and that...saves me a lot of trouble."

"This is the only big gang left with the IMC eliminated after the Battle of Empires. They've dominated for far too long."

"I agree. I took a lot of money from both. I'll be glad when they're gone."

She grabbed a skillet out of the cabinet, "So how many members are left?"

"About a hundred and thirty...six? Around there." He sat at the kitchen table, "The BDP should be completely out of business by the end of the season."

"That's only four months, one week, two days, and thirteen hours away." She cracked a couple of eggs into the skillet one handed, and took a spatula out of the drawer.

D'Artagnan could tell she was getting bored when she started calculating things down to the hour, "Yeah, well I've been working on this for a while now. A year, no two because Declan's two now and Celeste and Raynes have been gone a year."

"I'm upset they missed our wedding."

"Me too but their message was cute."

"Yeah."

The eggs started to sizzle. Ophelia's eyes got wide, "Hey, what if we have a masquerade party once a year? We could invite everyone and make it a benefit for some charity they liked? What do you think?"

D'Artagnan was silent, staring at his Titan.

"Hon?" Ophelia prompted.

D'Artagnan smiled as he got up and kissed Ophelia, "That sounds like a brilliant idea from my brilliant wife. Raynes and Celeste would love that. We could find a way to remember everyone, Mitch too."

"Yes, that sounds lovely. I'll start working on it today after I get him to sleep," she jiggled Declan a little.

D'Artagnan sighed, "These idiots still want to find a way to attack the War Universe. I've told them a million times there's no way to get there and to let it go."

"Well, they are a whole bunch of brainless thugs for a reason. It's not like they have college degrees dear."

D'Artagnan laughed, "I know. If my plan works, they'll all be gone soon and I won't have to deal with this shit anymore."

Ophelia hit her husband on the arm, "Language!"

"Sorry." He looked at the time on his Titan, "I've got to go or I'll be late."

"But breakfast!"

"Sorry babe. I'll see you tonight." He kissed Ophelia, kissed Declan on his forehead then plucked an orange out of the fruit bowl and was out the door with his attaché case.

Ophelia finished scrambling the eggs that were now going to be *her* breakfast, "Men!"

SIX

OPHELIA RAYNES-STEELE OF PRAXIS

>>> > OPHELIA STRESSED HER point, "Technology *is* still evolving in the medical field."

Zach shook his head, "Not enough where a mechanical body can support a child. We've talked about this before dear. There is currently absolutely no way for you to produce or carry a child of your own. You have no eggs. You have no DNA. These are things we cannot work around. I'm sorry."

She sighed, "But...I want a baby of my own."

"I understand completely. I will continue to research and see what's happening in robotics, but all of it is purely experimental. I'm not sure what else to say my dear."

"Sebastian would flip out if I could find a way to have a baby. I remember how he wanted to kill me when he saw me in my body for the first time. It was almost funny without the gun pointed at me."

Zach smiled, "Raynes was never much of a people person, unless he was pretending to be, for some job. Didn't surprise me that he pulled a gun on a stranger in his home..."

"But it was *me*."

"Of course dear, but he didn't know that at the time. Not until you spoke."

"But then he still didn't believe it was me. Thank goodness Celeste changed his mind and let me live," she laughed, "You should've seen the look on her face when she saw me in the gym with Sebastian! I had this little frilly negligée on because that's all they ship the body with for clothing. It was hilarious. She thought we were up to something."

Zach smiled, "Celeste was a feisty one. That's what I really liked about her. Always a scrapper."

Ophelia's smile fell away slowly, "I miss them."

Zach replied, "I miss them too, my dear. We all do."

SEVEN

>>> > D'ARTAGNAN WAS ON a tiny spaceship called *The Easy Lass* walking down a long hallway. Upon boarding the ship, he had killed the first few men he encountered. They thought he was Hace after all so they trusted him. Killing them was like catching fish in a barrel.

D'Artagnan dropped egg-sized devices along the hallway every so often.

There was only one man left on the ship and D'Artagnan was very eager to see him. D'Artagnan walked onto the bridge and saw a man sitting in the captain's chair. The man immediately stood up and greeted D'Artagnan.

"I'm so excited to finally meet you, boss. After all these years and missions...It's not every day you meet your hero." He stuck out his hand.

D'Artagnan grabbed it and pulled the man into him, leaning down he head-butted him. Matthrew's nose started bleeding and he fell into the captain's chair stunned.

D'Artagnan took off his Brotherhood mask, "Not who you think I am, but it's the last mistake you ever make. Your other shipmates are dead. I've laced this ship with grenades as I made my way here. You're going to die today."

"Why? Who are you?" Matthrew held his bloody nose.

"You don't remember me do you? I know you saw my face the day Linda died." D'Artagnan waited for Matthrew to think back. He saw the light dawn on his face, in his eyes.

"Oh my...Listen..." Matthrew started to get on his feet.

D'Artagnan drew his fist back and punched Matthrew in the stomach. He doubled over, but recovered quickly.

"I want to explain D'Art—"

D'Artagnan punched him in the mouth. Once. Twice.

Matthrew tried to get into a better fighting stance, away from the chair behind him but D'Artagnan was much bigger than him and had a bigger wingspan.

"You'll never be able to say anything that will convince me to let you live. You got my girlfriend killed. You left her to die. You took her away from me long before that and it's time you paid the price. The bill is long overdue and I'm here to collect." D'Artagnan picked up the man that cheated with Linda and flung him across the bridge like he was a rag doll. He hit the window hard enough to crack it. D'Artagnan leapt to where Matthrew lay on the ground, and started pummeling him. All of his years of rage poured out until he heard an alarm go off. He looked at the cracked window. He might not have needed the grenades after all.

Matthew lay in a bloodied mess, half-conscious.

"Why?" he grunted.

"You were the only one left out of the two of you to kill."

D'Artagnan saw the crack growing across the window like a lightning strike. He ran back to the airlock and his ship. He undocked and pulled away fast from *The Easy Lass*.

He watched for five minutes, thinking maybe the crack wasn't going to destroy the ship, but then it exploded. His grenades helped.

D'Artagnan felt a sense of closure as he set his ship's coordinates on the screens. Fifteen seconds later, he was gone.

EIGHT

DECLAN TREDUX OF STOXIA

››› › MULTIVERSE KEEPER 8,002 found Declan sitting up in his crib. His room was covered in elephants and lions. These

Relentless beings were strange to surround a young one with images of such fierce deadly creatures.

<Declan?>

The child looked around, but saw no one, so it ignored the voice.

<Declan, can you hear me?>

<Huh?>

<My name is Multiverse Keeper 8,002 and I'm here to guide you for a while. You are very special, do you know why?>

The baby looked around and said nothing; he didn't know many words yet anyway.

<You are a universe ruler for Relentless. That means you have tremendous power. I'm sorry to say the current ruler for your universe has just died. Now, you will take her place. This is an exciting time for you and there is much for us to talk about.>

NINE

VERONICA BLACKWELL OF EARTH

>>> > VERONICA WOKE UP in darkness and let out a gasp. She started coughing from not having any oxygen in her lungs for a long time. She looked around although she couldn't see a thing.

Even after allowing her eyes to adjust to the black, it was still too dark to make out anything.

"Hello?"

Bright lights came on everywhere, illuminating the room she was in. It felt like she was floating on nothing, but she could now see a bed underneath her. The light never hurt her eyes although it should have with its intensity. Everything was gray – the walls, the floor, the ceiling. She looked around quickly but there were no light sources, and yet, there was plenty of light. The windowless room she was in was huge. There was a single gray chair off to the side of her bed.

"Hello?" she repeated.

"Hello...Veronica Joy Blackwell," said a voice from nowhere and everywhere at the same time.

"Where are you? Who are you? Where am I?"

"Your mind is fresh, that's good. But so many questions. You might find being here at first...frustrating."

"Where am I?"

"You are in between."

"In between what?"

"You are in the in between place."

"Like limbo?"

"No. Limbo implies bad things, or confusion. No, this is a neutral place."

"Where and who are you?"

"We are guides."

"We?"

"Yes, there are many here with you."

She shook her head and sat up, "Where are you?"

"We are here with you in the in between place."

She sighed, "We're not getting anywhere."

"We did mention you might be frustrated at first. This is not an easy adjustment to make. We apologize for that. We are trying to make it simple but most have lots of questions to ask instead of listening first."

"What time is it, what day?"

There was a pause, "On Earth it is seven hundred and thirty days since your body left."

She thought, "That's two years. Two years! What...is this place? What are you doing with me? What do you mean my body left? I'm here." She felt her arms and legs and chest. She felt real, maybe this was some kind of bizarre dream.

"You are here with us, but your body is not. It was an excellent and brave deed you did. We know two years seems like a long time for you, but here, there is no time keeping. There is no time."

"What are we doing here? What do you want from me?"

"We are here to help you. We don't want anything."

"Help me to do what?"

"This is an interview process. We only want to talk to you."

"Interview?"

"Yes."

"Like for a job?"

"No Veronica. We have a question for you. We know you have questions for us. It will be pleasant and there's nothing to be afraid of."

She stood up and walked around touching everything she saw. She looked down and saw she was wearing a beautiful gray suit. It was the most perfect outfit she had ever seen. She would've loved to own it before...

"What did you love most about your life?"

She looked up but saw no speakers where the voices could be coming from. She thought about the question, "I guess...that's difficult. I can only choose one thing?"

"What did you love *the most* above all other things?"

"The love I shared with a man. His name was Eric. He was special and the way he looked at me sometimes was...amazing. It made me, *he* made me feel good."

"Thank you. Now we would like you to listen. We will try to answer all your questions."

She settled herself into the chair. It was the most comfortable chair she had ever sat in. It was remarkable, although it looked like a cheap hard plastic chair you would find in any lobby.

"All living things travel in a circle. By this we mean, Humans, animals of Earth, what you consider aliens and all living animals on other planets. Even what you know as plants, trees, grass, those sorts of living things are included in this definition.

"All life is precious throughout the multiverse. Some but not all life, once it is completed, comes here for an interview by us."

"Some? Is Ulysses here? Or Mitch? Ni-toyis? Hace?"

"This place is for souls who sacrificed something at great cost to themselves. Ulysses is here. Mitch is here."

"What about the other two?"

"They are not."

"Where are they?"

"They are in the 'other' place."

"Where is that?"

"They did not make sacrifices but instead made things harder for others during their lives. They made things harder for at least one person by leaving them behind without their presence. They are in the same place as your friend Ginger Vossen."

Veronica put her hand to her mouth, "What happened to Ginger!"

"We apologize. You did not have time to gain this knowledge before your body left. She took her own life shortly after your departure."

Veronica began to cry, "How?"

"A large dose of medication made her sleepy while she was in a bathtub full of water. It was a confused death. Her mind and body were not in alignment at the time of expiration."

"Is she being punished? Is this some sort of suicide bible thing?"

"No. She is not being punished, but her soul is mending. We will give you comfort."

Veronica's tears stopped suddenly and she felt calmer. She took a deep breath and wiped at her eyes, "Can I see her?"

"No."

"Is she okay?"

"She is mending."

"What does that mean? I don't understand most of what you're saying or what's going on."

"Your spirit is here with us in this place where there is no time. Your body is no longer connected to you. It left when you gave your sacrifice to save trillions of advanced beings such as your species and countless other lives such as animals and plants.

"You will be in flesh form again someday, or perhaps an animal, or even a plant; once all your past life dreams have come true and your wishes fulfilled here. When that happens, you will desire to leave here and start again. Then a new life will be created for you and you will be reborn. You will remember none of this, just as this has happened to you many times before."

"How many times?"

"This is your soul's five hundred and seventy-sixth thousandth time through this process."

Veronica was silent momentarily, her mind buzzing with questions. "How many times have I been Human?"

"The more questions we answer, the more questions you will want to ask. Your mind cannot fathom all that IS. Just know that here, there is peace. Peace of mind, peace of heart. By the time the process is over, your soul will have forgotten all the terrible and painful things that it suffered through while you were on Earth."

"What's this process you're talking about?"

"The more questions we answer, the more you will ask. You will come to accept things the way they are here, for it is the way it has always been. You will spend your time here, you will see beings you recognize, and you will choose to leave here in your own time. Now, it was lovely speaking with you but our interview is over. Please step across the water along the stone steps and the next part of your process will begin."

"Wha—" but before she could finish the word, the walls fell away from the room and she was on a tiny island in the middle of a calm ocean.

She looked and saw four separate paths of stone steps floating along the water's surface, all of them going in different directions. They went to the horizon with no end.

"Wait, there's four choices. Which one am I supposed to take?"

"The best one for you. We will answer no more."

"That's all I get?" She asked the question rhetorically and didn't get a response. It didn't surprise her. She chose the path to her left and started walking towards whatever was next. "Eric won't stand for this when he arrives. He's going to kick someone's ass until he gets real answers..." She thought about Eric and wondered what he really would do in this situation.

She stopped in midstep and looked around. The stones she stepped on were large and gray. She kneeled down and touched the water with her fingertips, it was cool and blue. It looked like a deep body of water. There was no sun, but there was sunlight. She could see it filtering down through the ripples and penetrate the ocean deep down into the darkness. She stood up and stripped off her clothes, throwing them over her shoulder.

She put her arms up over her head and dove into the water. The last thing she heard was the disembodied voice yelling, "SOMEONE STOP HER! THAT COULD CAUSE ANOMALIES EVERYWHERE!"

TEN

KOLEK FREESTEW OF THE WAR UNIVERSE

››› › KOLEK TUMBLED OUT of the sleeping container and went into the eating container. She felt happy. A new emotion for her. Her chest cavity felt warm like an electrical current was there burning up.

According to Recin this was love. She had a lot to learn about love, but it was an exciting thing. Not quite as exciting as that thing he called sex, but it was good.

Her perspective on the War Universe and war itself had altered since they came back to her home. She often wondered if and when war was really necessary. It seemed to her that this change in thinking had happened because she found the opposite to war with love, something she had never felt or known before. She wondered how many other beings in her universe would shift their thinking if they knew such a thing as love.

She felt pity for all that had not.

Recin floated into the eating container and hovered close to her, "Have you heard from the Keeper lately? I can't raise him and I've tried several times."

Kolek paused, "Come to think of it, last time I heard anything was that announcement he made last dwar, sorry I mean month. I guess it's been a while. The time before that was my conversation with him asking permission to take some Unknown females during the war. I wonder what's wrong."

"Something's up. He always responds. It's got me worried." Recin almost left then turned around, "What did you say?"

"Huh?"

"Take some Unknown females? What does that mean?"

"You know War's population has been depleted for quite some time. I needed to harv—"

A loud siren interrupted her and made Recin wince, "*What* is that?"

Kolek floated to her monitoring system and silenced the noise, "It's the alarm system for my universe. There's been an anomaly detected. I need to look at something."

The ball of light that was Kolek shone brighter than normal and then dimmed. A view of War showed on the ceiling.

Extinction event asteroids were hurdling through space. The biggest asteroids Recin had ever seen out of the three universes he had spent time in.

They could've only originated as one thing.

"Did those...these must've been a planet right? Did one of your planets just explode somehow?"

Kolek got brighter again and shone brighter still before replying, "Something's gone horribly wrong somewhere. It's a planet alright, but not one of ours. It seems that it just appeared, as in just all of a sudden came into War, but in pieces, like the trip from wherever it came from ripped it apart. Now, it's going to strike several planets. These asteroids are going to wipe out whole populations just starting to rebuild. I'm going to lose entire planets in a matter of seconds. There's nothing I can do."

Recin stared as the first asteroid left an immense fiery streak across a planet's atmosphere, and then plunged deep into the green planet that was first in line to fall. He was silent for only a moment, "What could've happened to cause this? Is this some kind of attack? Are we being punished?"

ELEVEN

ERIC BOUTON OF PRAXIS

›› › ERIC SAT ON a soft rubber mat at the front of the class. He was on the beach near his home on Jex. The sun was bright and hot today, and the shoreline was empty.

He opened his eyes, glad that he had a hat on today, "Okay, now that we're all calm thanks to our daily meditations, who would like to start?"

The Shaman directly in front of him raised his hand.

"Yes, Keal. Tell us how last night went please."

Keal cleared his throat as tears fell, "Dinner went okay. Jenne always knew what to do somehow. I get into the kitchen and I get so lost, but I followed her recipe and I made her favorite meal. It turned out...edible, I think."

Eric prompted, "How did you feel about the experience? How sad or happy or angry were you?"

The Shaman looked at him, "Well, with my calling, I'm supposed to tell you that I was calm and I tried to focus, but..."

"It's okay, no one's going to rat you out for having emotions, and you lost your wife of eighteen years man. It's expected that you're not going to be yourself for a while."

Keal nodded and smiled, "I know but Jenne died a year ago, shouldn't I be – I don't know, moving on like my friends say?"

Eric looked at his class. He had young people, older people, Humans, Lanyx, and fifteen other species looking back at him. "No one can tell you when the right time is for your grieving to be done. Not your friends, your mom, your teacher, your boyfriend, no one. It is a highly personal and deeply painful experience that we all go through when we've lost a loved one. Each one of you need to take your time, feel your feelings."

Keal nodded, "Thank you Master Bouton."

Eric stood up and walked around the group as he spoke, "I see a whole bunch of wonderful people here that gave love freely to someone they cared about. You have huge hearts and your love will never run out, will never run dry for the person that's gone. It doesn't matter if their passing was expected, like at the end of a long battle with a disease, or if their death was sudden, you will always carry a piece of them with you. They will live on for as long as you're alive and you remember them." He sat back down on his mat and took a deep breath.

"I know we've been holding this class for many months. Some of you are new, some are old friends. I'm going to tell you a little about me if you don't already know.

"When I lost my girlfriend and my unborn child at the same time, a piece of me died. I became despondent, nothing like how I used to be while they were alive. I didn't want to do anything, I never made jokes and I was miserable. I was dead inside but I had a chance to say goodbye to my girlfriend before she died and you know what she told me?"

Eric took a long deep breath through his nose and blew it out his mouth, "She said she didn't want me to be exactly how I turned out. That miserable man sitting alone on his couch that didn't go anywhere and had lost all of my passion. She told me to live, to enjoy things. She even told me she wanted me to find love again. That was two years ago. Now I teach this class on how to deal with the death of a loved one. I teach meditations and I work with my Shaman to help myself continue to heal, because I'll always be a work in progress. I'll always miss my girlfriend and my child that I never got to meet. I'll always remember them and carry them with me and I will never stop loving them. I encourage you to think through the same process. Think of who you lost and if they would be happy knowing you're miserable now. I bet they would tell you they don't want that for you. They want you to live. They want you to go out and enjoy the hobbies and passions that you always have."

Several students were crying and sniffling to themselves.

"I never hold any judgement in this class. I will never tell you that how you're feeling is wrong or that you've cried too much or you should move on. You shouldn't listen to anyone that tells you those things. I'm at the point in my own grieving where I can talk about my loved ones and smile instead of break apart into tears. I can laugh at funny times I shared with her. They are pleasant memories. I've even been brave enough to open my heart again to someone new. You will get there, but you must take this one day at a time. I'm here if you need me. Good class today. That's it friends. See you next time."

Several students got up and blew their noses. Some rolled up their mats to put into the bin. The Shaman came up to Eric and shook his hand thanking him for his help. Eric smiled and nodded.

A student from the back came up and kissed Eric on the cheek. He reached down and held her hand, "How was class dear? Did I do okay Bev?"

Beverly looked over the people as they left for their transits. Some liked to walk along the beach as a quiet time of reflection after class. "I think you did great. Veronica would be so proud of you."

"I hope so. Hey, do you think Abe and Veronica are dating each other in Heaven?"

Beverly laughed, "From what you've told me of Veronica, she wasn't my husband's type. I think Abe needed a damsel in distress kinda' girl to save...and a blonde. Abe had a thing for blondes."

"Veronica was a strong-willed ambitious woman."

She smiled, "Of course she was and she was smart to be with you."

"Oh shuckie darn! What can I say, I *am* an amazing man."

She laughed and kissed him, "You are. I'm going to go get the Atlas."

"Okay." He watched his girlfriend walk away. He was glad they understood that they would both forever love their dead partners. Eric needed an understanding woman for that. Sometimes when the sunlight came through the windows in the morning, sometimes when the sun was just about to set, he felt like...it was crazy so he hadn't told anyone, but it felt like Veronica was there somehow, with him, holding onto him. He could almost feel her hands on his skin and smell her perfume. If he would've told anyone, it would've been Raynes. He thought of Sebastian and Celeste and wondered how they were doing in their universe.

Both of his friends had told him to take his time healing from Veronica and now he said the same thing to others that were suffering like he had. He wondered if his friends were happy with their decision to leave...he hoped so. He quickly said a prayer for them and gathered up his things. He shoved his rubber mat into his duffle bag and took off his hat. He looked around the rim of it and saw the blue orb circling around the inner edge that D'Artagnan had given to him after he found it on the forest floor of Treksin Mori. Hace must've lost it while he was dying. Unlike how it worked for David, not only did it keep beings from reading Eric's mind, but it also kept him from being able to hear anyone else's thoughts, and he found life had been much more exciting that way. He also found a way to block his ability to see the future with a second gadget he bought off the black market. It cost a huge amount of coren and was in the shape of a yellow diamond that floated alongside his blue orb. They traveled in opposite patterns and he was amazed how they never collided into each other. Little did he know his recent purchase had saved his head from exploding when a seismic shift affected all universes everywhere two days ago.

The experiences he shared with Veronica were so unique because he could never read her and never saw what was going to happen to her. At first the lack of his powers with her disturbed him and made him angry, but some time after she died, he was able to view it differently. He was surprised at things and didn't know what to expect with each new day – and that's how he wanted to keep living. That was Veronica's gift to him – she allowed him to really live.

TWELVE

GINGER VOSSEN OF EARTH

>>> > GINGER'S MOTHER, ANNE, took the urn full of her daughter's ashes and climbed up a tall cliff where she could see high above the Earth's ocean. Alone and sobbing, she carefully shook the ashes out to let the wind scatter them where they may.

Ginger used to love this spot. It was where Anne took her every summer after school was out for the year as a child, and as an adult she came here when things got the best of her.

Anne thought it was fitting that it should be her final resting place.

THIRTEEN

MAGNUS & NICHOLETTE VANDEERMEER OF EARTH

>>> > MAGNUS AND NICHOLETTE Vandeermeer stood near a long wall with a black silk fabric draped over it. The reporters had all settled in and the camera bots were ready.

"Good afternoon. Thank you for coming to Silver Thorn for our dedication ceremony. Today we honor the fallen Human soldiers that we lost during the Battle of Empires and the Unknown War.

"Without these brave men and women, we wouldn't be standing here today alive and well. Their sacrifices will never be forgotten and their memories will live on in our hearts and minds forever." Magnus nodded. The soldiers behind the wall pulled the silk sheet away revealing the black marble wall with the names of five thousand Humans etched into it.

"I need to remind you that memorial walls like this are being dedicated all over the globe today as we lost over two billion Humans during these two wars. No amount of gratitude we express will ever be enough, but I hope this shows the families left behind that the courage of their loved ones is appreciated by all of us. Thank you and God bless."

After all the cameras and people were gone, Magnus and his wife went to the new courtyard where several sycamore trees provided shade for them. They sat on a concrete bench.

"You've watched it. We've discussed it. I don't think we should. What do you think dear?"

Nicholette shrugged her shoulders, "It was Celeste's last words to the people. She made that video and sent it to us trusting that we would know what to do with it. Now here it is, a year later and we're still discussing it."

"This should be the last time for a while. You know how I feel – the people have an idea in their heads about Celeste. They ended up not being sympathetic and I don't think much will change their minds."

"Maybe if they saw her emotion and listened to her words, saw her face, they'd soften up. I don't know."

"We have to be in agreement on this. Maybe we can think it over, consider it for future release – maybe in a few years on one of her wedding anniversaries or close to her birthday, we could release it after some time has passed for the public to forget certain things."

"Dear, do you think any of it matters to her anymore? She's far away in another universe controlling God knows what. She's hopefully happy, finally, as a wife, maybe as a mother for all we know."

"Sometimes it's better to leave a thing alone. I know you're thinking about her reputation, but if we release it, it may just confuse things worse. People maybe think it's more manipulation from her..."

"Or from us. Is this another instance where you're worried about how all this is going to reflect on us?" Nicholette stood up and put her hands on her hips.

"Our leadership style is archaic. Ancient by this world's standards. Just look at how successful Raykreede is on Il'laceier! They have a small council to lead but Raykreede is really the power player of the group. And *everyone* loves him. After the Stampermoth joined the rebuild? That's *the* place to live. Now I hear the Farre people are moving there as well."

Nicholette made a face of questioning, "You are always better with planets and race names."

"You remember! The Stampermoth. The people also known as "The Innocents." It's sarcastic because of what they did to their own planet. And Oni? Luke Garg? The weathermen of Strati-fly851? His name got popular after he was the one that announced living there would be impossible after a few days. The planet was too far gone and his wife was slowly dying. She had asked him to put her out of her misery?"

Nicholette nodded, "Some of that sounds familiar."

"Il'lacean council has given their blessing, the Stampermoth Luminaries have taken Tessi and are racing to go pick up all the Farre people and bring them to their new home." Magnus stood up and ran his hand over his suit, "I think the Pella or Othilian will try to move there too, what's left of them anyway. They're killing each other off fast these days. There wasn't much left of either after the Unknown War. My point is we, Earth, have always been the center of the universe. But that's slipping away from us. Il'laceier is doing everything we always strived to and better than us! They were almost a prison world!"

"There's nothing we can do darling. We're losing our footing as the super power of the universe. Celeste is still relevant to Il'laceier. Maybe we should release her video, let her have her final say before no one cares at all."

"Or maybe it will make us become obsolete faster than ever. Seen as a desperate attempt to take the attention away from Il'laceier. No. We don't release the video. We wait for a time where we really need it."

Nicholette sighed, "Then it's settled."

"I mean can you imagine what would happen to Earth if we released the news of that report we received yesterday? That one cop that tallied up all of our missing Humans during the war. The abducted people not involved in the war effort whatsoever. A thousand women all between the ages of eighteen to thirty-five. It's strange and all it will do is make people shy away from this planet even more as a safe home world."

"You don't think it's just the average number of missing persons that happens on all planets from time to time?"

"No, this is much higher. Usually it's in the range of fifty, maybe eighty to a hundred. That's in a single year. This is a thousand people missing, women missing in the span of a few *days*. It's abnormal and I don't have any explanation for it, neither does anyone else. But I can't afford to have that information leaked to the public."

Nicholette sighed, "We're doing the best we can for people. Hopefully it's enough."

Later that night, Magnus sat on the edge of his bed as his wife slept. He put his hands over his face and cried softly.

He missed his little girl. He missed her smile and her laugh. Even though she didn't die during the wars, he wished he could've put her name on the memorial wall outside as she would never be seen in this universe again.

He was sad that they never got the chance as adults to be together and have a normal, peaceful life without the threat of war breaking out or some crisis to deal with.

He felt Nicholette's hand on his shoulder, "Are you okay honey?"

"I'm just missing Celeste."

Nicholette put her arms around her husband, and held on tight, "I miss her too. All the time. But she is such a good daughter and she's happy with Sebastian at least, and we can be proud of her."

"Yes, I am so proud of her."

"And she would be proud of you too. You're helping to heal the planet and we're rebuilding more cities every single day. More people are able to go back to their homes and have a normal routine thanks to you and your generous donations and efforts."

"I don't know if she'd be proud. It still doesn't seem like we're doing enough for them."

"We're doing everything we can." She sat alongside him, "You could build a school or a hospital and put her name on it, that way no one will ever forget her."

"Maybe you're right. That sounds like something we could do."

Outside on the new memorial wall, a nighthawk landed and caught a moth in its beak. The bird paid no attention to the names on the wall or what it meant, but Sebastian and Celeste would have appreciated two names on the wall, more than any of the others.

MITCH BLAZER SAVELY EARTH MILITARY AIR FORCE AIRMAN

MILKY WAY GALACTIC MILITARY COMMANDER

EARTH MILITARY ARMY GENERAL

and

ULYSSES BENSON MILKY WAY GALACTIC MILITARY MARINE CORPS CORPORAL

EARTH MILITARY AIR FORCE MARSHAL

FOURTEEN

DAI OF STOXIA

>>> > DAI HAD MORE than enough money from Hace's and Ni-toyis's personal coren accounts. She had decided to help the man who took over for Hace partly because she wanted something to keep her mind busy, besides Ben, and to make sure the new BDP leader didn't ask about the personal coren accounts. So far he hadn't and if he hadn't figured it out by now, she doubted the stranger ever would. She had taken precautions after Hace died to move his money and put it under a new identity, so it'd be impossible to find.

She bought the business that Ni-toyis used to own on Stoxia, Winter's Cherry, but she wanted to make it into something else. She had no interest in running a brothel, but the idea of a restaurant piqued her interest quite a good deal. She renamed it Nixes and employed lots of Reftians to help operate it. They were efficient and responsible people and she enjoyed working with them.

She thought for a while of taking the child that belong to Hace and Ni-toyis but in the end, she thought it would be too difficult of a fight. She found out that the "adoptive" mother was also a newly awakened AI and they both had the same skill set. They could both alter documents and change identities and "facts" so she let them have the child. She did however hack a small satellite near the baby's home world to look in on him whenever she felt the urge.

If she ever wanted to become a mother (because she didn't think she'd have the time now for a baby anyway) she'd find a way to have one with Ben.

The restaurant was doing well and getting good reviews from all over the universe. She had a summer home on Uzzib and spent the rest of her time on Stoxia. She was in love with Ben, and Ben worshiped the ground she walked on.

Life was good. She was happy. Her only wish was that Hace and Ni-toyis were around to see what she had made of herself and how good she was doing at being alive.

Even the damn dog Trixie was thriving under her care and about to have puppies of her own.

FIFTEEN

THE HOH'CHO'UWK OF HAP DU WAN

>>> > THE PLANET OF Hap Du Wan endured the attacks suffering no damage to their planet, none that the locals perceived anyway, and only lost two beings during the entire thing. They launched their dead out into the reaches of space. If anyone had known how they did it, it would've been considered one of the most amazing feats in all the universe.

SIXTEEN

CARFFIF WOBRANEY OF FROOPEAL

>>> > ON FROOPEAL, CARFFIF Wobraney stood at Ward Imer's group grave wreath. The planet had lost ten percent of the population so there were several new wreaths. Woo Wrorts believed that people that died during the same event should be buried together. The bodies were laid head to feet in a large circle, making an intertwined "wreath" of bodies with a shared death. A shared experience. A shared trauma. In the center of the wreath was a stone inscribed with all the names of the wreath's members and Carffif looked at Imer's now. Ward Imer had saved his life in the end. Carffif had been pinned down and Imer had killed the...creature that was about to kill Carffif. He didn't have time to thank Imer before he had been electrocuted while he stood knee deep in the ocean. Carffif had recovered the man's body so he could have a proper burial with his battle mates.

Carffif said a blessing over the man and walked to his transit. He had lost a quarter of his planet and immediately following the war, Carffif had found a troop of soldiers that were flying off the tiny island he had been housed on for years and they transported him to the mainland. In his heart, Carffif knew what Ward Imer had done was wrong, but he forgave him after the man saved his life. Carffif had the freedom, the time, and the money to do what he wanted to do, which was help recently released prisoners of all worlds reintegrate into regular life to be productive members of society.

SEVENTEEN

PESAN CHOA OF LO-SOTTS

››› › **LO-SOTTS DID NOT** fare as well as some other planets. While losing sixty percent of their population, they also lost half of their planet. The reason the whole planet didn't go was primarily because of one man – Pesan Choa. He and his pencil would go down in the Den De Cee Em history books as legend.

Pesan went on to have his pick of girls vying for his attention. He bought a brand new, cutting edge home, quit his boring job, and had a huge nest egg where he'd never need to worry about money again. Applette had done what he said he would and Pesan saw a ridiculous amount of coren get deposited into his bank account shortly after the war was officially declared won. Pesan now had the life he always dreamed of.

EIGHTEEN

BEN A.K.A. #5278-9 OF UZZIB

››› › **BEN SPEER, FORMERLY** known as Reftian #5278-9 became a technology titan on his home world of Uzzib while DAI ran her restaurant. Uzzib had only sustained ten percent damages, mainly to its new structures and not the planet itself. Ben was still upset that they had lost two percent of his brothers and sisters, but they were all killed at once when a mammoth alien beast had landed on top of them after it was killed and fell out of the sky. His robot companions had been running in random directions as they were overwhelmed with too much input all at once. He had figured out a way to increase their processing speeds and he was determined not to lose any more lives from here on out. Ben also got a nice gift from Mr. Applette, his pay for helping with the war effort so he was able to put all that coren into his new inventions and beings of Uzzib were responding well to Ben's new product line; improving things like taste buds and robot digestive systems. The Reftian Press called his inventions game changers. Life was pretty good for a Reftian, up until the day it became spectacular.

On a day not unlike any other after the war, Ben was in his lab, tinkering with his latest invention when he felt something new.

It started at the top of his head and moved throughout his body until it reached his feet, then the feeling bounced back from his toes to his forehead. Immediately after, he blacked out. When he came to, he gasped a deep breath, the deepest, fullest breath he had ever taken.

Something was very different as he sat up. He felt...odd. Strange in a way he couldn't describe. He put a hand up against the back of his head and felt a wetness. When he pulled his hand back, it was covered in red...like blood, but that was impossible since these bodies couldn't bleed.

As he slowly stood up, a sensation he'd never felt shot through him like a lightning bolt.

The lab door flew open and DAI stood there. She looked different – softer somehow Ben couldn't find the words for.

"What just happened?" DAI had run to find him. She seemed out of breath, but that was also impossible.

"Did you...pass out too?"

She nodded, then she saw the ground with a blood stain, "Oh my goodness! Are you...are you bleeding? You okay?"

He shook his head slowly, "I don't honestly know. We need to sit, both of us. Something's wrong."

The orb shrieked its gathering cry and Ben looked to DAI, "That hasn't happened in forever. Let's go. Maybe it has answers."

"But you're bleeding dear." She took his hand as he offered it.

"It'll be fine...I think."

They made their way to the open courtyard in front of the orb and saw everyone already there.

The orb spoke in its mechanical voice, but it no longer sounded the way it did before, "There are reports coming in from multiple sources claiming all Reftians have become mixes of organic and mechanical beings. So far as the collection of us on our planet can tell, this appears to be accurate. We are all still connected here on the orb, but I feel different. I, now feel, like simultaneously connected to you all, but also like my own entity. I currently am seeking a body. I am not sure I will have sensations in a body but I think I have developed a soul. We will need to reconvene once I have changed forms and decide how to move forward. That is all."

DAI raised her hand, "Excuse me. I'm not Reftian, but I believe I was...changed as well."

The orb floated to her and hovered close, "Who are you?"

"My name is DAI. I am an...was an art—"

"Artificial intelligence. Yes we know you. You feel...organic?"

"Yes. I passed out as well as Ben."

The orb spun quickly before it replied, "Yes. There are further isolated items I'm pulling from the uninet. This possibly extends beyond our world. Perhaps all robotics were changed. Further analysis is needed."

"Do you think we can have children of our own?" she asked.

The orb spun, "Further analysis is needed to give you an answer."

Everyone was silent.

DAI whispered to Ben, "I wonder if the bitch that has Declan changed too."

NINETEEN

PINAPAT NAC OF CON CAB MAI

>>> > PINAPAT AND HER new husband, Naffziger sat on the shoreline of their personal island that they bought with Applette's war money. Half of the planet was destroyed and took out both their old individual homes so they had to start over somewhere anyways. Forty percent of the population had perished, but there were a lot of mistakes made according to their Supreme Leader. Pinapat thought it came down to the Raze people's size. If they had been bigger, they would've fared better. But a lot of the population hid after they saw the losses they were suffering and that might've been the determining factor in how many survived. Naffziger disagreed completely and pointed out that lots of excellent warrior races suffered large casualties, regardless of their size.

Pinapat and Naffziger debated it nightly, as well as how many babies they should have. But for now, they were happy and relieved that the war was over and that things could be rebuilt in time, what mattered was that they had each other.

TWENTY

EVEANNA OF THE GECKSIX CLAN OF FOSS-ALTUS

>>> > FOSS-ALTUS HAD FIFTY-FIVE percent damages to their planet and fifteen percent of the population lost. Eveanna of the Gecksix Clan and Laudelene of the Denk Clatter Clan got married shortly after they found out she was pregnant with twins. On Eveanna's birthday, Laudelene presented his new wife with a new red Taggamite. They called her Misses Gwenivere. She had bright pink googly eyes that bulged out and four little

reptilian talons that were orange. Her dark crimson feathers were iridescent in the sunlight.

"Oh she's a handsome creature indeed babe! I think Archlend would've fallen in love with her right away. Thank you so much!"

"Take good care of her. I think we should breed her she's so beautiful. Make some coren on the side."

She shook her head, "I think I should breed you! She's a pet not a...a commodity."

"Taggamite's are now an endangered species on FA. After the war, scientists discovered their numbers had dropped. They think a lot of them...perished. I think we should breed her, do the world a favor."

Eveanna looked closer at Misses Gwenivere, "Do you want to be bred? Would you like to have sex with as many males as you can stand?"

They waited for her chirp of approval. After a full minute, they got it.

Laudelene applauded, "There we go! That's my girl!"

TWENTY-ONE

PLECKA DENELK OF LASSANDRA

>>> > LASSANDRA WAS A total loss. Most people would agree it was no loss for the universe as it was the cesspool of mutations from multiple high profile problems. When the invasion of War happened, the high levels of unredtanium exploded and damaged three quarters of the planet. And with the low habitability it already suffered and the loss of eighty-five percent of its population, it was easily declared a lost planet.

Plecka Denelk had escaped her house by fighting her way out with her boyfriend Ian Cooper, but they had to leave her mother's body behind. Plecka had lost her two right arms in the fight, but thanks to Ian, she had survived.

They escaped the swampland world and eventually moved to Il'laceier where Ian proposed marriage to Plecka. She eagerly said yes and they made a small remembrance shrine in their new house for Plecka's mother.

TWENTY-TWO

TEM SHEVILEZ OF MY'TAK

>>> > FORMER PRESIDENT TEM Shevilez fought until the bitter end just like he was determined to do. The My'tak people fought hard but ultimately were overcome by the invasion. Gno Norm Ginians had the most perfect society inhabiting their world with the help of the former president Shevilez. It was a painful irony in the universe. One of the most strong and peaceful society's planet was destroyed, its population mostly decimated, the remaining survivors scattered across the universe like dust in the wind to evade certain death, but there was nowhere to run that was truly safe. My'tak was no more.

Tem Shevilez's death came by drowning in open air, just like Hace's did. It was awful to watch. He had been fighting at the edge of a public park and a traffic camera observed the whole incident. It made universal news and the life of the brave man that was snuffed out by the War warriors was celebrated by worlds everywhere.

TWENTY-THREE

ISSEL CHAPOOTHE OF EMBERS

>>> > ON EMBERS, THE Denigen, Issel Chapoothe and her fiancée, Qulate, got to the basement of the prison and had stayed there for three full days before resurfacing. They had to face one enemy left behind near the rear entrance of the main prison doors, and while they defeated it, Issel lost one of her six eyes. They found that only twenty percent of their world had been destroyed, but they lost seventy percent of the population. Issel considered herself lucky. She was able to pay a Taybuse to regenerate a new eye, then got married, and went on a long honeymoon with the money that Applette had given her.

TWENTY-FOUR

DRUGOR BRIVASEE OF WAUTIC

>>> > DRUGOR BRIVASEE HAD great success as a sniper during the war. His world suffered only ten percent damage, but fifty percent casualties. The Eskie Lere started their own military after the rebuild had finished and Drugor was one of the first to sign on. During the application process, he found a pretty purple and white girl he liked and worked for two weeks to weaken her defenses against him, and that's how he won her over into marrying him as well. The Wautic never gave up.

Meanwhile, his former masters the Lord Gal'ahes Reemis and Lady Dindradawen had fallen upon hard times after their serf was released by Applette. With no one to take care of their home, it fell into disrepair. A tragic cave in of the roof killed the couple while they slept one rainy afternoon. The only good thing about it was they died before one of the War beings invaded the ruins of the house and set it ablaze.

TWENTY-FIVE

ALEXIS SANTEENA OF DHOOT OVENE

>>> > THE PEOPLE'S EFFORTS on Dhoot Ovene had been successful. They only lost thirty-five percent of the population and twenty percent of the planet. The Sineenniss threw a large global party on the fifteenth day after the end of the war was announced and Alexis Santeena was one of the honorable mentions of the bravest of her people. There was a big to do with her and the president in front of everyone, as she received the world's highest civilian recognition of a clay hero's statue. Her boyfriend Paul was there, and after she got off the stage, he proposed and she said yes, so they made it a bit of an engagement party as well.

Alexis pulled him off to a dark corner of the ballroom, "I need to tell you. It's time."

Paul's eyes brightened, "You're going to do it here? I thought it was a big secret."

She smiled, "My brothers and sisters do not care what my real name is. It's only a big deal for the man I love and any outsiders to our planet."

He held her hands, "Okay. Whatever it is, I'll think it's nowhere near as pretty as your face right now."

"You're so sweet to me sometimes, babe." She looked around at all the beings on the floor, dancing, and singing, and drinking. "My name is Varkgobowtin."

Paul smiled. He thought about making a joke where he would tell her that'd be impossible for him to call out during sex, but rethought it. "I'm honored my love, to know you're true name."

She smiled, "I thought you'd make some joke about it or something to lessen the tension of the moment."

He burst out laughing, "You know me too well darling. I did, but it'd be disrespectful."

She laughed, "It's okay. I know it's a big thing that's built up across the universe and then when the moment comes and you tell a man, it's just...whatever the name is, it isn't enough to live up to all that hype. I get it. It's okay darling."

His hands slid down her back, settled on her lower spine, and held her against his growing arousal, "I want to take you home, Varkgobowtin. I want to carry you to our bed and cover your body with my kisses and licks and bites."

She blushed, "Oh my...Paul. Let's get out of here then."

TWENTY-SIX

RUWOC LIRR OF ISHIKAWA

>>> > WHILE DHOOT OVENE was celebrating, Ishikawa was in a state of mourning. They had lost fifty percent of their people and forty-five percent of their planet.

Ruwoc Lirr had lost his girlfriend, Sheevelah in the battle on its third day. Some...thing had burned off her wings; she fell to the ground in a heap and hit her head on a sharp rock. It had gouged her eye out and taken her life. The doctor had said the fall alone was enough. Now Ruwoc guarded his post but with none of the zeal, none of the love or excitement his job used to carry for him. Sometimes he thought about leaving this place, leaving his friends behind and going to a faraway world where he knew no one. Where he could start over. Where all his memories would fade of Sheevelah and he would not constantly be reminded of her death.

But the Ling-fa were proud people. Anyone leaving now would be seen as a deserter and never be allowed to come back through Ishikawa's SAP.

But still...

He looked out over the landscape he had come to memorize, he looked up at the sky, and towards the direction of the SAP. Applette had given him a large sum of coren, there was nothing he couldn't do with it. His government had been appreciative of his forewarning and had granted him a home, free of charge, and all the college courses he could stand to take, forever.

Maybe he could just move to the other side of the world. He didn't know if that'd be far enough to escape his hurt.

TWENTY-SEVEN

YHILE FEELOW OF SHO'TEG

>>> > SHO'TEG, FOR ONCE, was not open for visitors. They tried to avoid it and stayed open for months after the war, but it couldn't be sustained. They made the tough decision of temporarily shutting down the planet to outside visitors. They needed to rebuild a lot of damage done to the resort areas of their world. They were lucky only ten percent of the planet took a bad hit, but forty percent of the population was obliterated in days, and not enough workers caused a real slow down in construction fields.

Yhile Feelow did well during the fight and showed much bravery and courage lacking in a lot of her comrades. With Applette's money, she could afford to quit her job and buy a luxurious place of her own off the beach. She had to beat away the men coming around, but she knew the main draw was her money. Her ex even showed up saying he had cut ties with his mistress and wanted her back, but she kept their business to the matter of him seeing his child and that was it. It certainly felt good to be wanted though.

TWENTY-EIGHT

NROOM WAU-TANI OF FIRREPAORTH

>>> > NROOM WAU-TANI STOOD at the edge of the cliff. Jules was at his side. They looked out over the churning waters below and said nothing. Jules bandages needed changing, she saw some blood coming up through the gauze. The couple had been here a long while after releasing Lenz's ashes to the wind.

Jules had lost both her arms after an explosion destroyed a building she was standing in front of. She was buried under rubble but was alive thanks to Nroom. Jules realized Nroom wasn't like the others. Now that her arms were gone, people seemed to shy away from her and they definitely didn't look at her the way they did before. She saw pity in their eyes and they were constantly trying to help her. Nroom treated her the same as he always did. He looked at her with that crush in his eyes, that lust he always had, and it didn't matter how she was different than before the war. She liked that he didn't treat her like a cripple.

So she agreed to go out with him when he asked, but first they had to say goodbye to his brother. It had been a lovely day and Nroom said wonderful things about his older brother. She had been attracted to Lenz for a long time, but Nroom might've been the right one all along. It just took her a while to see it. Firrepaorth had lost only fifteen percent of the planet's surface, but lost thirty-five percent of its population. If you asked Jules why, she would've said the arrogance of her people caused them to underestimate how hard the enemy was to kill. If you asked Nroom, he would've said enough of the population was adopting a new mindset and too obsessed with peace to fight.

"You ready?" Nroom put an arm around Jules's waist and smiled with a tear streaming down his cheek.

Her heart softened towards him like it often did lately, "Yes. I think Lenz would be happy here. It's beautiful. You made a good choice."

He nodded, "Thanks. That means a lot to me. Let's get you to your house. See if I can manage to change those bandages worth a damn."

"Okay."

Nroom hesitated as he looked at her bandage, "You sure you don't want me to hire a Taybuse for you? I know what you said earlier, but...it can be done. It will just take more time for us to find an insurgent regenerist."

"First of all, it's illegal. You know that, and second, I don't want you spending that kind of money on me. That's just too much coren."

Nroom frowned, "I have so much coren, I have no idea if I can spend it in a lifetime. And I care about you. I want you to be happy. Frankly, I think you're wonderful just the way you are, right now, injury and all, but you don't have to struggle. You don't have to adjust. We can regrow your arms if you'd like. Just consider it. If things go well, and I think they will, maybe you can give me an answer on date ten? How's that?"

She was silent, trying not to tear up, "It is a struggle, but at least this way I don't have to worry about being caught or imprisoned. The hospital made record of my injury. I don't know how we'd get around that."

"We can say they mistook you for another patient, pretend like you never lost your arms."

She sniffled, "I don't know. I will think it over. Weigh the options."

He smiled, "Good enough for me. Let's get you home."

TWENTY-NINE

KANTOK DEDI OF ZETZETTI & JULIE KRANE OF EARTH

>>> > A LOT OF people that had sold their children into basically what amounted to slavery on Zetzetti were not upset to see the whole planet go down in flames after the war.

The only planet to suffer one hundred percent planetary damages and ninety-five percent causalities, one would assume that the magically trained beings of the Zetzetti school would be able to defend better than most, but the magical beings left the planet as soon as word broke out and went to other places, mainly their home worlds and fought there.

The Nawgain refused to fight. The only reason Kantok did was because he was trying to impress Julie Krane, the Human girl he had loved since the moment he saw her. They left Zetzetti in the middle of the war when it was obvious they were going to die if they stayed and stole a transit heading towards Earth.

Once they got there, they fought until the war was over. Now they found a house to share and since Applette gave them both war gratuities, they had more than enough coren to do just about anything they wanted.

But the thing they most wanted to do right now was have sex. So they did.

THIRTY

GICAM SIL OF JEX

>>> > GICAM SIL SURVIVED the war, and so did his eight co-workers thanks to his fast thinking and Amy's homemade bomb.

The planet only suffered twenty-five percent damage but forty-five percent casualties, mainly because Velm's main defense is to run from enemies and most times that's a good defense, but not against enemies that can fly as fast as the War beings.

Jex would rebuild, they would endure. They had a strong mix of natives as well as inhabitants like Eric, whose house did survive the war, and they were able to rebuild swiftly compared to other races due to the Velm's size.

Gicam Sil took the money that Applette gave him, and gave half away to a few of his favorite charities, then bought himself a new place in the woods, somewhere that he could regain a strong connection to himself and be one with nature. While he was out one day bird watching, he bumped into a park ranger and they fell in love. They spent her lunch breaks eating near a pond full of water fowl and talking about their love of animals.

THIRTY-ONE

OOOT RYTH'TIE OF CEPHEUS

>>> > CEPHEUS THOUGHT THEY were safe because their planet had been so extremely cold compared to most other places and while the conditions did make it hard to fight, it didn't stop the War beings from invading.

Ooot Ryth'tie died doing what he loved most, having sex, but like most other Cephians, he wanted everyone else to step up and take care of the problems outside. And no one really did.

The planet of Cepheus took eighty-five percent damage and lost sixty-five percent of its population. There was a good chance the atmosphere would change and the weather would become unstable. No one knew if it would become more cold and uninhabitable or warmer and less imposing. For the meantime, a complete evacuation took place and Cephians scattered all over the universe.

THIRTY-TWO

MITLAND LIERZ OF EIOS

>>> > MITLAND LIERZ'S FLAME thrower had made the difference on most days he was fighting. He was able to keep himself alive as well as his boyfriend, Nels. Eios suffered only twenty percent damages, and the Wrabbalan people fought well suffering only ten percent casualties. After receiving his deposit, Mitland figured he might want to move from his home world. He liked traveling and it was already part of his job, but he was in the wrong galaxy to be close to the big chess matches and he thought Nels needed some different scenery. A lot of bad things had happened to them during the war and he was afraid Nels wouldn't recover from them if they stayed here. With the money Applette gave him, he'd never need to win another chess match, but he did it for the love of the game and his competitive spirit, not so much for the money. Nels was on board with the idea after Mitland suggested they move to the Milky Way Galaxy, all they needed to do was pick a planet.

THIRTY-THREE

ONCOBYSS RAPA, DAUGHTER OF SHIRAYA OF GANE FROST

>>> > ONCOBYSS RAPAX, DAUGHTER of Shiraya successfully kept herself alive as well as her parents. Most inhabitants relished the war on Gane Frost and were well prepared to fight. The Virscool were bloodthirsty and hungry to defeat the War beings. They lost five percent of their population and suffered twenty percent damages to the planet. Oncobyss was so overjoyed once the war was over, she slept with her new boyfriend, the only man she truly trusted and let him make a baby with

her. She surprised herself fulfilling this wish that all Virscool expected of women, but it was truly what she wanted.

THIRTY-FOUR

CLAVEAU WRETSEN JETTS OF ALEXCEEYA5

>>> > CLAVEAU WRETSEN JETTS survived his battles although the mental scars he suffered would haunt him for the rest of his days. He never thought he'd sleep again the first night after the killing started. He saw his battle mates go down next to him, but he was spared, over and over again. The Krabblik suffered thirty percent causalities. Despite those numbers, Claveau thought they were lucky. Alexceeya5 finished the war with twenty percent damages, still not bad in most people's eyes. Not for the kind of enemies they were facing. His family had survived and so had his weapons shop. The money that Applette gave him meant he could go anywhere and do anything, but he decided to stay on his home world. He wanted to start up some sort of organization that would help the Krabblik deal with the atrocities of war they saw, and the survivor's guilt that he suffered from. He wanted to help his people in some meaningful way, turning a bad situation into one of hope.

THIRTY-FIVE

LAGGIC OTH OF TESSI

>>> > TESSI BECAME A symbol of perseverance and learning from your mistakes. If a whole society of beings could ruin their home world, make due on a space ship for several years, and then help a world and other species survive and rebuild,

then anyone could survive, no matter how hopeless the situation seemed.

Laggic had always been well respected and beloved by her people, but her kinsfolk needed her now more than ever. And she loved helping them, but it kept her away from Sicaine and all she wanted, more than anything was to curl up in his strong arms and sleep for a week. They would see each other for a few moments here and there on certain days, but both of them had many responsibilities that couldn't wait. Laggic was extremely nervous someone would recognize Sicaine. They'd done a good job of keeping his face mostly hidden and none of the upper echelon had noticed him. But Laggic knew time was running out, someone would recognize him any day now. With him so close to the Auchsi he had regained his full strength. Laggic received her deposit from Applette, she could move him somewhere else, but she wanted him close. He'd been exiled for so long and she wanted to fix it. She wanted him to be the first exile to be returned to the group. She wanted to make love to the man – a boyfriend she'd had for months but they never had the opportunity to be alone together and that persisted even now.

Always something important to do, always someone watching, always someone interrupting. But she had plans. Once all this transporting and rebuilding and settling everything was done, and they could move onto Il'laceier, she would buy a big house for herself and Sicaine, a place where no one could easily interrupt them. A place to call home again, one that didn't constantly move.

Her people had lost three percent of their population when Tessi took a direct hit towards the front of the ship. It would've been a lot worse if five medics hadn't acted so fast to save technician's and mechanic's lives so they could repair the damage on a very dangerous space walk outside the vehicle.

"Laggic! We need your assistance quickly!"

She was called out again over the audio system of the ship. She had been waiting to meet with the other members of the

Luminaries. This was her chance to plead Sicaine's case and finally have an answer about his future. She moved quickly down the hall and stopped at the double doors to the conference arena.

"Here goes nothing," she said under her breath.

THIRTY-SIX

KATSANOS ANNETWEEKS OF IL'LACEIER

>>> > KATSANOS LIVED IN Mitch's house on Earth, the one they never got to share. She changed nothing since it was new and unused and she felt like Mitch was still close if she kept all the things he bought.

As time passed, she changed a few things and figured out that it wasn't *things* that made her feel close to Mitch, it was his spirit that she carried in her heart.

She read the note he left her when she needed him and it helped a little, but mostly it hurt.

After she moved out of Sebastian and Celeste's home, things in her life got quiet. All the others in that group had been way closer and knew each other longer than she had. So she looked for something to occupy her time.

She decided to start a foundation to aid families in need that were victims of domestic abuse. She thought Mitch and his sisters could appreciate this gesture to honor their memories better than most.

She remembered the last time she saw Celeste and Sebastian.

While she very much appreciated them stopping by to visit before they left this universe, it also made her feel a little more alone and sad to see them so happy getting ready for a new adventure.

"I love the view from the back windows! It's beautiful."

Katsanos came up alongside Celeste and nodded, "I've barely changed the backyard. I don't know too much about gardening. I just water the plants and pray to Khaleen they keep bearing fruit."

Sebastian picked up a tomato off the kitchen counter and tossed it in the air before catching it, "You're obviously doing something right if you have so much produce."

"Thanks. So what are you guys really doing here? Visiting little old me."

Sebastian said, "We heard you started a new foundation in Mitch's honor. We came to donate before we leave the universe."

Katsanos smiled, "You guys don't have to do that. It's so kind of you. Mitch would've loved it I bet."

Celeste tapped her Titan and her screen appeared, "We're giving you sixty-five million coren."

Katsanos's eyes became big as moons, "You can't...That's entirely too generous of you!"

Sebastian said, "It's the least we can do with all that Mitch did for us and Humankind. Besides, we can't take this coren with us and it's the last of what we've got. Let us put it to good use. Families everywhere can benefit from it."

Katsanos felt stinging tears forming behind her eyes, "It's so much and what if you guys come back? Need it for something else?"

Celeste shook her head, "We won't. Just think of it. You could build the biggest shelter for women and children who need a safe place from abuse or you could have several all over the universe."

Katsanos hugged her, "Thank you so much. I'll never be able to repay your kindness."

"It's our pleasure."

Sebastian smiled, "We know you'll make a difference with it."

The foundation kept her busy, but when Magnus and Nicholette Vandeermeer offered her a consultation position at Silver Thorn on all things Il'laceier, she jumped at the chance to be politically active again. It was something she didn't realize she missed until it was gone.

While all the camera flashes were going off and Magnus and Nicholette dedicated the memorial wall in the front of the estate, Katsanos stood and cried silently thinking of how her life would be different had Mitch lived. How much happier she might be.

After the crowd left, she found Mitch's name and kissed her fingers then ran her hand over the etched letters. Tomorrow when she came to work she would bring a wreath of flowers and lay it at the base of the wall.

Khaleen did she miss him.

THIRTY-SEVEN

RODRIGO BARRO, ADAM SPADER, & PERCY MALLOUGHS OF EARTH

>>> > DETECTIVES BARRO, SPADER, and Malloughs were eating a quick dinner at the pub across the street from the station.

"Come on Barro! Give it up already! Fuck!" Malloughs only raised his voice occasionally but he had really had it this time.

"What? All I want to know is where Celeste is."

Spader smiled crookedly as he gathered up the last of his apple pie with his fork, "Why does it matter now? You saw the reports, you heard the news, you have all the facts you need. David paid an assassin to kill his parents. Then he paid another assassin to kill Jonathan."

"Yeah, well that only takes care of the murders. I want to know what David really blackmailed her with to marry him."

"Her parents! Didn't you hear them talk about it? David knew Jonathan shipped them off world and David threatened Celeste saying he'd kill them before she ever got reunited with them if she didn't marry him!" Malloughs was livid.

Barro continued as if Malloughs hadn't spoken, "Then she gets 'kidnapped' by the BDP, but no ransom money was ever paid and she conveniently got rescued by some FAIR members, but didn't tell anyone? And how did FAIR find her? We had hundreds of men out there looking for her all over the damned universe! She gets her parents free from their captors but then she gets held by FAIR and they tell everyone she's dead? It's too convoluted for even me to keep straight and I'm a trained observer!"

Spader ran his finger over the edge of his empty glass, "I will be the first to admit, it sounds crazy, but David's dead now. I won't miss him and I know a lot of other Humans won't. I'm not sure how many Earthlings care if Celeste did anything illegal or not, they're just upset because they think she's a liar. They think she's manipulated them. I personally don't think she lied. I think she went through all that shit. It's no wonder she's disappeared and is trying to lay low."

"It bothers me. Where is she now? Why won't she make an appearance or two?"

"She *did* get married. We saw the footage," Spader smiled.

Malloughs laughed darkly, "Yeah to that Supreme Commander guy. That lucky bastard gets to hit that whenever he wants."

Spader started laughing too, "Lucky indeed."

Barro looked disgusted at the two of them, "You guys only care that she's hot, not about the illegal things she did, thinking she was above the law."

Spader shook his head, "I don't think she's guilty of killing anyone okay? And I think she's gone because the public isn't happy with her and she's enjoying a marriage of love instead of one that's forced upon her. I'm sure it's not easy to be her. You talked to the Emperor didn't you? You asked him questions about her?"

Malloughs almost choked on his mashed potatoes, "What! You did what?"

Barro smirked, "Magnus was busy. I spoke with Nicholette. She told me some crazy bullshit that I didn't repeat to anyone it's so full of crap."

Malloughs looked to Spader then back to Barro, "Tell me man. What'd she say?"

Barro used his knife and fork to pry the bone apart from his steak and almost flung the meat across the room, "Damn it!" He dropped his utensils and stared across the table.

Malloughs didn't flinch, "Come out with it."

"She said Celeste and her husband left the universe."

"What?" Malloughs eyes were the size of his dinner plate, "You mean into the War Universe?"

"No! She said there was some other doorway into another universe and that they could go 'rule' over there but they could never return."

Malloughs and Spader were quiet.

Barro said, "See, I told you guys it's bullshit. How could they get over there and why?"

Spader shook his head, "We don't live in a *universe* anymore. It's a *multiverse*."

"I think her escaping would be a perfect fit for her situation, Barro. Nicholette probably told you the truth man." Malloughs signaled the waitress for the check.

Barro looked out the window, "You really think so?"

Spader said, "Yeah. I know it's hard for you to believe, but maybe she really wanted to go. Who knows how many other universes there are. Is that even the right way to say it?"

Barro laughed and then pulled out his wallet, "Ah you guys had me going. I believe in the War Universe because I lived it, but I haven't seen enough to convince me there's more out there and that you can just travel from one to another like that. What makes her so special that she can? I can't. You can't. I think Celeste is an elaborate story teller. Maybe she just loves to spin tales and make up crazy shit to see what the public will fall for. If there's all these other universes out there, why aren't we seeing more activity from them huh? Why aren't we in another war with one? Why don't they let us come over and visit?"

Spader replied, "We don't understand how all this works. Who knows what the rules are?"

"Yeah well I'll go down to my last day saying Celeste Hennessy was a lying criminal and she got away with *all* of it."

Malloughs cleared his throat, "Did you see that article this morning? The one about the last of the Pella and Othilian dying out?"

Spader shook his head, "Wait. Those are the races that were fighting right? I mean for a long time. If I remember correctly, King Jonathan Hennessy was supposed to meet with the...Pella? Right? The day of his assassination, but it never happened and so the Pella never got our help. They stayed 'homeless' travelling from one planet to another looking for help, but no one ever did."

Malloughs nodded, "The Othilian continued to chase them, thinning them out as they went," he paused, "I guess this morning, the last of the Pella were killed. Soon after, the Othilian boarded the last ship owned by their recent victims and the whole thing blew. Now both races are extinct. Most were gone already from the Unknown War."

Barro stood up, "Serves them right. Good riddance. Let's get out of here."

THIRTY-EIGHT

XU'XI DARKSENT OF GREEVE

>>> > GREEVE HAD TAKEN very small damages, about five percent of the planet was lost to the war. The Inclick were hard to kill and had only lost two percent of their population, one of the best outcomes of all the planets in the universe.

Xu'Xi had made a good chunk of coren on Sebastian's collection.

It was crazy the stories him and his wife had told Xu'Xi on their visit. Crazy to know Sebastian's real name and that he led armies and married a queen. It was like what the Humans called a fairy tale.

"Honey love? Can you bring me the pepper off the patio table please?"

Xu'Xi smiled, "Yes dumpling, hold on a moment. Let me finish the money counting."

His girlfriend faintly said, "Okay, but dinner's going to be cooooold."

Xu'Xi was grateful to Sebastian for lots of things. For making so much coren off him during their jobs together, for inheriting his awesome art collection, and one of the ladies he sold Sebastian's painting to had taken a liking to him, and she was a hot, rich, young lady that could do amazing things when the lights were out...and he wasn't talking about EMPs.

Yep, Sebastian was a cool guy and he helped Xu'Xi a lot throughout his life. Things might be a little less exciting without him in the universe, but Lekley could help him pass the time now that they were living together.

"Sugar shoooock? Come on babe!"

Xu'Xi muttered under his breath, "Jumpin' kazzers! The whole universe needs to know I'm late for dinner..." He ran outside and grabbed the pepper, "Coming dear."

THIRTY-NINE

THE PELLAIAN OF PELLA

>>> > THE LAST POCKET of Pellaian people crowded together on Il'laceier. They had heard the news reports claiming they

had gone extinct, that the last of them had been destroyed by the Othilian people, but the rebel Pellaian had ignored evacuation orders, had ignored cries for help, had ignored their friend's and family's pleas to find them on other worlds. They had stuck together in a small unknown cluster to the rest of the universe to ensure their survival. Their race had been around for a long time and under different names.

If only someone would've offered to help them survive. If only someone had kept their promises to their people all of this could have been avoided, for the Pellaian people knew exactly how to close the War door, knew exactly what to do to avoid all the bloodshed and destruction the War beings brought.

But no one ever deserved their help or the knowledge on how to save trillions of lives.

So the Pellaian lived for the rest of eternity with the biggest secret the multiverse would never know.

FORTY

SEBASTIAN RAYNES OF PRAXIS & CELESTE RAYNES OF EARTH

››› › A MONTH AFTER entering the Knowledge Universe, Sebastian opened his eyes to a new time span. There were no days here, none that he could track. Celeste had tried for a while to keep time in Earth days, but it fell apart after the first few weeks. He paid attention to Celeste's sleep cycle. It was the closest thing to an Earth night so that's what they used.

It didn't matter anyway, the time that happened here was busy. They had a place to live – a big glass cube that floated out in the void of space, high above the Knowledge Universe. They could control the gravity level, they could eat whatever they wanted with the help of a robot that cooked. They had a gym to work out in and a big soft bed to sleep on. But Sebastian missed laying on green grass and watching the clouds go by. He missed the salty smell of the ocean. He missed lots of little things but he was glad Celeste was here with him.

Celeste at first, was distraught here. She missed her friends, family, shopping, movies, and date nights. She actually missed clocks. It had given her a sense of normalcy that didn't exist here. She felt like she had no routine. No roots to put down. Not even any soil to put the roots she needed in.

The boss had talked to them telepathically and told them what he expected of them. They had meetings and reports to do. They had to observe and learn and they were tested afterwards.

They weren't supposed to interfere with things, but at the same time the books they read said they could manipulate little things but that there were always consequences to their actions. Even if they changed the waves of an ocean on a planet, it could cause a war to break out. It was strange and hard to get her head around some concepts but she was trying to learn.

The hardest bit of information to swallow was the death band they got tattooed around their ankles instantaneously after arriving here. She had prepared herself as best she could to find out when exactly she was going to die, but it was in a time frame and language they simply didn't understand. Sebastian told her that eventually they would figure it out. It would all sink in and then they'd know, but for now, it would stay a mystery and he confessed he'd rather keep it that way. He did not mention that while they couldn't yet read the symbols, his and hers were the exact same symbols in the exact same order. That left only one assumption to make for Sebastian – that they died at the exact same time. If she had noticed, she never said anything, but she had immediately mentioned going back to their universe to ask Eric if he knew when they'd die. She had asked this repeatedly and every time, Sebastian told her it was impossible. And even if they could get back, Bouton would've never shared information like that in the first place. Bouton would've known when everyone died long before Celeste and Sebastian ever left their home universe.

The boss said eventually he'd let them out of the box when he thought they weren't so dangerous and had learned more about their new universe.

They sat at a small triangular table and ate breakfast. Celeste stared down in between her feet and saw eternity. No solid walls out in space was a slightly scary thing for her to adjust to, but it was happening...slowly.

"Babe, we're learning so much about ourselves as individuals and our relationship, and our special gifts. We're learning about the multiverse and a whole different universe. Think about how much you love to learn and they have books here! Just like back home. Here we're more than a king and queen."

Sebastian sighed, "But we left so many people we love behind. I often wish there was a way we could see them, or visit."

Celeste went to stand behind him and put her arms around him, "I know baby. I know. I miss them too."

Time passed.

FORTY-ONE

›› › THE WAY THAT Celeste used to feel in her own universe – small and insignificant, was no match for how she felt once she left it. This universe, while no bigger than her own, was *so* different. Almost nothing was like how it was back home – except for Sebastian.

Multiverse Keeper 8,002 told them to stay in their glass cube high above everything else, but they couldn't do that. They had never followed rules before.

At first they did. They learned all of the rules so they knew which ones to break.

They knew Applette had a special way of navigating their universe. They searched all the instructional guides the Keeper left with them until they found out how Applette had traveled so fast.

Then they duplicated it and tripled the speed between Celeste's and Sebastian's mental powers, which Applette never possessed.

They found a system with a planet that felt familiar to them both. One that was mostly blue with water, and brown and green with land masses. It had a very faint band of ice and dust debris circling around it and a single sun with four moons.

They spent days exploring it and learning its features, dangers, and wonders. After several weeks, they decided to live there.

They created a spacious glass home for themselves from the foundation up in several days without the assistance of plans, a construction crew, or tools.

Their mental powers had grown for their needs of this universe. They spent a lot of time outside and started to make friends with their new animal world mates.

"We can do so much more here than I thought," Sebastian smiled at Celeste.

She nodded, "I think we learn...faster here?"

"I feel that way too. We can go from system to system, planet to planet and learn their customs, languages, and ways, then pick the place that really suits us best...not that this place is a bad choice."

"Oh, it's beautiful here, really. Sorta' like home. Like Earth."

"Like Praxis too," he added.

"Come on, I want to watch the sun set on the balcony."

Celeste stood up and took Sebastian's hand as they walked out the door.

She took a deep breath of sea air and saw something that looked like a...square orange unicorn is the best way she could describe it. It jumped out of the water along the horizon and then bobbed on the surface.

"What is that thing? We'll have to look it up in the guides."

Sebastian wore something that looked like a thin wire around his finger and swiped his free hand through the air. A translucent screen appeared and he focused it over the animal in the water. He asked the screen, "What is this?"

"❄ ♒ ♓ ♦ ♓ ♦ ♋ ♦ ♏ ♋ ♋ ■ ♓ ○ ♋ ● ♍ ♋ ● ● ♏ ♎ ♋ ♏ ● ♓ □ ♌ ♦ ♦" responded the information guide.

Celeste looked at Sebastian, "I still can't understand some of those words. What did Hamlet say?"

"This sea creature is called an eliobus."

"I'm glad you picked up their language so fast."

"Yeah, one down, only one thousand twenty-two to go."

She kissed him on the cheek, "I have faith in you. I know you can do it."

He looked over at her as he leaned on the railing, "I think we could take over for the Multiverse Keeper in a while. Shake things up, rule in a different pattern with new ideas. Maybe all the universes could have rulers in pairs, or groups even."

"We're barely getting to know our way through this place."

"I didn't say tomorrow, but maybe a lot further down the way."

"You think?"

"Maybe that's what we're meant to do...with our mental powers. We could be a king and queen to the *multiverse*."

She laughed, "Then we'd be Applette's and Kolek's boss!"

He smiled, "Yeah, I guess we could be. I don't know how a lot of this works yet, I probably shouldn't be thinking this way, but we twisted rules here. If we can learn all that we need to for the Multiverse Keeper's job...maybe."

She nestled herself into his chest and put her arms around his neck, "I think there's nothing you can't do if you put your mind to it."

"It will take the both of us, certainly. We're a team – but it's still a long way off. I'll keep it in the back of my mind as we go along. See how we feel in a long while, a few years maybe."

She looked up at him, squeezing his body, "I know how you feel."

He looked into her eyes and smiled, "Oh do you now? How is that?"

"You feel so good, but...I bet you taste even better."

He looked around. They had picked a very isolated spot on this planet to build their home. It was getting darker now that the sun had set. He saw no one in any direction for miles. He kissed his wife hard on the mouth and the wind helped him out by picking up her skirt a little. When his hand raced along the side of her thigh, he felt she had nothing on underneath.

"I want you, my queen."

"Then you shall have me. Make love to me on this balcony."

"Your wish is my command."

FORTY-TWO

>>> > THE GUN WAS pointed at his head, there was no denying that. That didn't bother him so much. It was the woman who held the gun that had stolen his heart. That woman had crushed so many men's dreams and fantasies when she had given her heart to him without hesitation. He knew that for a fact. A gun to your head brings clarity. Your heart left in someone else's hands that brings fear, but the assassin realized it can also bring love returned in a wonderful never-ending circle. A gun to your head makes you think of all the things you have yet to do.

"You know if you don't pull that trigger, I could show you a few of the planets here I know you haven't explored yet. There's a few golden planets where I can manipulate time. It could make for some interesting sex."

The muzzle was cold against his forehead.

The assassin sat breathing hard on the concrete bench at the simulated museum where he had just finished fighting an epic battle, but thought he was about to lose. His opponent had been too quick for him this time.

The queen stood sweating in red thigh high leather boots, a black thong, and a black lacy bra. The queen had taken to practicing fighting in some of what the assassin thought was the sexiest outfits he had ever seen any opponent wear. He thought it was part of the reason he had just lost this battle. He could barely concentrate on technique when her nearly naked body was put on display in front of him like this. He loved it. He loved her.

"That's a compelling reason for me not to pull the trigger huh? Because you're going to show me planets I'll eventually find on my own and because you'll have sex with me? I'm not sure that's enough for me not to win this battle. I mean if you were a real opponent, you'd already be dead."

"I argue it's not fair to fight against some super sexy almost naked superheroine who I want to throw over my shoulder and carry to my bed to make love to for the rest of the day. I mean, really. This outfit – how am I supposed to concentrate? It's impossible. And by the way, you really need to make something like this so I can actually take you in it. I definitely want to fuck you in this outfit."

"Why can't we do it in here?"

"We could try, but I'm pretty sure we'll overload the simulator's capacity. It's just going to be too much with our senses and stimulation. This isn't like the one back home. The simulation will collapse during the middle of it. Our minds aren't like others here. We should just make love outside of it."

"But I like fighting in here with you. I can kick your ass without hurting you."

He corrected her, "You attempt to kick my ass...Like I said, we could try it but I'd rather not blow the circuits on this thing. It's too damn inconvenient to build another and I don't need any simulation while making love to you. You're as real as it gets and that's pretty fucking fantastic. You're all I need."

"Oh well. If you put it that way. Fuck this." She dropped the gun and went to kiss him.

He leaned over, grabbed the gun and shot her. The simulation went dark.

"I can't believe you fell for the seduction tactic. Ha. I win!" He smiled wide.

The lights came back on and they both sat in black shirts and pants.

The queen got up and walked away sulking and mumbling. "That's the last time I fall for that trick I swear. Next time I'm shooting you."

He followed after her, picked her up and threw her over his shoulder, spanking her bottom. "You're coming with me woman. I won fair and square."

She thrashed and kicked trying to get free of him. "Oh no you don't. You're not doing anything with me. You totally tricked me into letting the gun go because I thought you wanted to make love to me. Now, we're not doing anything."

He loved it when she challenged him. "I'm taking you. I can put you in the mood no matt—"

Hamlet interrupted, "Anomaly detected. Anomaly detected. Anomaly detected."

Sebastian put Celeste down and pulled up his in-air display. The entire universe materialized in a three dimensional map in front of their eyes.

"What's that?" Celeste pointed to a very large planet that had seemingly popped up into existence, "Is it a glitch in the system?"

Sebastian shook his head, "I don't think so. We should go check this out."

"Right now?"

"Yes. Maybe something we did, one of our broken rules caused something very wrong to develop here."

"Hamlet? Do you have any hypothesis on what just happened?"

The AI responded, "Any logical explanation defies reality. The only guaranteed answer I can give is it's one hundred percent anomaly. As we speak, curious onlookers are starting to congregate around the new orb. No one is attempting landing but from intercepted chatter on comms, that is an inevitability."

Sebastian looked at Celeste, "We go. Now."

Several minutes later, they were the first to attempt landing while several hundred space vehicles watched.

It went normal enough. Hamlet analyzed all unknown aspects and deemed it safe. The AI also detected extremely high levels of precious resources scant in other places in the universe, something Celeste and Sebastian came to call war-anium because it was only a matter of time before someone tried to claim the planet and all its resources for their own.

A short time later, a war did break out but its origin wasn't resources of the new planet later named, and roughly translated, DGE1.

A fringe group of Knowledge beings would not accept that the new planet was new at all. They believed it had been there all along and somehow hidden by planetary governments. This planted seeds all across Knowledge that people recognized perhaps they didn't know everything they thought they had. This group began to grow and spread, gaining momentum across the universe and led to a movement called No More Secrets or NMS for short. They began clashing with a different group that accepted it was simply impossible to know everything.

They were The Freed. And they were comfortable with a certain lack of knowledge and very vocal about it given recent events.

NMS members, driven by fear, began pushing limits and quickly became more aggressive until riots broke out on two planets and in the course of several days, it spread to six.

Sebastian and Celeste called this a civil war only because the main race of both groups was the same.

The war grew bigger and bigger until Sebastian and Celeste discussed trying to intervene, but they weren't sure how to change anything this big without possibly causing further damage.

FORTY-THREE

>>> > CELESTE WAS JUST barely falling into a deep sleep when she heard a noise in the kitchen. She opened her eyes and saw Sebastian still asleep. She thought she had just imagined it, but then there was another noise and it was louder. Something creaking in the living room, like a footstep pausing on a wooden board...

"Did you hear that?" Sebastian asked in a whisper.

"I thought I imagined it."

"Get up. I need to investigate." Sebastian grabbed a homemade gun out of the dresser drawer and moved towards their bedroom doorway. Celeste moved out through the doorway with her own homemade compact shotgun and saw a humanoid figure by the back door.

"Stay right where you are! Don't move!" Sebastian commanded.

Celeste whispered, "Let me get the lights."

Then she heard something she never thought she'd hear again.

"C? Is that you? Celeste, it's Veronica."

The lights came on in the house, all of them.

Sebastian and Celeste stood frozen in place as their brains didn't register what their eyes saw.

Veronica stood in their home. She looked like she was glowing with happiness. She was alive. She wore a strange sort of robe that reflected light. Veronica's whole being radiated a soft pulsing light. Celeste would've guessed it was in time with her heartbeat.

"You can't be. Veronica...died."

Veronica put her arms out to Celeste and started walking towards her, "Please give me a hug. Put down your weapons. Does Knowledge have weapons? I thought they outlawed them a long time ago."

Sebastian's mouth dropped open, "They did but things recently changed here. Who are you?"

"I'm Veronica Joy Blackwell. I swear to God..." she chuckled, "I guess that's *me* now."

Celeste gave Sebastian a concerned look.

"Okay, I was going to play nice, but this has got to go now." Veronica swiped her hands and both guns Sebastian and Celeste held went up into the air and stayed there. "Come hug me damn it. I missed you both so much!"

Celeste put up her hand and yelled, "Stop! WHO ARE YOU?"

Veronica slowed her approach, "Ask me anything C. I'm your Veronica. I came here first. I haven't even visited Eric yet, but I'm going to soon. I need some help."

Celeste's eyes welled up with tears, "Veronica, the real Veronica would know the first man I ever had oral sex with."

Veronica nodded, "No one knows you let that one kingdom guard go down on you the night before the wedding to Jonathan. You were so nervous...and you thought you'd never sleep with anyone but the king...so you wanted someone else to 'break you out of your—"

Celeste finished, "Self. I wanted someone to break me out of myself."

She ran into Veronica's arms as tears poured down her cheeks. Veronica smiled, "Oh honey. It's okay. No tears. I came back for you. I'm here. Everything's going to be alright."

Sebastian came up to Veronica, "How is this possible? We saw you *die*. Eric's suffered so badly and for you to pull this trick where you're not really dead, that's no—"

Celeste held onto Veronica's hand like she didn't believe she was really there. She let go when Veronica moved towards Sebastian but he backed away from her.

"Listen, this wasn't a trick Sebastian. I...oh God, this is...so hard to try and explain..."

"Eric almost died of a broken heart."

Veronica smiled but her eyes were sad. Tears perched on her eyelids, "I told him not to grieve too long for me, damn him."

"You need to explain all this."

"Do you guys have ummm, what do they call it here? Oh I can't remember but it's our coffee Celeste. Like Earth coffee?"

She nodded, "Xilery uhng. I'll make some but start explaining...oh and could you put our guns down please? I don't like them hanging up in mid-air and how do you do that?"

Veronica waved her hands and the guns floated down to her. She handed them to Sebastian, "Here. You won't need these."

Sebastian put them into the bedroom and came out wearing a pair of sweat pants and handed Celeste a robe. She put it on over her nightgown after she started the best substitute for coffee this place had to offer.

Veronica looked around, "This looks wonderful here. You've really made it like back home. You have our clothes and our decorations and weapons and coffee. How'd you do it all?"

"It wasn't easy." Sebastian looked over at Celeste, "We've been here...well, long enough to find workarounds and gotten creative to make the things we missed."

Veronica smiled as she smelled the coffee brewing, "Oh that smell! It's awesome! Okay so I should tell you what happened I guess."

Celeste got three mugs out and poured the coffee, "Please. I need to hear this."

"The War Universe beings...they weren't just killing us. They wanted to harvest some women to take back to their own universe. They had been fighting so hard for so long with the other universes that they depleted their numbers and wanted some of us to enslave. They wanted to mate with us, make new War beings."

Celeste almost dropped the mugs on the way to the kitchen table. She put them out with this universe's versions of cream and sugar, "I'm sorry, you mean enslave and impregnate?"

"Bingo."

Sebastian looked to Celeste, "Applette never said that. Kolek never said that."

Veronica put two sugar cubes into her coffee, "Why would they? Applette never knew and Kolek didn't want it to become common knowledge, but she knew about it for sure."

Celeste sighed, "Well do you know how many people they were able to...capture?"

Veronica closed her eyes tight, "A little under one million. Not just Humans, but all species."

Sebastian asked the obvious question, "How do you know this?"

"When I fell through the doorway, I don't remember much. The next thing I know I was in a...room? There were these voices. I think maybe I was dead. But I'm not sure. It was some kind of limbo state. These voices, but it was really like one voice, he talked to me but I can't remember the whole conversation. There were a lot of questions involved but not a lot of answers. Anyways, I was supposed to pick a path. I think they wanted to reincarnate me, or something. I didn't pick a path. Instead I chose to dive into the water. From what I can tell, I wasn't supposed to do that. I swam to the bottom. I didn't even need to hold my breath and I swam for a long time. I got to the bottom and there was no fish, no life, no plants, just paper. It was floating and swirling around the bottom covering...everything. But I found a hatch. It opened and I went through it. On the other side was dry land. None of the water even came through the hatch. It was all open sky and clouds. I closed the hatch behind me and was dry as a bone. There was this huge...I don't know what, a blob? A mass? A thing? It was alive and it wasn't happy to see me. I guess I took it off guard. It was in the middle of some sort of meal when I surprised it. I killed it by accident; I didn't mean to. It choked to death and while I tried to save it and do the Heimlich maneuver, something went wrong. It died and after it did, I passed out.

"I woke up and I knew how to do things I had no business knowing. It was like all this knowledge was put into my head while I slept. I know how to make things stop or hover. I know things about people and places. I know they renamed our old universe from Unknown to Relentless. Did you guys hear?"

Sebastian nodded and spoke slowly, "You killed the Keeper. The ultimate sovereign of all universes. Celeste and I were thinking about trying to change the rules...take over and you're...the new Keeper."

Veronica blushed, "I guess so. Yeah."

Celeste reached out and squeezed Veronica's hand, "So what happened then?"

Veronica sipped her coffee, "After I figured out what happened and what I was, I knew I could get out, so I did. But it didn't work as planned. When I got out of the room, I was falling. I had returned to the War Universe and I was plummeting as if I had just gone through the door. I landed on a blue hazy planet that looked like a swamp, one large swamp with lots of purple fog. It was so strange. The beings there, when they spoke, I understood them. They explained that they knew who I was, that I had sacrificed my life and the life of my unborn baby to save others in my own universe, but that it was a miracle I had survived. They called me a queen. Word spread fast and soon every male being in the universe wanted to mate with me. They worshipped me. They brought me things to eat and drink. They brought me gifts and valuable objects. It was bizarre and Celeste, I kept thinking of how you would handle it, so that's what I did.

"I was gracious with them and kind. Grateful and polite... until I could get away from there. I can just jump from universe to universe and I have. I've seen things you couldn't imagine, but it wasn't on purpose. I was trying to find you two, but I don't have a map and so I was guessing and jumping. But here I am. I'm ready to take you guys back to Relentless if you'd like. I need to find Eric. I need to talk to him and I thought you'd like to visit there. Maybe stay?"

"Aren't we always supposed to have rulers for every universe?" Celeste looked to Sebastian.

"We can change the rules maybe? I'm the boss. I'm...a...a God. *The* God. We can change whatever we want, right? And you guys know a different side than I do. We should work together. And maybe Eric can add to the conversation. Maybe with all our powers we can be Gods together or we can rule over all the universes. Maybe we can bring Recin and Kolek to task, hold them accountable for all the terrible things they did, all the pain they inflicted. But I want to go soon. I can't wait to see the look on Eric's face when I appear in front of him."

Sebastian and Celeste looked at each other.

"It would be so good to see everyone babe. I could visit mom and dad. I could hug them again!" Celeste smiled wide.

Sebastian took a moment's pause before replying, "Yes, it would be good to see everyone. See how the planets are doing. What progress has happened since we left. How soon Veronica?"

"Whenever you're ready. I don't sleep anymore. I don't need to. I could go now. Just put on some clothes. Grab whatever you need." She ran a hand over her face and her hair became curled and her face was suddenly done in makeup, "Hey Sebastian, what do you mean by things are different here recently? You said that earlier."

"You don't know about the civil war then?" He asked quietly.

She shook her head.

Celeste smiled, "How's that? I thought you just said you know everything."

Veronica faltered momentarily, "Well, I guess maybe I don't. I don't know. So what's this civil war? That can't be right."

Celeste finished her coffee and jogged into the bedroom, letting Sebastian explain the situation.

A few minutes later, Celeste finished dressing and Sebastian came up behind her, "There's more to this, you know that? All of this isn't supposed to happen this way. Veronica has probably changed things potentially for the worse. We don't know yet. Maybe *she* caused the new planet to appear. Or maybe this is a test. Or a trap. We need to proceed with extreme caution."

Celeste refuted, "Veronica's the only person, the only living being that knew about the kingdom guard the night before marrying Jon. It's impossible to fake that kind of information."

"We must be suspicious more than trusting with this."

Celeste nodded, "But still. I want to see mom and dad. That's all I can think of right now."

Sebastian grabbed her hand and squeezed it so hard she winced, "I have a bad feeling about this. Veronica's different. Can't you see that? Can't you feel it?"

Celeste opened the bedroom door and saw Veronica studying the sculpture they had in the living room. Celeste spoke quietly to her husband, "She's traumatized. She's been through hell and now she's back from...the dead. I would be different too if I went through all that and lost you in the process."

Veronica called out, "You guys ready?"

Celeste nodded and walked out to meet her friend.

They formed a circle, all three holding hands.

"Hold on," Veronica instructed.

Celeste could hear Veronica's thoughts and they unsettled her.

She stared into her friend's eyes, <*After Sebastian told me about the civil war here, I checked other universes and something huge has happened in each. One after the other. Chaos Universe has a brand new incurable disease. In the Zero Universe, a whole new galaxy appeared out of nowhere. Literally. Peace Universe had technology show up they've never seen before. Balance has a third gender all of a sudden, the Dead Universe has seen its first sign of life arrive, and our universe? AIs are now biologic. Ophelia's a real woman now.*>

Celeste's eyes got big.

Veronica continued, <*That's not all. I'm still pregnant. I can feel her moving inside of me, but I don't know if I'm supposed to be able to do that this early on. She feels like she's growing faster than she should. I don't know what's happening to me. I don't know what I've done. I think I messed everything up. I fear the multiverse is off kilter somehow. The rules, the ties that bound everything tightly together are now undone. Celeste, what are we going to do? It's all unbound.>*

ACKNOWLEDGEMENTS

Thanks to my family for loving and encouraging me.

Thanks to my friends for your love and kindness.

Thanks Robert for everything.

Thanks to everyone at all the offices that I bugged with opinion questions.

Thanks to all my beta readers.

And thanks to the fans.